**Her encounter with that undead creature
had left permanent damage.
Some kind of supernatural scar.**

She slumped down and hugged her knees to her chest. Was this what it meant to be fae? To be this vulnerable? She wasn't tough and street-smart like Augustine, she was a computer geek who preferred the indoors to direct sunlight and email to actual conversation.

What would her mother do in a situation like this? Olivia had been strong and fearless. The kind of woman Harlow would love to be someday, but getting there was going to take courage. Something she wasn't sure she had. At least not in the kind of quantities she was going to need.

She should talk to Augustine and hope that all this craziness happening to her wouldn't scare him away. He *had* promised to teach her to defend herself. Maybe that would help somehow. And if it didn't...he'd know what to do. Or he'd find someone who would. He was the Guardian of the city. It was his job to protect the citizens of New Orleans and now that she lived here, that included her.

Praise for HOUSE OF COMARRÉ

"Painter scores with this one. Passion and murder, vampires and courtesans—original and un-put-downable. Do yourself a favor and read this one."
—Patricia Briggs, *New York Times* bestselling author

"Gripping, gritty, and imaginative. If you love dangerous males, kick-ass females, and unexpected twists, this is the series for you! Kristen Painter's engaging voice, smart writing, and bold, explosive plot blew me away. Prepare to lose some sleep!"
—Larissa Ione, *New York Times* bestselling author

"Kristen Painter's *Blood Rights* is dark and rich with layer after delicious layer. This spellbinding series will have you begging for more!"
—Gena Showalter, *New York Times* bestselling author

"Prophecy, curses, and devilish machination combine for a spellbinding debut of dark romance and pulse-pounding adventure."
—*Library Journal* (starred review)

"Kristen Painter brings a sultry new voice to the vampire genre, one that beckons with quiet passion and intrigue."
—L. A. Banks, *New York Times* bestselling author

"A world full of rich potential. Excellent!"
—P. C. Cast, *New York Times* bestselling author

"Exciting and interesting!"   —*RT Book Reviews* on *Bad Blood*

"The romance is tense and fresh...I highly recommend this if you enjoy fantasy and want an original take on vampires."
—*USA Today*'s Happy Ever After on *Blood Rights*

CITY OF
ETERNAL NIGHT

CITY OF ETERNAL NIGHT

CRESCENT CITY:
BOOK 2

KRISTEN PAINTER

www.orbitbooks.net

Copyright © 2014 by Kristen Painter
Excerpt from *Charming* copyright © 2013 by Elliott James
Excerpt from *Full Blooded* copyright © 2012 by Amanda Carlson

Orbit
Hachette Book Group
1290 Avenue of the Americas, New York, NY 10104
HachetteBookGroup.com

Printed in the United States of America

RRD-C

First Edition: December 2014
10 9 8 7 6 5 4 3 2 1

Orbit is an imprint of Hachette Book Group, Inc. The Orbit name and logo are trademarks of Little, Brown Book Group Limited.

The Hachette Speakers Bureau provides a wide range of authors for speaking events. To find out more, go to www.hachettespeakersbureau.com or call (866) 376-6591.

The publisher is not responsible for websites (or their content) that are not owned by the publisher.

Library of Congress Cataloging-in-Publication Data:

Painter, Kristen L.
    City of eternal night / Kristen Painter. — First edition.
        pages ; cm. — (Crescent city ; Book 2)
    ISBN 978-0-316-27833-1 (softcover) — ISBN 978-1-4789-3087-7 (audio download) — ISBN 978-0-316-27831-7 (ebook)
1. Vampires—Fiction.   2. Fairies—Fiction.   3. Paranormal romance stories.   I. Title.
    PS3616.A337845C58 2014
    813'.6—dc23
                                                                2014017826

ISBN: 9780316278331

To my readers, the real reason I do this.

Chapter One

*Life is an unwinnable game. Only the playing
time may be prolonged.*
—Elektos Codex 13.4.1
New Orleans, Louisiana 2068

Harlow woke with a gasp. Her heart raced in her chest. She swallowed, trying to get air. Sweat glued her tank top to her body. A few deep breaths eased the nightmare's grip on her, but its claws still dug deep into her subconscious. A few more breaths and the sharp edges wore away, leaving her with a residual fear that clung like secondhand smoke.

She forced herself to lie down and relax. *It was just a dream.* The coolness of the dark room eased the heat of her skin. *This is reality, not the nightmare.* She grabbed her Life Management Device off the nightstand and tapped the screen to see the time. A little after three in the morning.

Tossing the LMD onto the nightstand, she kicked the covers off. The whirling ceiling fan wafted cool air over her as she tried to concentrate on something besides the terrifying dream that had yanked her from sleep. She failed. The nightmare filled every synapse. She couldn't recall exactly what the dream had been, but the dread of it remained, impossible to shake. Something—or someone—had tried to drag her into an abyss. Or had chased her toward it.

Either way, she never wanted to feel that bone-deep sense of fear again.

Minutes slipped by, taking the panic with them. At last she closed her eyes, praying the nightmare wouldn't return.

It didn't, but neither did sleep. She focused on the whir of the ceiling fan. The subtle hum drowned out all other sounds. Except for one.

The unmistakable eddy and lap of water.

She got up and padded barefoot across the room, pushed back the sheers, opened the balcony door, and stepped out into the cool night air.

Augustine was swimming laps in the pool below.

She sighed. Seeing him anchored her firmly in reality. His lean, muscled form cut the water cleanly, sending smooth ripples to kiss the pool's edge. In the submerged light, his skin seemed a darker gray, sleek and seal-like against the water's aqua blue.

She walked closer to the railing. There was something otherworldly in the way he slipped through the water, the effortless way he spun and pushed off the wall as he turned, the boneless way his body undulated. Even if his horns hadn't grown back, with his gray skin and the six fingers on each hand—and now she could see six toes on each foot as well—no one would mistake him for human. He was utterly, completely, regrettably fae.

And she was utterly, completely, regrettably attracted to him. She exhaled the breath she'd unwittingly held. Sure, she was fae, too, but she'd spent her entire adult life trying to live as if she weren't. Now her new life in New Orleans made those bloodlines impossible to ignore. She was the daughter of the city's most famous fae, movie star Olivia Goodwin. And thanks to her mother's curious will, Harlow and Augustine had become co-owners of the house. And roommates. Hard to ignore your true heritage when you shared a house with the city's fae Guardian.

Who was practically naked in the pool below her.

Steam rose from the water but the trails evaporated before reaching her second-story balcony. He must be using some of his fae skills to heat the water. That would be a wicked cool power to have. Unlike hers, which were mostly bothersome.

She leaned against the metal railing, causing it to creak.

He lifted his head, twisting seamlessly into a backstroke to smile up at her. "Hey, Harley. Come on in, the water's fine."

She pulled away from the railing. "I was just going back to bed." *And don't call me that.* But those words never left her tongue.

"Funny. Looks like you're standing there watching me." With a smug look, he ducked under, flipped around and pressed off the wall to glide the length of the pool underwater in one long, easy movement. The water calmed, bringing into definition just how very small his black trunks were.

When he surfaced, he picked his head up and made eye contact again. "You can't sleep or you'd already be doing that. You might as well swim." He spread his arms out and floated lazily.

"I don't have a swimsuit."

His wicked grin returned. "I can ditch mine if it makes you feel better."

She bit her bottom lip and tried to keep her gaze from traveling below that smile. "Okay. Wait. No. Keep your suit on. I meant okay I would come swimming." Her tank top and boy-short underwear would work fine. It was dark. Sort of. And all that seemed to matter at the moment was that she get in the water.

She slipped back into the house, wrapped herself in a towel from her bathroom and then went down to the first floor as quietly as she could so she wouldn't wake Lally, the housekeeper. Outside, the grass muffled her steps. She shivered despite the towel. The unseasonably warm weather they'd been having was gone. At the pool's edge, she stopped, clutching her towel. She shouldn't be down here. She should be in bed. Asleep. *Alone.*

Augustine stood in waist-deep water. Vapor trails rose off his sleek gray skin to mingle with the steam from the surface, making him look like some kind of horned god of the underworld. He coasted his fingers over the surface, but his eyes stayed on her.

She shivered again. Standing beside a pool shouldn't feel this dangerous. This *wicked*.

He sank down to his neck and pushed back, sending out a small wake. "I can make the water as warm as you like."

If she didn't move forward, she was going to turn and run. She willed herself to drop the towel, then forced her feet down the steps. She could do this. She could be this bold. The pool was like a bath. She kept going, sinking down until her hair floated around her. "It's warm enough."

Warmer toward Augustine. Like the heat was radiating off him, which she guessed it was. She didn't know exactly how his power worked, but as skills went, this was a pretty good one.

He kept his distance, drifting about arm's length from her. "Couldn't sleep, huh?"

"No." When he didn't say anything, she filled the space with, "I had a nightmare."

He nodded. "Those suck." Then he moved a little closer, his brow furrowed. "You okay?"

She stayed put. "I'm fine. I'm not eight. I can deal with it." She hoped.

He shrugged. "I had nightmares after your mom died that felt as real as anything."

She dropped her gaze to the water's surface. "It wasn't about that. I don't even remember it now, really." Mostly true. Just the sense of that dark, threatening abyss remained.

"Cylo and Dulcinea should be back with your stuff today."

He was less than a foot from her, his voice soft. Lally's room was on the first floor, not that far away. She nodded, keeping her voice down, too. "I appreciate you sending them to Boston to clear out my apartment."

His face went serious. "Not something you needed to be doing with Branzino unaccounted for."

She backpedaled to lean against the pool wall and rest her head on the rounded edge. "I don't want to talk about him." Her biological father was a monster, not someone she wanted in her brain after that nightmare.

"Me either." Augustine joined her at the wall, so close his shoulder almost kissed hers. The heat coming off him felt like a blast furnace. He pointed skyward, water dripping off his hand. "See those five stars forming that wide W shape? That's Cassiopeia."

"Who was she? Some Greek goddess, right?"

"Close. A Greek queen."

"They're very pretty." She glanced over at him but his eyes were still on the sky. "How do you know about the stars?"

He turned toward her. "I like beautiful things."

A dark light flickered in his eyes. Her insides knotted with rare, unused feelings. She faced him, gripping the pool's edge with one hand while she pushed at him with the other. It was like trying to shove a stone wall out of the way. "Nice line, but I'm not falling for it." He'd have to try a lot harder than that.

He inched closer. The steam rising off him left little droplets in her bangs. "It wasn't a line. You're beautiful."

She swallowed, unsure how to respond. She didn't have to. His mouth closed on hers, the kiss unexpected, but not entirely unwelcome. His hands slid up her arms, stopping below her shoulders. She leaned into him, into his warmth. Into the press of a mouth both soft and firm. The surge of emotion she expected never came. Had he figured out how to squelch her gift? Or maybe he'd found a way to control what came through him.

She kissed him back, pleased that for once the only emotions skin-on-skin contact made her feel were her own.

His fingers tightened on her arms and his mouth bore down on hers. The pressure became painful. She pulled back to end the kiss and failed. He forced his mouth against hers harder. Panic jolted down her spine. The water chilled. She opened her eyes and struggled to break away.

A shadow passed in front of the pool light, causing it to sputter.

Except it wasn't a shadow. A crack had opened in the bottom of the pool. The blackness spilled out of it and spread toward her. The abyss had returned. She hit Augustine with her fists, but he didn't budge. They were locked together. She screamed into his mouth. The abyss came closer as a great emptiness opened inside her.

Augustine was sucking the soul out of her, draining the light and spirit from her body. She could feel it leaving as the blackness reached her. The water lapped over her, climbing up her arms, covering her body, choking the breath from her—

She bolted upright, gasping for air, clutching handfuls of the sheet like they were a lifeline. She was still in bed. It was just another dream. But the pounding of her heart was very real. She panted open-mouthed to get enough oxygen into her lungs. Just a dream, she repeated. *Just a dream.*

She checked the time on her LMD. Quarter after four in the morning. Her pulse was easing, but the panic was slower to subside. The water, the kiss, the heat of his skin…it had seemed so real. She jumped out of bed, ran to the balcony doors and peered out. The pool was empty and dark, lit only by the moon.

She turned and leaned against the door, her back flattening

the sheers to the glass. She spread her hand over her heart. The darkness was still there. Darker than the room she was in. She could *feel* it. Feel the way it strengthened with every nightmare. It sat in the empty place she'd always had inside her.

She'd lived with that all her life, a longing she'd thought had been created by not knowing her father, but she'd met him and that introduction had done nothing to take away the ache. Maybe because Branzino had turned out to be a horrible, manipulative monster of a man, but maybe there was another reason. Maybe she was defective in some way. Like a part of her was missing.

Either way, touching the vampire who'd killed her mother had awakened something in her. Made the hole more apparent. Created a sense of emptiness so intense, she'd assumed it was just temporary. Obviously she'd been wrong. Her encounter with that undead creature had left permanent damage. Some kind of supernatural scar.

She slumped down and hugged her knees to her chest. Was this what it meant to be fae? To be this vulnerable? She wasn't tough and street-smart like Augustine; she was a computer geek who preferred the indoors to direct sunlight and email to actual conversation.

What would her mother do in a situation like this? Olivia had been strong and fearless. The kind of woman Harlow would love to be someday, but getting there was going to take courage. Something she wasn't sure she had. At least not in the quantity she was going to need.

She should talk to Augustine and hope that all this craziness happening to her wouldn't scare him away. He *had* promised to teach her to defend herself. Maybe that would help somehow. And if it didn't ... he'd know what to do. Or he'd find someone who would. He was the Guardian of the city. It was his job to protect the citizens of New Orleans, and now that she lived here, that included her.

Augustine came down to breakfast to find Lally cooking eggs and Harlow already at the table. She was bundled in Olivia's old chenille robe, her cranberry-black hair knotted on top of her head. Even rumpled with sleep she intrigued him. Or maybe that disheveled look just fueled the fire she'd already started in him. He wanted to plant a kiss on the side of her neck. Smiling at what the consequences of that might be, he grabbed a mug for coffee instead. "Morning. Cool out there today, huh?"

Lally nodded. "Morning, Augie. I like that cool weather. Makes for good sleeping, don't you think?"

"It does, but Mardi Gras's going to be on the cold side this year if this spell doesn't pass."

Lally grinned. "Guess that means people just have to drink a little more to keep warm."

He glanced at Harlow. She'd yet to speak. "You okay?"

She nodded, but said nothing. Her gloved hands were wrapped around her coffee cup as if she were afraid it might try to get away. Purplish-gray semicircles bruised her under-eyes.

He took the chair next to her, fighting the urge to touch her. To comfort her. He stopped himself because she wouldn't welcome it. "Didn't sleep well, huh?"

She shrugged, her gaze never leaving her coffee. "I was...up late playing Realm of Zauron."

He'd passed her room at midnight. There'd been no light under the door from her computer.

She sipped her coffee. "My stuff should be here today, right?"

The sudden change of subject wasn't lost on him. Obviously whatever was bothering her wasn't something she wanted to discuss. Maybe if he'd been human she would have felt differently, but she was still coming to terms with being fae and that included him. He pulled out his LMD. "Uh-huh. I got a text from Dulcinea around seven a.m. She figures they'll pull in from Boston sometime this afternoon."

"Thanks for taking care of that." She raised her head a little, but still didn't make eye contact. She seemed reluctant to be around him this morning, more so than usual, and he had no idea why. Whatever had kept her up, maybe. He hoped whatever she wasn't telling him wasn't serious.

"Of course. With Branzino in the wind, it was the smartest way to handle it."

Lally set a platter of eggs and bacon on the table, followed by a basket of biscuits and a bowl of grits sprinkled with cheese. "I'm glad that man has stayed away. I'm guessing he knows when he's been beat."

"Let's hope so." Augustine took a biscuit and slathered it with mayhaw jelly. Truth was, it was more likely that Branzino was biding his time, and he was sure Lally knew that, too; she just didn't want to put the truth out there in front of Harlow. "That reminds me, I can't hang out too long this morning. I've got to meet Fenton." Fenton Welch served as the Elektos liaison to the Guardian, a role the member of the fae's high council took very seriously.

Harlow looked up. "I thought we were going to train today."

Was that part of what was bothering her? "I know, I promised I'd give you some self-defense lessons—and I will. Fenton just needs me for a bit this morning, then I'll be home."

She nodded. "Okay. Good." But her mouth bunched to one side and she sighed.

Damn it. She was obviously disappointed. He'd do whatever he could to make the morning meeting quick. "I'll be back as soon as I can."

Lally sat at the end of the table and helped herself to a

spoonful of scrambled eggs. "Do you have a lot to do to get ready for Mardi Gras? As Guardian, I mean."

"Some." Mostly he was going to nudge Fenton about getting the house warded before they returned to finalizing the investigation into the death of Dreich. The fallen fae had been the late Guardian's cousin *and* one of his lieutenants. Hard to believe the man had been involved in letting vampires into the city. Vampires who'd killed not only some tourists and the last Guardian, but Harlow's mother, Olivia Goodwin.

But the man both Augustine and Harlow truly suspected to have been behind the whole thing was Joseph Branzino, Harlow's biological father, raptor fae and known killer. They just didn't have any hard evidence, and without hard evidence, there was no lawful action Augustine could take. Unlawful action, on the other hand, was something he was coming to believe would be his only recourse. He was okay with that. Before becoming the Guardian, unlawful action was all he'd known.

He shifted his attention to Harlow. She stared at the table-top, taking a sip of coffee now and then and looking very much like a troubled soul. Maybe he should tell Fenton he needed a day off. "I could try to cancel, maybe push the meeting until tomorrow—"

"No." Harlow shook her head and the briefest of smiles bent her mouth. "I'm not even awake yet. Go do your Guardian stuff and we'll train when you get back."

Lally pushed the platter of eggs toward her. "Eat something, child. You need the energy just to keep yourself warm."

"Thanks." She took a piece of bacon, finally seeming to perk up. "I was thinking about how nice it will be to have all my stuff back. If it's okay with you two"—she turned her gaze to Lally—"I'd like to set up shop in one of the spare rooms."

"Shop?" Lally asked. "You're not going to get yourself into trouble again, are you?"

"No. Nothing like that." Harlow glanced at her. "But I still have clients and I need to work. It's not in me just to live off my mother's estate. If it was, my life would have been very different."

"True words." Lally nodded.

"I need to do *something*."

Augustine sat back. "What about the business you were already doing? Hacking into companies to test their security."

"Penetration testing. Word about my conviction has spread through the community." She frowned. "The jobs have dried up. And while I realize New Orleans may not have the same kind of business going on that Boston did, there's got to be some opportunity in a tourist town like this. I'm thinking I could do web work, maybe some graphic design stuff. I'll even do repairs. Whatever people need. There have to be people in this town who'd like a website designed. Most businesses here still have them, right?"

Lally shrugged. Augustine raised one shoulder. "I guess. Is that a thing most businesses do? My LMD is the closest I've been to a computer in a long time." The Great War had created a huge divide in who could afford things like electricity and technology. Once upon a time, connectivity had been an almost inherent right. Now it was a luxury for those who had the funds.

Harlow toyed with her fork. "I hope so. I'd like to do something with my time besides read my way through my mother's library. Not that that's such a bad way to pass the time…"

"You'll be plenty busy when we get this training schedule figured out." Augustine would keep his promise, but that didn't mean he wasn't having mixed feelings about teaching her to fight. It would be good for her to be able to defend herself, but he worried she'd get overconfident and do something with lasting results.

"I know." She chewed a bite of bacon. "But I still want to start this new business."

"I get it," Lally said. "No shame in wanting to feel productive."

"Take whatever space you want. It *is* half your house," Augustine added. "Just don't take the ballroom, that's going to be our training space. I'm requisitioning the stuff from Fenton today." If lack of activity was behind Harlow's unhappiness, then he was all for her starting up a new business. How busy she'd actually be, he had no idea, but it would give her something to do. With that and the training, she should be well occupied. And, hopefully, starting to feel like this place was really her home.

He popped the last of the biscuit in his mouth and pushed his chair back. "I should be back before Cy and Dulcinea get here."

"Wait." Harlow dug something from the pocket of her robe. "Take these." She held out a handful of business cards. She shrugged. "You know, in case you run into someone who needs computer help."

He took them. "Sure. Happy to spread the word." He pulled his coat on, covering his only visible weapon, the sword that hung at his hip, and tucked the cards into his pocket before heading out to the Thrun, the amazing piece of machinery he now drove thanks to his position as Guardian.

He trailed his fingers over the car's sleek black hood as he approached the driver's side. He tapped the unlock icon on his LMD, then opened the door and got in.

He smiled at the quiet-as-a-tomb interior when the door shut. Being Guardian came with a lot of headaches. This was not one of them. He pulled out one of Harlow's business cards and studied it.

His LMD vibrated with an incoming call. He tucked the card back into his pocket. "Answer."

The com cell behind his ear allowed the conversation to take place in his head, something that was still taking some getting used to. "Augustine, it's Fenton."

"I'm on my way." He started the engine and pulled the car out of the garage. The Pelcrum, their headquarters, was only a few blocks away in the heart of the Lafayette Cemetery. "I'll be there in five."

"No, meet me at Loudreux's." Fenton sounded tense.

"What's up?"

"I can't discuss it on an unsecure line."

"*This* is an unsecure line?"

"In this situation, yes."

Augustine rolled his eyes. Hugo Loudreux's position as Prime, head of the Elektos, had certainly filled him with a grand sense of importance. What the man wanted now, Augustine could only imagine. "On my way."

But he kept the car going in the same direction. Being called to the Prime's house was a lot like having the police come to your door. Even if they weren't there to arrest you, they probably weren't bringing you good news. And that could wait a little while longer.

With Dulcinea out of town, he wanted to check in on Beatrice. The late Guardian's widow had agreed to become one of his lieutenants, only finding out afterward that she was pregnant. There'd been no reason for him to displace her from the Guardian's house, since he'd become owner of half Olivia's estate, so he'd let Beatrice continue living there with the understanding that Dulcinea, who'd never had an address since he'd known her, would also live there. It wasn't that Beatrice couldn't take care of herself, but her pregnancy was proving difficult and Augustine felt a certain responsibility for her going through it alone.

Her late husband had been killed by Branzino's vampires, after all.

The Guardian house was technically his, but he certainly didn't need it to live in. Not after Harlow had asked him to stay at Olivia's. That house was half his, but if she'd asked him to leave, he probably would have. Although staying was definitely the option he preferred. Especially since the beginning of something unexpected and wonderful had blossomed between them.

At least it *might* be wonderful. Harlow was still adjusting to claiming her fae side and living in a city where it was all fae all the time. And he was about as fae as you could get. If she couldn't accept her heritage, whatever was happening between them would die on the vine. Being fae was who he was.

Regardless, he'd promised Olivia he'd protect her daughter and that was exactly what he was going to do. Hell, as Guardian it was his job to protect every citizen of New Orleans. Getting to live with Harlow was just a bonus. A really good bonus. Now if he could just figure out what was bothering her.

He pulled into the driveway at the Guardian's residence and turned off the engine, but his head was stuck on Harlow. Since the night the leader of the vampire gang had taken her hostage, she'd started pulling away from him in small increments.

Was it because she'd seen him slip inside the vampire and destroy the leech in a way only a shadeux fae could? Harlow had wanted nothing to do with anything fae when she'd first arrived at the house, though she was opening up to her heritage more and more with each passing day. Seeing him in battle mode like that must have been quite a shock.

Hell's bells. Of course it had shocked her. He tipped his head back against the seat. He'd vowed to protect her and yet he'd killed that creature right in front of her. No wonder she'd been avoiding him these past few days. He'd scared her. Damn it. That had not been his intention. He smacked the steering wheel, his anger at his own stupidity blinding him.

If she needed some space, he'd let her have it, but there was no way he was letting this go. He'd find a way to fix things. To show her she had nothing to be afraid of from him. There *was* something between them. Something he wasn't willing to give up just yet.

But as much as he'd begun to care for her, he couldn't change who he was. He'd spent his childhood pretending to be human for his mother, and all that had done was make him miserable. He was not about to spend his adulthood the same way.

Chapter Two

The walls of Olivia's vast library made for a beautiful prison, but Harlow was done feeling trapped. She had to do something about the ever-present hollowness inside her. She scanned the shelves for a book that might give her some insight into what was going on. The emptiness was as impossible to ignore as a toothache, except there was no pain involved. To the contrary, the hollowness seemed to absorb any overflow of emotion. Made her almost crave the onslaught that skin-on-skin contact brought. She'd hoped to get a moment with Augustine after breakfast to talk about it, but his job as Guardian took precedence.

She was torn about that. Part of her was disappointed they wouldn't be spending time together today and part of her was okay with it, because she was knew training with him would put her face-to-face with being fae. And face-to-face with her growing feelings for him. She rolled her shoulders, trying to come to terms with what being in a relationship with him might mean.

Definitely that she was okay with being fae, right? How could she admit to liking him without liking herself? And she did like him. So that had to mean she *was* getting more comfortable with being fae herself. Or did it? She sighed. It was all so confusing.

She knew he liked her. Knew that his skipping out on their training this morning was only because of his job. Being

Guardian wasn't something he could put off. Which was part of why she needed a job herself. To occupy more of her time and get her mind off whatever was happening to her. Which she still intended to work on. She *would* find a way to make herself right and hope that her descent into madness was stoppable. The Guardian of the city couldn't exactly spend his time with a sociopath. Not that she was that far gone *yet*.

She blew out a hard breath. None of her mother's books seemed to deal with suddenly coming into your own as a fae. She wasn't giving up, but maybe it was time to take a break and think about getting her stuff back and setting up shop for her new business.

She already had a room picked out for her office. It was a small one on the third floor that faced the front of the house and looked like it might have been used for an office before, based on her finding the blank stock she'd printed her cards on in the closet. The room got nice light, but not so much that the sun would overheat her precious equipment.

Besides giving Augustine the cards, she'd already emailed the *Times-Picayune* and taken out a classified ad. Websites weren't exactly her first love, but with her fae ability to read computers as if she were part of the machine, designing them was fairly easy.

If only her other *gift* were as useful. She sat on the couch and spread her gloved hands on her thighs. Skin-on-skin contact filled her with a rush of emotion from the other person, often bringing with it visions, sounds and scents. To make matters worse, the same thing happened when she handled recently touched objects. She was slowly learning to control it, but the fae who was helping her with that, Dulcinea, had been in Boston the last few days packing up Harlow's old apartment.

She'd been practicing, but the truth was, the idea of doing anything that might widen the emptiness within her made her hesitant. She'd put more effort into learning to control what she felt when Dulcinea was back to help. Harlow liked Dulcinea better than she had when they'd first met, but they weren't about to get matching tattoos.

Dulcinea's loyalties clearly lay with Augustine. And while Harlow was over being upset that the two of them had slept together as teenagers, she couldn't help but feel she'd never be as confident about being fae as Dulcinea was. Harlow wasn't sure she could get half that comfortable. The woman wasn't even full-blooded. Dulcinea was, as she'd explained, a remnant. A mix of fae and varcolai, or shifter, with no real idea of exactly what her bloodlines were.

But two reasons kept Harlow from ditching the changeling's help altogether.

One, Harlow truly wanted to be okay with her faeness. It would be so much easier to embrace who she was than fight it, but that meant learning to control the power that had handicapped her life. And two, there was the added bonus of being able to find out more about Augustine. About his life before he'd been taken in by Olivia, about how he'd met Olivia in the first place, what had happened with his own mother.

All the past history Dulcinea had been a spectator to. Harlow knew that she and Augustine had run in the same gang during their wild youth and they'd slept together. Both claimed it was a singular incident that had happened during those gang years, and Harlow had let it go at that, but that didn't change the reality that the bond between them was greater than friendship.

Theirs was the kind of relationship Harlow had never had with anyone. The kind of relationship she had no clue how to create. Or nurture. But that didn't stop her from wanting one. With Augustine. The hole in her heart called out to be filled and she was afraid that if she didn't find an answer for it soon, it was going to swallow her alive.

The doorbell rang and Harlow jumped, happy for the interruption, but then immediately wary. Branzino's return seemed more of a *when* than a *what-if*. She peered into the foyer from the library, but the figure behind the leaded glass double doors looked nothing like the man who'd fathered her. "I'll get it, Lally."

Harlow opened the door as Lally murmured a response from the kitchen, but Harlow's attention was focused on the man before her. He was both beautiful and intimidating. She tried not to stare at the band of silver tattoos that ran across his nose and cheekbones. They almost sparkled against the blue-black of his skin. A few more draped his knuckles, but leathers covered the rest of him from head to toe. Here and there, the hilts of a few blades protruded. If this was one of Branzino's men she was in trouble. Panic crept into her throat, tightening her voice. "Can I...help you?"

"I'm Nekai." The gravel of his voice was softened by the slightest edge of bayou honey. "I'm here to ward your house. Augustine requested I come."

If Augustine had asked him, he definitely wasn't one of Branzino's. She relaxed a little. "Ward the house?" Tiny silver hoops and studs lined the pointed ears peeking out from the mass of braids that fell to his waist. She really needed to stop staring. Making eye contact seemed far too intimate.

"I'm a weaver. You've had some problems?"

"You're fae." Brilliant response. Of course he was fae. "Yes, we've had some—do you have some kind of badge or something?" Speaking of problems, she didn't want to add another one and she was past the point of taking people at their word. Just because he knew Augustine's name didn't mean he was one of the good guys.

"No. I suggest you call Augustine. He can confirm who I am."

"I'll do that." She pulled her LMD out and hit Augustine's number while Nekai waited on the porch. She tugged her sweater coat a little tighter.

Augustine answered on the third ring. "What's up? Everything all right?"

"There's a guy here, a weaver. Name's Nekai. Says he's here to ward the house?"

"Hang on. Fenton, what's the name of the weaver you sent over?"

Harlow heard talking in the background but couldn't make it out.

Augustine came back on. "Yep, Nekai. Fenton says he's a tall dude, dark skin, long braids, silver tattoos. Sound like him?"

"Exactly. Thanks." She hung up and nodded at Nekai. Maybe a little too much. "Okay, all clear. Come in." She stepped out of the way. "Sorry about that, but these days—"

He held up his hand. Six fingers. Just like Augustine. *Definitely* fae. "Don't apologize. I wouldn't be here if you didn't have a reason to be concerned. You're Harlow, I take it?"

"Yes. My mother was Olivia Goodwin. She owned this house." Another completely irrelevant response. Apparently beautiful, intimidating fae rendered her dim.

"My condolences." He nodded as he entered. The foyer shrank in his presence. "I understand someone else lives here?"

She closed the door, then looked up at him. "Me and…" His pupils were ringed in silver. Her tongue got a little stuck to the roof of her mouth. "And…Augustine. But you already know that. Lally. She lives here, too. I mean, Eulalie Hughes."

Nekai shifted to look around, then back at Harlow. His eyebrows lifted. "Could you call her?"

"Oh. Sure." Harlow turned toward the rear of the house, happy to have something to do. Nekai's presence was a little overwhelming. "Lally? Could you come here, please?"

Lally walked out from the back, her gaze latching onto their visitor. "You the weaver Augustine called for?"

"Yes. I need to sample both of your energies in order to keep the wards from affecting you."

Living in this city with these people had prepared Harlow for a lot of weirdness, but this was new. The oddness helped shake off some of her nerves. "Sample our energies?"

Lally crossed her arms. "You don't need mine. No ward is going to keep me from finding this house. I been here long enough."

Nekai smiled patiently. "Everyone who lives in the house must have their energy included in the ward or it *will* affect you."

Lally looked like she wanted to argue. She raised her brows. "How do you propose to 'sample our energies,' exactly?"

Nekai held out his hands. "I need to touch you. It won't hurt and it won't take long."

Harlow stepped back, whatever curiosity she'd felt about this man replaced by panic. "No."

Nekai sighed. "It *won't* hurt. You won't even feel it."

Lally took a few steps forward to stand at Harlow's side. "She *will* feel it. The child is real sensitive to touch."

Nekai studied her for a moment, his gaze slipping from her face to her gloves. "Haerbinger?"

"Yes," Harlow whispered. Would she ever be comfortable admitting her fae bloodlines? "Isn't there another way?"

"No. But I'm skilled enough to keep you from reading me." Nekai looked at Lally. "How about you go first? Then she can see it's nothing to be worried about."

Lally nodded, reaching back to give Harlow's hand a reassuring squeeze. "All right then, I will." She moved toward Nekai. "What do you need me to do?"

"Just give me your hand."

Lally held out her hand, a tentativeness in her movement that Harlow was unaccustomed to seeing. Lally was afraid of no one.

Nekai closed both his hands over hers and shut his eyes for a moment. The air around his clasped hands wavered for a second before returning to normal. His eyes widened as they opened. He released Lally and looked like he was about to speak.

"Keep your knowledge to yourself, boy." Lally's stern expression underlined the warning in her voice.

"All the energies I sample are kept confidential. I use them for the ward and nothing else." But Nekai's gaze shone with the brightness of new information. What on earth had he read from Lally?

Lally interrupted Harlow's thoughts. "It's okay, child. I didn't feel a thing. A little warm, that was all."

But *what* had he read off her? Harlow's head spun with questions. She bit her tongue and focused on the task at hand. "I have to take my glove off?"

"Yes." Nekai tipped his head. "I can't do it any other way."

Reluctantly she shucked her glove and offered her hand. "Do your best to control what comes through then."

He dipped his chin and the corners of his mouth turned up the slightest bit. "You have my word." He took her hand between his, the warmth of his skin seeping into hers immediately. She inhaled, expecting the flood of emotion, sights and sounds that always accompanied such contact. But nothing happened. The warmth increased, the air wavered as it had with Lally, and then he released her.

"See?" He held his hands up. "Not so bad."

She tugged her glove back on. "I guess not."

He turned to Lally. "Thank you. That's all I need."

If that didn't sound like a dismissal, Harlow hadn't heard one. Lally looked at her before leaving. "You want me to stay?"

"No, it's fine. Thank you."

Lally gave Nekai one last appraising glance before she left.

Harlow lifted her face toward his. "Now what?"

"Now I need to walk the perimeter." He looked once in the direction Lally had gone. Was he checking to see if she was coming back? Was Nekai afraid of Lally? That was an interesting thought. "Would you like to join me?"

Not exactly, but she was curious about what he was going to do. "Okay."

He opened the door. "After you."

They walked across the property until they were in the farthest corner of the backyard. He pointed to the wall. "I'll start and end here. Once I'm done, the ward will repel unkind forces."

"Unkind? So it knows who the good guys are?"

"I've designed it to read intent. Neutrals, like neighbors or the mailman, shouldn't be bothered by it."

"Why did you need our energies then?"

"Ever come home in a bad mood?"

"Ah. I see." She thought a minute. "So if a messenger is delivering a package that contains a bomb, but they don't know it contains a bomb . . ."

"That's a gray area." He rocked his head back and forth. "They *might* get through, but this is a tough ward. Let's just say it has bomb-sniffing capabilities. Anyone willingly bent on harm won't stand a chance."

She leaned against the high plastered wall that surrounded the estate. She'd never been this deep in the property before. Even the gazebo stood between them and the house. "So this will keep out vampires?"

He shifted his weight. "Are you asking me if the ward could have saved your mother from them?"

"Would it have?"

"Possibly. It's a line of defense but it's not an absolute. Very little is, when dealing with such . . . *darkness*."

The way he said the word made the breath catch in her throat. She already knew he'd picked up something from Lally.

Had he picked up something from her, too? Did he know about the hollowness inside her?

He peered at her. "You okay?"

She nodded, probably too quickly. "I'm fine. Just wondering how you kept me from reading anything off of you. No one's been able to do that." Except for the vampire she'd been held captive by, and comparing the very alive Nekai to the undead wasn't exactly apples to apples.

"I am a weaver." He'd positioned himself facing the corner of the wall. Now he turned to look at her, his gaze too guarded to read. "I am highly trained to shield myself against intrusion and to prevent any of my power being siphoned off."

"Siphoned off?" The idea that his power could be stolen was interesting. "What kind of fae has that sort of skill?"

He shrugged. "There are a few, but they're rare. More likely to come from a magic crafter who isn't fae."

She tried not to dwell on what that implied. "So you can cast spells?"

He looked down his nose at her, amusement sparkling in his gaze. "I *weave* spells."

What the difference was, she had no idea. She shrugged. "I have a lot to learn about the fae. All the different types and what their powers are."

"*The* fae?" Those dark brows rose again. "You talk like you're not one."

"That's kind of how I lived my life until I got here, but I'm working on it. Slowly."

His eyes narrowed but he said nothing. He turned back to the wall.

"Do you mind if I stay? If I watch?"

"No." He lifted his hands, spread his fingers and began to work them through the air, as if he were conducting an invisible orchestra. Trails of pale light drifted in their wake, lines filled with odd shapes. Letters from an alphabet she'd never seen. Faeish, she guessed.

"Holy cats," she muttered. "That's amazing."

He stopped to look at her again. The lines of light disappeared.

She cringed. "Sorry. I didn't mean to interrupt. I've just never seen anything like that before. Those...things you're drawing, they kind of look like your tattoos."

He smiled. The wattage almost buckled her knees. "These marks aren't tattoos. They're my spells. Once my skin is covered, my ability to create new magic is gone. That's why each weaver only does certain spells, because only new magic creates new marks."

"Amazing." She shook her head. "I really should take a class or something."

His smile finally reached his eyes. "I'd be happy to teach you." He walked toward her, then leaned against the wall a few feet away. "If I'm not doing spellwork, I have a lot of free time."

She stared up at him and smiled back. The tingling in her belly was the same one she got when she was about to start out on a new quest in Realm of Zauron, her favorite RPG. He wasn't Augustine, but he also wasn't hard to look at. And Augustine was so busy lately. But Nekai was just as fae as Augustine was. She gnawed on her lip. "I don't know."

"I don't bite."

"That's what they all say." She couldn't find the words to explain that his being so very fae was the same thing that both made him interesting and scared her off. If she didn't get over feeling nervous about other fae, she was never going to be comfortable in her own skin.

He moved back toward the corner. "Your call. I'm free after I finish this."

Her desire to find peace with who she was won out. "Strictly educational." That wasn't exactly true, unless you called pumping someone for information educational. She really wanted to find out what he'd read from Lally.

He nodded. "Of course. I know you're the Guardian's woman."

Her mouth dropped open. She belonged to no one. "What? Like hell I am. Who told you that? Augustine? Phht." She spun on her heel and stalked back toward the house. "Hurry up and do your warding. I have a lot to learn and you're going to teach me."

When Augustine walked into Loudreux's, Fenton's narrow face announced plainly that the delay in his arrival had caused some consternation.

"Where've you been?" the cypher fae whispered. "Loudreux's been waiting. All the Elektos have. They're getting impatient."

"I can hear that." From the study down the hall, the sound of many voices discussing something serious filled the air. "I promised Dulcinea I would keep an eye on Beatrice while she and Cy are in Boston."

Most of Fenton's displeasure disappeared. "How is Beatrice?"

"She's definitely carrying a wysper's child. She's losing her voice more and more as the days go by." It wasn't unheard of for a pregnant fae to pick up some of her child's powers during gestation, and Beatrice's late husband had been more than half wysper fae. Full-blooded wyspers were mute except for a powerful scream that could kill a vampire, a skill that could have been the late Guardian's saving grace had the vampires who'd killed him not slit his throat. "She needed help with a few things around the house, so I took care of them before coming over here."

Fenton seemed mollified with that answer. "She might lose

her voice entirely. Khell's bloodlines must be stronger than we thought."

Augustine shrugged. "Even if she does, it'll come back after the baby's born. She's a hundred percent ignus fae." He gestured down the hall. "Is this about the investigation into Dreich's death?"

"No." Fenton sighed. "But I got word from Detective Grantham that he's hit a dead end. His grandmother confirmed that the powder found at Dreich's was *bokura*, but she had no idea which of the voodoo practitioners might have made it."

"Great. Does that mean we have a problem with the voodoo-ers then?"

"I don't know." Fenton shook his head. "Might be worth you going to see Father Ogun, though."

Augustine squinted. "Remind me who that is?"

"He's their most powerful practitioner. If anyone knows who made that zombie powder, it would be him."

"Or maybe he made it himself. Either way, talking to him sounds like Grantham's job. If he can't get anywhere, then I'll take a crack at Ogun, but I don't want to start something I don't need to."

Fenton nodded. "Agreed. I'll ask Grantham to speak to him."

Augustine peered down the hall. "What am I here for if not the investigation? I'm not trying to shirk my duties as Guardian, but I promised Harlow I'd give her a few lessons in self-defense. I need to make time for that." He turned back to Fenton. "That reminds me, I need training equipment at the house. Some mats, a heavy bag, that sort of stuff."

Fenton nodded. "I'll take care of it, but maybe you should hire someone else to teach her unless it can wait until Mardi Gras is over. I'm going to need your full attention these next few days."

"Then you really need to tell me what's going on."

Fenton pushed his glasses up on his nose, gritted his teeth and sighed. "Loudreux tried to pass a motion at the council meeting last night prohibiting the Guardian from attending the Exemplar Krewe Ball tomorrow night."

"*Sturka*, the ball's tomorrow night? I knew it was coming up."

"Didn't you get an invitation?"

"No."

Fenton rolled his eyes. "Loudreux."

Augustine snorted. "So what if he doesn't want me at the ball? Did it ever occur to him I don't want to go to the damn ball?" Except that he did. The Exemplars were the oldest of the Mardi Gras krewes and the only one that was exclusively fae. He'd never *officially* been invited to any of their balls, but he'd crashed the legendary party a few times in the past. Being there as an invited guest? He shook his head. From street kid to city Guardian…how far he'd come.

"You must go." Fenton's eyes rounded in emphasis. "It's part of the Guardian's job to be there. To show your support for your people and our traditions and—"

"Of course I'm going. Especially if Loudreux doesn't want me to. He doesn't have the power to keep the Guardian out anyway. I'm his equal, not his underling. But what's his beef? Why would he try to keep me out? It's just a party."

Fenton tugged at his cuffs. "I'm sure he thought most of the Elektos would vote with him, but after you took care of the vampire situation, the Elektos are almost entirely on your side. Loudreux keeps bringing up your history. He's claiming there's no guarantee you won't cause some sort of…embarrassment." Fenton snorted. "He's just an old fool who can't stand having a Guardian in charge who doesn't kowtow to him."

Augustine stared down the hall. "*Bala'stro*." He adjusted the sword on his hip. "All of the Elektos are in there?"

"Yes. Like I said, *most* of them are on your side, but there are a couple who would rather stay in Loudreux's graces by voting as he wishes. Passing such a resolution wouldn't keep you from attending; it would just be Loudreux's way of making his objections public record."

"I'm a very different man than I used to be."

"*I* know that, as do many of the Elektos." Fenton sighed. "But Loudreux doesn't care."

"Then it's time I remind him who I am *now*." Augustine strode down the hall with purpose. He was tired of Loudreux's constant undermining. Tired of being judged by his wild, reckless past. He hadn't been Guardian long, but his actions since taking on that title should have been enough to prove he was serious about the job. He stormed into the study, Fenton trailing behind.

Quite a few uncertain faces looked up at him. Loudreux's held a scowl and his tenor matched his expression. "I see you finally deigned to grace us with your presence."

"Excuse me for being unable to rush over here to discuss whether or not I'm invited to a *party*. A pregnant widow needed my assistance."

Yanna, one of the Elektos known to support him and an ignus fae like Beatrice, smiled. "How is she doing?"

"Well. Although losing her voice. If you could stop by and see her, I know she'd appreciate it."

Yanna nodded. "I will make a point of it. Regularly."

"Thank you." He returned to Loudreux. "What's your issue with me attending the Exemplar Krewe Ball? It's part of my job to be there and we both know you don't have the authority to keep me from attending. Even so, you'd better have a damn good explanation for what you're trying to do."

Loudreux stood, adjusting his vest. The man was cypher like Fenton, tall and thin and lightly freckled with birthmarks that were actually tiny numbers. Legend said that if you could "get a cypher's number," you'd own him. There were times Augustine thought about doing just that, but then he remembered that would require stripping Hugo down to his altogether and checking every inch of the man's skin. Never going to happen.

Loudreux cleared his throat. "There is some concern—"

"You mean *you* have concerns or the entire council does?" In his peripheral vision, he saw Yanna cross her arms and stare Loudreux down.

Loudreux's jaw jutted out in frustration. "Whose concerns these are is none of your business."

Augustine held his stance. "It is if the entire council that voted me in is now suddenly doubting their decision."

Yanna sighed loudly, her gaze still directed at Loudreux. "Augustine, I have no concerns about your presence at the event, but there are *some* who believe you would forget your position at the Exemplar Ball. That you might not behave in a fashion suited to your rank."

He pushed his coat back to put one hand on his hip and the other on the hilt of his sword as he surveyed the room. "So some of you think I might forget my position as Guardian because I'm in the same room as booze and pretty women? Would that be because of your own behavior? Because I've been to the ball numerous times in years past, and I've seen the way some of you carry on."

A few who'd been glaring at him suddenly found great interest in the carpet.

He narrowed his eyes at Hugo. "Do you think I'd also forget that I got this position because vampires killed the woman who raised me? That I'd forget the amount of bloodshed that put me here? That the burden of protecting every citizen within these parish boundaries could be so easily tossed aside?" He leaned in until barely a breath separated them. "If so, you're an idiot."

A few of the Elektos gasped. Yanna's mouth curved toward

smugness. Hugo *hmph*ed. "I am the Prime. I will not be spoken to in such a way. You agreed to abide by my wishes when you were sworn in—"

"Actually," Yanna interrupted, "he didn't."

Fenton nodded. "She's right. He didn't. And as Guardian, he's not required to. Prime or not, Hugo, the Guardian doesn't answer to you."

It was possible the top of Loudreux's head might explode. He pointed a finger at Augustine and took a step back. "My daughter is the Faery Queen this year. I will not have Rue's moment ruined. Do you understand me?"

Augustine frowned, although he was glad to finally know the real reason the ball was such a big deal to Loudreux. "I understand your desire to protect your daughter. It's admirable, in fact. But if you think that I would do something to ruin her night just because she had the misfortune of being saddled with you for a father—or for any reason—you're wrong again. Why would you even suggest such a thing? I won't be anywhere near her."

Loudreux's pale skin flushed with anger. "Your ignorance is showing, Augustine. Of course you'll be near her. The Guardian is part of her court. You're her escort for the presentation." He jabbed his finger for emphasis. "I suggest you bring a date. One you attach yourself to. I don't want Rue or any of her friends on the court getting stupid teenage romantic notions about the city's wild new Guardian, understood?"

Augustine raised a brow. "I will be the perfect example of a Guardian, something I'd do regardless of who the Faery Queen was, but beyond that, I can promise you that yours is the last family I want to get any further in bed with."

He wheeled around and strode out of the room, Fenton on his heels. Anger coursed through Augustine's veins. He put his hand on the front door, ready to shove it open. "Let's go to the

Pelcrum and discuss whatever it is we need to discuss. I'm done with Loudreux's nonsense."

"Guardian Robelais?"

The soft, small voice stopped him. He turned. A slip of a girl stood behind him, eyes wide, mouth bunched to one side with nerves, hands clasped behind her back.

"Yes?"

"I'm Rue."

He'd guessed that much. She was a slight thing, clearly the child of two cyphers with her wispy build and lightly freckled skin. "What can I do for you?"

"I…" She swallowed as she looked down at the floor for a moment. "I wanted to give you this." She took her hands from behind her back and held out a purple foil envelope. "It's your invitation. I know my father didn't send you one because…"

"Because he thinks I'm going to ruin your evening."

She held the envelope up a little higher. "But I don't. He's just overprotective." She lifted her chin. "I'd be happy to have you as my official escort, so I hope you're going to be there."

He took the envelope and smiled, then bowed at the waist. The kid had guts. "It would be my honor. I wouldn't miss it for the world."

Chapter Three

I don't know," Harlow said. "Tell me more about it."

Nekai grinned. "Well, then, at the end of the evening, right before the ball is over, a horde of monsters come in and pretend to kidnap the Faery Queen." He sat back. "Of course, they're just members of the Exemplar Krewe in masquerade. Her ransom is paid, which goes toward funding next year's ball, and she's released to eventually ride front and center on the Exemplar float. Which the tourists will be clamoring to see this year with the covenant gone. A real live Faery Queen." He threw his head back and laughed. "They'll be insane."

"You know, this whole ball sounds weird enough to be really entertaining." His mood was infectious. She grinned as she sipped her sweet tea, then set the glass down on the table so it stood exactly on the ring of condensation it had left behind. Lally had stayed well away from the kitchen after Harlow had announced she was inviting Nekai in for lunch. No matter. Harlow had managed some roast beef sandwiches and chips. Nekai had been tight-lipped about what he'd read off Lally, refusing to do more than repeat it was a matter of confidentiality.

He wiped his mouth after finishing the last bite of his sandwich, then draped one arm over the back of his chair. "It can be. Depends on how theatrical they make it, and I expect them to really push it at this ball. The Faery Queen this year is Rue Loudreux. She's the Prime's daughter." He rolled his eyes skyward. "She's also an only child and I think her mother's been planning for this day since Rue was born."

"The Prime is the head of the fae council. The Elektos, right?" Nekai was a pretty decent teacher. The sight of him occasionally made her forget what he was talking about, but then she'd always found beautiful men distracting.

"That's right." He picked up a chip from his plate and used it to gesture at her. "You're a quick study."

She shrugged, feeling the heat of his compliment rise in her cheeks. "I have to be, now that I live here."

"So what do you think about my question? You never really gave me an answer." He popped the chip in his mouth, the sparkle in his eyes making her want to say yes.

She started to respond but Augustine's sudden entrance through the back door interrupted her.

"Hey, Harlow—" Augustine paused, glancing at her lunch partner. "You must be Nekai. Everything go alright with the warding? I didn't feel anything when I pulled in, but I assume that's because I was already included in the ward."

Nekai stood. The otherwise spacious kitchen seemed cramped with him and Augustine in it. "The warding went fine. And yes, you didn't feel it because I'd already added you to the ward."

Augustine stuck out his hand. "Thanks for taking care of the house."

Nekai shook it. "It's my job." He turned his gaze to Harlow. "And Harlow was very accommodating."

The look on Augustine's face said that was new and different. She refrained from kicking him in the shin. He turned toward her. "It's good you're here." Where else would she be? "Can you find a ball gown and mask for the Exemplar Krewe Ball by tomorrow night? I have to go and I'd love for you to be my date."

She bit her lip as her stomach sank with regret. She'd love

to go with Augustine, but his late request complicated things. "There might be a problem with that."

"What? Why?" He looked puzzled. "Is it the crowds?"

Nekai shifted and crossed his arms, his gaze filled with curiosity.

"Not exactly." She flipped her gaze to Nekai before returning it to Augustine. "Nekai already asked me."

Displeasure flickered in Augustine's gaze. Or perhaps it was jealousy. She hadn't had enough experience with men to really recognize that emotion. In fact, there was definitely some disappointment there, too, and that tugged at her. He was the last person she wanted to disappoint. "And you agreed to go?"

Was this what it felt like to have the interest of more than one man? She'd always wondered. It was a heady feeling. Like a flush of power. Even better than the rush she got right before her guild set off on a quest. She hadn't been on a decent quest in a long time, so she decided to let this new game play out. "I didn't get that far."

⚜

"A word outside." Augustine tipped his head at Nekai, trying to temper the anger heating his blood. "Now."

"Why?" Harlow asked. "Why can't you talk right here? Because you're going to be talking about me? You can hash it out here."

With a look that might have killed a lesser fae, Nekai shoved his chair back and stood. "No, maybe we should go—"

"Sit." Augustine stood his ground. "She's right. Let's have it out here." He crossed his arms. "Why would you ask her to the Exemplar Ball?"

Nekai sat. "Why not? She wasn't going with anyone and she's

trying to learn what it means to be fae. What better place than the ball?"

"Fair enough, but she should go with me."

Harlow leaned back, the bemused expression on her face a sure sign she was enjoying the conversation.

Nekai snorted. "And why's that?"

Augustine put one hand on the counter and leaned in. "Because she and I are already..." He looked at Harlow. What were they exactly? Certainly not a couple. Not yet. She tipped her head like she was eager for the answer.

"You're what?" Nekai pushed.

"We're friends." Hell's bells, he wanted them to be more than that, but that would have to suffice for now.

"Really?" Nekai looked nonplussed. "You're friends but the ball is tomorrow night and you *just* asked her."

"So did you and I'm sure you've known about it for more than a few hours, which is all I've had. This is settled." Augustine turned to Harlow. "I really do want you to go with me."

Nekai jumped to his feet. "Not so fast. I asked first. It's a done deal." His gaze sparked with a new emotion that looked dangerously close to self-satisfaction. He gave Harlow a little nod. "Besides, Harlow is clearly interested in getting to know me better. She made me food with her *own* hands."

Augustine stilled. *Sturka*. When an unattached fae woman made a meal for an unattached fae man, it was a clear sign she was interested. "What kind of food?"

"Sandwiches." Harlow frowned. "Why does that have anything to do with it?"

"It doesn't," Augustine assured her. He glared at Nekai. "You know she doesn't know our ways. She has no concept what that means. And a sandwich is hardly a meal." Why hadn't Lally made those sandwiches? She was pretty strict about no one else messing up her kitchen.

Nekai shrugged. "Doesn't matter. I know when a woman is interested in me, and Harlow is." He grinned at her. "Aren't you?"

Augustine spoke before she could answer. "Excellent idea asking her. It is *her* decision, after all." He almost smiled. Obviously Harlow would want to go with him. They had history, even if it had been brief, and there was definitely something *else* going on between them. If she was interested in Nekai, it was probably just because she was trying to learn more about being fae.

"Agreed." Nekai looked smug. *Bala'stro*. "Harlow, what do you say?"

Harlow sighed and shook her head. "Dates must be hard to come by in this town if you both want to take me." She smirked in obvious self-deprecation.

"Dates are easy," Augustine answered. "But I'm not interested in anyone but you."

"Me either," Nekai quickly added.

Her brows lifted with shock and the kind of appraising look that caused Augustine to wonder if he'd done the right thing. Or maybe she just thought she was watching two overgrown teenagers fighting over her. If she chose Nekai...

"I don't know." She tapped a finger on her chin. "The ball is tomorrow night?"

"Yes." Nekai shot Augustine a vicious look.

She sighed. "That's short notice. *Really* short notice. From both of you."

Nekai straightened a little. "I'm a well-respected member of fae society. We'd be sitting close to the head table."

Augustine snorted. "I'm the Guardian. We'll be sitting *at* the head table." He shook his head. Amateur.

"My point exactly," Nekai shot back. "Harlow may not want that kind of scrutiny."

"Scrutiny?" Harlow's brow furrowed.

Damn it, Nekai had figured out one of Harlow's weaknesses.

Nekai nodded with sudden concern. "Harlow, you should know there will be a lot of people there. Almost exclusively fae. If you don't feel comfortable going at all, I understand."

She paled a bit, then squared her shoulders. "It's a masquerade, right?"

"Yes."

She swallowed and nodded gently. "I can handle that."

"I would never let anything happen to you." Nekai put his hand on his chest. "I swear it."

"Neither would I. Obviously." Augustine barely controlled the urge to growl at the fool next to him.

An amused sparkle lit her eyes. "That's very noble of you, Nekai. Can I assume you have some dangerous spells at your disposal then?"

He nodded. "I can be as tough as Augustine when necessary."

Augustine snorted. "I doubt that." Then he remembered she'd seen him kill a vampire by slipping inside it shadeux style and was now acting a little afraid of him. "But then what do I know about weavers?"

Nekai growled softly before returning his attention to Harlow. "So which one of us would you like to accompany you?"

She picked her LMD up off the table, tucked it into the pocket of her sweater and shrugged, her eyes alight with pleasure. "I don't know. I guess you'll both have to show up tomorrow night and find out."

Giselle knocked at Zara's door, her nerves tripping with anxiety. Not a feeling she was used to, but then it wasn't every day she told her sister that their mother's suicide was a lie perpetuated by their father in an effort to protect them from the truth.

Zara didn't make her wait long. She opened the door and for a moment Giselle's heart stuttered, thinking somehow their mother *was* still alive. But it was just Zara with the same piercing hazel eyes and the same fiery red hair that fell in soft waves around the same heart-shaped face. Zara had even adopted most of their mother's wardrobe, the long skirts and flowing dresses and bohemian beads many humans associated with women of their kind. The only thing Zara hadn't inherited was the full force of their mother's gifts with nature. Zara was a skilled green witch, but Giselle doubted any of their coven could compete with the talent their mother had possessed.

"Hello, Giselle."

"Hi, Zara. Can I come in? I need a few minutes of your time."

"Of course. My home is always open to you." Zara smiled and moved to let Giselle enter, the stack of bracelets on her wrist clinking against one another. "It's been a while since you've visited."

"It's hard for me, you know that. There are so many memories here..." Giselle walked inside, the herbaceous scent of the house thrusting her back into her childhood. Zara had changed almost none of the furnishings. Maybe there were more plants, which was saying something, since their mother had filled every space with green, growing things. They were her source of power, just as their father had his antiques to draw from and Giselle her crystals. Each witch had something that magnified their inherent abilities.

"But they're good memories, aren't they?" Zara closed the door. "You should take comfort in those. I do."

"I don't think we share all the same memories."

Zara smiled. "Maybe not, but there are *some* good ones. Especially of the fun we used to have. Remember the old tire swing?"

Giselle nodded, her smile coming easy. "I think that's where I developed my hatred of dirt." She laughed softly. That was one of the good memories, but it didn't make the bad ones any easier to bear. Instead it felt like a reminder of what was gone. Her smile faded. Their parents had separated when she and Zara were still young, then their mother had moved to this house in the Garden District. Close to their father's house, but not so close that Evander would think there was anything he could do to win Vivianna back. There had been arguments that turned into screaming matches, the shuttling back and forth between homes, the constant battle to see who could be the better parent.

"I know you're thinking about the fighting," Zara said softly. "Try to focus on the good days we had with Mother."

"Those were our best days, weren't they? She's the reason I'm here." Giselle tried to smile again, but too much sorrow weighed on her heart.

"Let's go out to the garden then."

Giselle hesitated. That was where Vivianna had died. "I don't know if that's the best place for this conversation."

Zara took her hand. "It's very peaceful there, I promise. Sometimes it seems like Mother's spirit fills that place."

Giselle closed her eyes and took a deep breath before opening them again. "It probably does. That's where she died."

Zara's sweet expression faltered. "I know."

"You knew that?"

"I sensed it. Follow me." Zara led her through the house to the garden that took up the entirety of the walled property's outside space. In the center was a gorgeous pond. That was new. As they walked toward it, hungry koi rose to the surface to greet them, a rippling mosaic of orange, pearl and red. Zara dug into the pocket of her ankle-length patchwork velvet skirt, pulled out a handful of feed and tossed the pellets to them. They gobbled the food down, their mouths opening and closing silently. "You know Father tried to stop me from moving in here, but

Mother's will left specific direction that whichever of us wanted the house was to have it."

"I remember." Probably to keep her from finding out what had really happened to their mother.

Zara smiled, her gaze still on the fish. "It was kind of you not to fight that."

"You always loved this house. It would have been cruel of me to take this garden away from you." Living here would have been a nightmare. The constant reminder of their mother... Giselle didn't understand how Zara could manage it, how she seemed to thrive in this environment, but of course, Giselle knew. It was the garden. Zara's source of strength. Which made Giselle wonder if Zara was actually stronger than she seemed. "Why do *you* suppose Father tried to keep you from moving in here?"

"When I moved in, the garden was destroyed. Purposefully. Like it had been done to cover something else up. Or remove something."

Because it had. "Any idea who might have done that?"

"I have a few guesses." Zara finally made eye contact. "But I can tell you it took a long time and a lot of effort for me to restore it. The spellwork I put into this..." She sighed, her fingers toying with the scrying glass that hung from her neck by a long gold chain. "It was a labor of love, though. Besides being a greater source of energy for me, I wanted it to be a memorial to Mother."

"You did a beautiful job. I'm sure she's amazed by what you accomplished." The garden had never looked this vibrant that Giselle could remember. Perhaps she'd underestimated Zara's talents. And how perceptive Zara was. "What do you think someone was trying to hide?"

A dark look flitted through Zara's gaze. "In the process of restoring the grounds, I unearthed a huge, burnt crater that had been filled in. Nothing would grow here, so I turned it into the pond you see before you." Her eyes went steely. "The ground reeked of chaos magic. It still does after a strong rain."

Giselle sank onto one of the marble benches surrounding the pond. Did Zara already know the truth of what had happened to their mother? She felt like they were dancing around it. "What do you make of that?"

Zara turned, the softness of her expression twisted by pain. "I don't know. But I'm hoping you can explain it to me, because that's what you've come here for, isn't it? Why you're asking me all these questions?"

"Yes." Giselle's grip tightened on the edge of the marble bench. Telling Zara the truth about their mother wasn't going to be easy. "Zara, what I have to tell you might come as a shock."

"I can handle anything. Just don't lie to me, Giselle. And don't try to soften the blow because of what you think I can and can't handle. Just tell me the truth." Zara took a step toward her and the garden . . . followed. Tree branches bent and plant stems curved in Giselle's direction. The koi in the pond gathered at the edge, swimming over each other to get closer to Zara. Their unblinking eyes stared at Giselle, mouths gaping like brainless zombies.

Nodding, Giselle stood, the backs of her knees bumping the edge of the bench. "That's what I'm here for. To tell you the truth. Even though it isn't an easy one. I also want you to know that the information I'm about to share, I just found out."

A stray breeze lifted the ends of Zara's hair, making it fly out around her face. "Found out what, exactly?"

Something tickled Giselle's ankle. A tendril of ivy reached toward her from the bench supports. She pulled her foot away. "Something I think you've probably already figured out. Our mother didn't kill herself. She died doing the chaos magic you found in your garden. She was trying to cast a spell that would destroy the fae and bring the witches back into power." The wind whipped up. "Our father knew this but thought it would be better if we didn't. He kept it all secret, according to him, for our own good."

Zara's eyes flashed with anger. A tree branch cracked. Then she closed her eyes and took a breath. The wind died down and the plants returned to their original positions. She exhaled and opened her eyes. They still held anger, but this time it was controlled. "None of this surprises me. It's what I've suspected all these years. He's done things all our lives that he thought were in our best interest but weren't. Why should Mother's death be any different? I'm glad you told me what happened. It's good to have closure." She glanced at the pond, where the koi had disappeared beneath the surface again. "Now I can move forward with some things I had planned, knowing exactly what was done here."

"Things? Like what?"

Zara stared out at the garden. "A cleansing ritual for the ground, for one." She shrugged. "Trying out a few new things after that. I'll be interested to see what this ground is capable of once I've finished preparing it."

Giselle smiled. Delivering the news about their mother to Zara hadn't been the ordeal she'd anticipated. "Let me know if you need any help." But she wasn't sure that request was likely to ever be made. Zara had never been the kind of witch who wanted or needed the help of others to make things happen, much like their fiercely independent mother. Giselle understood that, but there were times when an ally was invaluable.

Zara nodded. "I will. In fact, you can plan on it."

If Giselle's shock showed on her face, so be it. "I'm surprised to hear you say that. You're so much like Mother, I just thought…"

"That I'd keep my work secret? We're family, Giselle. Sisters."

She hesitated like she wanted to say more but couldn't find the right words. "Change is coming. If we don't have each other, what chance do we have of surviving?" She smiled tentatively. "Mother hid her work and look at the result."

Giselle nodded. "You're right." They'd been distant too long. "I guess I'll talk to you soon then."

Zara smiled brightly. "I guess you will."

Chapter Four

Harlow perused the gowns in her mother's enormous walk-in closet, enjoying the lingering scent of the lemon verbena perfume Olivia had always worn. A few of the dresses Harlow actually recognized from pictures she'd seen of Olivia online and in magazines, gowns that had graced red carpets and movie premieres and charity events.

Bittersweet emotion filled Harlow as her fingers lingered on the gorgeous fabrics. What fun her mother must have had in these gowns. What stories they could tell. Stories Harlow would never get to hear.

With a long sigh, she returned to her search. Somewhere in this endless row of feathers and sequins and silk and lace there had to be something she could make work for the Exemplar Ball. Something that would keep the interest of two men. She rolled her lips in to keep from laughing. How on earth had *that* happened?

Nekai was beautiful, but she wasn't really as interested in him as she was in Augustine. She wanted Nekai for a teacher. What she wanted Augustine for was something very different. Something much more primal. Not just sex, which she was so not ready for, but the way he made her feel. Because even though he was fae and that should bother her, most of the time she felt more at ease around him than anyone else.

She smiled as she remembered the look of jealousy on Augustine's face when he learned Nekai had already asked her to the ball. Oh, she was in big karmic trouble for enjoying that as much as she had. And for not doing anything to alleviate it.

A breeze danced around her ankles. She'd felt it before. It leaked in through an old hidden door in the back wall of the closet. She'd found it about a week ago, but hadn't given it much thought. Most old houses—and this one was really old—lost rooms to renovations and such. This time the breeze seemed more forceful than usual. She pushed the dresses out of the way to have a look at it again.

"Finding what you're looking for?"

Harlow jumped, the dresses she'd been holding back falling into place again. "Lally, you scared the crap out of me." The breeze disappeared.

She laughed. "Sorry about that, child. I didn't mean to. You trying to find a dress for the ball tomorrow?"

"Yes." Harlow adjusted the hanger of the black satin. The door could wait. "Can I ask you something?"

"Anything, Harlow. Anything, anytime, any subject."

Harlow smiled. "I don't have a lot of experience with men—"

Lally held her hands up, her eyes widening. "If this is gonna be a birds-and-the-bees kind of thing, I might need to revise my earlier statement."

"No, no. I know about that." She lowered her voice a bit. "I'm not exactly a... I mean, it's not that kind of question." Just the thought of having that conversation with Lally made her blush a little. "The thing is, I haven't dated a lot. Was it wrong of me to tell Augustine and Nekai that I wouldn't make up my mind until the night of the ball? I probably should tell Nekai that I'm going to pick Augustine so he can get his own date. That would be the right thing to do."

Lally's brows rose in obvious disapproval. "If that boy don't have a date already, he wasn't planning on having one and he'd probably have left you at the ball for someone more to his liking anyway. You want to play games, you play games because I promise you, he's been playing one."

"You don't like Nekai much, do you?" Why, though, that was the question. And Nekai wasn't about to spill his side of it. Maybe he would if she got to know him better.

Lally straightened the rack of clothes nearest her, adjusting what already hung in evenly spaced lines. "I don't like when a person can see into you more than you want them to."

Sadness swept Harlow. "You mean like I can."

Lally turned, the realization of what she'd said plain on her face. "No, child, I didn't mean..." She sighed. "It's different with us. You're family to me, just like your mama was. And family trusts family. But Nekai? He just came here to do a job. I'd rather he just do that and keep his distance."

The sadness dissipated. Harlow leaned against the center island of drawers. "Are you afraid he's found out some secret about you and he's going to tell someone? Because he said he keeps all that stuff confidential." She laughed, trying to diffuse the tension that hung in the air. "It's not like you have any secrets, anyway, do you?"

Lally's hand froze on the hanger she'd been adjusting, her whole body going still except for the rise and fall of her chest. "We all got secrets."

"I don't. You know all mine."

Lally smiled and swatted her hand through the air like she was trying to shoo a fly. "It's nothing. Just an old woman's silly opinion, that's all." Her smile stayed fixed. "Now, we need to find you a dress and you'll have to have a mask to go with it. That's easy, though. Your mama went to a lot of the different krewe balls over the years and it wasn't her style to throw anything away. What colors do you like?"

Harlow gave Lally a pass and let the topic of secrets drop. She
didn't want to upset the sweet woman who'd been her mother's
closest companion. "I tend to wear mostly black."

"I've noticed." Lally raised her brows. "Shame, too, with your
mama's pretty amber eyes and that beautiful hair of yours. Do
you know the theme?"

"There's a theme?" Harlow sighed. "This is getting more
complicated."

Lally dipped her head. "The boys asked you. One of them
should know. Personally, I'd check with Augustine as I believe
he's in the house."

"Good idea." She ran out of the room to the landing, leaned
over the railing and yelled down. "Augustine, you down there?"

A few seconds went by before he appeared on the first floor.
He wore his coat. "Getting ready to head out again, so training
will have to wait a little longer. What's up?"

"I don't have time to train right now anyway. I need to find a
costume for this ball, which is why I yelled for you. What's the
theme? Without that, I might not wear the right thing."

"Theme? I have no—hang on." He held up a finger. "Call
Fenton." After a beat he spoke again. "Fenton, Augustine. What's
the theme of the Exemplar Ball?" He nodded. "Okay, thanks.
Yes, on my way." He looked up at her with a smile that made her
stomach do funny things. The thought of a night at a fancy ball
with him was kind of amazing. "Fenton says Enchanted Forest."

"Okay, good enough. Thanks. See you later." She waved,
then went back to Lally in the closet. "Enchanted Forest. Whatever that means. I guess I should be some kind of animal?"

Lally squinted as she scanned the line of dresses. "Lemme
think now…"

"You know, I have a pretty fancy bird mask I bought for
Nokturnos. Maybe I could just wear that with a black dress
and call it done."

"Black? Please, child. Too boring for a ball like this, especially on the arm of a man like Augustine." Her eyes rounded and she slapped her leg. "I know! Your mama went to one of her very first balls as Mother Nature. Beautiful emerald-green dress, hair all done up and this mask that looked like tiny leaves. There was more to it, but I can't quite remember—"

"Don't you think a green dress with this hair would make me stand out?"

"That's the point." She came to Harlow's side and began riffling through the dresses at the far end of the rack, finally pulling out a long black garment bag from the very back. She laid it over the center island and unzipped it. "Yep, this is the one."

"Oh. My." Even with the walk-in's subtle lighting, the dress sparkled with life. Crystals, beads, embroidery and tiny velvet leaves covered emerald-green silk in a pattern of vines. She resisted the urge to pull her gloves off and touch the fabric. There was no way any residual emotions still clung to it this many years after her mother had worn it, was there? Probably not. She'd find out when she put it on.

Lally pulled the dress out of the bag. "Needs steaming and maybe a little alteration." She looked at the dress, then at Harlow. "Your mama might have been a tad more endowed than you when she wore this, but it was made by the same fae seamstress who did all her Mardi Gras ball costumes. Supposedly the dress adjusts itself to fit the wearer." She shook her head. "I don't know about that, but it sure fit her like a glove."

Fear replaced excitement as Harlow took in the dress's style. "That's strapless. I can't wear that."

Lally gave her a look. "You can't tell me you're shy about showing skin. Not your generation."

"No, it's because all that exposed skin is like asking to be touched." Harlow frowned. "You know how I feel about that and in that dress, skin-to-skin contact seems unavoidable. Add to that the crowd and…" She shook her head. "Even with gloves, I don't think I could stand it."

"Gloves. Hmm. You're giving me an idea." Lally hung the dress on a valet bar. "Come with me."

Harlow followed Lally downstairs to the kitchen, where Lally reached into the very back of the under-sink cabinets and pulled out a spray can. She held it up. "You ever try this?"

The label said "EZ Glove." "Never even heard of it."

"Spray-on latex gloves. Augustine got it for me for Mother's Day one year." She smiled. "That and a bottle of the vilest-smelling perfume you can imagine. Lands, it was like swamp water. But his heart was in the right place."

Harlow grinned. She loved these little insights into him.

"Supposedly you spray it on, covering your hands real good, and it works just like gloves for washing dishes and such until you peel it off."

"That would explain why I've never heard of it. Cleaning isn't my thing. Have you ever tried it?"

Lally shook her head. "I'm allergic to latex." She shook the can, rattling the marble inside to mix it up. "You want to give it a go?"

"Sure. I guess we'll never know otherwise." Harlow pushed her sleeve back and stuck out her bare arm.

Lally popped the top off and sprayed some on Harlow's arm above where her glove stopped.

"Ooo, it's cold. If this works, getting it on will be quite the experience." How amazing if it worked. To be able to be touched without having another person's emotions shoved into her. A whole night of not dreading contact. Of being normal. What would that be like?

Lally read the back of the label. "Says it dries quickly. What do you think?"

Harlow blew on it, but the patch didn't seem wet. "I think it's good." She held out her arm. "Let's give it a shot."

Lally hesitated.

"I won't share your secrets, I promise."

Lally smiled, but it was a weak effort. "It's nothing," she said softly. "I told you it's nothing." She reached out with a single finger, patted the latex-covered section, then pulled her finger back. "Did you feel anything?"

Harlow couldn't respond for a second, then she grinned. "Not a thing. This might work." She laughed. Not having to worry about people touching her would change her whole experience. "This ball might actually be fun."

As soon as Augustine had answered Harlow, he'd taken off to the Lafayette Cemetery and the crypt that held the secret entrance to the Pelcrum. It was the same cemetery that held Livie's urn. Her ashes had been spread on the fae plane.

Which reminded him that he hadn't been to visit her there in a few days. Right before she'd died of her vampire-inflicted wounds, he'd managed—at her request—to hustle the big foyer mirror outside and lay her body on it in an attempt to help her transport to the fae plane, but she'd died almost as soon as he'd done it. He'd thought his efforts had been too little, too late.

He'd found out differently after spreading her ashes on the fae plane. But while she could take on a solid form in that world, crossing back over to the mortal world in any form so far seemed impossible. The most she could do was appear in the foyer mirror's surface.

The fact that she was still alive in any form should be enough, but her refusal to tell Harlow she'd survived—or let him tell Harlow—had become a point of contention between them. He understood she feared Harlow would be repulsed by seeing her mother in such a state. Or further traumatized by the desolate spot where her mother had been trapped.

But Harlow was gradually making her peace with being fae, and it was high time she knew her mother wasn't really dead. Everything else Olivia wanted to keep secret, like Harlow's biological father, Joseph Branzino, being a raptor fae and one of the scariest of their kind, and that he'd killed the twin sister Harlow didn't even know about, could wait a little longer. Maybe tonight, after Harlow went to bed, he'd have a chance to slip through and talk to Olivia again. Dulcinea and Cy should be arriving with her stuff soon. Organizing all that would probably wear Harlow out and send her to bed early.

He walked through the cemetery gates, ignoring the few tourists to slip back through the rows of tombs to the Miller crypt. He glanced around, but he was alone. This decrepit part of the cemetery didn't get many visitors. The crypt looked like it hadn't been cared for in years, which was part of its disguise. He pulled the rusted sconce near the crypt's entrance and the door opened. Once inside, he pulled another sconce to shut the door and open a panel in the floor that revealed a set of steps.

He jogged down into the rough-hewn stone halls of the Pelcrum. "Fenton? You here?" His voice echoed off the phosphorescent walls as the gas lights flickered.

The double doors at the end of the hall opened and the cypher fae stuck his head out of the war room. "Come in, I have news."

Augustine joined him at the massive round meeting table inlaid with a fleur-de-lis. It matched the silver one that had been branded into his chest, a symbol worn by all those who served the fae, including Augustine's lieutenants. That mark on his chest also granted him access to this place. Somewhere, under Fenton's buttoned-up shirts and tweedy jackets, he bore one, too. "What did you find out?"

"I talked with Grantham about speaking to Father Ogun. He tried. The man acted like he had no idea about anything. You're going to have to take a crack at him. I sent his info to your LMD."

"I can't today. I have to be back at the house to help Harlow move her stuff in. I've already missed out on our first training session, I can't miss that, too. I'll do it first thing in the morning, though."

Fenton nodded. "All right. Was Harlow excited about the ball when you asked her?"

"About that—"

"Did you ask someone else?"

"No. I asked Harlow."

"So you're taking her."

"I'm *trying* to take her." Augustine sat back in his chair.

Fenton frowned. "I don't know what that means."

"Well, thanks to that weaver you sent over—"

"Nekai? Yes, he's very good."

"He's also very irritating. He asked Harlow to the ball, too."

Fenton's face scrunched up. "I don't understand. Are you taking Harlow or is he?"

"I don't know. She's making both of us show up and then she said she'd make her decision."

The line of Fenton's mouth bent oddly, then he broke out laughing. "That's good. That's very good."

"It's not good at all. It completely sucks. I don't want to share Harlow with that spell jockey."

Fenton's grin remained. "Loudreux was worried you wouldn't be occupied. Sounds to me like you're going to have your hands plenty full." The smile vanished. "Unless, of course, you think she's going to pick Nekai instead?"

"Hell, no, she's not going to pick him." *Sturka*. She might. "Damn it. I better go back home and talk to her."

"As much as I'd like for you to talk to Ogun today, I agree. Go home and see what you can do." He pulled his leather satchel onto his lap and rummaged through it. "Wait a moment. I have something that might help sway her. I was going to give it to you, but knowing Harlow, I think she'd need it more. Plus, a little gift never hurts when trying to impress—"

"I know how to impress a woman. Flowers, chocolates, sparkly things." The problem was he doubted any of those standbys would work on Harlow.

"Harlow isn't just any woman." Fenton steepled his fingers. "She doesn't strike me as the type to be easily swayed by your . . . shenanigans."

Augustine stood. "Shenanigans?"

Fenton snorted. "Your reputation as a lady-killer is well known, Augustine."

"Was," he corrected. "I'm not like that anymore."

"Since how long? Two weeks?" Fenton pointed to Augustine's chair. "Sit down. I really do have something for you. For Harlow, now."

Curious, Augustine sat.

Fenton pulled a small round case from his bag. "You can give it to her, take the credit and be the hero."

"I told you I don't need help."

"So you mentioned." Fenton unscrewed the top. The case held a small pool of clear liquid.

Augustine looked at it, then looked at Fenton. "I'm still getting to know Harlow, but unless that's magic water, I don't think it's going to impress her."

Fenton sighed. "This case holds a specially designed contact lens that's imbedded with facial recognition software. If Harlow wears this to the ball, it will identify the people around her. I know she's uncomfortable in crowds. With the help of this device, she hopefully won't feel so ill at ease."

Augustine peered closer into the case, picking up the subtle edge of something transparent floating within the liquid. "How about that. She loves technology. She's going to geek out over that. You were going to give this to me. Did you just make it?"

"No, this was originally developed for the Haven City Summit in 2057 as a way for attendees to recognize each other."

"It's very cool." Augustine sat back. "One small thing. People are going to have masks on. Won't that be a problem?"

Fenton screwed the top back on and slid the case toward Augustine. "Fae masks aren't the same as what most humans wear. And this software is pretty powerful. It's been programmed with the information on the fae most likely to attend but yes, because of the masks, there will be some it won't be able to identify. Still, it will give her quite the advantage."

"Better than nothing." Augustine slipped the case into his pocket and got back to his feet. "I'll talk to you tomorrow after I speak with this Father Ogun."

"Very good. Oh, one more thing, what are you going as to the ball?"

"I...damn. I hadn't actually thought about it."

"What's Harlow going as?"

Augustine growled softly. "I don't know that either. But she was working on it when I left, going through Olivia's old costumes."

"I thought as much." Fenton wagged a finger at Augustine. "Call her and ask her, then I might be able to help you."

Augustine nodded. "Call Harlow." A second later the com cell behind his ear sent a ringing through his head.

She picked up just before it went to voice mail, sounding breathless. "What's up?"

"What's your costume for the Exemplar Ball?"

"Looks like a Mother Nature sort of thing."

"Okay. That's all I need to know."

"Why? What are you going as?"

"I'm working on that. Home in a bit. Dulce and Cy get there yet?"

"No, but she texted a little bit ago to say they were getting close."

"All right, I won't be long." She hung up, and he looked at Fenton. " 'Mother Nature sort of thing.' Her words."

Fenton rested a finger on his chin. Then lifted it to point toward the back of the room. "I think we have something for that." He got up and started walking toward the rear right corner of the war room.

"We?" Augustine went after Fenton as he disappeared around a row of shelves. "This place is even bigger than I thought." The path ahead was blocked by a substantial metal door. "Is this a vault?"

Fenton unbolted the door. Rivets outlined the frame. "More storage."

"And that includes costumes for the Exemplar Ball?"

Fenton opened the door. "Yes. It's an important event and not one our Guardians and their lieutenants are always prepared for." He paused to wave his hand at Augustine. "Case in point." Then he went through.

Augustine followed. The room beyond was massive. More of a warehouse, really. He shook his head, awed by the space. "I know this is more fae magic but damn, this place should not be able to exist." Solars, sun-powered lamps, dotted the vast ceiling, shedding enough light for the room to be on the bright side of dim. The rows of shelves were numbered at the end of each stack with the same phosphorescent paint that marked the Pelcrum's main hall.

"It is a marvel." But Fenton's mind seemed elsewhere. He glanced up and down each stack as they passed it, checking and double-checking the numbers at the ends. "Ah, here we are." He started muttering under his breath so softly Augustine almost couldn't make out the words. "Jungle theme, not quite right... gods and goddesses, no...creatures of the forest—ah, yes, excellent." He stopped in front of one of the shelves. Labeled boxes were crammed against each other. He wheeled a rolling ladder over, climbed five shelves high, extracted a box and climbed back down. "This should do."

Augustine wiped dust off the label. "Satyr? What the hell is that?"

"In this case, half stag, half man. And your costume. Unless you're rather be a tree."

Augustine's brows shot up. "I'm good with satyr."

"Don't look so skeptical." Fenton rapped the top of the box, causing more dust to fly off. "That costume was made by a very skilled fae seamstress specifically for a horned fae. It should be a very good pairing for Harlow's Mother Nature."

"I just need a costume. Doesn't matter what it is."

"Yes." Fenton drew the word out like he was contemplating something. "I'm sure that's exactly the approach Nekai is taking."

"Point taken." Box in hand, he turned to go, then paused. "If you help Nekai out with a costume, give him the tree. Or better yet, make him a nutria."

Chapter Five

Harlow, they're here."

Lally's voice carried when she wanted it to. Harlow jumped up from her desk and headed downstairs, pulling her gloves on as she went.

Lally stood at the bottom of the steps. She tipped her head toward the back of the house. "Dulcinea and that big fellow just pulled into the drive in the moving van."

"Thanks." As Harlow's feet hit the first floor, a sleek black machine sped past the front of the house, screeching slightly as it rounded the side of the property. "And I see Augustine's home."

Lally *tsk*ed. "That boy's lucky he's the Guardian or he'd be losing his license again with the way he drives."

"Again? You'll have to tell me about that sometime." Harlow laughed. It was good to be getting her stuff back. To have something new to focus on. The ad for her new web design business would be in the paper tomorrow. Not a lot of time to get her system back up and running, especially with the ball coming up, but being busy was good. It kept her mind off the hollowness growing inside her.

She went outside, the slight chill hardly comparable to years of Boston's freezing weather. In fact, it felt good. Bracing. The kind of air that cleared out your cobwebs when you breathed it. With a little wave to Augustine, she went to greet Cy and Dulcinea, who were getting out of the van. "I'm so glad you're back. I owe you guys for getting my things."

Cylo, the enormous ethos fae, grinned. The smile helped diminish the intimidating nature of his towering height and massive build. "Nothing owed. Happy to help the boss's... friend."

She glanced at Augustine, but he was already talking to Dulcinea. "I guess we should get my stuff off the truck."

"Don't worry about it." Cy shrugged one mountainous shoulder. "I got it. Not much to get, really."

She canted her head. "I suppose not."

He hesitated. "That came out wrong."

"No, it came out fine." She smiled as she walked around the back of the truck with him. "I've been so wrapped up in computers all my life, I never paid much attention to stuff. Well, some stuff." Like all her geeky memorabilia and collectibles.

He grinned back. "I wrapped your *Star Alliance* light blade myself. Special edition like that, have to be careful."

"Thanks." She narrowed her gaze. "You knew what that was?"

He pressed his first two fingers together and placed them over his heart. "Ever starward."

"Is there any other direction?" She shot the answer back to him without even thinking, then stared at him in amazement. He knew the *Star Alliance* salute. And the catchphrase! "You're an Ally?"

His smile went shy and he nodded, glancing toward Dulcinea. "Nobody else I know is. Dulcinea called your light blade a toy." He snorted. "Civilians."

She laughed. "I never thought I'd meet another Ally in my driveway. Cool." The connection gave her a little courage. "Can I ask you something?"

He nodded. "Sure."

"I don't know if it's okay to ask this, but is your size your power? Or can you do something else?"

He grinned. "Watch this."

She kept her gaze on him, but before she could blink he was gone. Her mouth dropped open and words failed her. In his place stood Captain Finn Brakston, commander of the *Sanctuary* spaceship and the face of her favorite sci-fi show, *Star Alliance*. "Cy?"

Captain Finn saluted. "At your service."

It was even Finn's voice. She shook her head. "How...?"

In a flash, Cy was back in front of her. "Pretty cool, huh?"

Her heart was actually pounding a little. "Cool? That might be the most amazing thing I've ever seen." Why on earth hadn't she been born with that skill? "Can you do anybody?"

"Anybody I've seen, sure." He shrugged like it was no big deal. "I better get back to work."

"Okay." Still smiling at his amazing display, she watched while he unlatched the truck's big overhead door and shoved it up. Her smile disappeared. "That really is pitiful." Her entire life fit into so few boxes almost half the truck was empty. The bulk of the load was her desk and ergonomic chair.

"Would've been more if we'd had the rest of the furniture."

She nodded. None of it had been worth anything. "You found a place to donate it?"

"Yep." He jumped into the truck and presented her with a long, bubble-wrapped object. "Your light blade, safe and sound."

"Thanks." She took it from him. "Any chance you play Realm of Zauron?"

He bent, picked up three stacked boxes and turned. "Once in a while."

"Oh. I was going to ask if you wanted to join my guild, but if you only play once in a—"

He jumped down out of the truck. "I play whenever I'm not on duty. I'd be up for joining your guild."

"A guild?" Dulcinea sauntered over, Augustine right behind her. "What are you two talking about?"

"Realm of Zauron." Harlow crossed her arms, daring Dulcinea to start something. "It's one of the most popular multiplayer games online."

"For people who don't have a life, you mean." Dulcinea barked out a laugh. "Just kidding with you. I know what it is. Not my thing, though. Although, now that I'm living at the Guardian's house and the 'lectric is paid for, who knows?"

"I know," Cylo muttered.

Harlow bit back a smile. "Two minutes in Gyloon Tavern and she'd be toast."

Cy snorted.

Augustine clapped his hands. "Enough chatter. Let's get this truck unloaded. We're wasting daylight."

Harlow frowned at him. "Go do whatever it is you need to do. Cy and I can handle this."

Augustine grabbed her gloved hand, surprising her with the sudden intimacy. A tickle of intrigue danced through her. "Cy *and* Dulce can handle it. I need you."

"You do? For what?"

He tugged her gently toward the house. "C'mon. I'll show you." With his free hand, he pointed to Cy and Dulcinea. "Stack the boxes on the porch, then Harlow can decide where she wants what."

Back in the kitchen, a hint of a smile played across his mouth. He let go of her hand and reached into his coat pocket, pulling out a small round case. "For you."

"What is it?" The case was plastic and too small for jewelry. Not that Augustine had any reason to give her jewelry.

"Open it."

She unscrewed the top and stared at the contents. "Wow, a teaspoon of water! How did you know?" She gave him a look. "What is it?"

"There's a contact lens in there. Go put it in."

She jiggled the container. "I guess there is. Just one?"

"Yep." He dug something else out of another pocket. A compact. He flipped it open, revealing a mirror, and set it down on the counter. "Here you go. Put it in. Whichever eye you like."

"You realize this requires a lot of trust on my part."

"It's a brand-new contact. No one else has touched it. Fenton assured me."

"Fenton gave this to you?" That was a whole different story. He seemed like a helpful sort of guy. "Okay."

Augustine looked hurt. "So if it's from him it's okay but if it's from me it's questionable?"

"Pretty much." Laughing, she scooped the contact onto one finger, leaned over the mirror and popped it in. She blinked as it righted itself. "That's going to take some getting used to." She faced him. "I don't get what it's supposed—" A blinking cursor appeared in the corner of her field of vision. "Whoa. Hold on." Lines of type followed: *Augustine Robelais : Guardian : Shadeux/smokesinger fae : Analysis—friend*

Her mouth dropped open. "This is crazy. What is this thing?"

He grinned. "What *is* it doing?"

"I looked at you and it told me who you are, that you're the Guardian, what kind of fae you are, and then it determined you're a friend. How does it know you're a friend?"

"I think it's more like I'm generally not a threat. Sounds like it's working exactly as Fenton said it would. It's got facial recognition software in it and Fenton had it loaded with the expected guest list for the ball tomorrow night. He thought if you knew who people were it might help you feel a little less overwhelmed."

She pointed at her eye. "This is ridiculously cool. Like *Star Alliance*-level cool." She hugged him, thankful for the barrier of fabric between them keeping his emotions at bay. "I love it. I have to thank Fenton. Let's call him."

"He'll be at the ball. You can thank him in person."

"Oh! I have to go try it out on Cy." She ran out onto the porch. Cy was coming toward her, a stack of boxes partially obscuring his face. The cursor blinked, but no information followed.

Augustine stood beside her. "Well?"

"Nothing yet."

He nodded. "Fenton said the software has to have a certain percentage of visibility to recognize the face, which means it won't work on everyone at the ball due to the masks, but it will work enough to give you a serious advantage."

Cy put his boxes down and stood. "You want any of these inside yet?"

Cylo Greaves: Lieutenant : Ethos fae : Analysis—friend

"And there it is," she said softly to Augustine. She raised her voice to answer Cy. "The desk, chair and anything that's computer equipment goes into the third-floor room I cleaned out. Gimme a sec and I'll show you. The clothes can stay out here for now." She had a ton of winter clothes to sort through, which coming from Boston meant more than half her wardrobe. New Orleans got some cooler weather like they'd had these past few days, but nothing that necessitated keeping the three thousand chunky black sweaters she owned.

"You like it then?" Augustine asked.

She faced him, grinning. "I have some pretty high-end tech, but this tops them all. I love it. And it will definitely make me feel more comfortable at the ball. Thank you." She leaned in and gave him a quick kiss on the cheek.

His emotions were her reward. His happiness suffused her, warming her with the sense of how pleased he was to have been able to do this for her. Good emotions like that were like a shot of energy, boosting her mood and her general sense of well-being. They seemed to momentarily soothe the emptiness, too.

She tipped her head. "Maybe I should call Nekai and tell him I've made my choice for the ball."

Augustine smiled, bright and big, then looked away, his mouth bending into a wicked smirk. "I say let him show up." His stormy-sea gaze came back up to meet hers. "He should at least get to see how beautiful you're going to look."

Heat rose in her cheeks at the compliment. Those kinds of words unbalanced her. She stared at her gloves. "You have no idea what I'm going to look like."

"Doesn't matter." He lifted her chin with his finger, flooding her with more pleasant feelings. "I know what you look like now."

Giselle shivered despite her long cashmere tunic, leggings and tall suede boots. The gloom of the gray skies made the hour feel later than it was. She pulled her keys from her purse and let herself into the house, flipping the light switch to chase the shadows away. Zara's plans, whatever they were, stuck in Giselle's mind, tempting her with possibilities. What could Zara be up to? She'd never shown much ambition before this, but that was clearly no longer the case.

"Hello, Giselle."

Startled, Giselle lifted a hand, prepared to throw whatever defensive spell necessary. Father Ogun sat in one of her living room chairs. The *ivory* silk.

"Father Ogun. I'd invite you to make yourself comfortable, but I see you've already done that." She dropped her hand to hang her keys on the little hook next to the door where they belonged, but the comfort of that orderliness wasn't enough to displace her anger at his intrusion. Still, she'd known this day would come. She just hadn't guessed it would come this early. "I assume you're here to collect on our agreement?"

He sat for a moment, just staring at her. Trying to intimidate her, no doubt. "I am not here because of our flesh debt, no."

That was some relief. She'd paid a very high price for his help, but it had kept her free from the entanglements of the fae, cleanly severing her connection to the one who'd been letting vampires into the city. Of course the fae had their suspicions, but no proof. "Then what brings you here? Into my *locked* house." He'd obviously broken through the spell locks. She'd have to work on those.

Father Ogun smiled. Not a pleasant sight. "Locks. What do they really do? Give comfort to those inside the house. Someone who is determined to come in is going to come in."

"And now that you're in, can we get to the heart of that matter?" She was in no mood for games. "What brings you here?"

He nodded. "Very well." His smile flattened. "The police have been to see me about some *bokura* found in the house of a fae who *killed* himself." He waved one finger slowly through the air. "This should not have happened."

"I paid your price. What I did with that powder—"

"I do not care what you did with the *bokura*. I care that you allowed it to be traced back to me."

"That *bokura* could have been made by anyone."

"Anyone who practices voodoo. Which is why I had a police detective sitting in my parlor just as I am now sitting in yours."

Her pulse raced. "What did you tell him?"

"Nothing. That he had a dead end."

She nodded, her breathing evening out. "Then it's over."

"You'd better hope that's true." He shook his finger at her. "We have worked long and hard to clear the name of voodoo in this town. To free ourselves from the stigma our religion has carried for so long." He stood. "We will not be subject to the kind of control the witches are, and trouble like this is what brings that sort of regulation."

That regulation was a noose around her neck, tightening a little more every day that the fae were in power and her father did nothing about it. But at least Evander *had* some power. A coven behind him. What did Ogun have? A handful of priests and priestesses? "This won't come back to you."

He walked toward the door. "You best pray to your goddess it doesn't." As he passed her, his hand snaked out, fingers catching a few strands of her hair and yanking them free.

"Ow! What the hell?" She pressed her hand to her head.

He wound the strands into a little coil and tucked them in his pocket. "Fix this, witch. Or I will fix it for both of us."

Chapter Six

Augustine hadn't counted on Harlow's being occupied with setting up her computers for the entire evening, but it was the kind of opportunity he'd been waiting for. He knocked on Lally's door.

"Come on in."

She set her book down and waved him over from the sitting area by the big bay window that looked onto the side yard. She kept a garden there, one that supplied them with a decent amount of vegetables. "You hungry for dinner already? I wasn't going to start it for another hour or so. Give Harlow some time to get her things situated."

"No, I'm not hungry. I'm going through the mirror to see Olivia. Just wanted to let you know so you can cover for me in case Harlow asks where I am, although she should be pretty occupied for a while."

Lally nodded. "I'm glad you're going to see Miss Olivia. I miss her fiercely. You tell her that, you hear?"

"I will."

"Any chance she's gonna make it back through?" Her gaze turned misty. "I'd love to see her again."

"I don't know."

Lally smoothed the ribbon holding her place in the book she was reading. "She has to let that child know she's still got a mother. It's not right."

"Agreed. That's the main thing I'm going to talk to her about."

With a smile, she looked at him again. "I'm glad you didn't leave us for the Guardian house. I like having you and Harlow here. It's like...never mind." She shook her head and laughed softly. "Go on now. Go see Miss Olivia."

He sat in the chair across from her. "It's like what? Tell me."

She reached over and took his hand between hers. They were warm and smooth despite the work she did with them. "It's like you're my children." Her smile held a little sadness. "I like having someone to look after."

He placed his hand on top of hers. "I can't speak for Harlow, but I love having you look after me. Without you and Olivia, I'd probably be dead."

"Augie, don't say such things."

"You know it's true. You know what I was like when Livie first found me. The first night I was here."

"Mmm-hmm." Lally sat back, her sadness replaced by humor and a tiny bit of judgment. She drew her necklace between her fingers, making the cross, key and locket on it dance. "You stole some of Miss Olivia's best jewelry."

"And you caught me and beat me with the broom."

She laughed. "I'll do it again, too, if you get out of line."

He stood, kissed the top of her head and made for the door. "Good, because you never know."

"Get now, go see our girl."

"On my way." She was still laughing as he shut the door and went to stand before the ornate mirror in the foyer.

He let his fingers graze the glass as he filled his head with thoughts of Olivia. Magic pulled him through with a gentle tug. He opened his eyes to survey the desolate section of the fae plane she'd been relegated to.

This part of the fae world was a sprawling gray field pressed down by an endless gray sky. The mountainous horizon only added a deeper shade of soot to the distance. The seemingly ever-present wind whistled past to tear at his clothes and dishevel his hair.

Horrors resided in this wretched place, but this was where Livie had been pulled through to and there seemed no way for her to get out.

He turned, dreading what lay behind him but needing to see it anyway. To remind himself of how awful his kind could be.

The great black rock formation of the Claustrum towered in the distance. Slivers of jagged stone along the front edges guarded the gates leading in. *In* almost exclusively, because few who entered ever came out. The place was the fae equivalent of Alcatraz. A prison for those of their kind who'd committed crimes against other fae or humanity and couldn't be held in a human jail. Hell, there were very few fae who could be.

It was at moments like this he could understand Harlow's not wanting to be fae.

"That place gives me the creeps."

He turned. Olivia was at his elbow. He grinned and swept her into a hug. "Livie!"

She laughed, a sound that recharged his soul. "I've missed you, Augie. Don't wait so long between visits." She pulled back to look at him, his face in her hands. "Did something happen? Did Branzino show up?"

"No, nothing happened. And there's been no sign of Branzino." Despite the fact that buried close to the gates of the Claustrum was the enormous sum of cash Branzino had tried to pay off Harlow with. Augustine expected something to come of that someday. "We've just been busy. Harlow's moving in, you know. We got all her stuff from Boston. And the Exemplar Ball is tomorrow night, which we're both going to. Harlow's wearing one of your old costumes."

Her eyes lit up. "You're going together?"

"Yes, together." He laughed despite his uncertainty. "Don't

go making wedding plans." He'd keep the part about Nekai to himself.

"Oh, that daughter of mine could use a man like you in her life, Augie. Someone to shake her up, make her realize there's nothing wrong with being fae."

"I'd say she's coming around a bit. Slowly, but she's less horrified and asking more questions." He put his hands on her shoulders and looked her square in the eyes. "Which means there's no reason not to tell her about you."

Olivia pulled away. "No, Augie. Not while I'm here." She threw her hands up. "Look at this place. It's hell. Would you want a child of yours to see you in a place like this?"

No. "Livie, it's not hell—"

"Yes, it is."

"I'll give you purgatory." He sighed. She was so stubborn when she set her mind to something. "This is your daughter we're talking about. Your flesh and blood."

"Who lived her entire life voluntarily having no relationship with me."

Knowing his past with his own mother, he found that hard to believe. Harlow wasn't the easiest person to be around at times, but her grief over Olivia's death had been real. "She *never* reached out to you?"

"She did, but it always led to her wanting me to tell her who her father was."

He sighed. "I know you had reasons for not giving Harlow that information, but she has no idea about those reasons. All she knew was that you disliked the man and made the decision to keep him from her. Yes, she knows more about it now that she's seen for herself what a monster he is, but you can't blame her for being upset all those years."

He dipped his head. "If you were to explain things to her now, I'm sure, having met Branzino, she would understand.

And this..." He lifted his hands to gesture to the world around them. "It's going to be a shock. But don't you think she'd rather endure the shock and know her mother is still alive in some dimension than not at all?"

Livie took a few steps to a large boulder and sat. "I've been trying to cross back over using that mirror you left me."

And just like that, the subject was changed.

She shook her head, her gaze fixed on something in the distance. "I can't. There's no magic there. Not enough, anyway. Or not the right kind. Or maybe I used it all up getting here. It took everything I had just to call out to you through the mirror that first time."

"It hasn't been that long. I'm sure you're getting stronger every day. Keep trying."

She smiled sadly and turned toward him. "I don't remember you being such an optimist."

He exhaled and let a minute pass before he returned to the reason he'd come. "Olivia, I love you. You know that. But Harlow needs to know you're alive. I care about your daughter, and being a part of keeping this kind of secret from her could destroy the friendship between us. I will not allow her to hate me because of something I could have prevented. It was your will that made her the joint owner of the house with me, so clearly you wanted me in her life. Now that I am, I have to protect whatever it is that's begun between us."

"Augie—"

"No more excuses, Livie." He pulled his mirror out to travel back. "I'm giving you one more day, then I'm bringing her here."

"Augustine." She stood, a familiar, indignant fire snapping in her eyes. "Don't you dare give me an ultimatum." She huffed out a breath. "You don't even sound like the Augie I know and love."

"That's because I'm not that person anymore. I'm the Guardian now." The position she'd wanted him to take. "That carries a lot of responsibility. I can't let things slide anymore." He flipped the mirror open. "I'll see you in a day. And Harlow will be with me."

"There." Harlow tapped the enter key, finalizing the reprogramming. Everything was hooked up and operational, the last of her settings adjusted and each piece of equipment communicating with the other pieces like it should be. The third-floor room she'd taken over was finally starting to feel like an office and this place was finally starting to feel like... a home. Which it was. *Home.* That would take some getting used to.

She sat back in her desk chair, its ergonomic curves instantly familiar. She'd missed this chair. An odd thing to miss, but when you spent as much time as she did in front of a monitor, a comfy chair was an important thing.

"Home." She said the word out loud to taste it on her tongue. To let it ring in her ears and see if it sounded true. It did, almost. There was still something a little strange about that word being applied to this place. Thinking about this house as hers and not her mother's would take more time. In a way, it would *always* be her mother's. Olivia's fingerprints were all over this house, from the framed movie stills to the expensive antiques and massive library. Even the lemon verbena perfume that Harlow still caught a whiff of now and then. Her mother was in every room. Fitting herself into that picture was the hard part.

She logged onto her email and scanned the waiting messages. The ad for her web design company had come out in today's paper, both print and digital. She'd found her business card blanks in the stuff Cy had brought up and whipped up a bunch of q-cards with her information embedded in them. Anyone with an LMD who scanned the card would automatically be taken to her website. The techie q-cards made the plain old cards she'd printed earlier look totally amateur. Which they were. Q-cards were much techier.

Last she'd sent out some e-notices to a bunch of the design loops and boards she belonged to. So far no takers. She'd set her prices competitively. Her slim portfolio probably wasn't helping.

Her email held one bona fide penetration testing job offer, which was a bit of a surprise, and one hacking job offer, which was not. She deleted that one and started to answer the legit one, attaching her standard pricing info, contract and release of liability.

She paused before she hit send. Maybe Lionel Cuthridge, her mother's attorney—and now hers, since she was half owner of the estate and he was the executor of the trust—would take a look at the release of liability for her. It certainly hadn't done her any good when she'd been set up by a client to unknowingly hack into another company's files. That client had turned out to be the one man she'd longed to meet her entire life. Her biological father, Joseph Branzino.

Instead of the loving parent who'd missed her as much as she'd missed him, he'd turned out to be a monster. He'd deliberately put her in a bad spot so he could swoop in and take advantage of the situation. And what a situation it had been— pay a fine of eight hundred and fifty thousand dollars or go to prison. He must have expected her to jump all over his offer of money, but her mother's untimely death—a death Augustine was working to prove Branzino was also behind—had meant the estate's money had made it possible for her to refuse Branzino's unsavory offer. Branzino must have thought the same thing she had, that the estate's money would be tied up in taking care of the estate. Or maybe he'd thought Olivia had been broke. Or that Harlow was too proud to ask for the money for her fine and that accepting it from her father would be easier.

Whatever the reason, his plan had been thwarted, but not before he'd tried to physically force her to do what he wanted. Thank all that was holy that Augustine had been home. He'd come to her rescue, trading blows with Branzino before throwing the man out of the house and threatening bodily harm if he ever came back.

Was she totally convinced she'd never see Branzino again? No. And she prayed when that day came she would have a better grasp of her skills, Augustine would have taught her some incredible self-defense moves, or he would be with her.

A knock on her door brought her out of her thoughts. Had to be Augustine because Lally was probably fixing dinner, which Cy and Dulcinea were coming back for. "Come in."

He poked his head into the room. "This place looks like you could launch missiles. You sure have a lot of computer equipment."

She shrugged. "It's what I know."

He smiled. "You have a minute?"

"Sure." She tapped her monitors into sleep mode, the multi-panels going dark. She grabbed a few of the q-cards and held them out as she spun her chair toward him. "Take these and ditch those other cards."

He took them, inspecting the small rectangles of clear plastic. He held one up to the light. "What's in this? Some kind of chip?"

"Exactly. If you scan that with your LMD, it takes you right to my website."

He nodded. "You made these?"

"I have the machine, yes." Feeling pretty good about herself, she sat back. "So what's up?"

He tucked the q-cards into his pocket and the burdened look in his eyes returned. It was something she was becoming more accustomed to seeing. The responsibility of being Guardian weighed heavily on him at times. She wished she could do something to alleviate some of that load. "Nothing really. Just wanted to see if you needed anything for the ball tomorrow or had any questions about it. I have a few things to take care of that will eat up my morning, but if there's time when I get home, we'll start training tomorrow."

"As long as it's not too close to when we have to get ready for the ball." She pointed to a small upholstered chair she'd appropriated from another room. "You can sit."

"Thanks." He perched on the edge like being this close to her made him uncomfortable.

"What kind of stuff do you have to take care of? Are you still trying to link Branzino with your lieutenant's murder?"

He nodded. "Yes. I have to interrogate someone tomorrow."

"For real?" She sat up a little. "That sounds exciting. And maybe a little scary."

"I'm scarier than he is, so the odds are in my favor." He grinned as he looked around. "You know, you really should take over your mother's rooms. They're three times the size of the guest suite you're in now."

She nodded, running her fingernail along the seam on the arm of the chair. "Probably, but I can't do that yet. It's too soon." She tucked one leg beneath her. "What would I do with all her stuff anyway? Have you been in that closet? Hey, speaking of which, did you know there's an old door in there?"

He shook his head. "That's news to me."

She shrugged. "I'm sure it's nothing. Old houses have all kinds of weird things in them, right?"

He nodded. "They do. And who knows how many times this house has been remodeled? As far as all of Olivia's stuff goes, we could convert some of the attic space into storage. More storage, I should say. Do you know she's got a prop room up there?"

"Really? I had no idea. I haven't done a lot of exploring in the house yet. I haven't even seen your room yet." She hesitated, realizing how that sounded. "Not that I'm angling for an invite or anything."

He laughed. "You can see my room any time you like. It's nice, for an attic space. Bright. You should at least come up and see it." He leaned back in the chair and crossed one ankle over his knee. "It's only one flight up from here."

"I'm good." She spun back to her desk, finding something to occupy herself with until the heat in her face disappeared. The idea of being in his personal space made her slightly giddy, which just underlined the knowledge that Augustine was the only one she really wanted to go to the ball with.

"Let me know if you change your mind. Or if you need anything else to get ready for the ball."

"I should be fine. Especially with that contact."

"If you feel at all like you're going to have a panic attack, just say the word to me or Cy and we'll get you out of there."

"Okay." She didn't want to let him down. Maybe she should tell him about how the hollow place inside her had grown. How it sometimes felt like it was on the verge of taking over. Just in case something happened. She opened her mouth, but couldn't find the words to explain that she might be losing herself to something she couldn't explain. Instead, she turned to face him and said, "I *will* be fine."

"I don't think there's too much expected of the Guardian's date." A tiny smile lifted the corners of his mouth. The word *date* made the giddiness come back, but it was a good feeling. The hollowness gobbled it down like candy. He waved a hand nonchalantly. "You'll be introduced to a lot of people, have to make some small talk, that sort of thing."

"Small talk? With strangers?" She swallowed. Of course there would be small talk. How had she not realized that?

"All you have to do is ask people about their costumes. Most of these people have been planning their getups since the end of last year's ball. They'll be more than happy to fill all available air space with the details. If that fails, tell them you're new to the city and ask if they can recommend a few places to eat or what their favorite cocktail is. In this city those are never-ending conversations."

"Okay." She exhaled. He always had the answers. "I can do that."

"I'll have some official duties as Guardian during the ball, which is actually why I'm okay with Nekai being there. If I or Cy can't be at your side, I'm happy to have him there. Well, not happy, but he should be capable of protecting you if something happens. Dulcinea hates fancy events like this, so unless I give her a direct order, she won't be coming. Instead, she and Sydra will be running patrols, but like I said, Cy will be there and he's hard to miss."

She turned back toward him. "Patrols? You think something's going to happen?" Tiny alarm bells clanged in her head.

He waved her fears away. "No, I don't. Not in the city and not in that ballroom. It's going to be full of fae. It's the last place anyone would try something."

"All fae, huh?" She'd known that, but hearing him say it and then imaging herself in a room full of strange people with strange powers... she blew out a breath and sat back, putting her feet on the front edge of the chair. "Maybe the possibility of a panic attack isn't *that* remote."

"Hey, it's going to be fine. I know it's probably a hard concept for you to grasp, but they're your people. This is your culture. Even if you don't know much—"

"Anything."

"You know some. And you'll find most of them willing to help." He smiled. That never stopped being a good look on him. "I'll introduce you to Yanna, she's one of the Elektos. I think she'd be a good person for you to get to know. She'd probably be willing to teach you a bit, too."

"You mean instead of Nekai?" She dropped her feet to the floor and made a noise deep in her throat, a sort of purring thing. Specifically designed to rile Augustine. "I know he's fae, but my, that man is something to look at, don't you think?"

Augustine jumped up and stalked to her chair, put his hands on the armrests and leaned in, blocking her view of anything else.

She yanked her ungloved hands back. "What are you doing?"

"Giving you something else to look at." He grinned wickedly. "You like Nekai? Because I'm sure he likes you. Maybe I should put a good word in for you. Tell him what a good kisser you are."

The heat coming off him made her breathe openmouthed. Or maybe it was his sudden proximity. Her pulse raced. "Don't you dare tell Nekai anything."

Augustine nodded. "You're right, I won't, because I'm not sure if I really remember how you kiss." He rolled her wheeled chair close enough that he straddled her legs.

"I don't..." She had no idea what she'd been about to say. He bent down and brushed his mouth across hers so gently she almost couldn't feel it. And she wanted to. She leaned into him, driven by the need to have more than just that whisper-soft caress.

He held still, let *her* kiss *him*. Let her choose the pressure and the intensity and the duration. Something about that, about being in control, only made her want more. His emotions flowed into her, doubling as his fingers twined with hers on the arms of the chair, filling her with a lightness that few other pleasurable things could measure up to. He was *there* for her in whatever way she needed; that seemed to be what ran through him, like a promise that sang in his blood, spilling into her through the points of contact between their mouths and their fingers.

Nekai could never compare to this, he seemed to be telling her. *I dare him to try. I dare you to let him.*

She opened herself to him, listening, sensing, trying to feel more of him. And ran hard into something dark and hidden. She broke the kiss, not wanting to think about what that meant. She pulled her hands away and calmed her breathing. "What was...that all about?" Every breath tasted like him. Dark and sweet and wicked. The hollowness was, for a moment, filled. She ignored the other thing. Like Lally said, everyone had secrets. Augustine was allowed to have his.

But the sense that his secret was somehow tied to her remained.

"That was about you pretending to like Nekai because you thought it would get a rise out of me." Not a trace of smile on his face, but the spark in his eyes ignited a fire inside her that threatened to burn down every wall she'd ever erected. "Well done. It worked." He winked. "You know, in case you want to try it again."

Chapter Seven

The fog that muted the colors of the Treme houses did nothing to quiet Augustine's mood. This morning was an exercise in futility. He had no reason to believe that Father Ogun would tell him anything more than he had told Detective Grantham, and yet here Augustine stood. About to take a crack at the impossible.

Voodoo was considered off-limits by fae, the same as witchcraft. The fae had their own kind of magic. No point in muddying those waters with something human-based.

He notched his collar up against the damp cold. There were a hell of a lot of places he'd rather be this morning than here. Harlow's image filled his head. He'd checked in on her this morning as had become his habit when he left the house before she'd woken up, which meant most mornings after she'd spent the night gaming. She'd been curled into the covers like a bird in a nest. A wild, beautiful bird. Until Olivia's secret was no longer between them, he would keep his feelings to himself, but the truth was, he was falling for Harlow in a big way. Then all that remained between them would be her coming to terms with being fae.

That had to happen sooner or later.

Funny to think that for the first time he could remember he was looking forward to the Exemplar Ball not because he would inevitably find a woman there to take home, but because he already had an amazing woman to accompany him.

If Harlow didn't think she had her own kind of fae power, she was utterly wrong. She had certainly cast a spell over him.

Realizing he was smiling, he forced the grin off his face. Serious was more the demeanor for this job. He walked to the man's door and knocked. The smell of chicory coffee drifted past. Damn. He could go for some coffee.

The creak of floorboards announced someone answering the door. The man who opened it wore purple silk pajamas and a black silk robe trimmed in gold, which seemed to fit, since Ogun was the self-proclaimed King of Voodoo. "Can I help you, young man?" He sipped milky coffee from a glass mug. "You seem to be lost. We don't get many fae round these parts."

No kidding. Augustine had a pretty good idea Ogun already knew who he was. "My name is Augustine Robelais. I'm the fae Guardian. I believe Fenton Welch contacted you some time ago to let you know I had taken over the job."

Ogun nodded. "Ah, yes. He did. I didn't expect the personal visit, though. Usually I like to prepare for these things."

"I apologize." Actually, being here this early was part of the ploy. An attempt to catch Ogun off guard. When he'd be more vulnerable.

"Mmm-hmm." His gaze ran the length of Augustine before he resumed eye contact, making a face like Augustine didn't amount to much of anything he should be worried about. "Anything else I can help you with?"

Augustine didn't have to work at keeping a serious expression now. "Yes. I need to speak with you about a matter that I'm sure you'd prefer your neighbors not hear." He raised his voice slightly. "Unless you don't care that your neighbors might hear about you being involved in a murder."

"More of this nonsense?" Ogun's knuckles went white on the handle of his coffee mug. "Get in the house." He brushed past

Augustine to stick his head out and glance in both directions, looking to see if anyone might have heard.

Augustine stepped inside and was immediately overwhelmed by the sheer amount of stuff cluttering the man's house. All kinds of voodoo-related paraphernalia by the looks of it. Bundles of bones and feathers, little drawings on scraps of handmade paper, strands of beads, sequined banners. Iron somewhere, based on the sudden itch crawling over his skin. And the deeply intense smell of incense, which made the otherwise pleasant aroma of coffee almost stomach-churning.

Ogun shut the front door and pointed to a chair. "Sit." He took another that was covered with some kind of African cloth. There wasn't much in the place that wasn't covered with something else. "What the hell are you talking about with this murder nonsense?"

Augustine stayed standing. "The *bokura* powder found at the scene of a recent fae murder. I understand you told Detective Grantham you knew nothing about that."

"Because I don't." Ogun set his cup down, his expression suddenly much less hospitable. *"Sit."*

To keep things cordial, Augustine took a chair.

Ogun continued. "This line of questioning, this intimation that I'm not telling the truth or that I'm holding something back..." He shook his head, his expression grave. "It's not doing anything to further the relationship between the fae and those of us who serve the spirits."

Augustine held Ogun's gaze for a little longer than necessary. "There is no relationship between the fae and your people." He kept his voice calm, his tone even. "But there might be very soon. The same kind of relationship that my people have with the witches." He gave Ogun another long, hard look. "Do I make myself clear?"

Ogun returned the look. "The fae think we're not a powerful

people, but I suggest you think otherwise." He held up a hand. "I wish to be at odds with no one, but neither do I wish to be bullied, Mr. Robelais."

"I'm not bullying anyone. I'm trying to get to the bottom of who is responsible for letting the vampires into our city that killed several tourists and two beloved members of the fae community." If he could just find enough evidence to connect it all to Branzino, he could put the whole thing to bed. "This murder that I'm talking to you about? It's just the tip of the iceberg. Does that help you understand what I'm about a little more?"

Ogun nodded. "I did not know there was more…these vampires…" He sighed. "I understand."

"Good." Augustine stood. "I'll give you a day to ask around, see what you can find out. Maybe *remember* a little more. Then I'm coming back and we're going to have this talk again." He adjusted the blade hanging from his hip. "This time your answers better be different."

⚜

Giselle topped off her father's coffee. Her hand shook just enough to send small ripples through the black liquid.

"Are you all right?" Evander asked.

"Fine." She smiled brightly before sitting back down to breakfast.

"You don't seem like yourself." He bit into the frittata she'd made. Far heavier a breakfast than anything she'd ever make for herself, but she needed her father happy.

"Just a lot on my mind with Mardi Gras around the corner and all." She ate a slice of strawberry.

He nodded as he chewed. "Should be a good season. Hopefully this weather will warm up a bit."

"Yes, that would be nice. After a few hours in the Square, the cold really seeps into your bones." She had a substantial roster of regular clients, but a good bit of her income came from telling fortunes in Jackson Square. Amazing how much some of those tourists had to spend.

"Surely you don't need me to teach you a warming spell?"

"No, of course not, but casting even a minor secondary spell like that can sometimes make my ability to read the crystals a little...foggy." She smiled. There were only so many spells any witch could sustain at once. Keeping her beautiful clothes clean was more important than being warm. She had a certain level of appearance to maintain, after all.

He sat back. "You don't have to work like that, you know." His eyes held a kindness she hadn't seen much of since her mother died.

"I have to earn a living somehow. And I generate a lot of personal clients by telling fortunes in the square." Until she took over for him as head of the coven, her bills were not going to pay themselves.

"Most of those people are tourists."

"Tourists with money and computers. I can counsel them via email." Computerizing the coven was something she'd been after him to do for years. "Besides, it's not that bad. I meet a lot of interesting people."

He snorted. "You hate people."

"Daddy, I do *not* hate people." She grinned. "I like you and Zara."

He laughed. "First you cook me breakfast, then you tell me you like me. Now I know you're buttering me up for something."

Looking injured wasn't hard. "I haven't been the best daughter. I know that. We've had some words recently and I wanted to make up for that. Patch things up between us."

"Is that so?" His smirk mirrored his cynical tone. "Until what? The next time I do something you disagree with?"

She sighed. "I can't help that I crave progress. But that doesn't mean I'm not sorry when we argue. Or that I don't still love you."

The smirk softened into a smile. He reached over and squeezed her hand. "You're right. No matter what happens, you're still my daughter and I love you, too. I *am* sorry about hiding the truth of your mother's death from you. I was grieving. Not thinking clearly." He released her hand. "I just couldn't imagine you girls knowing what had really happened. That shame wasn't something I thought you two needed to bear. You have to understand that."

"I do." She didn't. Not for a single blasted second. How was thinking your mother had killed herself better than knowing she'd died trying to make things better for all witches? The very fact that her father thought their mother's actions shameful was telling. "We all have errors in judgment sometimes."

"Witches or wizards, we are still human underneath." Still smiling, he picked up his fork again. "I'm surprised by your grasp of this, but then perhaps that's not giving you enough credit. I love both you girls equally, that goes without saying, but I've always felt you had more of a head for the business. Like your old man." He ate another bite of frittata.

She wanted to roll her eyes, but the opening was as good as any. And she needed his support. "I wish that were true, but I feel like I've made a mistake."

"With what?"

She'd practiced her story, chosen her words, but making such a confession still felt like an enormous risk. At least she was only telling him about bespelling the charm. Revealing she'd created a deception spell that allowed a fae to walk as human would most likely incense him beyond helping her. With that in mind, she prayed to the goddess that her father's desire to protect her would win out over his anger at her actions. "I was hired to cast a spell recently that I fear has put me in danger."

All joy left his face. He set his fork beside his plate, lines of frustration bracketing his eyes. "Who hired you? What did you do?"

She put her napkin down, stood and paced to the other side of her small kitchen to put a little space between them. "A man came to me needing a spell put on a charm." The same man she'd created the deception spell for, although she couldn't be certain he was the one who'd used it. "He paid me for my work and I thought nothing more of it." She stopped to lean against the counter, head down, fingers twitching with anxiety. "Then everything exploded and now I fear…" She inhaled a deep shuddering sob. Tears had made Evander pliable when she was a child, but she hadn't cried in front of him in a long time.

"Damn it, Giselle. Why do you do such stupid things?"

She sobbed harder, hoping more tears would do the trick.

With a sigh, he came to comfort her. "Settle down." He pulled her into his arms and patted her back. "It can't be that bad."

"But it is." She sniffled into his shoulder, a little peeved that he hadn't been more moved. "The man I helped turned out to be one of the fae who was involved in bringing in the vampires."

Evander took her shoulders and pushed her away so he could squint at her. "You hate the fae. How did he get you to help him? I can only assume it came down to money."

"More than I've ever been paid for spellwork before." Her father seemed less surprised by her actions than she'd expected. "But he also used some sort of fae magic to make me think he was human." Actually, she'd done it for the possibility of the havoc it would create for the fae. Weakening those who oppressed her people never seemed a wrong move.

"How did this fae know to come to you?" Alarm rounded her father's eyes. "Did he say if someone had sent him?"

She shrugged, loosening his hands from her shoulders. "Not

that I can recall. He must have known about me by my reputation, I guess."

"I see." He exhaled with a relief she couldn't explain. "Well then. We should put this behind us. There's really nothing for you to worry about, since the vampire issue is resolved. The fae have tied up all their loose ends." He smiled patronizingly. "You're worrying for nothing."

She shook her head. "If only it was that easy. I was so afraid I went to someone for help and things have gotten . . . worse."

The tension in his jaw caused a muscle to pop. "Who? A coven member?"

She bit her lip. "No. Someone outside."

He groaned and shook his head. "Not a smart move. Not smart at all."

"I was trying to protect the coven from the fallout of my mistake." She dropped her head again, sniffling harder and trying to hide her anger. Her father wasn't exactly being the doting parent she'd hoped for. Perhaps she could at least get him to pity her. "I'm such a fool, Daddy. Why do I believe people when they say they'll help me? Why am I so trusting?" If he would believe that lie, she was home free.

"You're the least trusting person I know, Giselle. I'm not sure what made you act so differently this time." He returned to his chair, slumping into it with a kind of resigned sigh that gave her a glimmer of hope. "Tell me everything."

Little chance of that. "I went to Father Ogun."

"The voodooist?" Evander cringed. "Of all the—why would you pick him? He's not exactly a trustworthy character."

"I didn't know," she cried. "He seemed like such a nice man. Now he's threatening me." She swallowed. "Blackmailing me."

"What? Why?"

She looked away as if the pain of her confession were too much to bear. Really she was tired of the judgment in her father's gaze. "I went to see him—just to ask him some questions. I explained my situation, but his price was too high." She closed her eyes against the imagined horror. "Then the next thing I know, I find him here. In my *house*, Daddy. And he tells me he's taken care of the problem and that I owe him."

"What did he mean, he'd taken care of the problem?"

"That report in the *Picayune* about that fae who killed himself? I don't think it was suicide. I think Ogun killed him and made it look like suicide. Or maybe he used some kind of voodoo magic on the fae and made him kill himself." She twisted her fingers together and laid on the emotion as thickly as she dared. Her story was a mix of truths about two different fae she'd done spells for, but he didn't need to know the details. "I'm scared, Daddy."

Evander pushed to his feet, the hard set of his jaw at last reminding her of the father she remembered. The one who would do anything for her. "If anyone should be scared, it should be Ogun. He apparently forgot who your father was."

She smiled through the two tears she managed to squeeze out. "But I didn't. I know exactly who you are."

"That's my girl." Evander nodded, his happiness at being needed by his daughter evident. "You did the right thing by coming to me with this."

Finally, the result she'd hoped for. She kept up the act a little longer. "What do you think I should do?"

"Not a thing." He kissed her forehead. "You let your father take care of this."

Chapter Eight

I told you. Not a damn word." Augustine scratched one horn. They were almost completely grown out now, the points a little sharper every day. "But I can smell it on him like cheap cologne. Ogun knows something."

"I have no doubt," Fenton said.

"Is it a matter of being more persuasive?" Yanna Quinn, one of the other Elektos, had joined them in the war room this morning at Augustine's request. He liked her better than most of the Elektos and she seemed trustworthy. He hoped she was as willing to help him out with Harlow as she'd been with Beatrice.

He shrugged. "Maybe, but I don't think this is a man who's going to respond well to physical intimidation unless that's our only option."

Fenton's LMD vibrated on the table. He held up a finger, indicating his head was about to be occupied by the incoming call. "Answer." His eyes rounded in surprise. "I'm fine, Evander, and you?" Fenton shot Augustine a look. "You don't say? Really? I'll send him over." Fenton nodded. "I think today, yes. All right." A pause. "End call."

Fenton glanced at Yanna, then Augustine. "Evander wants to talk to you. Says he has information on the recent fae suicide."

Augustine raised his brows. "Evander has info on Dreich's suicide?" He snorted. "What? Is he turning his daughter in?"

Yanna's eyes rounded slightly. "Giselle's involved? Do you know that for sure?"

Fenton put his fist to his mouth as he cleared his throat, his gaze flicking to Augustine. "I hadn't read her in on that yet."

"Ah. Sorry." Augustine turned to Yanna. "No, we don't know that for sure. All we have right now is her involvement with the silver cross that was used to kill the vampire we were holding for questioning."

She nodded, clearly in thought. "The one captured the night of Olivia's murder?"

"Yes."

Her fingers drew small circles on the tabletop. "What else don't I and the rest of the Elektos know?"

Sensing Fenton might be in trouble, Augustine spoke first. "Fenton held back information at my request. You told me yourself not to trust anyone. All we knew was that whoever was involved with bringing in the vampires had deep roots."

She nodded. "I understand. I do. And I'm glad to be a part of this now, but if you don't trust me enough to share, why did you ask me here?"

"I do trust you." So far. "You've given me no reason not to." And he hoped that would remain the case. Perhaps it was time to test that. "I also believe that the man who's truly behind the vampire invasion is Joseph Branzino." Yanna nodded, but didn't interrupt, so Augustine continued. "Flooding the city with vampires was just a way to create chaos and cover his real intent, which was to kill Olivia Goodwin."

She canted forward. "Who is this man? And why Olivia?"

"He's fae," Fenton interjected. "Raptor to be exact, and he's got a criminal history that includes almost every crime you can imagine."

Augustine sighed. "He's also the father of Olivia's only child, Harlow."

Concern bent Yanna's mouth. "That poor girl. First her mother is murdered, then to find out her father is this horrible creature."

"She doesn't know he's a raptor." Augustine flattened his hand on the table. "And it needs to stay that way a little while longer."

She nodded. "I'm sure you have a reason for that. Something else you're not telling me?"

"Yes, but it also needs to be kept secret."

"I can do that."

"Olivia Goodwin made it through to the fae plane the night she was murdered. She's not what any of us would call a hundred percent, though. She's stuck on the same plane as the Claustrum."

Fenton wiped his hand across his mouth. "The Claustrum? You didn't tell me that."

"She didn't want anyone to know."

"How did she end up there?"

"It was the last place on her mind when she passed." Augustine narrowed his gaze. "She was worried about me. That the Elektos were about to send me there if I refused the Guardianship."

Yanna sighed. "Can't she just cross back over?"

"No. And she's refusing to let me bring Harlow to her."

Yanna glanced at Fenton. "She doesn't want her daughter to see her in that place. I understand."

"So do I, but I'm about to take the decision out of her hands. It's unfair for Harlow not to know her mother's alive, no matter where she is. And personally, I'm done keeping the secret. I've already told Olivia I'm bringing Harlow through tomorrow one way or the other."

Fenton pushed his glasses up on the bridge of his nose. "Has Harlow ever traveled by mirror? You might want to give her a little test drive first. Show her it's nothing to be afraid of."

Augustine hesitated. "You know...probably not. That's a good idea." He let out a breath. Maybe she'd enjoy it or think it was cool. It might even make her like being fae a little more. "Back to Branzino. Harlow and I both believe he orchestrated the vampire influx with the purpose of killing Olivia and putting Harlow in a position to own the house. Granted, he didn't count on Olivia leaving me half of it. See, Branzino also set Harlow up to need a large sum of money. When the house became hers, he figured he'd just swoop in, help her out financially and end up being able to use the house as a base of operations here in New Orleans."

Yanna nodded. "Because a felon can't own property in a Haven city."

"Right," Fenton said.

She sat back and crossed her arms. "And Dreich?"

Fenton tapped a pen on the tabletop. "He was absolutely involved, we just aren't sure to what extent. Yet. We know he had access to the Pelcrum, so he could have delivered the silver cross to the vampire in custody."

"Which means he's probably the one who contacted Giselle about bespelling the silver cross in the first place." Augustine tapped his fingers on the table. "Why Dreich would work with Branzino remains a mystery."

Fenton sat forward. "Dreich's account showed a large, recent deposit. It could be as simple as money."

Yanna shook her head. "What a mess this is. If there is anything I can do to help, please let me know."

"Actually," Augustine began. "I have a favor to ask you."

She exhaled and dropped her shoulders. "Name it."

"Thank you. Harlow needs some...fae tutelage. She's coming to the ball with me but she's not great with crowds."

"I sensed that at the funeral," Yanna said.

"Fenton's supplied her with some info on the fae who will

be in attendance." He wasn't sure if the facial recognition software lens was general knowledge. "But I'm still concerned that the ball is going to be a real test for her. She fought being fae her whole life and never learned to use her powers. As a result of being suppressed, they're very difficult for her to control. Dulcinea's been helping her, but I need someone who can teach her some of the basics of fae life. Our history, our traditions, that kind of thing. Enough to make her more comfortable with the event."

Yanna smiled. "It would be my honor to help Harlow with that." Her smile faded a bit. "Is she on board with this or is this something you hope I can talk her into?"

"I think she's on board with it. At least she was when Nekai offered to help."

Yanna's face screwed up in a barely suppressed smile. "There aren't many of us who wouldn't get on board with Nekai. Whatever he was offering."

He grimaced.

She laughed. "I'll head over there shortly if you like. I'm sure she'll have some questions about the ball this evening."

"Thank you." Augustine stood. "And on that note, I'm off to Evander's to see what his news is." He nodded to Fenton, then Yanna. "I know you know where the house is, but since it was just warded you might not be able to find it."

Yanna stood, Fenton a second behind her. "All members of the Elektos are automatically included in any wards."

Augustine narrowed his eyes. "Since when?"

"It's always been that way." Fenton shrugged. "Don't look so put out. The Guardian is included. Why do you think you've never had any issues accessing Loudreux's? His house is heavily warded. It just doesn't affect those of us in fae government."

Augustine let that information sink in. The only thing more startling was being labeled "fae government." Olivia must be laughing at him right now. "I guess Harlow's not the only one with more to learn."

An order of groceries had just been delivered, so Harlow stood in the kitchen, gloves off, practicing her object reading skills. She dropped a can of tomato paste as quickly as she'd picked it up. "Whoever boxed these up was having a bad day. Everything in here feels like..." She picked up a bag of rice. Grimacing, she let the images ride out. She shuddered and put the bag down. "I think the stock boy's girlfriend broke up with him."

Lally laughed. "That is some skill you got there."

"I guess." Her LMD buzzed. She checked it, anticipating a message from someone interested in her new web design business. She sighed and put the device down after deleting yet another unimportant email. Obviously it was going to take a little more than q-cards, an ad in the paper and a few posts to some loops. Maybe she needed to sacrifice a virgin or something.

"What's wrong?" Lally asked.

"Nothing, just hoping I'd get some kind of interest in my new business venture."

"Give it time. In the meanwhile, you want a cooking lesson?"

"Sure. Just be prepared. I can barely boil water." Lally had promised to teach her how to cook, something Harlow had never really learned. And after eating Lally's food, turning down her offer seemed foolish. Why not learn from the master? The woman had skills in the kitchen.

"You made sandwiches, didn't you?" Lally stood, grinning. "I can work with that."

Someone knocked at the front door.

"I'll get it," Harlow said, grabbing her gloves. "Back in a sec."

The figure visible through the fancy leaded glass panes was female. She opened the door. "Can I help you?"

The woman smiled. "Actually, I'm here to help you. If you're interested." She held out her hand. "I'm Yanna Quinn. I'm one of the Elektos and a friend of Augustine's."

Thankful she'd remembered her gloves, Harlow shook the woman's hand. Her high cheekbones and strong jaw made her starkly beautiful, but nonetheless intimidating. "Not that I doubt you, but how do I know you are who you say you are?"

She nodded. "Very good. You should always be sure. And don't ever feel like you'll offend someone by questioning them. Women often feel that way. I do not." She pointed at the porch floor. "You recently had the house warded, yes?"

Harlow nodded. Okay, so the woman knew that much.

"If I was a foe, the ward would have made it rather difficult for me to find the house, forget about walking onto your porch." She leaned forward, a conspiratorial twinkle in her eye. "All Elektos are automatically written into the wards. It's one of the perks of the job."

"I had no idea."

"No one does, really, but you live with Augustine. I'm sure it's something you'd have learned sooner or later." She clasped her hands in front of her. "I'll wait here while you call him to confirm who I am."

"Ah, okay." The woman's straightforward attitude made Harlow like her immediately, but she pulled her LMD out anyway and tapped the button to direct-dial Augustine.

"Hey, Harley." The Thrun's hybrid engine purred behind his words.

"Don't call me that," she muttered. Then, louder, "Yanna Quinn is here."

"I asked her to stop by. Red hair, strong features. Says what she thinks."

"That's for sure." That described the woman perfectly. "Thanks. Bye."

"Bye, Harley." He hung up.

Bugger. She smiled at her visitor. "He confirmed you're you. So how did you want to help me?"

"May I come in?"

"Sure, sorry." Harlow stepped out of her way.

She strode into the house. "I came to your mother's memorial, but sadly missed meeting you on that occasion."

Because she'd been upstairs, escaping the crowd that had thrown her into a panic attack. "I don't do so well with crowds sometimes."

"Then it's good I'm here. With the ball coming up, Augustine wanted to see if there was anything I could do to help you get ready. Answer any questions you might have. Anything to make you feel more comfortable." Her smile matched the sparkle in her eye. "It was good of him to recognize men aren't always the best at such things."

Harlow grinned. "He talked to me about it. Which I thought was sweet, but..."

"But he's not a woman. And he's only just learning the intricacies of our society himself. There's no way he can know the kind of etiquette required at a social function of this level."

Harlow's grin vanished. "Etiquette? He's not the only one in trouble then."

Yanna waved her worries away. "It's not hard to learn and much of it is common sense. You'll see."

"I don't know. What if I do something wrong and offend someone?" Harlow rubbed the tips of her fingers together.

"It's a ball, not an inquisition. Besides, I'm here to make sure that doesn't happen. And it won't. Now, we'll start with the dance tickets—"

"Dance tickets? There's going to be dancing?" Harlow's chest constricted. "Of course there's going to be dancing, it's a ball." She swallowed, her mouth suddenly as dry as a desert. Dancing meant touching. That spray latex better do its job.

Yanna pressed a hand to her cheek and clicked her tongue. "I see I should have gotten here sooner. Well, nothing we can do about that but press on." She swiveled, then pointed toward the library. "That space will do." She headed in, gesturing for Harlow to follow. "Time's a-wasting."

"No wonder Augustine didn't give me details," Harlow muttered. "Lally, I have a visitor," she yelled toward the kitchen. Then she followed Yanna, hoping the woman had some kind of fae ability to perform miracles, because without one, Harlow feared her night at the ball could go very, very wrong.

No sign of Giselle at Evander's, which was good. Augustine accepted the butler's offer of coffee, although the cup was too damn small for his liking. He drank half before setting it down on the side table. Across from him Evander sat at his desk, sipping from his own cup in a much more gentlemanly way.

Augustine hadn't come here to be gentlemanly. The coffee was a bonus, though. "You have news about our recent suicide?"

Evander smiled with the kind of long-suffering displayed by those who thought they had the upper hand. "You're not much for small talk, are you, Guardian?"

"Not when my task list gets longer but the day doesn't. The Exemplar Ball is this evening and I have a lot to do before that begins."

Evander nodded. "I'd forgotten about that. What's the krewe's theme this year?"

He thought about saying Witches Make Us Crazy, but didn't. "Enchanted Forest. Your news?"

"So impatient." Evander raised a hand. "But I understand. Too much work, too little time." He straightened the spoon resting on his saucer. "It's been brought to my attention by a reputable source that the voodoo community is gearing up for a power grab."

Interesting, considering where he'd spent his morning. "This has nothing to do with fae business."

Evander's brows shot up. "It does when their first step involved killing one of your lieutenants." He absently shuffled a few of the papers on his cluttered desk. "That suicide wasn't a suicide, but you already knew that, didn't you?"

"There's nothing to indicate that." Nothing they'd released to the public.

Evander sat back, snorting softly. "That's a lie. Otherwise you wouldn't be here."

"I'm here because you said you had information about the death. How does killing one of my lieutenants help the voodoo community?"

"Because it was done in such a way as to throw suspicion on my people." He sighed, shaking his head. "It's no secret that my daughter was peripherally involved with this recent business regarding the vampires—"

"No, it isn't a secret. And I wouldn't call her involvement peripheral. She admitted to casting the spell on the silver cross that killed the vampire we had in custody, effectively dead-ending our investigation."

"Just because she cast the spell doesn't mean she did it with ill intent. Now, if we could focus on what's important—"

"Which is?"

"Any evidence found at the scene of that supposed suicide was planted there by someone in the voodoo community looking to incriminate my people."

"And by people, I assume you mean your daughter? Because

if it was anyone else in your coven, why not just name them? It's clear you're protecting her."

Evander bristled. "My daughter is not the focus here." He jabbed his finger at Augustine. "You need to be looking at the voodoo practitioners."

Augustine sucked down the last of his coffee, then planted his elbows on the chair arms and laced his fingers together in front of his chest. "I'm not familiar with any of them. Care to give me an idea where to start?"

"Father Ogun. He's as close to a leader as they've got. He might tell you he's not in charge, but I guarantee he is." Evander was the epitome of seriousness. "He says jump, those priests and mambos ask how high."

"Father Ogun. I'll make a note of that." Augustine lifted a finger. "Just one question before I move on this new information."

Evander looked mollified. "Anything to help."

"Do you know what *bokura* is?"

He snorted derisively. "Of course. It's a very powerful tool of the mambos and priests. Makes people very biddable." He waved his hand through the air. "In layman's terms, it's what they use to turn people into zombies. Father Ogun is known for his especially virulent version."

"Is that so?" Augustine tried to look suitably impressed. "In that case, I have a second question."

"Ask all you want." Evander's chest expanded. "I'm here to help."

That was about to change. "If Father Ogun is behind this pretend suicide, how would leaving traces of *bokura* behind implicate the witches? Wouldn't he leave something more… witchy behind? Eye of newt, wing of bat, that sort of thing?" Augustine stood. "Seems to me he's the one being set up."

For a split second, confusion clouded Evander's eyes. "Are you saying you found *bokura* at the scene?"

Might as well tell him that much. "Yes."

Evander laughed. "Then Ogun is both a conniving fool *and* sloppy. The traces of *bokura* only strengthen the information I've given you. It proves he was there. We're innocent in this. Which means Giselle is innocent in this. You have to—"

"I don't have to do anything, but I *will* be talking to your daughter again. Thanks for the info, such as it was." Augustine headed for the door. "Tell Giselle if she leaves the parish before I speak to her, I'll assume she's guilty, so it would be best if she doesn't come back."

Evander spieled on about who was innocent, who was guilty, the danger of the voodoo community rising up and a few other things Augustine ignored as he walked out of the house. The man would probably defend Giselle to his dying day.

As soon as Augustine was inside the Thrun, he made a call, starting the engine as Cy picked up.

"Hey, boss."

"Hey, Cy. You have a minute?"

"Sure, boss, what can I do for you?"

He drove toward the Pelcrum so he could fill Fenton in before going home to get ready for the ball. He might actually have enough time to show Harlow a few simple defense moves. "Have you ever met Evander Vincent? You know what he looks like?"

"Head of the New Orleans Coven? I haven't really met him, but I've seen him and heard him speak enough times to be able to mimic him, if that's what you're asking."

"It is." Augustine smiled. "I have a job for you..."

Chapter Nine

Y ou what?" Rage coursed through Giselle's body until there was nothing else left to feel. "How could you?" Her hands clamped into fists. "You said you were going to take care of things, not make them worse."

Her father had suddenly shown up at her front door, looking very full of himself. He now sat in her living room. "It was in your best interests, Giselle. I needed to shift the fae's attention off you and onto Father Ogun."

"And you failed miserably. Now they're going to assume I'm the one trying to set Father Ogun up."

"Giselle, calm down and tell me the truth of what happened. It's the only way I can help you."

"You help me any more and I'll end up in jail." She'd never wanted to strike her father as much as she did in that moment. He had royally screwed her over.

"Sit. Down."

That tone of voice hadn't held sway over her in many years, but she sat anyway. It was that or collapse under her own anger. "You want to know the truth? I'll tell you the truth. I was scared that damn fae Dell or Dreich or whatever his name is was going to blame me for everything." No matter how truthful she was being at the moment, she'd never let her father know everything she'd done. "I went to Father Ogun for that *bokura* powder and yes, I used it on the fae to get him to write a confession, then convinced him to hang himself. Let me tell you, with that *bokura* in his system, it didn't take much."

"Giselle." Her father's face twisted in a mask of anger and grief. She'd expected the anger, but the grief was surprising. It only cemented her belief that the old man was in deeper with the fae than was right for any coven leader. "So Father Ogun isn't blackmailing you?"

"No, but he's threatening to tell the police I bought the *bokura* powder from him if I don't make this all go away." She shook her head. "You said you were going to take care of this. That's the last time I come to you for help."

"What did you think I was going to do? Kill Ogun?"

"Is that so much to ask?" She threw her hands up. "What good is this power we wield if we can't protect ourselves and those we love?"

His eyes narrowed and he frowned. "I can't believe you think that way."

"Don't look at me like you're suddenly disappointed in me. Like any of this is such a shock. One of us has to protect the coven. One of us has to make some headway in this struggle against the fae. And it sure as hell isn't you."

"There is no struggle against the fae. We're at peace with them. It's when something like this happens that the pot is stirred." He pointed at her. "You created these ripples. I've done what I can to help you. What happens now is up to you."

"You're in league with them, aren't you?" It suddenly seemed so clear. "That's why you covered up Mother's death. I don't know why I didn't understand it sooner. You weren't trying to protect us. You didn't want the fae to know she was practicing chaos magic. That she was trying to destroy them." Anger pushed her to her feet and caused her to do something she'd never done before. Lay hands on the man who'd given her life. She grabbed his coat and hauled his bulk up, gathering strength from her anger.

"Giselle, this is no way to treat your father!"

"Get out of my house, you traitor." She shoved him toward the door.

He opened it, but turned to look back at her. "You have no idea what you've done."

"You have no idea what *you've* done. Your time is fast coming to a close, old man. The need for new leadership has never been clearer. When the coven hears about how deeply in bed you are with the fae, they'll see my side of things."

"I am not in bed with the fae." He shook his head. "I'm glad your mother isn't alive to see this."

She lifted her chin, skin itching with barely controlled magic. "I'm sorry my father is." She lifted her hands. Energy snapped off her fingertips. "Get out of my house or I may do something about that."

Fear filled his gaze and he hurried out, slamming the door behind him. She dropped her hands and slumped into a chair. She'd tolerated her father's leadership of the coven for many years, blaming his age and adherence to old-school ways for his baffling allegiance to the fae's oppression. But he'd crossed a line by sharing information with the fae. One that couldn't be uncrossed. Augustine wasn't stupid. He'd know Ogun wouldn't have left evidence behind if he were really the one to blame.

She had no choice but to do things her own way. She might be able to rely on Zara, but not for this next task. Still, it had been good to reconnect with her sister and know that Zara took after their mother, who'd had no love for the fae. Zara seemed to share those feelings. Should she trust Zara with everything that had been going on? They were sisters. Family. But family was the reason she was in this position to begin with.

No, this next step was one she would take alone. She tipped her head back, exhausted tears burning her eyes. The weight of her world was almost too much to bear.

Something had to give, but it would not be her. With a long sigh, she picked her head up and steeled herself for what lay ahead.

Wearing only a strapless bra and underwear, Harlow stood in the middle of her mother's bedroom, her feet firmly planted on an old sheet that she and Lally had spread out to protect the carpet. Her hair was clipped up and tucked beneath an old shower cap. She held her arm out. "I'm ready."

"You sure you're dry?"

"Yep." She would have showered anyway, but after her first lesson with Augustine, she'd needed it. Amazing how sweaty you got learning how to incapacitate someone.

Lally shook the can of spray-on latex. "It's gonna be cold."

"I can take it." At least it would give her something else to focus on. Between Yanna's information and trying to remember the moves Augustine had taught her, Harlow's head felt like it might explode. She was starting to think all that info was adding to her nervousness. That and the prospect of dancing. She was so not ready for the dancing.

"Here goes." Lally popped the cap off and began spraying.

Harlow hissed. "Son of a—cold is right." She gritted her teeth and scrunched her eyes against the chilly onslaught.

From the tips of her fingers, up one arm and down the other, across her shoulders, back and chest, Lally covered every inch of exposed skin. "Lift your chin."

Harlow opened her eyes. "You really think someone might touch my neck?"

"You want to take that chance?"

She tipped her chin toward the ceiling and mumbled "No" while trying not to inhale the latex.

When the last spraying was done, Lally set the can down and picked up the hair dryer. She set it on low, then turned it on Harlow.

She shivered. "That feels good. I wasn't sure I'd ever be warm again."

Lally smiled. "You get in that ballroom and I bet you'll be plenty warm with all those people."

Harlow exhaled. "Don't remind me."

Lally clicked off the dryer. "You sure you're going to be okay?"

"I'll be fine." Actually she wasn't so sure, but she planned on having a drink as soon as she got there. Alcohol definitely took the edge off. "Can I get dressed?"

Lally tapped Harlow's forearm gently. "Seems dry to me."

Harlow dropped her arms, half expecting them to stick to the rest of her body, but they didn't. She grinned. "I really hope this stuff works as well as anticipated."

"Me, too. Ready for the gown?"

"Yes."

Lally rolled the valet rack in from the closet. "I put the rest of the accessories on your mama's vanity table, then I steamed the dress while you were having your lesson with Augustine." She unhooked the dress from its hanger.

"Thank you. I would never have thought to do that. It looks brand-new." Harlow stepped into the dress and held it in place while she turned for Lally to zip her. "You sure this is going to fit? It seems big—"

As soon as Lally pulled the zipper up, the top of the dress constricted around her, fitting itself to her like it had been custom-made to her measurements.

"—in the chest." Harlow turned. "What was that? A self-adjusting dress? That's crazy!"

Lally laughed softly. "I told you it was made by a fae

seamstress. Those women got skills you can't imagine. Also explains why it was so expensive."

"I'd say."

"Although I remember there being more to the dress somehow..."

"Whoa, what's happening?" The vines on the bodice of the dress grew over her skin, slithering over her shoulders and winding down her arms.

"That's it." Lally nodded. "That's what I remember it looking like."

Harlow checked her reflection in the full-length mirrors on the closet doors. The vines twisted over her shoulders and arms in a lacy pattern. "Wow." Plenty of skin still showed but the effect was straight out of a Hollywood special-effects studio. "My mother must have loved this. It's like a movie costume."

"Wait until you put the mask on."

"I'm a little afraid." Harlow laughed. "But not so much that I don't think this is one of the coolest things I've ever worn." She twirled once in front of the mirror. "I better do my makeup and hair. Augustine will be ready and Nekai will be here soon."

Lally clucked her tongue.

"I know, I know. You don't like him." Harlow settled at her mother's vanity table. The mirror was lit with bulbs all the way around, making the lighting much more complimentary than in her guest suite, so she'd brought her makeup in here. "Speaking of men you do like, would you mind checking on Augustine? He wouldn't tell me what his costume was and I'm a little afraid he's just slapping a mask on and calling it done."

"That's something he'd do, too." Lally wagged her head back and forth. "That boy. Sometimes I just don't know. I'll see what he's up to. You need me, you holler."

"Will do." Harlow picked up her favorite eyeliner. Wearing a mask would only bring more attention to her eyes and, with the two particular men she'd be spending the evening with in mind, she carefully began to make up her eyes to equal her amazing dress.

"Augie? You got clothes on?" Lally's voice rang out from the hall.

"Yes. Enough for you to come in without having to go to confession." He stood in the middle of the room, a towel firmly tucked around his hips.

She walked into his room and stopped cold. "Harlow's already got her dress on and you're still in a towel? Child, you need to get a move on."

"I was about to, then I opened the box Fenton gave me. Look at this." He pointed toward the box on the coffee table in front of his sofa. He'd looked through it twice, trying to find the rest of the costume. "That's not a costume. It's two horns, a leather breastplate and a pair of furry tights. There's not even a mask in there. Which is kind of the point for a masquerade." He'd be laughed out of the ball going in like that.

She peered into the box. "It's pretty fur."

He frowned at her. "You're not helping."

She pulled something from the box. "What are these?"

He took the two pointy, fleshy triangles from her. "As best I can tell, they're ear tips. Like my ears aren't pointy enough already."

She covered her mouth with her hand, but the edges of her smile showed through. "You got this from Fenton?"

"Yes. He dug it out of some fae storage area." Augustine growled. "And if he thinks he's getting away with this, he's dead wrong."

"Now, now. If that man gave this to you then it's got to be fae and I have a feeling I know how it works. You just need to put it on."

Augustine cocked his brow. "You used to be such a nice woman—"

She laughed at him. "Don't you trust me? Put that stuff on."

"Just remember, you asked for this." He grabbed the edge of his towel.

She shrieked and turned around. "Augustine Robelais. I do not need to see your business. Again."

Laughing because she'd reacted exactly as he'd suspected, he dropped the towel and grabbed the fuzzy tights from the box. They were fawn-colored, patterned after the hindquarters of a stag, but darker near the feet like hooves. He tugged them on. *Tight* was an understatement. "It might not be legal to go out in these."

The tights moved. He froze. *"Sturka."* Not just moved, but transformed. The dark ends of the tights didn't just resemble hooves, they *became* hooves. Without feeling any different, his legs had taken on the shape and bone structure of an animal's. He went to the mirror, an unmistakable clip-clop accompanying his steps. "You have got to be kidding me."

Lally's hand still covered her eyes. "Is it safe to look?"

"I . . . guess."

She turned, peeking through her fingers. "Land sakes. You look like that Greek fellow who plays the flute."

"Pan. Fenton said this was a satyr costume. Apparently he wasn't kidding." The fur from the tights traveled up his thighs until it blended into a natural waistline, leaving his chest bare. The leather breastplate would take care of that, though. He glanced at her. "How did you know these tights were going to do this?"

She shrugged. "I didn't really, but Miss Olivia used to get all her gowns for the Exemplar Balls from a fae seamstress and they worked pretty much the same way." She clasped her hand against the side of her neck. "Does it hurt having your feet all crunched into those things?"

"It doesn't feel any different than if I just had shoes on."

"My, my."

"Since you're here, help me buckle this on, would you?" He grabbed the breastplate and dropped it over his head. The matching pieces of leather were worked in gold and held together by brass buckles on the sides. He adjusted it, then held it in place while Lally did up the first side.

"You're going to be a good match for Harlow's Mother Nature."

He grinned. "Yeah? How's she look?"

"Beautiful. Like a goddess." She patted his side. "Turn."

He did, resting his hand on the back of his neck to lift his arm out of the way. "Yes, but how does she look in the costume?"

Lally's fingers kept working but her gaze came up to meet his, her smile gleaming. "You like her, don't you?"

"I do. Very much."

"Then why don't you do something about it?"

He sighed. "Because Olivia's secret lies between us. I can't open myself up to her while I'm hiding something that big."

She nodded. "You've got to tell her soon. Child deserves to know."

"I agree. And I plan to tell her. Maybe tonight."

"Good." She went back to buckling. "Speaking of tonight, you keep that Nekai away from her, you hear? He's the kind to sway a woman with gentle words and sweet lies."

"Harlow's a good judge of character. I think it would take more than that to fool her."

"I hope you're right." She patted him again. "All done."

He dropped his arm. "But we're on the same page as far as that goes with Nekai." He winked at Lally. "I don't trust him either. But I doubt he'll do anything out of line, seeing as how I am basically his boss." He looked at himself in the mirror. "This is either weirdly attractive or something that belongs in a fairy tale."

She settled into his one easy chair. "Put the rest on."

"Might as well." He pulled the horns out and inspected them. "These are hollow on the ends, so I guess they go over mine." He fit the first one on, then the second. As soon as that one was in place, they began to grow, branching out and curving slightly inward until he sported a very impressive set of antlers. His eyes widened. "I'm glad I don't have to carry these around on a daily basis."

"Are they heavy?"

"No." He turned his head back and forth, testing them out. "Just like the tights, they don't feel any different."

She nodded at the box. "Now those ear tips."

"I don't need those."

"Augustine. Put them on. Sometimes these outfits don't work properly until all the pieces are in place."

"When did you get so bossy?"

"Since Olivia passed on and left me in charge." Her smile was a little sad. "She would have loved to have seen you and Harlow all fancied up like this."

"She would indeed. I thought about taking Harlow to see Olivia before we left for the ball, but I'm not sure if Harlow could handle that much."

"She's already worried about the ball."

He nodded. "Plus she's probably never traveled via mirror before. Depending on how the ball goes, I might take her through when we get home."

"Good plan."

He scooped the ear tips from the box and wiggled them at Lally. "Ears going on."

He went closer to the mirror, turning his head as he fitted the rubbery triangles over the slight points of his ears. When the second one went on, the pair instantly matched themselves to his skin tone. He turned so Lally could see. "Happy? I still need a mask."

Her eyes widened and her mouth slowly dropped. She shook her head. "Child, the mask is taking care of itself. Look."

He went back to the mirror. "When you're right, you're right." He rubbed a finger across his cheek, but it wasn't paint. Somehow, the tiny white speckles and darker strokes that resembled fur were just there, on his skin, without any sort of makeup. His now-thicker brows winged up. His eyes were rounder, his nose broader and the tip shaded dark like an animal's. As he watched, the effect continued, darkening his shoulders and dappling them like a deer's hide.

At last he turned. "What do you think?"

"You look like nothing I've ever seen. But very handsome. And...a little wicked." She laughed. "Nekai's got no chance of beating that."

Chapter Ten

Lally hadn't come back yet, so Harlow could only assume Augustine had needed help. She finished her eyes and picked up the mask Lally had left on the vanity table. The edges of the green satin were trimmed in vines that matched the dress. Clear sticky dots outlined the back and since there was no strap she figured it must just attach to her skin. Given what magic the dress held, there was no reason the mask couldn't stay on without being tied into place.

She should probably try it on, then figure out what to do with her hair. She held the mask in place, then finger-combed her hair around it. Maybe half up, half—

The mask moved. She pulled her hand away. The mask stayed attached, so she sat very still, watching in the mirror to see what it would do. The satin cooled her skin with the same sensation as a breeze blowing over her while the vines decorating the edges branched out past her temples and into her hair. They grew into a crown, winding through her hair and weaving strands into the circlet until it was beyond anything she could have created.

When the last vine stopped moving, she noticed a ring in the mask box. She picked it up and smiled. It was exactly the kind of thing her mother would have loved, a huge pink flower, the petals and leaves encrusted with crystals. She almost put it back in the box, then, on a whim, slipped it onto her finger.

A gorgeous floral perfume floated up around her. She glanced down at the dress. The vines had *bloomed*. Her mouth dropped in amazement. A thousand tiny flowers covered the gown and the mirror revealed the wreath in her hair had blossomed, too. Here and there insects emerged—butterflies, dragonflies, honeybees— all glistening like jewels as their wings fluttered. She breathed out a sigh of wonderment. There were no words for what she was seeing.

She ran to the full-length mirror again. Okay, there were *some* words. "Fae magic is freaking amazing."

Lally walked in. A huge smile brightened her face. "I forgot about that part! You look like a faery princess." She laughed. "I guess, in a way, you kind of are."

Harlow turned. "Did Augustine's costume do this?"

Lally nodded. "In its own way, yes."

"I can't wait to see him."

"He feels the same way about you."

She lifted her head at a strange noise. "Do you hear that? It sounds like…a horse. Upstairs."

Lally laughed. "That's no horse. That's your date."

"What? I have to see this." Harlow picked up her skirts and started up the stairs to Augustine's room. She almost ran into him on the third-floor landing. Or at least a creature who looked like him. She stared, speechless.

He stared right back. "You look…wow."

She nodded. "So do you. You're a satyr, right? Of the deer variety?"

"You know about them?" He grinned. "Is it okay?"

"Totally." He looked like one of the forest guards from Realm of Zauron. Which was pretty hot. Not that she was going to tell him that.

He exhaled. "Good. Because you look beautiful beyond words."

"Thank you." Before she could stop herself, her fingers reached out to stroke the fur covering his thighs. Even through the latex spray she could sense how soft and *real* it was.

"Hey!" He grabbed her hand.

"Sorry." Her cheeks went hot and she was thankful the mask covered part of that. She jerked her hand back but he held on.

"I don't care that you touched me." He lifted her hand. "But you're not wearing gloves."

"I am. Sort of. It's that spray-on latex stuff you bought for Lally." She wiggled her fingers. "Works really well. So far." She held out her arms. "It's all over me, actually."

"So I can touch you and it won't bother you?"

There was no good answer to that question. "Depends where you touch me." Which proved the no-good-answer part. "Ignore that. Most of me is covered, so I won't be able to pick up your emotions." That was a safe response.

The wicked glint that made her skin tingle returned to his eyes. "What parts of you aren't covered? No, wait. Don't tell me. This could be fun—"

"Augustine." Her face must be red because her cheeks were on fire. "Behave. This is a fancy thing we're going to. I don't want to embarrass myself." But she couldn't help but be amused by his response.

"Little chance of that. You look, I mean, it's kind of hard to describe how amazing you look." He whistled long and low. "Harley Goodwin, you are going to be the most stunning woman there. And hot damn, you're my date."

The doorbell rang before she could tell him not to call her Harley. She let it slide. There were worse things to be called. Full of new confidence, she put her hands on her hips. "Nekai might have something to say about that. Let's go see, shall we?"

⚜

"I'll get it." Augustine headed for the door, his good mood tempered by Nekai's arrival. Why had he thought having the weaver come along was a good idea? He wanted Harlow to himself. Maybe he'd tell the guy to get lost. As Guardian, that was within his right.

Harlow trailed him all the way down, standing beside him as he opened the door. Augustine almost laughed when he saw Nekai. "You forgot to shave."

"I'm a *wolf.*" Nekai squinted at him. "The kind that eats deer for breakfast."

"I'm a satyr." Augustine crossed his arms. "And still Guardian."

"You both look very nice," Harlow said. She gave Augustine a little hip check. "Why don't you come in, Nekai? We're just about ready to go."

He walked in, smiling in the most irritating way possible. The wolf costume had given him bigger teeth. He lifted her hand to his mouth and kissed her knuckles, his whiskers brushing her skin and making her laugh. "You look enchanting. Perfect for the theme."

Augustine refrained from making a gagging sound. "What are you again? A German shepherd?"

"A wolf." The angry glitter in Nekai's eyes told Augustine he was getting through.

"And what's enchanted about being a wolf?"

Nekai stared at him a little too long, then spread his arms, leaned forward and growled. His nose elongated into a snout, he sprouted extra tufts of fur and his eyes went silver. When he stopped growling, he returned to his regular wolfy appearance.

"So you're a werewolf then."

Nekai smiled at Harlow, who thankfully didn't look that impressed. "Same thing happens when I howl. Or sneer."

She nodded. "Do you do that often? Howl, that is?"

"Only when I see something worth howling about." He winked at her.

Augustine rolled his eyes. "Some*thing*? I hope you mean some*one*. She's a person, not an object."

"Enough, you two." Harlow held her hands up before Nekai could respond. "I need to grab my purse. I'll be right back. Try not to kill each other while I'm gone." She backed away, glancing at them a few times like she expected a fight to break out any minute.

Augustine waited until she was gone. Then he leaned into Nekai's personal space. "Watch yourself, weaver. Harlow isn't one of your usual cheap thrills."

"You're one to talk." Nekai snorted. "Is there a woman in this city you haven't slept with?"

Augustine's hands knotted into fists. He fought to keep them at his side. "Just keep your distance. Watch over her tonight, make sure she's safe, but that's it."

Nekai growled softly, lighting his eyes with the preternatural glow of his costume's magic. "She asked me to teach her our ways." He smiled, all traces of wolf disappearing from his gaze, and touched his hand to his chest. "I'm not going to turn down her request just because you said so. She's a grown woman and she can make her own decisions about who she spends time with."

"I've already arranged a teacher for her."

Nekai shrugged. "Yes, but the things she could learn from me...you might even get to enjoy them when I'm done with her." He laughed wickedly.

Augustine lifted his fist. "What the hell is that supposed to mean?

Nekai sighed like the conversation bored him. "What did you think? I planned on marrying her? Don't pretend you're a saint all of a sudden. You wrote the book on love 'em and leave 'em."

"Those days are over."

"Mine aren't, so don't get in my way of having a little fun."

"Okay, all ready," Harlow called out as she descended the stairs.

Augustine dropped his hand, but the unfulfilled urge to lay the guy out made him twitchy with pent-up energy.

"Wonderful," Nekai said. Like nothing had happened. "Which one of us have you decided will accompany you to the ball then? Me? Or Bambi?"

Harlow smiled sweetly, but the light in her eyes seemed just this side of angry. "Oh, didn't I tell you? I'm allergic to dogs."

Giselle stood at her father's door, regretting what she was about to do but knowing it was time. She pushed the doorbell. Cormier, her father's butler, came a few minutes later. "Miss Giselle." He adjusted the collar of his robe before smoothing an age-spotted hand over his gray hair. "Apologies for my lateness, but your father had already dismissed me for the evening. Is everything all right?"

"No, it's not." She hung her head. "I need to speak to him. Is he still up?" Probably. Evander liked the night as much as she did.

"He is." Cormier moved to let her in. "He's out by the pool."

As she entered, she lifted the bottle of wine in her other hand, a peace offering. "Could you bring us a corkscrew and two glasses?"

"I believe Mr. Vincent is already enjoying a glass, but I'd be happy to bring fresh glasses for you both."

"Thank you." She walked through the house and into the backyard. Her father sat on the patio in one of the lounge chairs. All the lights were off, except for the glow of the pool. Cormier had been right. Her father was already drinking. An empty wineglass sat on the small table beside him. She nodded. Good. That would hasten the process and strengthen her story.

She shut the door softly.

"Cormier?"

"No, it's Giselle." She walked forward so he could see her. "I brought you some wine."

Cormier came out with the corkscrew and glasses and set them on the side table before disappearing back into the house.

"It's late. You didn't come all the way over here to bring me wine." Her father didn't seem as angry as she'd expected. Maybe he'd realized she was right. No matter. She was tired of being on this constant roller coaster with him.

She twisted the corkscrew into the bottle and freed the cork. "No, I didn't. I came to apologize." She poured them each a glass and handed one to him. Thankfully, he took it without further persuasion.

He clinked the glass against hers before trying a sip. "Apologize for what?"

She held her glass without drinking. This was not the conversation she'd expected to be having. Why was he acting like nothing had happened? Like there'd been no fight? "For not... believing in you more." She couldn't bring herself to apologize for calling him a traitor, because she still believed that was exactly what he'd become.

He patted her leg. "I never know what to expect from you, but that's my fault, not yours. You've always been the more emotional child."

Was that what this was? He thought their fight had just been her being emotional? Her resolve for what she was about to do redoubled. She topped off his wine, happy to go along with his idiotic supposition if it would make her task easier. Even so, her heart twinged at what lay before her. "Yes," she groused. "I'm practically bipolar."

With apparently zero notice of her sarcasm, he laughed and took another mouthful. "I wouldn't go that far, but you have certainly kept things interesting."

"I'm a lot like my mother, aren't I?" She almost dared him to disagree. To say something disparaging about the woman who'd died trying to wrest the witches' power away from the fae. To take away the guilt that crept in around the edges of her thoughts.

His face took on a solemn cast and she wondered if the sudden shift in emotion was due in part to the amount of wine he'd already had. "Yes, you are. I think that's part of why you're so easy to forgive, too."

She stilled, anger making her stiff. Now she was the one who had to be forgiven? Goddess help her, the man was insufferable. She'd definitely made the right decision. She poured more wine into his glass. "That's so sweet of you, Daddy." She stood. "Let's walk a little. It's such a beautiful night and you know I don't have a garden."

Without waiting for him, she headed away from the house and into the dimly lit yard. She tipped a little of her wine onto the ground to make it look like she'd drunk some, then turned when she was a few feet away. Her father lumbered after her, glass in hand. "You know you could always move into your mother's house."

"That house belongs to Zara now."

"I know, but your sister wouldn't mind. She spends all of her time in the garden anyway."

He assumed so much.

"She'd probably welcome the company." Already his words slurred a little.

"I'm not so sure." She lifted her glass, urging him to drink. "Don't you love a clear night like tonight? The moonlight recharges me."

"It does, doesn't it?" He swallowed some more wine, walking with her as she headed toward the deep end of the pool. His steps seemed heavy, his gait a little unsure. He shook his head. "This wine is hitting me hard. I need to go to bed."

"Don't leave me out here all alone."

"I guess I can stay a little longer."

She paused at the outer edge of the pavers. Time to draw him closer to the pool. Time to do what she'd planned. "Did you have the tile redone? I don't remember it being that color."

"No, no. Same as it's always been." He swiped his arm across his forehead. "Warm all of a sudden, isn't it? I'm not feeling so well."

"It is warm." She held her wineglass at her side, spilling a little more onto the grass. Then she kicked off her ballet flats and walked across the pavers to stand at the pool's edge. She bent to dip one foot in the water. Goddess forgive her. This was for the good of the coven. "The water's cool. Why don't we sit on the side and dangle our feet in? Like Zara and I used to do when we were little. It would cool you off."

He blinked, nodding and looking like he was having a hard time focusing. "O-okay." He tipped his wineglass back, draining the contents, then wobbled toward her, reaching for one shoe. "My head is spinning. That wine…"

He twisted like he was trying to look back at the bottle, but lost his balance at the pool's edge. He tipped toward the water, dropping his glass. She threw her hand out toward him. *"Mortus sonus."*

Dead silence entombed them. She held the spell, the effort gnawing at the edges of her strength. It was one thing to cast a spell and let it be, another to restrain it and hold it in place. His wineglass shattered on the bricks without the slightest crash of breaking glass. The water erupted around him as he fell into the pool, but made no sound. Water splashed her bare feet as he thrashed.

Fear overtook his face for a moment, then anger replaced it as he realized what was happening. He got one hand up to fling a burst of defensive magic at her, but sank beneath the surface as she dodged it.

The drug she'd laced the wine with had slowed his reflexes too much. A bead of sweat trickled down her spine from the effort of holding the spell. One last attempt to fight her and he sank under again, his limbs heavy with forced intoxication. A long moment passed before his body surfaced, limp and seemingly lifeless.

She released the spell, dropping her hand and gasping with fatigue. The repressed sounds returned in a riotous din. The shattering glass, the splash of her father's bulk hitting the water, his screaming her name, his cries for help, all resounded through the air as though they'd just happened.

She joined in. "Cormier, help me, we need help!"

Grimacing, she jumped into the chilly water. Her father floated facedown. She rolled him over, hooked her arms under his and started kicking toward the shallows.

Cormier came running out. "What's happened? Oh no—"

"Get the pole," she screamed. "Help us."

He ran for the shepherd's hook. She leaned her ear against her father's cold, damp mouth. He'd put up a good fight, but there was no breathing that she could discern.

Just the smell of wine and death.

Chapter Eleven

"Stop that." Harlow poked Augustine in the ribs as he leaned in a second time and woofed softly in her ear. She laughed anyway, because after she'd gotten over being angry at Nekai's words—words she'd heard every bit of from the landing—she'd realized that Augustine had once again been the one to stand up for her.

He stood next to her now as they waited in line to be announced at the Exemplar Ball, his fingers interlaced with hers. If he thought she hadn't noticed how much he was touching her, he was wrong. "That's the last of the Elektos. We're up next."

She nodded, wondering if the onslaught of information from her contact lens would be too much to take in. So far she'd avoided looking at anyone long enough to activate the software, but that would change when she was in the midst of everyone. The hum of the crowd vibrated beneath the soft music and the introductions of the guests by the master of ceremonies as they walked onto the stage.

"Just breathe. It'll be fine." He released her fingers to extend his arm.

Thanks to Yanna's info, Harlow knew to place her hand on his forearm. His softly speckled forearm. His costume really was amazing.

"Here we go." He started forward as the MC's voice reached them.

"Ladies and gentlemen, your new Guardian, Augustine Robelais. Accompanying him this evening is Miss Harlow Goodwin."

They walked out through the curtain to a round of applause. Harlow sucked in a breath. "It's beautiful," she whispered. The entire ballroom had been transformed according to the evening's theme of Enchanted Forest. In the center was a wide-open field capped by a starry evening sky that seemed miles above them. Trees lined the edges, their soaring branches creating a canopy that sheltered the tables made of squat, fat mushrooms. The chairs were dainty things built of twigs and moss. Enough fireflies dotted the trunks and branches to cast a golden glow over the dining space. "This is all fae magic, right?"

"Yep." Augustine nodded to people in the crowd and gently guided her toward the head table, where they'd be sitting. In the very center was a gilded throne.

"I can't believe we're in a building. This whole thing is just too much to believe." She deposited her green satin evening bag—another treasure from her mother's closet—by her place setting.

"It is, isn't it?" He pulled out a chair for her. "Do you want to sit?"

"No, I..." Fenton and Yanna's name cards were only a few spaces away, which was nice, but as she gazed out over the crowd, the realization of just how many people were there and how prominent the head table was made her pulse kick up a notch.

Augustine cupped her shoulder. "You okay?"

She turned away from the crowd, happy to face him instead. "I could really use a drink."

"What do you want?"

"I have no idea, but don't leave me here by myself." She picked up her evening bag.

"Come on, we'll head to the bar. You may have to meet a few people along the way. You can leave your bag here." He pointed to the ends of the raised dais the table sat on. Guards dressed as foxes were positioned at each end. "It'll be safe, trust me."

Her LMD was in the pocket of her dress, but she had a little cash, a lipstick and the case for the contact in the purse. Nothing too much to worry about. She set it back down. "Meeting a few people couldn't hurt."

He leaned in, his mouth so close to her ear his breath tickled her skin. "You know with that facial recognition lens, you don't really need me to tell you who people are, right?"

"I know, but I'm still feeling a little overwhelmed." Although with him this close, she was starting to feel overwhelmed for a different and not entirely unpleasant reason.

He stuck his arm out. "Let's go."

She took his arm and they threaded through the crowd, but they were stopped so many times she wasn't sure they'd make it to the bar. She leaned in. "A few people? I think you meant everyone here. You're kind of a celebrity, huh?"

He shrugged, looking slightly uncomfortable. "This is the first chance most of these people have had to meet me—and it's not really me they're interested in so much as seeing what fool was willing to take on the job of Guardian."

"Don't say that. You're not a fool."

He smiled grimly. "It's a known fact that this job doesn't have a long life expectancy."

His words sucked a little of the beauty out of the evening. "That's cheerful."

"Sorry." He raised a hand to the bartender, who rushed toward them. "What's the drink this evening?"

"Starlight punch. Would you care for some?"

She looked at Augustine. "What do you think?"

"Sure." He nodded at the bartender. "It's alcoholic, right?"

The bartender smiled. "Yes, it's this evening's signature cocktail."

"We'll have two," Augustine answered.

"Make mine a little stronger." Harlow almost hated to ask, but the feeling of being overwhelmed hung over her like a dark cloud about to storm.

The bartender nodded. "Yes, ma'am."

"Ouch," she whispered in Augustine's direction. "Ma'am? Really?"

"It's protocol," Augustine whispered back, smiling. "Don't get your panties in a bunch, Harley."

She pinched his arm. "I told you not to call me that, and leave my panties out of it."

He was about to reply when another voice interrupted them. "Harlow."

At the sound of her name, she turned. Nekai stood a few feet away. "Can I talk to you?" *Nekai Dupre : Spell crafter : Weaver fae : Analysis—friend*

Augustine made a move like he was going to defend her in some way, but she patted his arm. "I can handle this." She lifted her chin. "You've done enough talking, Nekai."

He gave Augustine a look, then frowned. "Just a minute. Please."

Everyone deserved a second chance, didn't they? "Fine, but one minute. That's it."

"Thank you." He gestured toward a more private spot.

She walked with him, neither of them speaking until they were away from Augustine. "Well?" She crossed her arms and stared at him.

"I wanted to apologize."

"For?" She expected him to do this right.

"For what I said about you to Augustine." He leaned against a tree and had the decency to look embarrassed. "What I said was just...stupid male ego. I'm sorry. You don't deserve to be treated that way."

"No woman does."

"You're right."

Surprised, she nodded. "That took some spine to admit to. I accept."

He righted himself. "Thank you. Do you think...would you be willing to dance with me later?"

She glanced back at Augustine. He still stood near the bar, but all she could see of him through the cluster of women surrounding him was his horns and his smile. She turned back to Nekai. "I'll dance with you—although I don't know all these fancy ball dances."

He smiled. "All you have to do is mimic what I do." He pulled a small leaf from somewhere in his costume. "Here."

She took it. "Is this what I think it is?"

"A dance ticket? Yes. It reserves one of your dances for me."

"I know what it does." Yanna had explained these. The female guests were bound by etiquette to accept the tickets unless they'd already received enough to fill their evening. There were twenty dances tonight. If she had to dance them all...

"You're not booked up already, are you?"

"No." She couldn't bring herself to lie. She looked at the leaf more closely. It was actually fabric, printed with the title of the ball and the dance information. "Seems like such an old-fashioned thing, doesn't it?"

"It does, but like so much of what makes up society here, it's tradition, which carries a lot of weight in this town."

"I'm starting to realize that." She held the leaf up. "I'll see you for the dance then. And look, just because I'm agreeing to this and I've accepted your apology doesn't mean we're suddenly best friends." He wasn't back in her good graces, but she was willing to let him try, and there were worse options for dance partners. She'd already met a few of them. Besides, she'd been excited about having him as a teacher and while it might not be possible to recapture that feeling, at least they might be friends. She had so few of those in this town.

"Understood."

"Good." With a nod, she turned to go. The crowd behind her seemed to have doubled since she'd been talking to Nekai. Her contact lens was going crazy, spitting out lines of info at a pace she couldn't keep up with. So much for that. The scrolling output made the vision in that eye like looking out a greasy window and at this point, it was just adding to her stress.

She veered away from the bar and headed for the table where she'd left her purse. Good thing she'd brought the case for the lens. It was time to take it out. It was that or go crazy from the information overload.

But getting to the table wasn't as easy as it sounded. She was stopped numerous times by different men requesting a dance and giving her a leaf. Yanna had prepared her for the possibility of this happening, Harlow just really hadn't believed it would. It was both flattering and slightly unnerving to have so much male interest directed at her. Why had she agreed to this?

Fenton stood behind his seat talking to someone as she finally approached the head table. She grabbed her purse as he broke away from his conversation to greet her. "Harlow, you look stunning." He gestured to the man beside him. "This is Salander Meer, another of the Elektos."

Salander extended his hand. "My condolences on the loss of your mother. She was a great friend to this city."

Salander Meer : Elektos : Saboteur fae : Analysis—friend "Thank you." She shook his hand, thankful she hadn't taken out the lens yet. "You're a saboteur fae, right? I'm still learning all the different types. Can you tell me what that means?" A small burst of panic struck her as she wondered if that was a polite thing to ask. Yanna hadn't covered that. Or had she? There was so much to remember.

Then he smiled and her panic disappeared. "Perhaps a small demonstration is in order…" He plucked an ivy leaf from the floral runner in the center of the table and held it on his open palm. "Watch."

The leaf wilted and curled up as it went brown, then dried up and turned to dust. He blew it off his hand and smiled. "Does that answer your question?"

Her face must have given away her shock because he laughed. "Don't look so alarmed. I can control it."

She nodded. "Oh, that's good. That's very good." Her images of everything around them decaying disappeared. "Can you do that to people, too?"

"Yes, but that would only be in self-defense."

Fenton smiled. "Sydra, one of Augustine's lieutenants, is part saboteur fae."

Harlow didn't know exactly how to respond to that. "How… nice for her." Once again, her powers seemed so weak compared to those of other fae. It was frustrating not to have defensive abilities and yet oddly comforting not to have to learn to control anything with real destructive powers.

"Hey, there you are." Augustine joined them. "I was starting to get worried. You never came back to the bar." He handed her one of the drinks he was holding, leaning closer.

She took it gratefully, hoping the alcohol would take the edge off her nerves.

"Everything okay with Nekai? He didn't try anything, did he?"

"No. Actually he apologized." She sipped the drink. It was slightly sweet, slightly tart—then it felt like bubbles were bursting on her tongue. She looked at the glass. "That's the craziest thing. More magic?"

"Is that the starlight punch?" Fenton asked. "If so, then yes. The themed drink always has a little something special added to it."

Salander gestured with his glass, the amber liquid looking more like whisky than the punch she and Augustine were drinking. "Last year the theme was Heaven and Hell. The Hades concoction actually had flames."

"That must have been something." But Augustine didn't look very interested in discussing drinks. "Fenton, Salander, if you'll excuse Harlow and me for a moment? They're getting ready to introduce the Faery Queen soon and I'd like a little time with my beautiful date."

Harlow occupied herself with her drink, but even the cold beverage couldn't keep the warmth from her face.

Fenton nodded, his gaze elsewhere. "Yes, I see Loudreux is here. Go on, you two have fun."

Augustine tipped his head at her as if to say, *Follow me*, so she said her goodbyes. "Very nice to meet you, Mr. Meer."

"Elektos Meer," Augustine whispered under his breath.

Crap. Yanna *had* told her that. "Elektos Meer," she corrected, but the saboteur fae smiled kindly as if no harm had been done. She followed after Augustine. "He seems like a nice man. Wicked cool talent."

"He is a nice man. He's one of the Elektos that's on my side, too." Augustine led them to a secluded area behind a few trees. "I wanted a minute with you before I go off to take care of my job as part of the Faery Court. How are you doing so far? The crowd is bigger than expected."

"I'm okay." Even better knowing he wasn't too caught up with official business to make sure she was handling things all right. "But after you go do your thing, I'm taking this contact out. It's too much information for me to process and it's adding to my stress. Sorry."

"Hey, it's okay. It was meant to help you. If it's not doing that, ditch it." He relaxed a little. "So Nekai apologized?"

"Yes, but don't worry. It doesn't mean I'm not a little wiser about him."

Augustine smiled.

"What?"

"Nothing." He shook his head. "You're so like Olivia. Which is good. She was one of the smartest women I've ever met." He looked back toward the crowd. "It's almost time for me to go." He rolled his eyes. "I have to walk the Faery Queen to her throne."

She laughed. "I think it's sweet."

"Loudreux's worried his daughter and her ladies-in-waiting are going to turn into a bunch of slavering, lovesick fools around me." He snorted.

She raised her brows. "I could see that happening. Especially in this getup." She waved her finger at him. "You're basically naked from the waist down except for the fur and that leather chest thing doesn't really cover that much and..." She swallowed, realizing too late that staring at him had caused her to lose her train of thought. She lifted her glass. "Um, so yeah, this drink is good."

The look in his eyes went from cynical to amused in half a second, the wicked sparkle something she recognized instantly. "Been checking me out, have you?" He took the drink from her hand and set it in the hollow of a tree, removing the one small obstacle between them. "And you think I look naked from the waist down?" He feigned indignation. "Just how closely were you looking?"

She swatted him on the arm. His hard, muscled arm. "Don't get full of yourself. Fuller, I should say."

He backed her against a tree. "I'm not the only one with a lot of skin exposed, Harley." His appreciative gaze swept the bodice of her dress.

"I'm covered in vines." Her voice came out as light as the center of her body felt.

His amusement turned into something darker. Something... feral. "*Covered* is open to debate." He planted his hands on the trunk, pinning her between them. He bent, nuzzling her throat. "You smell amazing." His words vibrated over her skin, raising goose bumps and causing the lightness in her chest to spill into her head.

"It's the... the dress..." She grasped his shoulders and arched her head back, giving him more access. Despite the latex protecting her, his touch came through just fine. The warmth of his breath, the softness of his lips, the gentle pressure of the kisses he feathered down the slope of her neck.

Unable to bear his teasing any longer, she cupped his face and drew him up to look at her. "You're torturing me."

Heat snapped off his skin like sparks. "I think you've got that backwa—"

She shut him up with her mouth, kissing him hard, and remembering too late that her lips had no protection against the onslaught of his emotions.

What spilled into her was a mix of desire, desperation and need so strong it bordered on possessiveness. There was anger there, too. And something hidden. Fear. But of what? She let him go. His chest rose and fell with his breathing. "What are you afraid of?"

His gaze narrowed. "I'm not afraid of anything."

"Don't lie to me. I could... taste it on you." Among other things she wasn't willing to put words to.

He stared into her eyes like he was looking for his answer. "I've seen the eyes of other men on you tonight. The way Nekai looks at you. I don't like it, but I also know I don't have the right to do anything about it. You don't belong to me." He opened and closed his mouth before finally speaking again. "I hate that...that..." He frowned and looked away.

She turned his face toward her. She brushed her thumb over his cheekbone. "That I might like one of these men better than you?"

He pulled back enough that her hands fell away. "How many dance tickets have you collected so far?

She'd hit a nerve and whatever moment they'd just been sharing was gone. "Eleven."

His eyes widened.

His response hurt more than she expected. "Shocked I have that many?"

"Shocked you have that few." He slid his hand into the side of his breastplate, pulled out a bunch of the leafy tickets and held them out to her. "Anyone else asks, tell them you're full." He hesitated. "If you're willing. Because I would hate for you to like one of those men better than me."

She took his tickets, trying not to smile and failing. "I don't think there's much chance of that happening." She didn't think there was *any* chance, not when he was willing to be so honest and open with her. If ever there was an aphrodisiac. Of course, her being able to feel his emotions made it hard for him to keep anything hidden for long.

He grabbed her and pulled her in for another kiss. Pleasure and unbridled joy came through, mingled with a sense of worry she hadn't expected. He wasn't sure if she felt the same way he did—if she'd ever feel the same. If she'd run from him at some point because he was so very, very fae. Or because his job forced him to do something that scared her away. Then those emotions started to morph into barely controlled desire, and he broke the kiss, eyes smoldering with a dark fire. "I should go get ready to escort the Faery Queen. I'll see you afterwards at the table."

"Okay. Have fun." She gave a little wave as he sauntered off. What was she doing? What was this breathless, light-headed giddiness threatening to turn her into mush when he was around? She knew what it was and it made her every bit as afraid as Augustine was. She grabbed her drink from the hollow of the tree, about to down some in an effort to cool the emotions burning through her, when she felt the emptiness inside her rise up.

She reached her other hand out for support, trying to hold on to the pleasure that had suffused her just a moment ago, but her grip was slipping.

The abyss absorbed the happiness and left her with the longing for more emotion, any kind, and a sense that the gaping hole she'd lived with all her life was going to keep growing until it swallowed her whole.

Chapter Twelve

Augustine's thoughts were so wrapped up in Harlow that he almost bumped into Cy backstage. Streaks of gray and brown body paint covered the ethos fae. "What are you supposed to be?"

Cy held out his arms. "I'm a boulder."

Not much of a costume, but a fitting one. Augustine held his tongue. "How did it go with you-know-who?"

Cy glanced around, but the chaos behind the curtain was directed at getting the Faery Queen and her court ready to be presented, not at eavesdropping on the Guardian and his hulk of a lieutenant. Still, Cy kept his voice down. "She was *not* happy. And she basically confessed, boss."

Augustine cursed, earning a sharp look from one of the mothers in attendance. He took a few steps farther away from the cluster of women, motioning for Cy to follow. "I knew it. What did she say?"

"That she bought the *bokura* from Ogun, then used it to drug Dreich into confessing and killing himself." Cy shook his head. "I don't think she had any idea I wasn't her father. She got so mad. She accused him of being in bed with the fae, then she called him, I mean, me, a traitor and threw me out of the house." He held up one thick finger. "She said Ogun was blackmailing her. Threatening to tell the police she bought that powder from him."

"If that's true, pushing him a little harder should be enough to make him spill this information. Then we can tie her to Dreich's death, finish that part of the investigation and take her into custody. Once that happens, I'm sure I can break her down. I have no doubt she played a bigger role in the vampire invasion than we know about. I can feel it."

"You think she'll lead us to Branzino?"

"That's my hope."

Cy shifted a little. "We might have one problem, though."

"What's that?"

"She also said something about going to the coven and telling them Evander was working with the fae. I think she wants to get him thrown out as coven leader."

Augustine crossed his arms. "I'm sure she's wanted that for a while. You know she doesn't agree with his tolerance of our rules. But her feeling that way and the coven feeling that way are two different things. They're not about to dethrone Evander. He's kept the peace and kept them comfortable. That's what matters to them."

"If you say so, boss."

"I—"

"Excuse me." A very stern, very petite cypher fae inserted herself between him and Cy. "*Mr.* Robelais, if you'd like to join us, the young ladies are waiting."

"Good evening to you, too, Mrs. Loudreux." Hugo's wife was not amused. But then that was pretty typical, from what he knew about Mimi Loudreux. She was one of those women who wielded their husband's position like an iron fist, and she used Hugo's to crush any opposition or obstacle she faced, whether it involved attaining the presidency of some organization or dictating exactly how her daughter would be presented to fae society for the first time.

Cy leaned down. "That's *Guardian* Robelais."

She wheeled on him. "And you, you're not even supposed to

be back here." She shooed him away with both hands. "Go on, now, the promenade is about to begin."

Cy backed away, eyes wide. Augustine nodded. "Go ahead. We'll talk more later."

Mimi Loudreux clapped her hands. "Please, Mr. Robelais. I will not have you wrecking Rue's big night with your tardiness."

Cy's news coupled with the taste of Harlow lingering on his lips had put him in a defiant mood. He stared her down. "If you ever interrupt Guardian business again, I will charge you with obstruction of justice and have the charge published in the *Picayune*. I doubt the Historical Society would want a felon as their president."

The ice in her eyes melted enough to give him satisfaction. Then she froze over again. "Please take your position, *Guardian* Robelais." She lifted her chin. "And I'd like to remind you that Rue is a child and should be treated as such. *Hands,*" she emphasized, "to yourself."

"I've never done anything to justify that comment." His hands tightened into fists, then he relaxed, knowing she was doing this on purpose to rile him up. "So if you think I'd do anything inappropriate toward a sixteen-year-old, you have a sick mind, Mimi." He curled his lip. "You should be ashamed of yourself."

He pushed past her to find her daughter, which wasn't hard. Rue stood in the center of a group of girls, all dressed in pastels to compliment their queen. She wore a froth of glittery white and, like her attendants, had been outfitted with a working pair of crystalline wings.

When he approached, they fluttered nervously. "Hello, Miss Loudreux," he said.

"Guardian Robelais! You came!"

"Did you think I wouldn't?"

"I wasn't sure." She blushed and looked sideways at her ladies-in-waiting, who'd begun to whisper and giggle.

"I'd never turn down a personal invitation from the Faery Queen herself." He moved to her side and extended his arm. She rested her hand on him so lightly, he almost couldn't feel it. After a moment he realized she was trembling. What on earth had her parents told her about him?

"Don't be afraid." He whispered so as not to share her discomfort with the other girls. "No matter what your parents said, I'm not going to do anything to embarrass you. I promise."

Her head dropped a little. "Thank you, but I'm not worried about you." She swallowed and turned toward him a little. "They're all going to be looking at me. I'm worried I'm going to trip. Or faint. Or do something else stupid."

Liquid rimmed her lower lash line. Panic struck him. He could *not* make the Faery Queen cry. He smiled. "Do you want me to faint instead? I promise no one would be looking at you then."

She laughed, covering her mouth with one slim hand. "No." The laughter faded. "I'm just so nervous."

"I understand. One thing that might help is actually hanging on to me." He flattened her hand against his forearm. "Lean on me if you have to."

She nodded. "O-okay."

He canted his head toward her. "My girlfriend is the same way about crowds." *Girlfriend.* Harley'd probably smack him if she heard him use that word, but it had slipped out so easily. "She gets panic attacks."

Rue's eyes widened. "She does?" Then she smiled. "I didn't know you had a girlfriend."

He didn't. Not officially. Not in any sense of the word, but the conversation seemed to be distracting Rue from her nerves, so he went with it. "She's dressed as Mother Nature tonight. I'll introduce you to her later, if you like."

"I would." She glanced at her mother, who was scolding one

of the ladies-in-waiting for wearing the wrong color of nail polish. "My mother said you were..." Her voice lowered. "Lecher-
ous. And that it was a crime against all things fae that I should
have to be escorted by you this evening."

He stared at Mimi, nodding slowly. "Are you wishing you
hadn't invited me?"

Her grip on his arm increased a little more. "No way. Neither
of my parents is that great a judge of character. Especially when
they think someone isn't quite up to their standards."

He almost laughed. "Pretty *and* smart. You've got a bright
future, Rue."

She blushed again. "I'm still a little nervous."

The chimes began to sound, announcing the entrance of the
court. She paled.

"Hey now, it's going to be just fine." He winked at her. "I can
still faint if you want me to."

A hint of a smile tugged at the corner of her mouth.

He stretched his arm out a little farther. "Stare at my fingertips if you don't want to make eye contact with anyone. They
won't be able to tell if you're looking at them or not."

She nodded, her gaze immediately shifting. The curtains
drew back and the master of ceremonies started announcing
Rue's court.

"Once around the ballroom, then you're seated on your
throne and dinner is served. You can do this, Rue." The line
moved forward as one by one, the girls and their escorts walked
through the curtain and out into the crowd.

"I can do this," she repeated. She didn't sound that convinced.

"And if you do feel like you're going to faint, pinch my arm.
Hard as you want. Just give me the signal and I won't let you
fall."

"Promise?"

"Promise." But she was still trembling.

The master of ceremonies' voice bellowed their introduction, making any more conversation impossible. "And now, ladies and gentlemen, our Faery Queen, Miss Rue Loudreux!"

They stepped through to an enormous burst of applause. Rue's hand turned to ice on his skin. He used his smokesinger abilities to raise his temperature and bring a little heat to her fingers.

She glanced over at him, a question in her eyes.

He raised one brow as if to say, "Yes, I did that on purpose."

And by the time they were halfway around the ballroom, the trembling was gone. When he brought her to her throne, she was smiling and laughing and waving. "You did great, Faery Queen."

"Thank you, handsome escort." Her smile was a little shy and a lot teenage girl. "You really helped me."

"That's what the Guardian is for." He sketched a courtly bow and made his way back to Harlow's side.

"How was it?" she asked.

He gave her a smug grin. "Let's just say someone might have a little crush on me."

She laughed and looked down the table at Rue. "Is that so?" She gave him a sly smile at the same time her hand squeezed his thigh under the table. "Should I be worried?"

He swallowed. The heat in his body now had nothing to do with his smokesinger abilities. He licked his bottom lip and tried to form words, but all he could do was shake his head.

Giselle sat in her father's living room, wrapped in her father's robe. Cormier had given it to her after he'd called 911, but she was still shivering, soaked through as she was with pool water. And guilt.

Her father was dead. By her own magic. She reminded herself it had been for the good of the coven. For the *future* of the coven.

The police had spoken to her and were with the paramedics in her father's garden now, leaving her alone at last. She stared at her hands, clutched in her lap. The lights of the ambulance parked out front washed the room in amber and blue. People from the neighborhood had begun to gather, drawn from their homes by the commotion. They knew exactly who lived here. Some peered eagerly toward the garden. Perhaps hoping to catch a glimpse of the body. She dropped her head into her hands. Parasites.

"Giselle."

She looked up. "Ian." A longtime coven member, but the newest member of the council of thirteen and a man she'd long admired for his belief that their people deserved more freedom. A man her father had never seen eye to eye with and a man Evander had made her swear never to become involved with, claiming he was the worst kind of influence for someone of her talents. Whatever that meant. Of course, that had only piqued her interest in the long-haired, eyeliner-wearing bad boy of their circle.

Interestingly, her mother had never had any objections to Ian, other than thinking he was a little too old for her.

Add to that the fact that he rode a motorcycle and worked in a tattoo shop and she'd spent the latter part of her teenage years crushing on him and conjuring countless love spells. Now he owned that tattoo shop and the decade's difference in their ages didn't mean nearly as much.

Maybe it was the concern in his eyes or just that he was the first of their coven to come to her side, but something in her broke. Her chin quivered and she bent her head to weep softly. "He's gone."

"I came as soon as I heard." He knelt at her feet and clasped his hands over hers. They were warm and calloused and the scents of ink and sage wafted off him. He must have come from his shop. His silver rings and bracelets glimmered in the flashing lights.

"I tried...to save him..." Tears clogged her throat and cut her words short. She told herself that her actions had been for the protection of her people, but that didn't erase the pain of losing her father. Or her guilt. Maybe her reasons had been a tiny bit selfish, but she *was* thinking of the witches' future. That future just happened to be hers as well. She sighed. If only he hadn't been such a traitor. If only he hadn't forced her to take such action.

Ian's hands squeezed hers a little tighter. "I know you did. Cormier told me what happened."

Cormier had no idea what had happened. She nodded and inhaled a deep cleansing breath while chanting a calming spell. After a moment she could speak again. "I need to tell Zara."

"I can tell her."

"No, she should hear it from me. From family." Despite her best efforts, her lip quivered again. "From the only family she has left." She looked at Ian, losing herself for a moment in his black-rimmed eyes. "We're orphans now." And she'd made them that way.

He brushed a strand of wet hair off her cheek, the creak of his leather jacket an oddly comforting sound. "You're both strong women. You'll get through this." He looked away for a moment before continuing. "I know the time isn't right, but that can't be helped. We must discuss the leadership of the coven and who's going to take over in his place."

She shook her head. "My father's body hasn't even been taken away."

Ian seemed unmoved. "His death is exactly why we have to discuss this."

"I can't. Not now." Although that was exactly why she'd done what she'd done. "Can't it wait until morning?"

He sighed. "When word gets out and you have not announced your intent, there are those in our circle who will take that as a sign of weakness."

"Only a fool would mistake me for weak." Anger crept through her grief. "How did you find out? He's not even cold."

"I have a friend in the police department." He studied her. "Do you plan on announcing your intent to take over as high priestess? The New Orleans Coven has always been led by a descendant of Aurela La Voisin. That means you or Zara, unless there's another relative I don't know about."

"There is an aunt. My mother's sister. But she doesn't live in New Orleans."

"Do you want me to track her down?"

She sighed. Aunt Geeta was the last person they needed. "No."

He stood. "I will support you, should you decide to challenge your sister."

"Should I decide to? Of course I plan on announcing." Giselle found the strength to rise. "You think Zara would want the position enough to oppose me?"

"I don't know." His gaze softened. "But I know where you stand on the things that concern the coven the most and with her, I don't. I like your ambition. Your drive." He lifted her hand to his mouth and pressed a kiss to her knuckles, never taking his eyes off her. "I would gladly serve under you, *Lady* Giselle."

A delicious shiver ran through her, one so at odds with how she should be feeling, she almost didn't enjoy it. Almost. But his touch combined with the honorific title that would be hers as head of the coven was too much to ignore. "My father never liked you, Ian."

The tiniest of smiles bent his mouth. He kept hold of her hand. Perhaps a little more possessively.

She frowned as best she could with the pleasure of his touch coursing through her system. "Never liked your ink and your piercings and your taste for the darker ways."

He brought her hand to his mouth again. This time his tongue darted between her fingers. She inhaled before she continued. "He warned me away from you. Told me you had only become a member of the thirteen because your mother was too powerful to deny."

"A lot of fathers warned their daughters about me." He smiled, as wicked a smile as there ever was. "And while my mother is quite a powerful hedge witch, I ascended to the rank of the thirteen on my own power and my own position. I have a fair amount of influence on my own, you know."

"I know." She wound her fingers through his and drew him closer. "Let it be known that I am willing and capable of succeeding my father. I'll go to Zara's and give her the awful news and gently let her know I plan to announce my intent to take the coven's reins." She narrowed her gaze slightly. This was a man she'd lusted after for many, many years and the one reason she'd never done anything about that had drowned along with her father. Those years of longing drove her now. "Do you know where I live?"

He nodded. "Edge of the Quarter, off Orleans Avenue. Do you need me to drive you home?"

"No." Outside, the paramedics wheeled a gurney toward the ambulance. A sheet draped her father's body. She pushed away, maintaining an appearance of propriety for the sake of the cops making their way back into the house. "Just be there. I'm going to need comforting in my time of mourning. You do know how to comfort a woman, don't you, Ian?"

Heat smoked his gaze and his jaw tightened, but he managed an almost imperceptible nod. "Until then, my lady."

Chapter Thirteen

As the night rolled on, Harlow came to the shocking realization that she was actually having a good time. She'd danced with all the men who'd given her tickets, except for Nekai and one other, but Augustine, when he was available, was by far her favorite partner. He was surprisingly graceful and whispered sweet things—and some wicked ones—into her ear whenever they were close.

Sadly, he was in great demand as a dance partner and although he broke away to spend time with her as often as he could, she was pretty sure he'd been around the dance floor with each of Rue's ladies-in-waiting more than once. Despite not having him all to herself, Harlow smiled. Seeing him at work in his official role made her proud.

How strange to be proud of the same man she'd hated a few weeks ago, but the Augustine she'd come to know, the Augustine who was here tonight, was nothing like the man she'd imagined him to be. He was so in charge and so charismatic that several times she found herself doing nothing but standing and watching him. She imagined her mother would have been very proud of him as well.

"May I have this next dance?"

She looked toward the voice that had interrupted her reverie.

The gentleman smiled. "You have my leaf."

She recognized him by his outfit, an elaborate version of one of the evening's more popular costumes, the Green Man. "Yes, of course. As soon as the new song starts."

The software-impregnated contact lens now rested in its case, but it wouldn't have helped even if she'd left it in. The man's mask completely covered his face, a sort of leafy getup that looked like it could have been made by the same fae who'd made hers. "We kind of look like we go together."

He laughed. "Yes, we do. And so do about half the other attendees tonight. Green was a popular choice."

His voice seemed familiar, but then she'd talked to him earlier. She couldn't remember his name, causing anxiety to trip along her nerves. Best to just confess her social blunder and hope for the best. "I'm Harlow. But you know that already. And I'm very sorry, but I don't remember your name."

"I'm sure you've met a lot of people this evening. Please don't worry about it." He held out his hand. "I'm Arlis Moore."

His grace about his forgotten name was kind, but she still hesitated. Shaking people's hands without her gloves on wasn't easy to get used to. She told herself to stop being silly and took his hand. "Nice to meet you again, Arlis."

He tipped his head as he released her hand. "I know your mother was haerbinger, so you must have some of her skills." He smiled nervously. "Are you going to tell my fortune now that you've touched me?"

His knowledge about her was unsettling, but Olivia had made no secret of being fae when the covenant had been broken, causing humans to finally see the othernaturals living among them. "No, I . . . took precautions against that. I can't tell anything by touching you."

He looked relieved. She didn't blame him. He nodded. "I guess that must be quite a burden to bear, being able to read people like that."

She changed the subject. "So are you from New Orleans then?"

"I'm actually from Baton Rouge, but I own the company that makes the throws for the Exemplars, so they always invite me to the ball."

"Throws?"

He dug into a pocket and pulled out a large, shiny gold coin. "Things the krewes throw from the floats during the parade. Beads and coins are pretty popular. You can have this one if you like. A lot of people collect them year to year."

"Thank you." She took it. One side of the coin was printed with the Exemplars' signature fleur-de-lis and the date, the other was printed with the tree of life and the words "Enchanted Forest." The song ended and a new one began. She tucked the coin into her pocket. "Sounds like they're playing our song. And thankfully it's a waltz, I can do that one."

With a smile, he extended his arms to her. She took her position and they began to dance. Augustine and Nekai were both on the floor as well, their partners looking thrilled. She could imagine.

"You've just moved here, right?" Arlis asked.

"Yes." Amazing how much strangers knew about her life.

"How do you like the city?"

"So far, so good." She'd given that answer more times than she could count this evening, but no one wanted to hear that her adjustment wasn't going as smoothly as she had hoped.

He nodded. "Do you have any family here? Outside of your late mother, of course, may she rest in peace."

"No, no family."

Arlis's eyes narrowed a bit. "That's too bad. There's nothing like the support of family."

Augustine twirled by, looking suitably entranced by the teenage girl he was dancing with. Harlow couldn't find that level of pretend within her. "I wouldn't know, Mr. Moore. I grew up without much of one." She smiled coldly, daring him to push the subject.

He bowed slightly. "I see I've hit a nerve. I am very sorry. Not my intention. I talk too much when I'm nervous and it's been a while since I've danced with a beautiful woman." Sadness took over his gaze. "My wife passed away recently and I thought the ball would be a good way to take my mind off things, but this is the first year I've attended without her and it's...hard."

Now she felt like an inconsiderate beast. "I'm so sorry. Ignore me. I'm known to be a pain in the ass, even to strangers."

He dropped his hands and they stopped dancing. "It's okay, you didn't know." He swallowed.

"We should finish our dance."

He exhaled, a soft, shuddering sigh. "I'm just going to find a quiet place to sit. I shouldn't have come. I thought I could handle being around people..." His voice trailed off.

"Let's go get a drink and we'll find a place to sit together and you can tell me all about her." She looped her arm through his and started leading him toward the bar. "Have you had the starlight punch? It tastes like it's made with real stars."

He smiled. "You're very kind."

She winked at him. "That's rarely a word applied to me, so take advantage of the opportunity."

He looked at her, his eyes suddenly sparkling. "Okay. I will."

Fenton stood at the edge of the dance floor, discreetly but frantically waving Augustine over every time they made eye contact. At last the song ended. He bowed to his partner, yet another of Rue's ladies-in-waiting, then headed toward the twitchy Elektos. "What's going on?"

"Don't you have your LMD on you?"

"Yes, but I can't exactly whip it out on the dance floor and I turned the cell com off. It's loud enough in here without voices in my head."

Fenton frowned. "Something has happened."

"Such as?"

"Evander Vincent drowned in his pool this evening."

Augustine's mouth opened slightly but it was a moment before he could speak. "Drowned. As in dead."

Fenton nodded. "The report so far is that he was intoxicated, fell in and drowned. Giselle was there—"

"Of course she was."

"You think she had something to do with it?"

"Do people drink on Bourbon Street? Hell yes, I think she had everything to do with it."

Fenton sighed. "It doesn't matter. She tried to save him, from what Grantham told me. They're not ruling it suspicious, and there won't be an autopsy."

"So Giselle came up with the perfect murder." Augustine growled softly. "There's no way she's not involved. Not after what happened earlier. In fact, I might be the reason she went to see Evander in the first place. If that's true, I never dreamed she'd retaliate like this."

"What are you talking about?"

Guilt shadowing him, Augustine filled Fenton in on how he'd sent Cy to Giselle's disguised as Evander, how she'd confessed and called Evander a traitor. "I pray that wasn't enough for her to kill her own father, but I also don't know her that well. Other than she's ambitious and hates the fae."

Fenton blew out a long breath. "You can't feel guilty about this. You were just trying to get to the bottom of things, to prove her involvement in Dreich's death once and for all. If she killed Evander, that's all on her."

Augustine looked away, his stomach turning at the thought of what he might have set in motion. "I'm not sure I can sign off on this that easily."

"You're going to have to. Things are about to get interesting and the city is going to need your full attention."

That brought his head back around. "How so?"

"The New Orleans Coven is a matriarchal society. The line of succession runs through Aurela La Voisin. That means Giselle or Zara will now preside as high priestess. There is an aunt in another city, but that would be unusual."

"If Giselle becomes coven leader, will the coven side with her?"

"I don't know. The witches are a curious group. They're fairly divided between those who seem content with the status quo and those like Giselle, who are vocal about their resentment of the regulations placed on them centuries ago." Fenton's attention shifted to his LMD. "Just a moment." He tapped his screen, then nodded. "And there it is. Word has it Giselle has announced her intentions to step up."

"And you really don't think she was involved?"

Fenton's expression was grim. "I don't know. Evander liked his drink. That much seems plausible. Giselle as coven leader..." He shook his head slowly. "Evander was at least predictable and mostly level-headed. Giselle is...not." He met Augustine's gaze. "We must be wary of her."

"Shouldn't we get some sort of official word from her that she's taken over? That is the custom, right?"

"It is, but I wouldn't be surprised if breaking that tradition is her first act of rebellion. We should expect her to do the opposite of what Evander would have." He looked past Augustine. "It's almost time."

"For what?"

"For the mock kidnapping." He narrowed his eyes and

gestured toward the far reaches of the ballroom. "See them, back there in the trees? The hooded figures."

"They look like executioners."

Fenton snorted. "Considering half those men are probably members of the chamber of commerce, they'd be amused you think so."

Augustine glanced toward Rue. She was dancing with a boy about her own age, laughing and looking very much like she was having fun. "She certainly isn't acting like she knows what's about to happen." Because if she didn't, she was about to be scared out of her mind.

"She knows. Every girl who dreams of being the Faery Queen knows about the kidnapping. They probably look forward to it as much as the ball. She'll be whisked off to a suite at some hotel where her ladies-in-waiting will meet her. I imagine they do whatever teenage girls do during a sleepover. Eat pizza? Talk about boys?" He shrugged like the behavior of teenage girls was more foreign to him than quantum physics. "The ransom request will come in the morning, Loudreux will send his payment and she'll return home in time for lunch." He smiled. "It's all harmless fun. It happens every year." He leaned in. "It's the bulk of how the Exemplars fund this ball and their parade float."

Knowing the fae in those hoods were local businessmen made Augustine feel a little better. "It's still a strange thing to do." He scanned the crowd for Harlow but couldn't find her. Or Nekai. His jaw tightened in irritation that had no real basis. Other than jealousy. "Have you seen Harlow? Or Nekai?"

"I saw Harlow not too long ago at the bar, and Nekai was dancing with Mimi Loudreux."

Augustine snorted. "Of course he was."

"He's not a bad sort, Augustine. Minus the juvenile record and street fighting, he's actually a lot like you used to be."

Augustine crossed his arms and leaned against a nearby tree. "That's the part that worries me the most."

Power and grief were a heady cocktail. Giselle's hand trembled as she knocked on Zara's door. "Zara, wake up. It's Giselle."

Lights came on in the front of the house. A few moments later, Zara opened the door. She wore one of their mother's old robes: midnight-blue velvet, the edge stitched with a pattern of vines and berries in silver thread. The kind of thing their mother used to wear to do serious spellwork. Zara's eyes were bright. "Is something wrong? It's late."

Zara had clearly not been in bed. "Can I come in?"

"Of course."

Giselle waited until the door was shut behind her. "I have terrible news."

Zara clutched the ties of her robe. Sap stained her fingers. "What is it?"

Giselle took a breath. "Father…" She'd rehearsed this on the way over, but nothing sounded right. "He's gone, Zara. Drowned. I couldn't save him." She dipped her head and let the tears come. "There was nothing I could do. He'd been drinking and he was too heavy for me to pull out of the pool. By the time Cormier got there, he was…gone."

Zara was quiet a long moment. Too long. She began to nod slowly as she wiped her eyes. "So turns the wheel of life." She sniffed once. "He always was one to overindulge. Food. Drink." Her eyes met Giselle's. "Adherence to rules and regulations." She pushed her flaming hair out of her face. It hung wild around her shoulders and contained little bits of leaves.

"That was him." Giselle had to bring up the subject of who would take over the coven, but that was something she hadn't figured out how to do gracefully. Although maybe Zara wouldn't care. She certainly didn't seem broken up over their father's death. "Ian came by. He heard from someone in the police department what had happened."

"Good of him to do that, considering Father never did like him." Zara's mouth turned up in a restrained smile. "Although you did."

"Zara."

She spread her hands. "There's no one standing in your way now. If he still interests you, I say go after him. We aren't teenagers anymore, Giselle. There's no reason not to live our lives the way we want to." Her brows rose. "Does that shock you? If so, I'm surprised. You never struck me as someone overly concerned with what anyone thought." She frowned for a second. "Anyone except Father, and now…" She lifted one shoulder in a gentle shrug.

Giselle nodded. Zara was right. "Thank you."

Zara tipped her head. "For what?"

"For calling me on that sort of ridiculous behavior. And for not being an emotional wreck over this. You really are like Mother, you know that? In the best possible ways." She sighed, relief washing through her. "I love you, Zara. I know we haven't been as close these past few years, but just like there's no reason not to live the way we want to, there's no reason we can't be better sisters."

Zara smiled. "I'd like that." She stood back. "Do you want some tea or something? Obviously, I wasn't asleep. I was doing some spellwork in the garden. As if you hadn't guessed that."

Giselle shook her head. "Thank you, but I can't. There's too much for me to do right now." And Ian was waiting for her.

Zara's hand went to her mouth. "Oh, the coven. You're going to take over, aren't you? You have to. I can't, Giselle. You know me. I'm not cut out to be a leader. You are, though."

"You aren't even the slightest bit tempted?" Giselle didn't want to fight Zara over this in years to come.

"No. Take it with the blessing of the goddess. I'm happy to support you." Her eyes narrowed. "I think you and I are on common ground when it comes to the fae oppression."

Her admission confirmed what Giselle had guessed. "We are. Although I must admit I used to think you were content to just putter in your garden and sell your tinctures at the farmers' market."

"That what I've wanted people to think." Zara smiled slyly. "You always say how much I'm like Mother." Her smile grew. "I'm probably more like her than you can imagine. Especially where the fae are concerned."

"I'm happy to hear it." And surprised. "Then I can count on you for whatever I might need in that fight?"

"You can. Do you have a plan?"

"Not exactly, not yet, but I will figure something out. I'm tired of being under the fae thumb."

"We all are. Well, that's not exactly true, is it? There are some in the coven who will oppose you. They're happy with the status quo. They fear change and the possibility that the fae will tighten things further."

"Ian won't oppose me. He's said as much."

Zara's sly smile returned. "Is that so?"

"Yes." A wave of giddiness overtook Giselle and she almost laughed. "I should go, but I'll talk to you soon about the details for the funeral and such."

Zara leaned against the wall and crossed her arms. "What aren't you telling me?"

"Nothing." But the thought of Ian brought another smile to her face.

Zara's expression turned incredulous. She waved her finger at Giselle. "Silence now your lying tongue or pray the goddess you go dumb."

Giselle rolled her eyes, but her sister's spell was cast. She certainly couldn't go home to Ian without being able to speak. The words spilled from the tip of her tongue. "Ian's waiting for me at my house."

Zara's eyes twinkled. "Well, off you go then to a night of earthly pleasures and I back to my spellwork. Tomorrow we can grieve suitably, but I see no reason to derail our evenings over a man who did little more than complicate our lives. So mote it be."

Giselle nodded. Her conversation with Zara had gone so much better than she could have imagined. In fact, the whole night had turned out much better than she'd expected. "So mote it be."

Chapter Fourteen

Arlis seemed in better spirits after a drink and a few stories about his late wife. Harlow was happy for the break in dancing. As poorly trained as she was, even following someone's lead became something of a chore. Especially when she was trying to carry on a conversation and not step on his feet at the same time.

"Thank you for listening to me." He smiled at his drink. "You remind me of my daughter. Well, I'm guessing. We lost her when she was just a baby. It's wishful thinking that she would have grown up to be a lovely young woman like yourself."

She shook her head. "That's a sweet thing to say. You've certainly had your share of sorrow, haven't you? Was she your only child?"

"No." He smiled wistfully. "But our only daughter."

"I'm so sorry." The tragedies of his life put hers in perspective.

He patted her knee. "Now, now, can't live in the past, can we? Forward. That's the only direction worth focusing on." He looked over at her. "Speaking of which, how many dance tickets do you have left? I fear I've taken up too much of your night."

"Hardly any."

"You're a bad liar, my dear." He stood, grunting softly. "Too much sitting and I stiffen right up these days. I think I'm going to call it a night. Maybe take a little walk and loosen the old bones." He hesitated. "I'd ask you to come, but I think one of your dance partners is waiting." He tipped his head toward the bar.

One of the men she'd met earlier, whose costume could only be described as over-amorous rabbit, waved from the bar. She looked back at Arlis. "Actually, that walk sounds great." It was getting a little stuffy in the ballroom. The noise and people were almost too much.

He laughed. "Don't get me into trouble, now. My days of fighting off suitors are long gone."

"Suitors? Oh no, no, no. Let's not go there. I'm not remotely interested in any of those guys." Just one in particular.

"Well, I shouldn't take you away from all this. I'm sure you'll be missed."

A loud shout erupted from the ballroom and the crowd on the dance floor parted as a group of men in hoods and monstrous masks slipped out from the shadows. "No one's going to miss me. That fake kidnapping thing is going on." As much as she wanted to see how they pulled that off, Arlis seemed like he needed the company. She took his arm. "Let's go get some air."

They slipped out of the ballroom by a side door and then went through one of the service areas of the hotel hosting the ball until they found an exit. The night was cool and clear and surprisingly quiet, given how close they were to the Quarter. "I don't know this area that well."

"I do," Arlis answered. He pointed behind them. "The river's just right back there. Have you walked along it? Too cold with the wind coming off it now, but during the day it's nice. Especially if you like watching the boats go by. Which I do." He laughed. "That's an old man's pastime, isn't it?"

"No, I don't think so. What else do you like to do?" A few minutes and she'd go back to the ball, but for right now the quiet was just what she needed. What they both needed.

"I try to stay busy with my work."

The conversation carried on without much effort. He was easy to talk to and she couldn't help but feel sympathetic.

Minutes passed and she realized she wasn't quite sure where they were. The street was dark and deserted. "I should get back."

"You're not going back."

"What?" She pulled away from him, panic spiraling through her. She dug in her pocket for her LMD.

He held it up. "Looking for this?"

She snatched at it, but he threw it into the dark. He grabbed her arm. "Enough, Harlow. Do you really not know who I am?"

"No." She racked her brain, but she knew so few people in this town.

Arlis smiled and shook his head. "My dear, sweet, gullible girl." Then he leaned in and the faint chlorinated smell of pool water triggered her memory as he spoke what she already knew. "You know exactly who I am."

"No," she whispered. She jerked away, but couldn't break his grip. "Leave me alone. I don't want anything to do with you."

His hand tightened and the face she'd once thought kind took on a cruel twist beneath his mask. "Too late. You took my money. Now we need to talk about what comes next."

"I didn't *take* your money. You sent it. I never asked for it. Never wanted it." She glanced around but there was no one in sight and she couldn't remember a single move Augustine had showed her. "Help," she screamed. The sound reverberated through her, echoing in the deep abyss of her soul.

A thread of power unwound within her, tensing like a serpent about to strike. Its presence would have been a comfort if she had known how to control it. Or could she?

"Your precious Augustine is busy at the ball." He yanked her against him.

"He's the Guardian. He'll find you." She tried to open herself to the power, the same way she did when trying to hack an unfamiliar server. It blossomed, filling her senses . . . but seemed to have no other effect.

Branzino shook her hard. "I'm done waiting on you, Harlow. I need that house and you're going to give it to me."

With a low growl, a dark form dropped onto Branzino, taking him to the sidewalk. Nekai. The weaver fae jumped to his feet. "Get behind me." He thrust his hands out, pale-green fire crackling from his fingertips, which his costume's magic transformed into curved talons.

She slipped behind him partially, the pounding of her heart shaking her whole body. The thread of power disappeared.

Branzino got to his feet. "This doesn't concern you, son. This is between a father and his daughter."

"What kind of father makes his daughter scream for help?" The fire snapped like a hungry, living thing.

Branzino's lip curled and his gaze shifted to Harlow. He lifted a hand to her. "Let's go, Harlow."

"Like hell." She held on to Nekai's arm, more thankful for his presence than she had words for. "Augustine warned you not to come back."

Branzino seemed unfazed. "But he's not here, is he?"

"No," Nekai answered. "But I am."

"Fat lot of good that's going to do you." Branzino lunged for Nekai.

He stretched his hands out. The fire leaped from his fingers to Branzino, crackling over his skin like webbing.

Branzino went to his knees, spasms shaking him. His eyes rolled back in his head and his costume began to smoke. She realized in that moment there was no denying Branzino was her father. He had as little defensive magic as she did.

Nekai balled his hands into fists and the fire died away. Branzino fell to his side, twitching and groaning.

Nekai slumped against her. "We need...to go...before he gets a second chance."

"Are you okay?" His blue-black skin had gone dusty gray.

Suddenly he tensed and pinpoints of light burst off his forearm. He cried out, gritting his teeth as an unseen force etched new runes onto his skin. When it ended, he breathed openmouthed. "Need to rest."

She stared at the runes. "That was a new spell?"

He nodded. Branzino rocked back and forth like he was trying to get up.

"Lean on me. I'll get you back." She looped his arm around her shoulder. "Which way?"

He lifted a finger to point ahead of them and kept directing her at every turn with a tip of his head or a grunt of approval. She got him into the ballroom and helped him into a chair in the same back corner where she'd sat with Branzino. Nekai leaned his head against the wall and closed his eyes. His color looked a little better.

She shivered thinking how close she'd been to Branzino. To being taken by him. Was she that vulnerable? That stupid? Apparently. Look how easily she'd been led astray. She sank into the chair beside Nekai, grasping his hand between hers. The man had marked himself permanently in her defense. What he'd done to upset her was completely forgiven. "Thank you. You saved my life."

His eyes slitted open, his head still propped against the wall. A hint of a smile curved his mouth. "Does that make up for me being an idiot earlier?"

"Absolutely. It's forgotten."

He closed his eyes again. "Thanks."

"Thank you." She glanced at the fresh runes marking his arm. It was a little humbling to know that he'd been willing to do that for her. She leaned up and kissed his cheek.

"Harlow, I was—"

She turned to see Augustine standing in front of her. Anger practically vibrated off him. She dropped Nekai's hand and stood, putting herself between the two men. "Relax. All you need to know right now is that Nekai just saved my life."

Concern replaced most of the anger in his eyes. "Why? What happened? Are you okay?"

She looked around. There was no way of knowing if Branzino had anyone else here. She kept her voice low. "I'm fine. Branzino happened. I don't want to talk about it here, but if not for Nekai, I wouldn't be standing here right now."

Augustine nodded, glancing past her to the weaver fae. "We're going home right now."

"Don't you have duties here?"

"They're finished."

"And the kidnapping?"

"Over." Steel glazed his expression. He was also apparently done. With the evening, with her questions, with not knowing what had gone on between her and Nekai. But nothing would change that the weaver had saved her life. She couldn't just turn her back on him.

"Nekai should come with us. At least until he's feeling better."

"Fenton can get him home."

"I can get myself home." The voice came from over her shoulder, where Nekai now stood. "New runes always take some adjusting to."

"New runes?" Augustine looked at her, then back at Nekai. "What the hell happened that you had to create new runes?"

Nekai slipped his arm around her waist and leaned in to whisper in her ear. "You better get him home before he pops a vein."

She frowned. He didn't seem completely recovered. More like he was hiding how he really felt. "Are you sure you're okay?"

"Never better. I'll be in touch." He winked at her, then walked away with a slightly slower gait than he'd had earlier in the evening.

Augustine actually did look like part of him was about to blow up. She tipped her head to one side and pointed toward the head table. "I need my purse."

He didn't move, except to put his hands on her shoulders. "And I need some answers. Please, just tell me if you're okay? Why did he need to create a new spell?"

"I'm fine. Mostly. I'm shaken up, but I'll get over that." She shrugged. "About the new spell... I guess he didn't have much in the way of defensive magic."

Augustine's eyes rounded. "Why did he *need* defensive magic? What did Branzino do?"

"Can we discuss this at home? I really don't want to be here anymore."

His jaw tightened.

She reached up and pressed her hand to his cheek. He felt like fire. "All that matters is I'm okay, right?"

He closed his eyes briefly, leaning into her caress. "I agree. But I hate the fact that something happened to you and I wasn't there to protect you."

"I get that you're the Guardian, you're not exactly my personal bodyguard. Besides, Nekai was there."

A soft growl left his throat. "That's not helping me feel better about this."

"I can't do anything about that and neither can you, so let it go." She slipped her hand to his chest. She wanted to tell him about the power, about how she'd summoned it, about how it had felt like something greater than she understood, but now was not the time or the place. "Please, let's just go home."

Chapter Fifteen

Giselle sighed contentedly into her pillow as Ian traced the bones of her spine with his rough fingers.

"So much blank, beautiful canvas." He followed the path of his fingers with his mouth. "You should let me ink you."

She glanced over her shoulder. Goddess, he was beautiful in the morning light. Like some kind of fallen angel. The contrast of his dark hair and eyes and tattooed body tangled in her white sheets made him somehow more forbidden. Or maybe it was just the way he looked at her. "I don't think I'm the tattoo type."

He pulled her close, curving the length of his body against hers so that his mouth rested in the hollow of her shoulder. "Everyone's the tattoo type. You just need the right tattoo. And I already know what that is."

"You do, do you?" She closed her eyes. There was so much work to be done today, but not so much that she couldn't indulge in a few more minutes in bed. "What's that?"

"The source of your power. Your crystals. That is where your power comes from, isn't it?" She could hear the mischievous grin in his voice as his fingers splayed over her hip.

She scowled at him. "That's bold of you." It was considered impolite to ask about a witch's source of power.

His hand stayed on her hip but he cocked one brow. "It's not such a secret. You read them in the square, they're all over your house…am I wrong?"

She sighed. "No. But you're still bold." She planted her elbow on the bed and rested her head in her hand. "So what about this tattoo?"

"It would be my gift to you, my new high priestess. We'd both benefit from it."

"How so?"

He kissed her shoulder. "My power comes from those I ink, but I can also pour it into the work I do. By tattooing you with an image of a crystal, I could actually increase your power."

She sat up, wrapping the sheet around her. "Couldn't you also steal it?"

He rolled onto his back and crossed his arms behind his head. "No, my gifts don't work that way."

She studied him, the feeling that he wasn't being completely truthful gnawing at her. "Then how do you get power from the people you work on?" He'd already asked about her power. Seemed only fair he divulge a little about his own. Besides, she didn't want him siphoning off any of her ability, if that's what he was capable of.

He shrugged. "The same way you get your power from the crystals."

She planted her fingers on his chest and leaned over him. "I am your high priestess. I demand you answer me."

"You demand it?" His eyes sparkled.

"Yes." Judging by the way the rest of his body was responding, Ian wasn't opposed to a dominant woman.

"As my lady wishes." He wrapped a strand of her hair around his finger, brought it to his nose and inhaled, sighing with pleasure. "My power comes from the pain I inflict. Which doesn't mean I cause any more than necessary. Pain is a by-product of tattooing. Fortunately for me, that pain is also power."

She sat back, pulling the strand of hair out of his fingers. If he was trying to show her his loyalty by telling her the source of his power, it was working. "That doesn't exactly make me want to get tattooed."

"I have ways of lessening what you feel, but I can't eliminate your pain entirely."

"You wouldn't get anything out of it then, would you?"

"No, but that's not why I can't do it. Pain is just a part of the process."

The increase in power was a heady possibility. How much stronger could she get? Enough to handle chaos magic? To complete the spell her mother had died doing? "I have a lot to take care of today, but I'll think about it." She pushed at his hip. "Get up and make me some coffee."

The familiar spark of desire lit his eyes again. His tongue worked against his cheek before he finally answered, "Yes, my lady." He rolled out of bed, not bothering to dress, and sauntered out of the room.

She watched him go, admiring the view and thanking the goddess for his sudden and unexpected help. Taking over the coven would be so much easier with him at her side, willing to do her bidding.

Whatever that might be.

Harlow pulled out her new LMD. Amazing how fast Fenton had procured one for her. She unlocked it. Still no answer on the text she'd sent, but then it was early and last night had been long and difficult for all of them. She put the device back on the desk next to her coffee cup and returned to building another sample website for her portfolio. Augustine had slept through breakfast, which she understood. He'd been out so late she had no idea when he'd actually returned home from hunting Branzino with his lieutenants, and she also knew that meant she might have to skip today's training session. But if last night had taught her anything, it was that she was done feeling defenseless.

She rubbed her hands together. The room she'd chosen for her office was a little chilly, but when the sun rose higher that would change. A car door closed. She tensed at the sound, further underlining her need to be able to defend herself. Could Branzino have come for her? She went to the window that overlooked the front of the house, saw the car and smiled. No wonder her text hadn't been answered. Nekai had come straight to the house.

Harlow flew down the stairs to answer the door before Nekai rang the bell. No sense in waking Augustine or getting Lally riled up after the lovely breakfast she'd made. Harlow pulled the door open and gave him a little wave. "Hey."

Nekai smiled at her. "Hi."

"How's your arm today?"

He walked in. "It's fine. How about you? I'm sorry I didn't respond to your text. It sounded..."

"Pitiful?"

"Important." He shrugged off his coat. "I thought I should just get over here and see how you were doing."

She sighed. Better, now that he was here. "I'm okay, maybe still a little freaked out."

"Totally understandable." He hesitated. "Can I ask why you picked me over Augustine?

"Because I think your skills are better suited for what I want." She took his coat and hung it on the stand in the corner. "Let's go in the library where we can talk."

She waited until he entered, then slid the pocket doors closed. "I want to learn to defend myself. If you hadn't been there last night, I don't know what would have happened. Well, actually, I can guess." She slumped onto the couch, not wanting to imagine the horrible possibilities.

"But I *was* there." He took the other end of the same couch.

She shook her head. "That time. But what about when you or Augustine aren't there? Then what? Branzino isn't going to leave me alone." Even having Augustine return Branzino's money wasn't going to stop the man. That much she knew. "I have to be prepared."

He looked oddly disappointed. "I'm not much of a fighter. Augustine would be better at that. You saw what I did last night. That was fresh magic. I've never used my skills that way."

"I get that. And Augustine's already started teaching me to fight, but I'm thinking that's never going to be my forte." She shrugged. "And I need to know how to defend myself now."

"So what can I teach you that he can't?"

She pulled her gloves off and wriggled her fingers. "Magic."

He snorted softly. "That's not something that can be taught. You either have it or you don't."

"Well, I have it. At least I'm pretty sure I could feel it inside me last night but I didn't know what to do with it, or how to harness it or anything, really." She tucked her gloves into the pocket of her hoodie. "I've already started learning how to control my ability to read emotion but if you want to help me with that, too, great. What I really want is for you to teach me how to weaponize it." She wasn't about to go into full detail about how touching the vampire had awakened the sense of power inside her. All he needed to know was that she had some kind of power. And the time had come to make it work for her.

"I can do control. But not all fae have the kind of powers that can be used defensively. Take Fenton for example. Cypher fae are some of the most vulnerable. And you're what, haerbinger and...what's your father?"

She bristled. "Please don't call him that. Branzino will do. I can't stand the fact that I'm related to that monster."

"Noted. What kind of fae is he? I couldn't tell from what little of him I could see last night."

"I have no idea."

"Hmm." He tapped his fingers on his leg, making the silver runes on his knuckles glimmer. "Let's go at it another way. What skills do you have?"

She took a breath. This wasn't a conversation she'd had with many people. "Two main things. One is being able to read people and objects. Skin-on-skin contact means I get flooded with emotions—whatever that person is feeling, I feel. All of it. Good, bad, sometimes things they're not even fully aware of themselves. With objects, I get more. Images, emotions, sounds, smells… like a little snippet of wherever that object just was interlaced with whoever touched it last. But those things fade over time from objects, so if I'm going to read something it has to be done within the last few days of being touched."

She looked around at the room. "Take one of these books off the shelf that hasn't been touched in months and I probably wouldn't be able to read anything off it."

"Interesting." He nodded, thoughtful. "That sounds like haerbinger mixed with something else. Probably whatever your fath—Branzino is. What's the second thing?"

"The second is I'm good with computers. Weirdly good. I've never come across a firewall that can keep me out or an encryption I can't break."

His brows rose. "Never?"

"No."

"How do you do this?"

She sat back. "I just… kind of… become a part of the system. It's like I'm one with the computer. I can feel my way through it, see the pathways in my mind. It's hard to explain because it's something I just do."

"Cyphers can figure out a person's passwords or codes just by touching them. You have freckles. Are any of them actually tiny numbers?"

"Numbers? Is that a thing?" He nodded. She'd have to get a better look at Fenton the next time she saw him. "Okay, that's new. All mine are just plain old freckles."

He sat for a long moment without saying anything, the wheels of his thought process almost visible. "What's easier for you to read? Paper? Fabric? Plastic? Metal? Glass?"

"Metal. Definitely."

"When you get this influx of emotions from people or things, how does it make you feel?"

She took a deep breath. Lately she'd almost been craving the sensations brought on by touch. Like she was hungry for them. Not *her*, really. It was the emptiness inside her that needed that onslaught of feelings and emotions. The way it swallowed down the pleasure of Augustine's kiss at the ball had frightened her. But not feeding it felt almost impossible. The urge was growing. Nekai didn't need to know any of that, though. "Like I'm being invaded."

"So it's a bad feeling?"

"Not always." Already she'd confessed more than she'd even told Augustine, but she wasn't comfortable telling Nekai about the ever-growing hole inside her. Not before she told Augustine. He deserved to know that first. "Sometimes, it's almost... pleasurable." That was as much as she was willing to say. "And it seemed last night that I could feel power within myself but I couldn't act on it. That makes me wonder..." She looked at her hands. Here and there remnants of the latex spray clung to her arms like a shedding snakeskin.

"Wonder what?"

"I had latex covering my entire upper body last night, protection against being touched. I wonder if the latex that was keeping sensations out was also keeping my ability in." She glanced up at him. "Is that possible?"

"I don't know, but it's an interesting theory." He leaned forward, his thoughts clearly churning with this new information. "Would you say traveling via mirror is easy or sometimes gives you trouble?"

She stared at him. "Traveling via mirror? I don't even know what that means."

He frowned. "You know, when you use a mirror to get somewhere quickly."

"Again, no idea what you're talking about."

"Have you never used a mirror for transportation?"

"Unless transportation is fae slang for putting on makeup or looking at yourself, no."

He grinned. "This is going to be fun." He stood up and pulled a compact from his pocket, then he held his hand out. "Come here."

She hesitated, finally slipping her gloves back on. "Just in case," she mumbled as she slipped her hand in his. She really didn't know what he could and couldn't read off her, and didn't want to chance his picking up on the emotional pit inside her.

"Whatever makes you comfortable." He flipped the mirror open with his other hand. "We'll start small and keep it local. Don't let go."

She squeezed his hand. "I won't. Is this going to hurt?"

"No, but you'll feel something. Maybe a little dizzy. Here we go."

"Where—" A sharp burst of sensation hit her. Falling, spinning, being pulled sideways and down. She blinked.

The library was gone. In front of her was the gazebo and beyond that the pool. They were standing in the backyard.

Augustine rubbed his eyes on his way down to a late breakfast. There'd been no visit to Olivia last night as he'd intended, but he would slip through the mirror to see her at some point today. Harlow needed to know her mother wasn't gone.

Instead, after finding out Branzino had nearly kidnapped Harlow, something that had taken her way too long to tell him about, he'd gone out with Sydra and Dulcinea to sweep the area around the hotel. Cy had stood guard at the house, but all had been for naught. The most he'd found was Harlow's shattered LMD and a scorched spot on the sidewalk about ten blocks from the hotel where the ball had been.

He wasn't fool enough to think that meant Branzino was gone, though. At least knowing the man was in town gave him a slight edge. And with the house now warded, something that unfortunately reminded him of Nekai every time he thought about it, Branzino wouldn't be waltzing up to the front door anytime soon.

Lally sat at the kitchen table, drinking coffee and reading her morning paper. There was no sign of breakfast, but the warm vanilla scent of French toast lingered.

"Damn it."

Lally frowned at him. "Augustine, you know I don't like that language. And at breakfast. Have some manners."

"Did I miss French toast?"

"Yes." She got up, a wry smile on her face. "But you know I saved you a plate." She grabbed a towel, opened the oven and pulled out a plate heaped with four fat slices of French toast and a pile of bacon.

He grinned. "You do love me." He poured himself a mug of coffee, then sat beside her. "Harlow still in bed?"

Lally's mouth thinned. "No. She got that weaver man here. They're in the library. I think she thinks I don't know he's here. Well, I do. And I still don't like him."

"I don't either, but he saved Harlow's life last night, so cut him a little slack. He's not the worst person she could be spending time with." Or maybe he was. He'd saved Harlow's life. That had to change the way she looked at him. The way she felt about him.

"My lands, what happened?" Lally clutched at the charms dangling off her necklace, rubbing her fingers over the cross.

He filled her in on the previous night's events.

She shook her head. "Augie, you have got to deal with that Branzino once and for all. That child can't live her life in fear of him."

Harlow walked into the kitchen, Nekai behind her. "Fear of who?"

Augustine ignored Nekai. "I was just telling Lally about last night." Harlow looked pretty good, despite the scare she'd had the night before. Maybe a little tired, but they all were. "How'd you sleep?"

"Okay, considering. Took forever to get that latex off, though." She rubbed at a spot on her arm. "It's still not all gone, but if I scrubbed anymore in the shower, I'd have taken skin off." Her expression darkened. "Did you find Branzino last night?"

He sipped his coffee. "No, but what's left of your LMD is on your bed."

"Thanks." She glanced at Nekai. "I guess you didn't kill him after all."

"Sorry," Nekai whispered.

She sat down at the kitchen table, looking a little shell-shocked.

Augustine shook his head. "I'm sorry I don't have better

news." Fear filled Harlow's eyes. He reached over and put his hand on top of her gloved ones. It gave him a perverse pleasure knowing she didn't want Nekai touching her either. "At least Branzino knows I'm not the only one looking out for you and willing to fight for you. That's a good thing."

"I'm glad you can find something good in all this." She pushed her chair back and propped her feet on the edge, pulling her knees to her chest. Nekai moved to stand behind her and put his hand on her shoulder.

Augustine wanted to shove that hand away, but his com cell chimed in his head. "Answer."

"Augustine, we have an issue." Fenton sounded frantic.

"What's going on?"

"You need to get to Loudreux's immediately. Something's gone wrong with the kidnapping."

He stilled. "Wrong like how?"

"The ransom note. They're not asking for money." Faint crying could be heard in the background. "They want the current Guardian to relinquish his position."

A creeping sense of dread took hold of him. "Fine. So tell them I relinquish, Rue gets released and then I go back to being Guardian."

Fenton stuttered something unintelligible. "They've specified that the relinquishment must follow standard protocol."

Augustine chose his words carefully, knowing Harlow was listening. "There's only one way that happens."

Nekai's brows lifted like he had an idea what was going on.

"Yes." Tension strained Fenton's voice. "By death."

"And if that doesn't happen?"

More distant crying filled the small silence. "They're going to kill Rue."

"*Sturka.*" He pictured the sweet girl he'd gotten to know.

She'd been terrified of the crowd last night. He could imagine what being truly kidnapped was doing to her. "You have the note?"

"Yes."

"I'm on my way. And I'm bringing Harlow."

Chapter Sixteen

The steely resolve in Augustine's eyes filled Harlow with dread. "What's going on? Where are you taking me?"

"Rue's been kidnapped—"

"We already know that." Nekai lifted one brow. "That's not news."

"The Faery Queen girl?" Lally asked.

"Yes. She's been kidnapped for real. The ransom note came this morning, but instead of asking for the money needed for next year's ball, the kidnappers are threatening to kill her unless their demands are met."

Harlow moaned softly. "Oh no."

Behind her, Nekai cursed.

Augustine ignored him and looked directly at Harlow. "I need you to see if you can read anything off the ransom note. Any clue as to where they might be, who they might be, anything."

Cold with shock, she nodded. "Okay, of course. Let's go. That poor girl."

"Is there anything I can do to help?" Nekai asked.

Augustine shook his head. "No."

Harlow stood and turned to him. "I'll be in touch as soon as I can. You just work on what I asked you about, okay?"

Nekai nodded. "Okay. Be safe. Don't be afraid of your abilities. Let them guide you."

She smiled and gave his hand a squeeze. That would be great

advice if she could control whatever was trying to swallow her whole.

"Why is she here?" Loudreux's left eye twitched. "This is Elektos business."

Augustine stood his ground, but Harlow cringed at his side. "She's offered to help. I understand you're upset about Rue, we all are, but now is not the time to reject someone with the ability to help find your daughter."

Fenton pushed past them to enter the house. He stood directly in front of Loudreux, blocking his line of sight. "Hugo, Harlow is a talented haerbinger. She can read objects in a way that may tell us who the kidnappers are or possibly where they're located."

Loudreux relaxed slightly. "That's not a typical haerbinger gift."

Fenton turned enough that Loudreux could see Harlow again. "She's not a typical haerbinger. Let her help, Hugo."

Muttering something, he nodded and turned away, disappearing down the hall.

Augustine looked at Harlow. "You okay?"

She swallowed. "I'm fine."

He wasn't totally convinced, but she was a strong woman and getting stronger every day. "Remember, you're my guest. Nothing he says really matters so long as you're with me. As Guardian, no one tells me or, by extension, you what to do."

"He's right," Fenton said.

She nodded. "Good to know. I really just want to help Rue."

"Me, too." He reached down and took her hand. "Let's go see what we can find out."

They followed Fenton down a hall into the living room. Most

of the Elektos were there. Loudreux paced, scowling. Harlow hung back. "It's okay," Augustine whispered.

"Hello, Harlow." Yanna smiled at her. "How generous of you to help." She moved to Harlow's side. "We're lucky to have you."

Harlow smiled, but looked only partially convinced that anyone else felt that way. "Thank you."

Augustine caught Yanna's gaze and nodded his thanks for her kind words before addressing the rest of the Elektos. "What do we know about the kidnappers?"

A man in a suit walked into the living room before anyone could answer. Loudreux stopped pacing. "How is she?"

"I've sedated Mrs. Loudreux. She's now resting in her room." He shifted his bag to his other hand. "If you need me for anything else, don't hesitate to call. Or if I can do anything to help . . ."

Loudreux just nodded. Fenton stepped up. "Thank you, Dr. Carlson. We'll be in touch."

"The kidnappers?" Augustine reminded them.

Loudreux turned on him, eyes filled with fury. "You caused this. They took my daughter because they want you dead."

"Was I mentioned by name in the note?" Augustine asked.

"No." Salander Meer clasped Loudreux's shoulder. "Hugo, Augustine wouldn't do anything to hurt your daughter. You can't blame him for this."

Loudreux finally sat. "I can blame whoever I damn well please, and just because they didn't mention him by name doesn't mean they don't specifically want him dead. Everyone knows who our Guardian is. It's public knowledge."

Augustine understood the man's anger and pain. "I'm going to do everything in my power to get her home safely. But I need your help to do that." He took a breath. "Why don't we go right to the note. Where is it?"

Loudreux stared at the floor. Another Elektos pushed a tumbler of amber liquid into his hand. "In my office. On my desk."

"Who else has touched it besides you?"

Loudreux sipped the drink. "Just me and Mimi." He looked up, eyes shining with unshed tears. "And the kidnappers."

⚜

Harlow sat in Hugo Loudreux's desk chair, staring at the antiqued paper and the scratchy calligraphy that made up the ransom note. "Why not just send a text?" Of course, that would have been cake for her to trace. Which might be exactly why the kidnappers had used paper.

"It's tradition," Salander supplied. "The ransom note is carried to the parents of the Faery Queen by messenger, just as it was done in the old days."

She frowned. "And I know how important tradition is." She looked back at the paper, and read the note a second time, but there was no misinterpreting it. Whoever had kidnapped Rue wanted Augustine's life in exchange for Loudreux's daughter.

Fenton's hands stayed clamped at his sides. She didn't know the man well, but he seemed unusually tense. He bent to talk to her, letting her see for the first time that his freckles really were tiny numbers. "Do you need anything, Harlow? Anything at all to help you read the paper?"

Augustine moved closer. "I can call Dulcinea. Unless you want to try this yourself?"

"I can do this. I don't need help." She glanced around. Besides Augustine and Fenton, they'd been joined by Loudreux, Yanna, Salander and the rest of the Elektos. The entire crowd had gathered in the office and now stood watching her expectantly.

Their gazes weighed on her, a thousand pounds of untenable pressure. "But I'd prefer less of an audience."

Augustine turned, arms outstretched. "Everyone out."

Loudreux twitched with anger and pain. "This is about Rue." He jabbed a finger onto the desk beside the note, making Harlow jump. "I'm not leaving."

Panic flared through her. Panic the abyss glommed onto eagerly. What if something happened while she was reading the paper? What if this hollowness inside her somehow manifested itself? What if it somehow got...out? There was no latex holding it in now.

She couldn't do this in front of Loudreux. Especially after what Augustine had told her about him. Loudreux was always looking for a reason to discredit Augustine. She was not going to fuel that fire. It took every ounce of daring she had to stand up to him, but her voice still came out only slightly above a whisper. She hated how confrontation made her tremble. "I would really prefer it if you left."

He shook his finger at her. "I'm the Prime and this is my daughter we're talking about. Do you know what that means? It means I get to stay."

She shrank back, angry at herself for being afraid of this blustering loudmouth. A small piece of the power she'd felt the other night rose up. It clogged the flow of fear in her system, pushing her to her feet. She stared across the desk at Loudreux, a heady surge of power filling her mouth with words she'd never have had the courage to utter on her own. "Get out or I'll leave and whatever happens to Rue will be your fault because you stood in my way."

Her new voice filled the room, booming with purpose and challenge. The hollowness had spoken. Perhaps it was not such a thing to be feared after all.

Loudreux's mouth dropped open. Even Augustine looked at

her with new respect in his eyes. Yanna's raised brows slowly lowered. She clapped her hands. "Let's go. Give the woman the space she needs."

Half the Elektos were already out of the room. Harlow sat back down. "Fenton, Yanna, you can stay if you like." They were the only two she felt comfortable enough with.

"Are you sure?" Fenton asked.

She nodded. "Yes. It's okay."

"Thank you." Yanna stood near the fireplace, hands clasped in front of her.

"We're ready when you are." Augustine closed the office doors, then came to lean over the desk. "That was impressive, by the way. Well done."

"Thanks." Harlow smiled despite her nerves and peeled her gloves off. She was more prepared than the last time she'd read an object for Augustine, but every piece was different, containing varying amounts of information. Until her hands were actually on it, she had no way of knowing how hard it would hit her.

She took a breath, cleared her head, then pressed her fingers to the edges of the paper, closing her eyes and bracing for the impact.

A wall of cottony silence rose up to meet her, enveloping her in a thick sea of nothingness. It clamped down on her senses, shutting off all other sound, blacking out her vision, numbing her fingers. She opened her mouth to cry out for help, but the unrelenting silence slithered down her throat, muting her voice. The silence suffocated her, coating her tongue with the ashy taste of death. Panic took over, tripping every alarm inside her.

Alarms that roused her new power once again.

It spiraled out of the hollow place and chewed through the silence, breaking her free of it. She gasped for air as she tore her fingers off the paper and pushed away from the desk.

She was trembling so hard her body spasmed with the relief of freedom.

Augustine rushed to her side. "What did you see?"

She shook her head as she looked up. "Nothing. Except maybe my own death." She swallowed. Her mouth was dry as dust.

Yanna stepped to the bar cart, poured a glass of water and put it in Harlow's hands. "You look like you could use this."

She tugged one glove on before she took the glass and gulped down a few mouthfuls.

Augustine sat on the edge of the desk. "Are you okay? What happened?"

"I'm not sure, but it felt like whoever sent that paper was anticipating someone trying to do exactly what I just did." Her fingers tightened on the glass. "If I'd held on any longer, I think it would have killed me. Knocked me out at least." She shook her head, staring at the paper. "There's no way I can get anything usable off that note."

"It's okay." He stroked her shoulder. "You tried."

"And failed." She stood up, the feeling of defeat compounding her existing sense of vulnerability. "Take me home."

Augustine could imagine how frightened Harlow must be. But not as frightened as Rue. He looked at Fenton and Yanna. "Could you give us a minute?"

They both nodded and left.

As soon as the door was shut, he faced Harlow. "I know you want to go home and we will, in just a moment. I don't want Loudreux to see you so shaken. Sit down and catch your breath first."

With a slight nod, she did.

He crouched by her chair. Her heart thumped in his ears. "Did anything about what you felt seem familiar?"

She shook her head, then stopped. "You mean like... Branzino?

"Yes."

He glanced toward the living room where Hugo was intermittently cursing whoever was responsible for holding his daughter hostage and begging no one in particular for her safe return. Most of the other Elektos were in the room with him, arguing tactics, making suggestions, but generally doing not much else. What could they do? Very few of the fae in that room had ever faced this sort of threat before, but this was exactly the kind of event they had a Guardian for. Now they just had to get out of his way and let him do his job.

He felt sorry for them, for that feeling of helplessness that must be coursing through them. But when he thought of Rue, of how kind and innocent and delicate she was and how utterly terrified she must be... the heat of his anger turned his vision red and his blood to lava.

Harlow blew out a long breath. "I don't know." She bit at her cheek. "It would make sense, though, wouldn't it? Whoever sent this note wants you dead. If you were out of the picture, the house would be mine alone. One less obstacle for Branzino to deal with. But why would he want to kill me?"

Augustine shook his head. "He wouldn't have known you'd be the one to read this note, and if he did, I'm sure he only meant to scare you again."

"Scare me? He would have killed me if..." Her lips pressed into a hard line.

"If what?"

"If I hadn't broken contact with the paper."

It felt like she was hiding something, but he didn't want to press her after what had just happened. He stood. "Why does he want that house so bad? What is it about New Orleans that he's so desperate for a foothold here?"

"I don't know, but I really want to go home." She sighed. "I wish I didn't have to walk by all those people. Loudreux is going to freak out on me when I tell him I can't help."

"I can get you out of here, but you're going to have to trust me." He hadn't planned to spring the whole traveling-by-mirror thing on her this way, but now seemed like as good a time as any.

"What does that mean?"

He pulled his compact from his pocket. "Just that there's a way to get you home without you having to see Loudreux."

She glanced at the compact. "Oh, right. By mirror."

He frowned. "You know about that?"

She nodded. "Mmm-hmm. Nekai just showed me that this morning. Right before you got home. We went from the library to the backyard and then back inside again. Made my stomach feel a little weird. Like riding a roller coaster. But the cool factor overrides that. Not that I'm ready to try it alone."

That damn weaver. "Oh." So much for being the one to share that with her.

She stood. "Let's go. I just want to be home."

He flipped open the mirror and held out his hand.

She pulled her other glove back on and took it. A few seconds later, they stood in the foyer of their house. He released her hand. "I have to get back. You okay?"

"I'm fine, I promise. I hope you find Rue. If there's anything else I can do to help, please let me know. I want to help."

"I appreciate that." He wanted to stay with Harlow. To take her to Olivia and get that last secret out in the air so there was nothing stopping him from telling her how he felt. But right now Rue needed him more. "I'll try to be home for dinner."

She smiled halfheartedly. "I'll tell Lally."

He looked into the mirror and returned to Loudreux's.

Chapter Seventeen

Harlow sensed Augustine's hesitation but was totally okay with him not sticking around. Being unable to read the ransom note bothered her more than almost dying. Her disappointment was quickly turning to anger, though. Why the hell did Branzino want this house so badly?

There was something she had to investigate. It might be nothing, but then again, it might be the very answer she was looking for. "Lally, I'm home," she announced. "Going up to my office."

She didn't wait for a reply. Instead she jogged up the steps, but not to her office. Her mother's room. All quiet. Wherever Lally was, it wasn't here. Harlow went into the closet, shoved the dresses away from the back wall and stared at the faint outline of the long-forgotten door.

Her fingers traced the seams. The air slipping through was cooler than the air in the rest of the house. Almost like outside air. But that couldn't be. Could it? She left the closet and went back through the room and into the hall. She looked in the room next door. There was no extra space between that room and the wall of her mother's closet that she could see. And no outline of a door in that room either.

Something was off.

She went back to the hidden door and tried to open it, but no amount of effort budged the thing. More air seeped through around the seams. She found an old metal nail file on her mother's dressing table and used it to pry along the edges, working her way down along one side, then across the bottom. Shouldn't there be hinges?

The file ran into something, stopping her progress. She jammed the file in harder, using a little more force. It popped free, taking a small portion of plaster with it.

A lock.

She brushed the plaster dust away from it. Roughly the size of a dime. She went back to her mother's vanity table and riffled through it in search of a key. The best she could do was a few hairpins. She poked one into the lock and jiggled it, but after several tries she hadn't gotten anywhere.

There was one person who might be able to help her, though.

She found Lally in the garden on the side of the house. Apparently there were still things to harvest in the cooler weather, judging by the big basket of green leaves at her side.

"Lally, I—"

"You wanna learn how to pick collards?" Lally sat back on her heels, a short hooked knife in one hand. "I'm gonna make a big pot of greens. I can teach you how to cook those, too."

"Sure." Harlow crouched on the grass at the garden's edge, her senses telling her there was a reason that door was hidden. A reason Lally might not be keen to reveal. "Can I ask you something?"

Lally went back to work, nodding. "What's on your mind, child?"

"Do you know where I could find a key for that old door in my mother's closet?"

Lally's hand stuttered and the hooked knife sliced halfway through one of the big leaves. "That old door? I doubt there's even a lock."

"There is. I found it. But it's really tiny, so the key must be small, too."

"Probably lost years ago then. You know these old houses. Full of forgotten things." She bent back to cut more greens.

Harlow stood and walked toward the shed. Was her hunch about to be proved right? "Guess I'll have to get a crowbar and pry that thing open then."

A sharp inhalation punctuated another soft whoosh of movement. "Harlow...don't. What's behind that door ain't anything you want to be messing with."

Harlow turned. Lally stood facing her, the basket of collards toppled over at her feet, the curved knife clenched in her fist. But her eyes held fear, not a threat. Neither one was going to deter Harlow. "Why? What's behind there?"

Lally shook her head. "Leave it alone, child."

Harlow lowered her voice, uncomfortable speaking too loudly outside, where anyone could hear. "Branzino wants this house for some reason and I need to know why. I need to know what's so valuable that he'd be willing to kill Augustine and maybe even me for it."

Lally gaped in shock. "He tried to kill you?"

"You already know Loudreux's daughter has been kidnapped, but they're asking for the Guardian's life in exchange. The ransom note was imbued with some kind of defensive magic so that I almost died when I tried to read it. I can't imagine anyone else being behind this but that man."

The fear in Lally's eyes took on a dark anger. She lifted her chin as her body shifted into the defensive stance of a warrior. She nodded. "It's time then." She scooped up her fallen basket and headed for the house. "Come with me and I'll show you what that man wants. Something no one's seen in many, many years."

Giselle hung up the phone, the last of the arrangements for her father's ceremony complete. His ashes would be delivered later today. She'd expected the police to ask for an autopsy but they hadn't. She wouldn't have argued if they had, because it wouldn't have made any difference. The intoxicant she'd put in the wine disappeared from the bloodstream in eight to ten hours. They'd find nothing and have no choice but to rule his death an accidental drowning. She laughed. "I almost wish they had pushed for the autopsy."

She sniffed. Her kitchen smelled suddenly of bleach. She opened the cabinet under the sink to see if one of her cleaning supplies had tipped over.

"What do you wish? What have you done now, you stupid girl?"

She whirled at the voice and stared up into the face of some kind of monster. Slick murky gray-green skin covered his monstrous frame. Eyes too human to be demonic sat just below a sloping forehead that curved back from his wide, slit nostrils. "Wh-who are you? What do you want?"

The creature opened his mouth, and a black, three-pronged tongue flicked out from between multiple rows of teeth that curved back toward his throat. "I'm the fae you've been working for."

She shook her head. "No. The fae I did some spells for wasn't...wasn't..." Fear choked her words off.

"Wasn't a monster? No, Dreich was just a greedy, easily swayed half-blooded wysper." The creature smiled, showing off his horrific teeth. "I don't normally look like this, thanks to the spell you created that allowed me to appear human, but I made the mistake of wearing a costume soaked in fae magic. Apparently the two magics don't mix and taking the costume off stripped away your spell, too. I need that one the most." He leaned in. "So you will make me another."

She backed up but the counter was right behind her. "I'm not making you anything."

He slapped her across the face. Pain shot through her cheek.

"You killed Dreich, so now you deal with me. Get to work on that potion."

"Or what?" She clung to the pain, using it to gather her last shred of courage. "I'm not just any witch now, I'm the high priestess of the New Orleans Coven."

"Which is the other reason you'll now be reporting directly to me. The death of your father. Shame that. He was my ally in all this. You'll have to do now."

Shock chilled her bones. "My father was *your* ally? In what? And who the hell are you?"

His eyes narrowed, his stare piercing her. "You really don't know?"

She shook her head.

"Then let me introduce myself. I'm Joseph Branzino. Evander and I had an agreement. He wouldn't prevent me from achieving my goals here in New Orleans—goals that involved bringing vampires into the city and the removal of some of its more prominent members—and once I was established, I would give your people the freedom they desired."

"Not preventing you from something and working with you are two very different things." She couldn't believe her father, the man who had believed the status quo was perfectly fine, could have had anything to do with the plans this fae spoke of.

Branzino's large brow crinkled. "Yes, they are, but your father served as a sort of concierge for me. He told me to contact you—through Dreich, of course. Knew you were eager enough for change to do the kind of questionable work I needed done. He was right. Too bad he didn't share those plans with you."

Too bad indeed. He might still be alive. But she was too afraid to feel guilt. "I don't want to be involved in this anymore. The fae already suspect me. I'm the high priestess. Just let me lead my coven and go away."

He edged closer and grabbed her arm. "I'm a raptor fae. Not full-blooded, but enough to be incredibly dangerous. Do you know what my kind are capable of?"

She shook her head, cursing her lack of knowledge about the fae. His long slender fingers curled snakelike around her wrist. Cold and smooth and yet pulsing with life.

"Raptors feed on emotions." This close, the stench of bleach burned the back of her throat. "We have some other talents, too, but this is the one that should concern you. What a lot of people don't know about us, though, is that some of us also have the power to flood emotion back into a person. Any emotion we choose. Joy, sorrow, desperation. Abject terror." His grip tightened. "Can you imagine what that might feel like?"

She swallowed and shook her head. "I'll make the potion. Just let me go and I'll get right to work on it."

"Yes, you are about to do exactly that. But I think first you should have a taste of what I'm capable of, just so we don't have to do this again the next time." His fingers warmed considerably. "Just a taste…"

"What are you…" Her words trailed off as a new feeling flooded her. She no longer cared what happened. Her mother was dead. Her father was dead. And at her own hand. Her life was in shambles. Why had she even gotten out of bed? Nothing mattered. Not her stupid obsession with her perfect white clothes or her beautiful house, which wasn't beautiful at all, but pretentious and ugly. Not her sister, because it was clear Zara was only tolerating her. Not Ian, because he was only using her.

Not her life. Nothing.

Maybe she should just kill herself and be done with it.

Branzino pulled his hand away and her suicidal thoughts fled as the residual feeling of his skin on hers vanished. Fear flooded in to take its place. She tugged her hand to her chest and rubbed at her wrist. If he had that kind of power over her…

how could she turn down Ian's offer to strengthen her skills now? "What did you do to me?"

"Something I could very easily do again." He smiled. Hideous. "However, I would prefer us to be partners in this, Giselle. There is far more for you to gain on that path than what you stand to lose by refusing me. Which is why I will return this time tomorrow to collect the potion you're going to have ready."

Her skepticism must have shown on her face.

He laughed, a grating sound. "I can see by your expression you don't believe I have anything to offer you. But I do. The same thing I promised your father. Assist me when I need it, stay out of my way when I don't, and I will lift every restriction ever placed on the witches. But that's only if you prove to be worthy of such freedom. Fail me, do the slightest thing to upset my plan, and I will destroy you."

"You think you can topple the fae? They've had power over this city for centuries. Others, more powerful than you, have tried and failed. Your offer is a heady one, I'll give you that, but one that seems impossible for even another fae to accomplish." She planted her hands on her hips, still shaken from his touch, but unwilling to let him see the evidence of that. "How exactly do you propose to accomplish all this?"

He shifted his bulk. "I'm going to take control of a very powerful, ancient magic, then I'm going to take over this city." He lifted one finger. "Right after I kill off the Guardian."

Chapter Eighteen

Harlow stood in her mother's closet, Lally at her side and before them the hidden door. "You have a key for this?"

Lally slipped her fingers beneath the chain around her neck and removed it. Three charms dangled there: a cross, a locket and a key. "I do."

She took the small gold key and fit it into the lock. It clicked when she turned it. She put her necklace back on before laying her hand on the door. "This isn't something you can go talking about, you understand? But I ain't about to let you and Augie be threatened over something you know nothing about. I know what that man wants. Don't know how he found out about it, but I guarantee he wants to put his hands on what's inside this house."

Inside the house? Harlow couldn't imagine.

Lally pushed the door open and ducked through the small passage. Harlow's heart thumped with the excitement of the unknown, her nerves pinging with anticipation. She went through behind Lally and came out on a narrow landing that butted against a trunk. She peered up. "Is that a tree?"

Lally nodded and lifted her hands, resting them on the enormous trunk. The bark looked scorched. She closed her eyes for a moment like she was praying.

The landing they stood on was connected to a spiral staircase that hugged the open space surrounding the tree. The tree rose up through the center of the house, stopped at the peak by a large section of glass roof. Here and there its branches grew into the framework of the house. Leaves sprouted in clusters, their shape fractured and twisted. And all of it, the trunk, the branches, the knots and the leaves, was charred black.

Lally pulled her hands away and brushed soot from them. "This here is a lightning tree."

"I don't know what that is. Or what it means." She reached out to touch the section of trunk closest to her.

"No." Lally's sharp command rang out in the enclosed column of space. "You don't want to touch this tree until you got no other choice. And even then, you still don't want to touch it."

"Why? You touched it. What's so special—or dangerous—about it?"

"I can touch it because that tree and me have a special relationship. Always have." Lally glanced at the tree once more, then moved to stand between the trunk and Harlow. "Let's go back inside and I'll tell you the whole story." She glanced at the tree. "This isn't the safest place for long discussions."

When they were settled at the kitchen table and a kettle sat on the stove, Lally began. "My mama was a *traiteuse*. That's what folks around here call a healer. She was the best of her day, so much so that the man who owned this land originally gave her a small portion of it in exchange for saving the life of his son."

"Impressive." And the first time Harlow had heard Lally speak about her family. Or her history. Or anything really personal.

"She was happy for the land. Built herself a little house, right in the shade of the biggest tree. But what she wanted more than anything was a good man who could give her children. My mama wasn't exactly what most folks would consider a typical woman. She was half Houma Indian, half free woman of color and a powerful *traiteuse*. On top of that, she was a landowner."

Lally shook her head. "Most men wanted nothing to do with her.

"The first night she moved into her little house, there was a terrible storm. Lightning struck the big tree and Mama was sure it was dead. All the green leaves fell off. The trunk was scorched all over. But she watched it and as the summer passed, it grew odd new leaves and stretched out new branches, and Mama, being the sort of woman she was, knew that tree was very special."

Harlow pointed upstairs. "That same tree that's built into the middle of the house?"

"Mmm-hmm. The lightning tree." Lally got up and fixed herself a cup of tea. "You want a cup?"

"No, thanks." Just more of the story.

Lally sat down and added sugar from the pot on the table. "A lightning tree is a curious thing. People believe they can do all sorts of things. Some true, some not. Mama knew word would get out and people would come around from all over to get to her tree. She called her daddy, another *traiteur*, the one she'd learned from and one more powerful than she had yet become.

"He was full-blooded Houma Indian and had the knowledge of secret things. For the length of one full moon, he chanted and prayed around that tree, but there was nothing he could do to destroy the tree. Finally, he warned my mother to leave it be and went home." She stopped to sip her tea.

"And then what happened? The warning didn't work, did it?"

"No, it didn't. And my mama, she still wanted that husband and child, so she laid her hands on that tree and made her most heartfelt wish."

Lally bent her head. "Two days later, Jeremiah Hughes showed up on her doorstep. He was also a free person of color. He was looking for work, but he found a whole lot more. They were married not long after and sure enough, I came along in due time."

Harlow sat back. "All this talk about free people of color…" She shook her head. "You make it sound like this was all so long ago. I know it's not nice to ask, but how old are you?"

Lally's brows lifted. "Old, child. Old."

Harlow couldn't help but press her. "Which is what in years?"

"Many." Lally frowned. "Centuries. Now do you want to hear the rest of this story or not?"

Centuries. Holy cats. "Yes." Harlow ran her fingers across her lips like she was zipping them shut.

Lally turned her cup clockwise on its saucer. "The tree wasn't done fulfilling my mama's wish but my mama didn't know that."

Her gaze took on the distance of memory. "Not long after I was born, Jeremiah fell off a roof he was patching and broke his neck. Nothing my mama did could save him. After that, she shut up the house and we moved to Baton Rouge. She had family there. But I got very sick and she ended up coming back here." Lally leaned forward. "She put her hands on the tree again. This time she offered me up to the tree. If the tree would heal me, she'd teach me to protect the tree for the rest of my life. Then she scraped off some of the bark, picked a few leaves, made a tea and spooned it down my throat. Within a day I was completely better."

"She knew then that my life was forever bound to the tree. Not only that, but she'd used the tree to wish for me and she'd got me, but she understood that Jeremiah had paid the price." She shook her finger. "That tree will give you anything your heart desires, but not without a cost."

"So what was the cost of her second wish to save you?"

"My life. I'm bound to this tree. To this land." Lally smiled sadly. "Mama tried to take me away another time and again,

I got so sick I almost died. I've never tried to leave since I've been an adult, but I suspect if I get too far from the tree, I'll die." She looked out the window for a moment. "Someday I imagine I'll see how true that is."

A shiver ran through Harlow. "How did this house come to be built around the tree?"

Lally took a deep breath. "Mama lost her mind a little as the years went on. People'd come to make use of the tree and she'd run them off. Took to carrying a shotgun. Soon no one wanted her services as *traiteuse* anymore either. She ran out of money."

Lally traced a pattern on the tabletop. "The witches were a lot stronger back then. They knew the power of that tree. Knew it well. They offered to buy the land at a price that would keep Mama for the rest of her life, but the fae found out and they came with an offer, too."

"Based on what I already know about this house, I'm guessing the fae made the better offer."

Lally nodded. "They did. They promised Mama that no matter what, I'd be allowed to live here, near the tree. They also promised her that the tree would be left alone, that no one would use its magic. One of their weavers even cast a spell over the coven to make them forget about the tree. The fae are good people. Most of them. You know this house has never fallen out of fae hands? No matter what went on here, the tree has always been protected and I have always been right here with it."

Harlow's stomach rolled. "Oh, Lally. When I said I was going to sell the house...I'm so sorry. I didn't know. You must have hated me."

"Hated you for something you didn't know? Phht. You're Olivia Goodwin's baby girl. I could never hate you."

"Did my mother know about the tree?"

"Yes. And that's part of why I'm telling you now. You own

this house. You deserve to know the responsibilities that come with it."

"Does Augustine know?"

"No, and he doesn't need to. This is a secret that's only been held by women, and even then as few as possible. My mama preferred it that way. Figured they were better secret-keepers than men."

"But Lally, if Branzino is after me to get this house—that tree—Augustine needs to know that. And how would Branzino have found out about this tree?"

"As far as Branzino and this tree..." Lally sighed. "The fae keep records of everything. Maybe he researched this place when your mother bought it. If he went back far enough, the truth of it was bound to be in there somewhere." Lally shook her head. "Now where Augustine's concerned, all he needs to know is that you're in trouble. He's already got soft feelings for you. He ain't gonna let Branzino do anything to harm you. You've seen evidence of that."

"True, but it feels dishonest." She couldn't imagine keeping something this big from him. "I don't think I can promise I won't tell him someday if it feels necessary."

"Hmph. You think he doesn't have secrets of his own?" She shook her head. "You really don't know much about men, do you?"

"Maybe I don't." Harlow exhaled, the weight of this new information clicking things together in her head like puzzle pieces. "The tree explains a lot. Like why my mother made Augustine and me half owners of the house. She knew I'd sell it if I could. And knew he wouldn't." She tipped her head. "But why not just leave the house to you?"

Lally laughed softly. "Because with ownership comes a lot of legal things, paperwork and questions, and for someone my age, those questions aren't exactly easy to answer. Your mama knew that. Besides, if she'd left the house to me she wouldn't have gotten you to stay in New Orleans."

"True, but…" Harlow's heart ached. "But it's not like she's here."

A funny look passed over Lally's face. "I should get supper on. Promise me you'll leave that tree alone."

"I will. I swear. And now I know why Branzino wants this house so bad. What do you think he would do with that tree? If it's made you immortal—I mean, I'm assuming that's what you are, right?"

Lally shook her head. "I suppose I am."

"Have you ever been sick since that day?"

"No."

"Have you ever been hurt? Like seriously hurt?"

"If you're asking me can I die, then my best answer is…I don't think so."

"That has to be it. If he becomes immortal, he'll be unstoppable." The weight of all this new information was almost too much to bear.

"Whatever that man wants with my tree, I can't imagine, but I'm sure it wouldn't be good."

"I don't think much of what Branzino does could be classified as good."

"You and Augie best make sure he doesn't get his hands on it then." Lally pointed toward the pantry. "Grab yourself an apron and I'll teach you how to fix these greens."

Harlow stared in amazement at Lally, not just because the woman could so casually move on from such amazing revelations, but also from a sense of privilege at knowing such a woman. The things Lally had seen, Harlow could only imagine. And now that she knew about the tree, nothing was ever going to be the same.

Lally pulled out a big pot and put it on the stove. "I know, you got questions. We'll talk while we work."

"Thank you." Harlow's voice caught in her throat.

"For what, child?"

"For trusting me with all of this."

Lally smiled. "I had a long history with your mama. I expect to have a long history with you." She waved her fingers toward the pantry. "C'mon, now, get that apron on. You still don't know how to cook."

"And I won't for a little while longer." Harlow got up from the table and turned to leave. "As much as I appreciate your offer, there's a sixteen-year-old girl out there who needs me more."

Chapter Nineteen

Hours of patrols, of talking to people, of following up possibilities, and not a single usable lead to find Rue. Augustine's gut ached with frustration. "We're getting nowhere."

Dulcinea nodded, her eyes watching the far end of the street. "If Branzino's behind this, he's got to have a connection in the city." She faced him. "Who would want you out of the picture besides him?"

He leaned against the wall, pulled out a half-smoked *nequam* cigarette and lit it, taking a long draw and releasing the burnt-sugar-scented smoke before he answered. "I can think of a few people."

"Like?" She took the cigarette from his fingers.

He narrowed his eyes. "Your old buddy Giselle."

Righteous indignation danced in Dulcinea's odd-colored eyes. She blew out a trail of smoke as she handed the cigarette back. "Oh, I hope it's her. Just so I can personally take her down."

He shook his head. "I don't know. She doesn't feel that... organized to me. She's a lot of talk. And yes, she was definitely assisting on letting the vampires into the city, but she's not the big cheese. She's not even the little cheese. At best, she's the cheese plate. She just doesn't have the authority to make things happen."

"But she's the high priestess, right?"

"Not officially, unless they've had the ceremony already. And from what Fenton says, her radical ideas aren't supported by the whole coven." He offered the *nequam* to Dulcinea again, who pinched it between her fingers. "No, Branzino strikes me as the type to want to deal with the head of the food chain. Father Ogun, maybe."

She blew out a thin stream of smoke. "Evander then."

"Evander was too much a by-the-book kind of guy." Augustine straightened. "He *did* give me a lot of grief when I was trying to get that list of names of coven members known to perform black magic."

Dulce handed the *nequam* back and shrugged. "Evander's dead, so if he was working with Branzino, that's over."

Augustine swore. "Maybe Evander had had enough. Maybe this kidnapping was a bridge too far."

"You think he wanted out so Branzino offed him? Made it look like a drowning?"

"Him or Giselle." Augustine dropped the smoke and crushed it under his heel. "I need to meet Fenton at the police department. Do you have to head back to the Guardian house?"

She shook her head, rattling the beads and shells stitched into her dreads. "Beatrice is fine."

"Then meet up with Cy and talk to anyone else you think might have seen something. Maybe go back to the hotel and talk to the employees who were on that night again."

"You got it." With a salute, she was gone.

A half hour later he was walking into the NOPD with Fenton. The cypher fae approached the front desk and spoke to the officer on duty. "We're here to see Detective Grantham, please. He's expecting us."

A uniformed police officer led them upstairs to Grantham's desk. He was on the phone but gave them a sign he'd seen them. A few seconds later he hung up. "Welch. You wanted to talk?"

Fenton nodded. "Is there somewhere private we can go?"

Grantham grabbed his coffee. "Interrogation room. This

way." He led them into the room, then closed the door and took a seat at the dented metal table in the center of the small space. "If this is about Ogun, I can talk to him again, but—"

"No." Fenton took the chair across from him. "We have bigger problems right now. Hugo Loudreux's daughter was kidnapped last night."

Grantham's brow furrowed as he looked at Augustine. "I thought that was some ceremonial thing?"

"It is." Fenton took a deep breath. "But not this year."

"I'll get a team on it immediately."

"I'm not sure that will help." Augustine leaned against the wall. "Dulcinea and I have scoured the area where the real kidnappers should have been, we've talked to the girls in Rue's court, talked to the members of the Exemplars who were in charge of setting up the ceremonial kidnapping…all dead ends."

Grantham took his tablet and stylus from his jacket pocket. "Tell me what should have happened and what actually happened."

Augustine looked at Fenton. "This is more your domain than mine."

Fenton laid out the whole tradition and what should have gone down, then started in on what had actually happened. "Rue was kidnapped as planned, but when her court arrived at the hotel suite, she wasn't there. They found a note saying she'd be there in an hour. Before the hour was up, the girls all fell asleep—we believe some sort of drugging agent was slipped into the air vents. They didn't wake up until after the real ransom note had been delivered to the Loudreux's."

Grantham scribbled on his tablet. "And what about the krewe members who were actually supposed to do the kidnapping?"

Fenton's gaze dropped to his hands. "They were found after the note was delivered also, locked in a storage area of the hotel where the ball was held. One had been killed as an example to the others."

Grantham lifted his stylus. "And none of them could identify the perpetrators?"

Augustine shook his head. "The girls from Rue's court never saw anyone and the note telling them Rue would be late was gone when they woke up. The krewe members only remember hooded figures with monster masks, which is the exact description of the kidnappers everyone at the ball saw, myself included."

"What about the hotel workers?"

"Same thing."

Grantham leaned back in his chair. "I'll certainly give you a team of officers if you want one, and it goes without saying that every cop in this city will be on the lookout for anything suspicious, but I'm not sure I can do better. What were the ransom demands? Was there a location for the drop-off?"

Fenton glanced at Augustine. He shook his head. "It wasn't that kind of ransom. They'll release Rue when Augustine relinquishes his position as Guardian, which by fae law isn't something one just resigns from. The Guardian's job ends only one way. Death. And whoever wrote the note knows this. They want Augustine dead."

Grantham's dark eyes took on a hard glitter. "Can we fake your death?"

Augustine shook his head. "That's a hard thing to pull off with fae. Most of us can hear heartbeats, shallow breathing, that sort of thing. I imagine the kidnappers would want the kind of proof that would require me to actually be dead."

Grantham frowned. "You're saying Rue was kidnapped by another fae. Who do you know who would want you dead?"

Augustine pushed off the wall and took a seat beside Fenton. "This isn't information we're sharing widely."

"Understood." Grantham set his tablet down.

"There are two possibilities. Giselle Vincent, daughter of Evander Vincent, the leader of the New Orleans Coven who just drowned in his pool. While it's no secret she hates the fae, my death wouldn't remove the rules and regulations the witches live under."

Grantham nodded. "And the second?"

"Joseph Branzino. He's the most likely. He's Harlow Goodwin's biological father and from what we've been able to gather, he's trying to gain a foothold in New Orleans by paying off Harlow to use the house she inherited from Olivia."

"Why that house? He could buy a place."

"He can't," Fenton said. "Fae law doesn't allow a fae convicted of a felony to own property in a Haven city."

Grantham nodded. "I see. What are his crimes?"

Fenton pushed back from the table, sighing disgustedly. "Pick one. But I doubt you'll find much in your databases on him. He employs erasers to keep his record spotless."

Grantham threw a hand up. "Then how do you know—"

Augustine tapped a finger on the table. "We have proof."

"Of what?"

Augustine hesitated. He didn't know Grantham like Fenton did. Didn't know what he could and couldn't be trusted with. "This information has to remain sealed until we tell you otherwise, understand?"

Grantham nodded. "You have my word. I'm not about to ruin the trust I've built with the fae over all these years."

Augustine looked at Fenton, who nodded for him to continue. "We have video of him killing an *infant.*"

Grantham's expression changed little. "Video can be faked. With modern technology..."

"It wasn't faked. We know the source. And we know who the child was. It can all be proved."

Grantham leaned forward to clasp his hands atop the table. "With that kind of evidence, we can put him away for life. Although I imagine he's not the kind of fae we could hold."

"No, he's not." Augustine shook his head. "Although we may need some backup to bring him in, but when we do, he's not going into the human justice system. We have a place for fae like him." He stood. "A place where we can make sure he's never heard from again."

Giselle lay facedown, her arms crossed and supporting her forehead. Her hair was twisted out of the way. Ian had prepped her skin and now sprayed a numbing solution on the skin between her shoulder blades. The medicinal smell mixed with the earthiness of the sage he'd burned to clear the space before he began.

"Here we go." His voice was quiet. Almost reverent. But that made sense considering this was his craft and his source of power. He would gain from this. Not as much as she would, but still, it was nothing either of them was taking lightly. Which was why they were in her home and not his shop. No one was to know about this power exchange.

At the sound of his machine, she began chanting a calming spell. It did little to drown out the buzzing. The sting of the needle followed. She squeezed the crystals clenched in her fists, calling upon them to soothe her.

"Easy," Ian whispered. His hand covered her bare shoulder. His touch was warm and comforting. "Tensing up will only make it hurt worse."

"I can't imagine that." She forced herself to relax.

"Better." He went back to work.

The sting became a bite, then the bite turned to burning, and just when she thought she might cry out and beg him to stop, the machine clicked off.

"All done." He wiped her tender skin gently, smoothing ointment over the ink he'd inlaid. "You want to see?"

She pushed up, clutching the sheet she'd been lying on to her chest. "Yes."

He gave her a hand mirror. She took it and walked to the bathroom, turning to view the new tattoo on her back. A crystal sparkled from between her shoulder blades. He stood beside her, his face tentative. She looked for a long moment before nodding. "It's...so much better than I imagined."

He smiled. "I told you I do good work."

She kissed his cheek. "Can I get dressed?"

"Let me tape it up. You have to keep it covered for a few days."

She followed him back to the table and sat while he applied the dressing. "Okay, you can put your shirt on."

She kept her back to him as she pulled her top on, then turned to face him. "Remind me again what I need to do to take care of it?"

His grin reappeared. "Just keep me around and I'll worry about that."

"And my power?"

"Try something simple. Something that maybe isn't your strongest ability, something that takes more than your standard effort."

She pursed her lips as she looked around the room. Finally she stretched her hand out toward a softball-size mercury scrying ball on a small stand. "Telekinesis isn't one of my best skills." She wiggled her fingers, commanding the sphere to come to her.

It lifted off the stand and hurtled toward her. She and Ian ducked as it smashed into the wall behind them.

Ian cursed under his breath. "I said something that takes some effort."

She stood. The floor behind them was covered with silvered shards of glass. "Trust me, I've never come close to moving anything with that kind of efficiency. Holy goddess." She laughed, then grabbed Ian's shoulders and kissed him hard.

He laughed along with her when she broke the kiss. "I take it you're happy with the results?"

She nodded. "Obviously there are a lot of other things I'd like to try before I know just how much more powerful I am, but yes, I'm happy." She tilted her head to one side. "I was skeptical, I admit, but this... this is amazing. Thank you."

"You're welcome, my lady. It was my pleasure to give my high priestess such a personal gift." He nuzzled her neck. "I'd be happy to give you a different kind of *personal* gift, if you're interested."

She leaned into his caress, but her mind was on other things. Like her next meeting with Joseph Branzino and how she would show him that she was as worthy a partner in his endeavors as her father had been. All she had to do now was whip up the potion he was coming to collect. She laughed softly, letting Ian think it was because of his offer, but in truth it was because of the knowledge that with Branzino's help, she was finally going to make her mother's dying wish come true.

The witches were about to control New Orleans once again. No matter what Branzino's plans were.

Chapter Twenty

"Hey."

Harlow jumped, yelping slightly, her hand clutching at her heart as she scowled in Augustine's direction. "Holy crap, don't do that to me."

He had the decency to look guilty as his lanky form slouched against the doorframe of her office. "Sorry. Didn't mean to scare you. You must be pretty involved with whatever it is you're doing."

She exhaled a long breath. "I am. And actually, I'm really glad you're home." She stood, stretching. How long had she been in that chair? "I've found something."

His brows lifted a little. "Like what?"

"Look." She sat back down, laid her hands on the keyboard and used her abilities to mentally access the cam sites she'd found and bring them up quickly. The monitors above her flickered as their screens changed. Excitement zipped through her, filling her with the happiness of being able to help.

Augustine moved to stand beside her, his gaze fixated on the monitors. "What is that?" He looked closer. "That's Bourbon Street."

"Yep." She tapped away at the keyboard, splitting each one of her six screens into two camera feeds. "And the one next to it is Jackson Square. The rest are traffic cams, ATM machines, a few personal security cams. Basically, I can monitor almost all of the city."

He glanced down at her. "Personal security cams? If they're personal, how are you using them?"

She shot him the side eye. "There are some questions you shouldn't ask. If you're not sure which ones those are, you'll know when I don't answer them." She went back to punching in the algorithms she'd come up with. "Fenton's facial recognition software gave me an idea…" She called up the image of Rue she'd entered as her target.

Augustine leaned in. "Where did you get that picture?"

She stayed quiet as she typed a little more.

"Where'd you get it?"

Sad that he was so pretty and yet such a slow learner. "Remember that whole thing about questions I don't answer?"

"No, Harlow, I want to know. Where did you get that picture?"

She sighed and leaned back in her chair. "When we were at Loudreux's. I touched his computer long enough to get his router information. Then from here I downloaded a backdoor into his system. Now I can come and go as I please. The picture was in one of his files."

Augustine stared at her. "It's really that easy for you?"

She nodded. "Yep."

The tiniest bit of alarm crept into his eyes. "Did you happen to go through any of his other files?"

"Maybe."

"Anything that might connect him to Branzino?"

"If I had gone through his files and found something like that, don't you think I would have told you?"

"So that's a no."

"Now you're catching on."

He shook his head slowly. "Have you hacked into anything else I should know about?"

"No."

"No, you haven't hacked into anything else or no, I shouldn't know about it?"

She narrowed her gaze. "What's more important? Finding Rue or me giving you information you don't really need?"

He sighed, but his eyes went back to the screen. "So how is this going to help us find her? Are you going to sit here and monitor these computers until you see her? There are way too many feeds."

"Not for a computer. I've programmed the system to use Fenton's facial recognition software to monitor all incoming feeds for Rue's face."

"You mean the contact lens? How?"

"Rue was already programmed into it, since she was at the ball." She shrugged. "I just had to provide it with a picture to search for. It's what I do. I've also set it up to search all archived feeds for the last three days. Any hit will ping both our LMDs."

"Both?" He gave her an incredulous look.

"Look, if you think there's any technology that's safe from me, including your LMD, you're wrong. I proved that when I tracked you into the Quarter when you were vampire hunting. Get over whatever weirdness you have about this as quickly as you can because it's not going to change."

He held his hands up. "You're right."

She almost fell off her chair. "I am?"

"I've used my skills to do things that weren't exactly aboveboard. Why should I give you grief for doing the same thing? Especially when you're helping me like this." He sat, leaning back while he glanced at the monitors again. "This is above and beyond. It's really good work. Stuff I never would have thought of. Hell, I've lived here all my life and it never occurred to me to access those cameras like that. Not that I would've known how."

She couldn't tell him about the tree, about how the need to

protect it and Lally had lit a new fire in her. "Rue's in trouble. Trouble most likely brought on by that piece of garbage Branzino. If he's willing to get physical with his own daughter, what do you think he's going to do to a kid like Rue?" She stood and moved for the door. "Anyway, this is all set up. No need to babysit it. I'm sure Lally's about to call us for dinner anyway."

Augustine jumped up, stepped into her path and put his hands on her hips. "The way you do all this tech stuff amazes me. It's pretty hot."

She grinned, but ducked her head. "It's just what I do."

"You know what else is hot?"

She looked up through a few strands of wayward hair. "What?"

"You." He bent like he was going to kiss her, then straightened. "Damn it. Incoming call." He growled, his hands holding her firmly in place. "Answer."

She bit her lip, enjoying the chance to study him so closely.

"Fenton, slow down, you're—what?" His mouth opened and he inhaled sharply, his expression going slack with disbelief. He blew out the breath and closed his eyes for a long moment. "I see. Okay. We'll be there."

"What happened?"

He swallowed and shook his head, looking like he might get sick. He let go of her. "Dinner's going to have to wait. The Loudreux's just got another delivery. Rue's little finger."

The pinky lay pale and bloody in the box, the nail oddly pretty with its glittery white polish. Harlow had never seen anything like it and hoped never to again. She stayed quiet and hugged the wall of Hugo Loudreux's office, out of the way of Augustine and the Elektos. Loudreux hadn't made a fuss about her being there this time. He'd barely acknowledged her. She got it. Things had escalated. In a big way.

Loudreux slumped in his chair, his elbows on the desktop, his head cradled in his hands. "My little girl," he moaned.

Augustine looked like he was about to ask a question when Fenton raised his hand. He motioned to one of the other Elektos, a man whose pale-green skin made him look like he'd been underwater too long. The man seemed to understand Fenton's directive and coaxed Loudreux into leaving.

When he was gone, Fenton looked at her and spoke. "I appreciate your willingness to help us yet again."

"Of course," Harlow said. She did want to find Rue, but she also very much wanted to stop Branzino.

"I thought what happened the last time you attempted to read something for us might have put you off trying again. Are you willing to give this another shot?"

She nodded. At least she knew what might be facing her. "I am. If the box is spelled with the same thing, I should be able to anticipate it sooner and keep it from hitting me so hard."

Fenton smiled weakly. "I was thinking differently."

Augustine frowned. "You have another way for Harlow to help us?"

"Not exactly." He pushed his glasses back on his nose. "It's not the box I think she should read."

"Fet'ka," Yanna muttered. "You want her to read the finger."

A chill lifted the small hairs along Harlow's spine.

Augustine stepped closer to Harlow. "Fenton, that's asking too much. The box is good enough."

"No." She put a hand on Augustine's arm. "Fenton's right. Reading the finger will tell us so much more. Like whether or not it's really Rue's." If Branzino was behind this, she didn't doubt it was.

"At least Rue will be able to grow that finger back." Fenton pulled out a handkerchief and wiped his brow. "Not that that makes this okay. Maybe it's not hers."

Augustine stared at the severed digit. "I'm pretty sure that's the same nail polish she was wearing. I remember Mimi yelling at one of Rue's maids because she'd worn something different."

Fenton sighed. "That sounds like Mimi."

Augustine looked at Harlow like he was searching for something. "You're sure you can handle this? That's flesh and blood we're talking about, not some inanimate object. The kinds of feelings and emotions that are attached to it..." He shook his head. "Even if it isn't Rue's, it belonged to someone who probably didn't enjoy having it removed."

"I know that." But the finger was also technically dead. She hoped that like the vampire who'd once touched her, she wouldn't read any of the emotions the person it belonged to had felt. Instead she planned to read it as she would any other object, to get a sense of where it had been, what had been going on around it and, with any kind of luck, who had touched it last. If that didn't work, then she'd attempt the box. "The sooner we do this, the more I can pick up."

"If you're okay with it—"

"I am." She wanted to do it and get it over with. If she thought about it any more, she might chicken out. Touching a dismembered finger wasn't high on her list of things to do, but for Rue's sake she would. Especially if it could lead them to Branzino.

Augustine motioned for the Elektos to leave. "Give us some space. This isn't a sideshow."

Yanna squeezed Harlow's arm. "You're brave to do this. Thank you."

Harlow smiled despite her nerves. "You and Fenton can stay if you like."

"We'll be by the door. Out of your way." Yanna went to stand with Fenton.

Harlow took a seat at Loudreux's desk. The memories of almost suffocating under the ransom note's deadly spell came rushing back. There was no reason to believe she wouldn't have that experience again. But this time she was expecting it.

Augustine crouched at her side. "Should we have some kind of sign? In case you run into that same spell again?"

"I'm not sure I could get a word out if I do. That spell shut everything down almost as soon as it hit me." Concern welled in his stormy-sea eyes. "But I'm ready for it. And just knowing you're here helps."

"If you look like you're in distress, I'm breaking your contact."

"Don't be too hasty. Sometimes it takes a little distress to get a good read." She patted his arm. It was nice to have someone looking out for her. Especially someone like Augustine. She grinned. "Now if I look like I've stopped breathing or I start turning blue, by all means, yank that thing out of my hands and commence the mouth-to-mouth."

He growled. "I don't know how you can joke about a thing like that. Branzino isn't the kind of fae you screw with."

She shooed him away with her hands. "I'm just trying to get through this." She interlaced her fingers and stretched them, cracking her knuckles. Then she pulled off her gloves. "Okay, here goes."

Without touching the box, she reached in and picked up the finger. The pain hit her instantly. She sucked in a breath and arched back. The feeling of her own finger being cut off punched her in the gut. A swell of sensations followed. The gleam of the blade as it sawed through flesh. The crunch of bone. A scream that sounded very much like it had been ripped from the throat of a sixteen-year-old girl. Harlow shuddered. Tears streamed down her cheeks at the torment of the experience, but she held on.

"Are you okay?" Augustine's voice was faint.

She nodded, unable to speak, but hoping he understood not to touch her or break the connection. More images. A froth of white spattered with red. Rue's dress? The metallic tang of blood. A dark, gravelly voice. Male. Harlow's teeth chattered at a sudden wash of cold.

Then the undeniable scent of bleach.

She dropped the pinky, partly out of shock and partly because she'd gotten the information she needed. The second she broke contact, the hollowness opened and drained down every horrible emotion lingering inside her with such ferocity that it sucked the breath from her lungs. She panted for air.

Augustine rushed to her side. "Are you okay?"

She nodded, finding enough breath to speak. "It's Rue's. It has to be." She swallowed. Her insides felt like they'd just been torn out. She grabbed Augustine's arm. His warmth seeped through his shirt into her bare fingers. "And it's definitely Branzino."

Augustine swore softly. "I knew it."

Liquid pooled in her mouth. "I need to go home." Her words came out a whisper. "Now. I'm—" But it was too late. She leaned over, grabbed the trash can and vomited.

Chapter Twenty-one

The foul odor of cigar smoke woke Giselle. She left Ian and came downstairs to find Joseph Branzino sitting in her living room, puffing away. He wore a hat and had turned up the collar of his overcoat, but there was no disguising his fae monstrousness. "Mr. Branzino, if we're going to be partners, there are a few things you need to get straight."

"Such as?"

She flicked her fingers at the window, then at the horrid length of rolled tobacco perched at the corner of his mouth. The window opened and the cigar flew out. Another flick closed the window. The ease of her new power pleased her to no end. "Such as there is no smoking in my house."

Before he could respond, she extended her hand, lifting him bodily from the chair. She held him there while she opened the door with the other, then she shoved him through it. "The other is you will knock before you enter and not until you've asked to do so." She released him and slammed the door shut.

In the excitement of her tattoo and the work of making the potion Branzino was here to retrieve, she'd forgotten to renew the protection wards around her house. She'd be sure the new ones were unbreakable.

He pounded on the door.

She sent a little sleeping spell upstairs to keep Ian from interrupting them, then tied her robe a little tighter before opening the door. "Mr. Branzino, what a surprise."

He glared at her. "You like to live dangerously, witch."

"Quite the opposite, actually. Which is why you'll abide by those rules and show me the respect I deserve if you expect my help. Do we have an understanding?"

Looking like he'd strangle her if he could, he nodded.

She left the door open and walked back toward the kitchen for some much-needed coffee. "Do come in then."

The door slammed behind her. "What the hell's gotten into you?"

She added coffee and hot water to her French press, then set the timer. "Nothing." He didn't need to know she hadn't always been this powerful. "You just caught me off guard yesterday, but we're going to move past that." She turned and smiled. "Aren't we?"

He was almost smoldering. "I don't think you understand who you're dealing with."

She dropped the smile and called upon her new strength to fill her with power. "No, I understand perfectly. You're a powerful fae who wants a foothold in this city, but you're also a fae who's underestimated me. You want my help? I'll give it to you, but only because we share a common goal." Her skin crackled with energy. "And I will expect everything you promised—the witches *will* regain their freedom. No one breaks their promise to me. No one."

His smolder disappeared, replaced by grudging respect. "I see. Perhaps I did underestimate you." He nodded as if considering that thought. "I won't break my promise about the restrictions being lifted off your people, but nothing changes the fact that I won't allow anyone to get in my way."

"Understood. And why would I when your end suits me?"

"All right then." His voice regained its earlier gruffness. "Where's my potion?"

She reached into the Eiffel Tower cookie jar on her counter

and took out a slim vial of emerald-green liquid. She held it out, her fingertips at the end so that there was no reason for any skin contact between them. She remembered too well what had happened the last time he'd touched her.

He took the vial. "This isn't the same color as the one you made me last time."

The timer buzzed. She turned it off and plunged the press down on the coffee. "Because it's a stronger version. One that should easily withstand the pressure of a little fae magic."

He grinned. Goddess, that was a horrifying expression on him. "Excellent." He yanked out the cork and held the vial out to her. "You first."

She poured herself a cup of coffee. "What?"

"Take a sip. Show me it's not poison."

Her patience was growing thin. She took the vial and lifted it to her lips. It tasted like mud and vinegar, but she swallowed down a small sip before handing it back. "There. Happy?"

"Yes." He took it and drained the whole thing. "One can never be too sure."

She snorted. "You're not very smart, are you, fae? If I had created a poison—which I haven't, as you're still alive—I know enough to create one that wouldn't affect me." She added a teaspoon of sugar to her coffee. The taste of the potion lingered on her tongue.

His appearance morphed from fae to human before her eyes, but the tiny flicker of doubt and surprise in his eyes remained, satisfying her that she'd made her point. She was not to be trifled with. "You're right. I've underestimated you." He smiled, this time without causing her to recoil. "You're more powerful than your father ever hoped to be, aren't you?"

She sipped her coffee. The hot liquid burned away the potion's remnants. "Yes, I am. And I appreciate you admitting what you just did. I agree to work with you."

He laughed, a harsh mocking sound that scratched at her nerves. "You agree? I never asked for your approval. Was there some chance you might decide differently?"

"Yes, there was." She put her coffee cup down, reached into the cookie jar again and took out another vial. This one held pale-green liquid. She slid it toward him before picking her cup back up. "So I suggest you drink this."

The look of derision left his face. "Why?"

She smiled sweetly. "Because it's the antidote to what was in your potion." Taking a sip of coffee, she flicked her gaze toward the clock on her oven. "And if I were you, I'd hurry up."

Augustine dragged a hand through his hair. They were at a horrifying dead end. And Rue was suffering because of his inability to find her. The bottom line was, he was failing at his job. He leaned his forehead against the big round window that took up the far wall of his attic apartment. The sun was barely up, so the glass was cold, but it felt good. As good as anything could feel right now. Rue was out there, somewhere, and he was powerless to help her.

He should head to the Pelcrum and see if Fenton had anything new. But Fenton would have called if that had been the case.

A soft knocking brought his head up. He turned to find Harlow standing in the doorway, her hair long and disheveled from sleeping, her robe and fuzzy socks as sexy a look as he'd ever seen on a woman. For her, he managed a smile. Didn't take much. "Hey. Good morning."

"I hope I'm not bothering you."

"Never." Hell's bells, she was gorgeous. "You come for the tour?"

She looked around but stayed where she was. "It's nice. A lot nicer than I expected when you said *attic*."

"You can come in, you know."

She took a few steps. "We need to talk."

The words sent a chill through him. "Everything okay?"

"No." She pointed toward the couch. "Can I sit?"

"Of course." He let her pick a side, then took the other. "I take it you're not totally recovered from reading Rue's pinky."

"Yes and no, but that's part of it. Or maybe it isn't." She sighed and shook her head like she was trying to clear her thoughts. "Look, I just need to get this out. Something…happened to me. Something that might not be so good. Or it might be. I can't tell yet. But when that vampire had a hold of me—"

"The one I killed in front of you?"

She nodded.

Damn it. He bent his head to hide his anger. "I should have handled that differently. I should have protected you."

She put a hand on his leg. No glove. The heat of her fingers burned through his pajama pants. "Augustine, that was shocking, yes, but seeing a vampire killed in front of me, especially one that had been a part of my mother's murder, wasn't exactly a life-scarring event. You should see some of the things that go on in the RPGs I play." She raised her brows. "No, what happened that night is hard to explain."

She took her hand back and stared at the cushion between them. "When the vampire touched me, I couldn't read him like a living being. He was a blank. Or so I thought." She waved her hands in front of her. "It felt like some of his undeadness leaked into me."

Augustine scratched one horn. "That doesn't sound good."

"It's more than that." Her mouth thinned to a hard line for a moment. "All my life I've had this empty, hollow place inside me. I always thought it was the part of me that was missing my father. It's why I wanted to know him so badly. Why it was such an issue between my mother and me. But meeting him did nothing to fill that spot."

"Probably made it worse." He had a feeling he knew what had caused that empty place in her. The twin she'd never known.

"Actually, that's what the vampire did. At first I thought it was the darkness in him, but now I think it was my reaction to him. For the first time in my life, I was faced with my own mortality, and even though I had no idea how to use my gifts to protect myself, on a subconscious level, I must have tried. That confrontation brought something new to life in me that night. It happened again the night Nekai saved me from Branzino."

She planted her hands against her torso. "I can feel it in me. That power sits in the hollow place and every time I feel some-thing intense, good or bad, it sort of rises up and…devours it." She peeked sideways at him like she suspected he might be about to call the men in white coats.

"Oh, Harlow…" There was nothing wrong with her, but he had promised Olivia not to tell her about the other half of her heritage. It was like Olivia had put shackles on him with that promise. "Being in contact with the vampire obviously awak-ened a part of you you'd never had to use before." A part of her that belonged to her raptor blood. All that darkness pouring into her…how could it not have? "It'll get better." Damn it. That was a perfectly useless response.

She frowned. "I *am* trying, you know."

"You are. You're doing really great, too."

She looked past him, her gaze somewhere beyond the win-dow. "I wish my mom was still alive. Besides being able to fix things between us, it would just be nice to have her to talk to." She glanced at him. "Not that there's anything wrong with talk-ing to you, I appreciate you being willing to listen, but a mother is…" Her mouth bunched to one side. "I'm sorry. You probably don't want to hear about how nice it would be to have a mother to talk to."

He smiled wryly. "Hey, my birth mother might have been a wash, but Olivia did a great job of filling in. And yes, I get it. She was great to talk to." He laughed softly. "Always had some advice to offer, even if I didn't want it."

Harlow almost smiled, dipping her head and hiding her face from him. "I was such a horrible daughter." Her voice cracked like she was on the verge of tears. She raised her head, her eyes shining. "What am I going to do about these new powers? I don't even know what they are. I've been having horrible nightmares, I'm starting to crave touch—me!" She tapped her chest. "I hate being touched, but I've got this growing hunger that seems like it feeds off emotion and I have no way of controlling it."

The time had come to ignore Olivia's wishes. He was taking Harlow through to the fae plane. "Harlow—"

"Tell me the truth. Am I going crazy? Or did the vampire infect me with some kind of undead virus? You have to know. Or at least know someone who can help me."

He smiled. "As a matter of fact, I do. Go change and meet me downstairs in the foyer."

"You know someone who can help me? Who is it?"

"No details. Hurry up. I need to get dressed, too."

"Fine." She made a face, but there were traces of excitement in her expression.

As soon as she left, he pulled on a jacket and boots, then tromped down to the foyer to wait.

A few minutes later, she jogged down the last of the steps to stand beside him. "Okay, I'm here."

He wasn't about to take her to see her mother without a little explanation first. This could go wrong, especially since Livie wasn't going to like it. "There's something I've wanted to tell you, but because of a promise I made, couldn't. I want you to know that I kept that promise because I'm a man of my word, knowing that it could upset you. That wasn't my intention." It was also the reason he hadn't pursued things with her to a greater degree, but now wasn't the time to explain all that.

She tucked her gloved hands into the pockets of her hoodie. "You're freaking me out."

Wait until she realized her mother wasn't dead. "It's going to get worse before it gets better."

"That's reassuring."

"I know you've traveled via mirror with Nekai. Did he also tell you about the fae plane?"

"You mean like there's an airline?"

"What? No." Augustine furrowed his brow. So much for Nekai's prowess as a teacher. "I mean like another dimension that exists outside this one that only fae can travel to."

"Wow, no. That sounds amazingly cool." A curious light filled her eyes. "You know, this is kind of like being part of a real-life guild about to go on a real-life quest. I know that doesn't mean anything to you."

"It's a gaming thing, right?"

"Right. I never looked at it that way, but it actually makes it a little less awful to be fae. Not that I still think being fae is awful. Hard. Whatever. You know what I mean."

He refrained from rolling his eyes. "I guess, but there's nothing hard about being fae."

"Easy for you to say." She pursed her mouth. "So, the fae plane. Is that where we're going?"

"Yes. But it's a big place and we're going to a very specific part of it. It's not exactly scenic, but there's a reason for that. It houses a place called the Claustrum. Think of it like a maximum-security fae prison."

She grimaced. "Let's go somewhere else."

"We can't. The person we need to see is stuck on that part of the plane."

"Are they in the prison? I don't really want to go to a prison."

"They're not in the prison. And while you'll be able to see the Claustrum, we're not going in it."

She shrugged like that was only slightly reassuring. "Will we be in any danger?"

He put his hand over his heart. "You're not in any danger. Not even a little bit." He, on the other hand, might be.

It all depended on how Livie reacted to this surprise visit.

Chapter Twenty-two

O kay then. I guess I'm ready." Harlow pointed toward the fancy gold-framed mirror that hung over the foyer table. "Is that the mirror we're using?" It certainly looked big enough to travel through, but she'd already been through much smaller mirrors with Nekai and Augustine, so clearly size had very little to do with it.

"Yep." He extended his arm, elbow first. "Grab hold of me. You could probably do this on your own, but—"

"I'm good letting you drive." She slipped her hand through the crook of his arm and held on.

"Okay. Here we go." He reached out and grazed his fingers across the mirror's surface.

She shut her eyes against the slightly queasy feeling she'd felt the last time she'd traveled this way, but it never came. Maybe she was getting used to it. Or they hadn't gone through yet. She opened her eyes.

They'd definitely gone through. The world around her was a wash of gray. A sudden wind whipped past them, scrubbing at their clothes with sandy grit. A moment later it died down. As far as she could see, everything was bleak and dry and scoured. The gray extended to the horizon, where darker peaks rose toward the dismal sky.

But all of that paled in comparison to the monstrous forma-tion of black rock that towered over them. An entrance had been carved in the rock's center but it was guarded by a pretty impressive metal gate. Shards of jagged stone stuck out all along the edges like teeth, making the whole thing resemble a giant, gaping mouth about to bite.

She backed up, bumping into Augustine. "I take it that's the Claustrum."

"It is."

She realized then that the whine in her ears wasn't the wind. The wind was gone. "Am I hearing the prisoners?" The abyss inside her seemed to close in on itself as if it were hiding, leaving behind a wholly uneasy feeling.

He put his hands on her shoulders. "Yes, but like I said, you're in no danger from them. None."

"Those voices are awful—"

"Augie? Is that you?"

Harlow froze, leaning back against Augustine because she was suddenly unsure she could keep herself from falling. *That* voice she knew without question. Regaining her senses, she spun, pushing Augustine out of the way to stare into the face of the woman she'd thought she'd never see again. "Mom?"

"Harlow!" The figure before her nodded. "Yes. It's me."

Harlow looked at her mother, then at Augustine, then back at her mother. "I don't understand. I thought you were dead. How are you here? Why are you here? Are you a ghost? You look real."

"She is. In a way." Augustine explained about the night Olivia had died, about putting her body on the mirror, but thinking she hadn't made it until well after he'd sprinkled her ashes.

Harlow stared at him, a very unkind feeling welling in her soul as the abyss slowly expanded. "She's been alive all this time and you didn't tell me?"

Olivia stepped closer. "I made him promise not to." She shot a look at Augustine, anger snapping in her gaze. "Which means that promise is broken. I didn't want you to see me like this, Harlow. I've been trying to cross back over, but so far, I can't make it happen."

Augustine shook his head, clearly upset. "Livie, I told you I was bringing her. I never wanted to keep this from her at all, but you made me." He dropped his head slightly, but turned enough to look at Harlow. "I know how this must feel."

Her hands clenched into fists. "I don't think you do." She turned toward Olivia. "And you. How could you not want me to know you were alive? Are you *that* mad at me?" She stalked forward, the hollowness driving her. "Because if anyone should be mad, it should be me. All those years you refused to tell me who my father was—"

Olivia backed up. "I told you he was a monster."

Harlow shook her head. "'A monster' barely scratches the surface of what he is. You should have prepared me. You should have given me some kind of warning—"

Olivia grabbed her and pulled her into a hug. "I'm so sorry, *cher*," she whispered into Harlow's ear. "I thought I could protect you." Sobs made her words jagged. "I thought I could keep him away from you."

At her mother's embrace, something she couldn't remember feeling since she was a very small child, Harlow's anger lost its bite. The hollowness shrank down, still there, but not as predatory. She returned her mother's hug briefly before pulling away. "I appreciate that. I really do. But Augustine brought me here because he thought you could help me. Now's your chance to make up for all those years of not telling me a thing."

Olivia wiped at her eyes, then looked past Harlow to Augustine. With a sigh she turned and sat on a large boulder, patting the stone beside her. "Come. Sit. There is a lot you don't know."

Olivia inhaled for strength as Harlow took a seat beside her. Augustine stood his ground a few feet away. She couldn't really be angry with him. He'd told her he was going to bring Harlow through and he was a man of his word, keeping her secret for longer than she'd expected already.

"How could you ever be involved with a man like that?" Harlow asked. "Did you love him?"

"Love, no. But was I charmed by him? Yes." This was a talk she'd hoped never to have with Harlow, but she'd learned a long time ago that *never* was a dangerous word.

Harlow looked skeptical. "By *that* man?"

"To the point I felt intoxicated by his presence at times. He always seemed to have the right words at the right times. Part of his power, actually. Not the words, but the way he made me feel." She stared at the stony ground beneath her feet. "I really had no idea what a monster he was until after you were born."

"Why? What happened?"

Olivia hesitated, finding the words. "I have to back up a little in order for it all to make sense." Her heart began to ache as the memories came flooding back. "Early on in my relationship with Branzino, I read his palm."

"Like you do to everyone."

She nodded. "You'd think I would have learned." Her breath came out as shredded as her insides felt. "I never should have told him what I read."

"Which was?"

"That his firstborn child was going to be the death of him."

"That's a pretty heavy thing to lay on a person—" Harlow's eyes rounded. "Wait a minute. Am I his firstborn? Is he planning on killing me? Why would you tell him such a thing?"

"No, you're not his firstborn, and I told him because I didn't know how dangerous he was then *and* because he already had a son. That child's birth hadn't caused anything to happen to him, so I didn't really believe what I was reading." She tipped her head back to stare at the clouded gray sky. "If I could change the past, I would."

"Why? If he already had a kid, what was the big deal?"

She brought her gaze back to earth. "The big deal was that the child was his nephew, adopted when Branzino's brother was killed in a car accident." She reached out to wrap her hand around Harlow's, to feel that her remaining child was alive and well and, for the moment, at her side.

Something dark flickered in Harlow's eyes. "So I *am* the firstborn?"

"No, sweetheart," Olivia said softly. "Your sister was."

Giselle sat on a chaise by the pool, reliving the night her father had drowned. Reminding herself that it had been a necessary thing. An act of love toward her people, really.

Tonight those people, *her* coven now, would gather here, on the grounds of her father's estate—the place he'd loved most—for a private ceremony to say goodbye to him and send him on his journey to the Summerlands.

She wanted to cast the circle they'd use well before that. To have a little private, uninterrupted time to prepare herself and say her own goodbye. She'd asked her sister to join her.

Giselle pulled her sweater a little tighter around her. The house was empty except for Cormier, who didn't have much to do now. She hadn't really figured out what to do with him or the house. She loved her place in the Quarter and couldn't see giving it up, but neither could she see taking on this new role and not living in this house. It had become the headquarters for the coven in many ways.

After tonight, she would officially be the coven's high priestess. Reading crystals in the Square was a little beneath her now. Private clients were another thing entirely. No one would bat an eye at that sort of commerce. She had to have a little income that didn't rely on her position, a little discretionary cash. Besides, her clients often made her privy to information she wouldn't otherwise have gotten.

"Giselle?"

She turned. "Zara. How are you?"

Zara sat on the chaise next to her. "Well enough, considering." She glanced at the pool briefly before returning her attention to her sister. "How's Ian?"

Giselle couldn't help but smile. "He's good. Very good."

Zara laughed. "I bet he is. I should take a lover. You look more radiant than I've seen you in a long time. Or perhaps it's because you're about to become our high priestess?"

Giselle took her sister's hand, something she hadn't done in a very long time. "You're really and truly okay with that?"

"Absolutely." Zara gave Giselle's hand a little squeeze. "I am perfectly content doing what I'm doing. Although that is not to say I won't enjoy the perks of being the high priestess's little sister."

They both laughed at that, then their laughter faded as if they'd both remembered the purpose of being at their father's house. Zara fiddled with the closure on her bag. No doubt it held her contributions for the altar they were about to set up in preparation for casting the sacred circle. She looked at Giselle. "You always had a better connection with Father than I did. He and I were never what anyone would consider close. Are you doing okay with his passing?"

Giselle's smile felt thin even to her, but the regrets she carried were hers to deal with. Being a leader meant making hard choices. Evander himself had taught her that. "I'm fine. It'll take some getting used to, but I'm...fine."

"You're going to move into the house, aren't you? You should. It's yours as far as I'm concerned, no matter what his will says. I got Mother's, you should get his."

"Thank you. I was just thinking about that. I don't know what I'm going to do. I love my place in the Quarter."

A shy smile turned up the corners of Zara's mouth. "It would be nice to have you closer. And nothing says you have to get rid of your place in the Quarter."

Giselle was touched that her sister genuinely wanted her nearby. "You think I should move in here?"

Zara looked over her shoulder at the house, then swept her gaze over the grounds. "You're about to be high priestess. This house is basically coven headquarters. And while your town house is lovely, this place—"

"This place is grand. You're right, I know. But I can't live here with so much of his energy clinging to every inch."

Zara lifted her brows. "I'm a green witch. If anyone can cleanse this house of bad energies, it's me. You're just making excuses. Look what you did with that town house, then think about how beautiful you could make this place. I'll even help you with the garden."

"You just want another one to work on when you run out of space in your own."

Zara grinned. "Maybe, but you'd benefit from it."

Giselle looked at the house. Really looked at it. If she could see it without the memory of her father attached to it, without his ghost haunting the halls, reminding her of what she'd done, then the potential was limitless. It had great bones, and the Garden District address didn't hurt either. She turned back to Zara. "You'll help?"

"With the garden. You want heavy lifting, hire it out. You've got the money now."

"I do, don't I?" Giselle nodded. "You've talked me into it."

"Good. Now which of his cars do you want?"

Giselle glanced toward the garage. "I...honestly, I hadn't thought about it. I don't have a car now. I'm not sure I need one."

"You have a driver's license, don't you?"

"Yes."

"You need the car. You're about to be the high priestess. You can't rely on the streetcars." Zara sighed in exasperation. "The black Mercedes convertible or the white Mercedes sedan."

"Why do you care about this so much?"

Zara's impish smile lit up her face. "Because I'm going to take whichever one you don't want."

Giselle laughed and shook her head. "Which one do you want?" After being so gracious about the issue of who would become high priestess, Zara deserved her pick.

"Do you really have to ask? The black convertible."

"Then it's yours. I'm perfectly happy with the sedan." She stood and brushed off her impeccable ivory wool trousers. "Let's get this circle cast. I've got work to do."

Chapter Twenty-three

Harlow wasn't sure how long she sat without moving or speaking. Trying to process the words that had just come out of her mother's mouth left her paralyzed. She wasn't even aware that she'd reached out with her other hand until she felt the comforting warmth of Augustine's grasp through her thin silk glove. "I have a sister?"

Olivia's lids were rimmed with liquid. "Had."

That one word shot a dagger into her heart. The hollowness suddenly made sense. Her whole body ached as the realization hit her. "She's...dead."

Olivia nodded almost hesitantly, like she was waiting for Harlow's cue before she said more.

Harlow looked at Augustine, now crouched beside her. "Did you know about this?"

"Only just recently."

She let go of both their hands to fold hers in her lap. "Did Lally know?"

Augustine nodded. "Some of it."

No wonder Lally had said Augustine had his own secrets. Keeping the tree from him might actually be doable, knowing he'd kept so much from her. "So everyone knew all of this except me."

"She never knew the details about the death of your twin," Olivia whispered. "Just that she had died at birth and it wasn't something I ever wanted to talk about."

A brand-new wave of grief washed over her. *Twin. Sister.* The words dug their sharp edges into her, forcing her to feel a kind of pain she'd never experienced before. The hollowness took on a new shape, expanding so that she was no longer hollow in one place, but everywhere. She *became* the emptiness. The longing. It clogged her throat until she swallowed the knot of sorrow. "What was her name?"

"Ava Mae."

"Ava Mae." Saying her name tore a new hole in Harlow's heart. "And she was firstborn?"

"Yes."

"How did she die? Why have you kept her death a secret?"

Olivia sobbed, sharp and sudden. The wind picked up the sound and reeled off with it. "I did everything I could to keep him away. I swear it. I did everything I could to protect you and your sister." A tear rolled down her cheek. "It wasn't enough. I shouldn't have put your names on your cribs, but then he might have killed both of you."

Harlow had too much of her own grief to feel any for her mother right now. "*How* did she die?"

"I was away on a night shoot. He killed one of my security guards and broke into the house, killed the nanny I'd hired." She wiped at her eyes. "He smothered Ava Mae in her crib."

Disgust and abject horror pushed Harlow to her feet. The chaos of emotions coursing through her made it impossible to sit any longer. Hate, anger, grief. She stared down at her mother. "Branzino killed her because she was firstborn? Because of what you told him?"

Olivia dissolved into tears, unable to speak. She nodded.

"How do you know this? How do you know it was him?" Harlow might have been yelling, but she didn't care.

Augustine stood, stepping between her and Olivia. "She has security footage. I've seen it. It's him. He looks right into the camera because that's the kind of monster he is. He wanted her to know what he'd done."

She pushed him aside to glare at Olivia. "Why didn't you take that video to the cops? Why didn't you have him arrested? He'd be in jail right now."

Augustine blocked her view again. "No, Harlow, he wouldn't."

She shifted her glare to him. "Why the hell not?"

"There is no human prison that can hold a fae like him."

That knocked her back slightly. "And exactly what kind of fae is that?"

He pointed at the boulder. "Sit down."

She did as he commanded, only because she wasn't sure she'd be able to stand after she got his answer. Whatever kind of fae Branzino was, she knew it was something awful. "Tell me."

As Olivia sniffled, Augustine continued. "He's raptor fae. They're mostly known for two things: their ability to read metal and their consumption of emotion. They feed off it. And some can actually force emotion into a person. Based on the reputation Branzino has for intimidation and the way he charmed your mother, it's highly likely he's got that skill."

"That's why I am the way I am then." It explained so much.

He nodded. "You're haerbinger and raptor, two types of fae with very powerful mental abilities. The power to read metal combined with how you can read objects explains your computer skills. The emptiness you've been feeling isn't just missing your sister. It's because you've kept yourself closed off from touch. After so many years, your body is hungry for the emotions it feeds off of. It's your raptor side. Being touched by that vampire definitely woke your defensive powers. You probably tried to push emotion into him without even knowing it, but you just didn't have the knowledge to make it happen."

She wanted to shed her traitorous skin. "I don't want to have anything that links me to Branzino. He's a killer."

Augustine knelt in front of her. "He is. But you're not. Don't you feel better understanding what's going on inside you? Knowing where you come from doesn't mean you have to go back there." He grabbed her hands, forcing her to look at him. "You move forward. Take this information and make it work for you."

She nodded, but she was overwhelmed.

Olivia laid a hand on her arm. "He's right. Please, *cher*, don't let this paralyze you. I know it's a lot to take in, but just because Branzino is your biological father doesn't mean he should have any kind of hold over you. You've always been a strong, inde-pendent woman. More than I wished you were sometimes." She smiled a little bit. "Don't stop being that woman."

"I need time to process this." Harlow pulled away. She was done talking about all of this. She felt like a raw nerve. One more thing and she might snap. "So you can't cross back over?"

"Not yet," Olivia answered. "Maybe never. I don't know. I hope you know that no matter what happens with me, the house is yours."

"And Augustine's." Harlow frowned. "You and your tricks."

"I had my reasons."

Harlow looked deep into her mother's eyes. "I know. Lally and I had a *long* talk."

Understanding registered. "Good. I'm glad. Lally is the best friend I ever had." She patted Harlow's hand. "You should take over my bedroom. Do it up any way you like. Whatever style suits you."

"I don't know. Feels weird."

"Why? I'm not actually dead. Just pretend I've moved."

Harlow shrugged. "Maybe."

"I don't care what you do with all my old movie stuff. Sell it if you like. Oh, so you know, there's a white ceramic box on my nightstand—there's a picture of you there, too—you'll see the box, it's got a lamb on the lid. Be careful with that. Those are Ava Mae's ashes."

Harlow stood, unable to take any more. "I'm happy you're still alive, Mom. I really am. But I need to go home now. I'll be back. I promise. I just don't know when."

Olivia stood and hugged her. "I know this is a lot of new and difficult information." She let Harlow go and looked to Augustine. "Take care of my girl."

He nodded. "I always do." He held out his arm to Harlow.

She slipped her hand through the crook of his elbow as the wind tore past again. The weight of what she'd learned was heavy, but poor Rue was still out there. Still Branzino's prisoner. And knowing what she did about the man now, there was no way Harlow could let him kill again.

With the threads of an idea weaving themselves together in her overloaded brain, she and Augustine slipped back through the mirror.

Augustine could only imagine what was going on in Harlow's head, but his LMD buzzed the second they got back in the house. Five messages, all from Fenton. Augustine scrolled through them. Fenton had a plan. It relied on a lot of things falling into place and still would only result in a slim chance of getting Rue back, but slim was all they had right now.

He texted back, *Messages received. On my way soon.* Harlow stood in the foyer, staring at the mirror they'd just come through. He hurt for her. Her plate had gone from mostly empty to overflowing. "I hate to dump all that on you and run, but I have—"

"Guardian business. I know." Harlow waved him off. "It's okay. After all that, I'd like some time alone."

"You're sure?"

She nodded, her mind obviously elsewhere.

"Okay. Call me if you need me for anything." She seemed numb, but maybe she really did need some time alone. With one last glance at her, he took off to his room for weapons and his coat and then he was in the Thrun and on the streets. He arrived at Ogun's fifteen minutes later with a firm plan. The skies were darkening and the wind picking up. Rain couldn't be too far behind.

The man opened on the fourth knock. He eyed Augustine with distaste. "I was hoping you weren't coming back."

"I keep my word. May I come in?"

Ogun sighed and walked away from the door. "Better inside than out where all the neighbors can hear you."

Augustine came in and shut the door behind him. The place still reeked of incense and herbs. "The daughter of our Prime was kidnapped. Have you heard anything?"

"You think my people had anything to do with that? We're not about harming children, Mr. Robelais."

"No, I don't think your people had anything to do with it. I just know that you're well connected. I thought you might have heard something that could be useful in getting her home safely."

Ogun nodded, seemingly mollified. "If I hear anything, I will be sure to tell you."

"Thank you. Now, how about you tell me what you know about Giselle and her connection to the fae who committed suicide. Give me that information and I'll leave you alone."

Ogun settled into a chair, switching off the holovision that had been on a news channel. "Fae, you don't understand the kind of war you're asking me to unleash."

Augustine sat without waiting to be asked. He leaned forward. "Yes, I do, but I have a feeling that war is already on its way. Are you aware that Evander Vincent is dead?"

"I heard. Drowned, they say." Ogun's jaw shifted to one side before he spoke again. "Evander was a good man. Liked his drink, but then who doesn't? His daughter…" He sucked at his teeth and shook his head. "Trouble."

"You think she killed him?"

Ogun's brows shot up and he chuckled. "You just say everything that's on your mind, fae? Or do you ever listen to it first, see if it might stir things up?"

"Is that a yes?"

After a big sigh, Ogun bounced his hands on the chair's arms. "I don't want to be involved in this."

"Too late for that."

Ogun swore in Creole. "I can't give you what you want. Not at the expense of my own skin." He brushed his fingers through the air. "Do what you will. You have no real evidence against me."

"Besides the trace amounts of *bokura* found at the scene, I have Evander's recorded testimony." That was a lie. Augustine hadn't recorded anything, but for the sake of Fenton's plan, Ogun had to believe they had actionable evidence. He sat back. "Before he died, Evander told me you were the one who killed Dreich, that you'd set it up to look like there'd been witch involvement and that you and your people were planning a power grab. His words, '*power grab*.'" Augustine crossed his ankle over his knee. "If you can't give me information that disputes that, I'll have to consider taking action against you and your practitioners. Put some *regulations* in place, that sort of thing."

Anger sparked in Ogun's eyes. "Do what you feel you need to, but be aware your actions will have consequences. If Evander actually did tell you that, it was to protect his daughter."

"So you're saying she needs protecting. Which means you must know she's involved."

Ogun groaned out a sigh. "I do not want to be involved in this."

"I get that you're afraid of incurring the wrath of the witches and making trouble for your people, but that ship has sailed. You know we found *bokura* at the scene."

"It's not a crime to produce *bokura*."

"Not yet, but I have a feeling that's about to change." Augustine let that sit a moment.

"You have no right to regulate what we do."

"As Guardian of this city, I sure as hell do. If you think I'm worried about whatever consequences you and your people might bring against the fae, you're wrong. No matter what magic you can conjure up, the fact remains that you're still human."

Ogun scowled. "What you want from me, I can't give you, Mr. Robelais. The cost is too high."

"You leave me with very little choice. I'll have to start questioning other members of your religion. I'll search homes if I have to." Wind whistled past the house.

"What if I can help you in another way?"

"How?"

Ogun took something from his pocket and wound it around his finger. A thread? A hair? "What if I can convince Giselle to confess the truth to you on her own?"

This was exactly what they'd been hoping for. To push Ogun to confront Giselle again. A little more publicly if they were lucky. Augustine furrowed his brow. "And you can do that how?"

"Is the how important if the end result is what you want?"

"It's not." Augustine shook his head. He honestly didn't care what Ogun did if it got Giselle to confess on the record. Or in front of enough witnesses. "You have an LMD. Make sure you record what you get."

"What if she detects it?"

"Not my problem. You've got a day to make this happen."

"I need more time."

"You've already had more than enough. Twenty-four hours. You know where to find me." If that didn't push Ogun to action, then they were back to square one. Augustine stood. "I'll let myself out."

Back in the Thrun, Augustine called Fenton. Thunder cracked above him and the sky looked like it was about to open up. "I baited the hook, now we just have to see if Ogun takes it."

"What did you tell him?"

"That Evander blamed him for the whole thing. Which is the truth. Ogun claims he can get Giselle to confess. I gave him a day to bring us proof of her involvement. If that doesn't push him to confront her, I don't know what will. Anything new on your end? Any new ransom notes?" Hopefully no new body parts.

"No. We're at a standstill."

"*Sturka*. If that girl dies..."

"I know." Fenton sighed. "I know."

"If this doesn't work, do you have a plan B?"

"The Elektos, sans Hugo, are having an emergency meeting tonight. Hopefully we'll come up with something."

"Do you need me there? I could have Cy cover the funeral. He's certainly more equipped in the disguise department." As it was, Augustine was going to have to rely on Nekai's weaver skills to hide his true identity at the last rites ceremony.

"No, you should be the one at Evander's. I'm messengering some equipment to your house: a tiny camera in a contact lens. If Ogun does show up, you'll be able to record what happens and then we won't have to rely on whatever he brings us alone. After Giselle performs Evander's last rites ceremony she'll officially be high priestess and in charge of the coven. It's a big night. The thirteen will be there and so will her sister, Zara. I think a little intel on that whole group could be very beneficial in the future. Giselle is not about to be the easy ride Evander was."

"I'm well aware of that."

Fenton snorted. "Good luck tonight. It's not going to be a pleasant evening with this weather, but I'm sure the witches will work some kind of magic so that it doesn't interrupt the ceremony."

"Are you sure they won't be able to detect the fae magic disguising me?"

After a long pause, Fenton spoke. "No. If you think you've been found out, I'd suggest evasive maneuvers. Tonight's ceremony is quite sacred. They're not going to take being spied on lightly."

"No pressure then." Augustine rolled his eyes. "I'll call as soon as I'm out of there." He hung up. Whatever risk he was about to take would be worth it if things worked out. Hopefully, Ogun would show and get Giselle to make some kind of confession. After that they could pick her up and use that info to pressure her into giving them Branzino's location.

He hated that finding Branzino might mean offering Giselle immunity for Dreich's death, but they were running out of time. And Giselle would eventually slip up again anyway. That much was certain.

Chapter Twenty-four

Harlow paced the length of her room. Thunder rumbled overhead. Somewhere, out there, a very scared Rue was in Branzino's clutches, who was probably doing unspeakable things to her. And all because Branzino wanted this house. *That* tree. There had to be something she could do. Some way she could harness her powers to help. If only her twin were alive.

Ava Mae. Her *twin*.

Harlow stopped pacing and sank down onto her bed as the hollowness in her gut threatened to undo her. How was it possible to love someone she'd never met? A sister. A twin sister. The ache was almost unbearable. No wonder she'd spent her life feeling like a part of her was missing.

She got to her feet again, driven by the unstoppable urge to be near the sibling she'd never known. If Olivia could survive in a different form on the fae plane, why was there no hope for Ava Mae? She was just as fae as the rest of them. Harlow kept moving until she got to her mother's room. To her mother's nightstand. There it was, the alabaster box with the lamb carved on the lid. Even in the storm-dimmed daylight, the creamy stone seemed to glow. Beckoning her.

With reverence, Harlow picked up the box. So small. But then an infant's ashes didn't amount to much, did they? She swallowed at the clutch in her throat. "Ava Mae," she whispered, her heart aching with the loss of a lifetime missed out on. "I'm so sorry I never met you. I wish there was something I could do—"

The sharp crack of thunder and brilliant flash of lightning filled the room. She glanced toward the closet, Lally's warning about the tree ringing in her ears.

What price would the tree want for what Harlow was thinking of? There was no way it could be worse than the pain she'd already endured.

And even if it was, she no longer cared. She was done feeling incomplete. Done hurting.

With the box in hand, she strode into the closet and shoved back the clothes that hid the secret door. But she had no key. If only her powers were more useful.

Maybe they were.

She set the box down, then knelt before the door and yanked her gloves off. She pressed her fingers to the lock. It was metal. She ought to be able to do this. She opened herself to it, a picture of the lock forming in her head—the way the tumblers sat, the way they needed to be moved. She ran back to her mother's vanity table and grabbed a hairpin.

On her knees before the lock again, she jammed the pin in and, with her fingers on the lock, used the picture in her head to guide the pin into the tumblers. She struggled with the lock, failing to get it open. With a soft growl of frustration, she tossed the hairpin away and sat back on her heels. She glanced down at her sister's ashes. "I'm sorry, Ava Mae, I'm trying…"

The lock snicked open.

She stared at it. How had that happened? She must have unlocked it without realizing. She wrenched the door wide, then grabbed the alabaster box and climbed through. The tree seemed bigger. The bitter smell of soot lay heavy in the air. Gray streaked the sky visible through the glass roof, but the rain held off.

Working on instinct alone, she took the top off the box. Inside was a white satin bag tied with gold cord. She loosened the cord and looked inside. Ashes, just as they should be. Hard to believe that dust was her sister. "Forgive me, Lally, but I have to do this."

She scooped up a handful, the ashes soft as feathers. "I hope you're still in there, Ava Mae." She planted her empty hand on the tree trunk while she lifted the one filled with ashes. The air around her snapped with energy. "Please, I want my sister back. It's my heart's desire. Bring her back to me. Fill this hole in my heart."

Another crack of thunder and lightning. In a trick of the light, an image of a girl seemed to sway in the higher branches. Harlow almost pulled her hand back. The bark was rough and oddly warm, but no emotion flooded into her, just the sensation of a low, almost electric hum.

A breeze built, sweeping up from the base of the tree. It sucked the ashes from the box and out of Harlow's hand and spun them into a whirling thread. It wound higher and higher until the wind died and the ashes disappeared. Harlow stared into the branches of the tree, waiting. The image she'd glimpsed was gone.

Seconds stretched by and nothing happened. She pounded her fist against the trunk. "Where is she? You took the ashes, I want my sister."

"Harlow?"

At the sound of her name, Harlow spun. On the platform behind her stood a paler, somewhat altered version of herself. "Are you...Ava Mae?"

The woman nodded and smiled shyly. Her skin was nearly translucent, her eyes overlarge and the hollows beneath her cheekbones too pronounced. "And you're my sister Harlow."

"I am." Was she real?

"Thank you."

"For what?"

"For bringing me all the way back." She moved closer. Floated, really. The movement caused Harlow to realize that the creature before her wasn't entirely corporeal. Still, she held her ground as the image approached. "Have you missed me?"

"Yes." Harlow didn't care what form Ava Mae had returned in. "But I didn't really know it was you I was missing. I just found out about you."

Ava Mae tipped her head, a curious, birdlike movement that made her large eyes and skeletal features seem more fragile. "I've always known about you."

"You have? What did you mean by 'all the way back'? How are you... that is, you look the same age as me. I thought maybe you'd be..."

"An infant?" Ava Mae smiled. "After Lally told Mama about the tree, she brought my ashes in here, planned to do the same thing you just did, I believe, but Lally anticipated that and caught her. All Mama managed was to drop the handful of ashes she was holding. That was enough to give rise to my ghost. But I couldn't become more without the rest of me."

"So you've... grown up as a ghost?"

She laughed. "Yes and no. I've lived here since then, listening and learning. Mama liked to watch a lot of her old movies in the ballroom and that's one of the spots I can eavesdrop on, since one of the tree's branches grows beneath that floor." She smiled. "I'm not a baby anymore by any stretch of the imagination, but when you were making your wish and picturing me in your mind, how did you see me?"

Harlow's mouth opened. "Exactly as you are. My age."

Nodding, she reached out and stroked a piece of Harlow's hair, her expression dreamlike. "So that's what you got. Are you disappointed?"

"No, of course not. Have you been... in the house all these years then?" She'd almost said *haunting*.

Ava Mae dropped the strand of hair and smiled. "Mm-hmm. Like Lally, I can't get too far away from the tree. Actually, I can't go into any room the branches don't touch. The tree won't let me."

"It won't *let* you?"

Ava Mae shrugged. "I don't think that will happen now that I'm all together. That's all that matters. Now I can finally explore the world out there."

Harlow bit at the inside of her cheek. "Do you know about the man who killed you?"

Ava Mae jerked like she'd been struck. Her bright amber eyes went black and her mouth stretched into an unnaturally wide grimace filled with sharp pointed teeth. "Joseph Branzino. Our father. An evil, evil man. I never want to hear his name again."

Harlow nodded as she retreated, stopping only when she hit the railing. "Ava Mae, you're scaring me."

Ava Mae's eyes widened farther and her mouth rounded into an O. In a blink of her eyes, her face returned to normal, but now it was warped with pain. She seemed on the verge of tears. "I didn't mean to, Harlow. Are you mad at me? I would never hurt you."

"Of course I'm not mad." Harlow knew unquestioningly she had to soothe the woman-child in front of her. "You're my sister. I love you." But it was definitely time to change the subject.

Ava Mae smiled, all bright-eyed and beaming happiness. "I love you, too. I'm happy you're not mad. I'm happy you brought me back."

Harlow chalked up Ava Mae's ability to shift moods so suddenly to her being basically alone and a ghost for the last twenty years. Which made her next words as cautious as possible. "I know you said you *were* a ghost, but I think you might still be one."

Ava Mae looked down at herself. "I don't know. Am I?"

"I don't know either, but you don't look like you're flesh and blood. Can I touch you?"

"Yes." Ava Mae stuck her arm out.

Harlow tentatively put her hand on her sister's arm. Her fingers passed through a cold mist, but never touched flesh. Harlow pulled her hand back. "Hmm. Looks like you might be a ghost after all."

Ava Mae's smile flatlined and her eyes darkened. "Does that matter?"

"No." Harlow laughed softly and waved her hand like it was nothing, hoping to defuse the situation and keep her sister from shifting into her darker form again. "It really doesn't. I'm just happy you're here. Next time I'll know to make my wish a little more specific, though." A thought occurred to her. She glanced back at the tree. "Can I ask you something?"

Ava Mae bobbed up and down like a puppy awaiting a treat. "Anything."

Harlow eyed the creature before her. "Do you have anything to do with the nightmares I've been having?"

Ava Mae went still, then her eyes crinkled with a little fear. "Would you be mad if I did?"

"No, I just want to know."

Ava Mae nodded, looking down and wringing her hands. "I was just trying to reach you. I didn't mean to scare you."

Harlow exhaled. "I'm just happy I'm not losing my mind. How did you do it?"

Ava Mae shrugged. "It wasn't hard to slip into your room and whisper things in your ear when you were sleeping." She clapped her hands. The gesture made no sound. "I had no idea you'd be able to hear me. I'm sorry you had bad dreams. I tried to give you a dream about us swimming in the pool. I've always wanted to do that, but you can't swim without a body. I guess you didn't like the dreams?"

"No, but they're over now, right?" Harlow hoped so.

"Yes, no more bad dreams." Ava Mae looked slightly chastised, which meant she was basically on the verge of tears again, but Harlow was okay with that considering what she'd just confessed to. "I'm sorry."

"I forgive you."

She pouted anyway. "I was just trying to make contact with you. I was murdered, you know."

"Yes," Harlow said softly. "I know. I'm so sorry."

The pouting disappeared. Ava Mae's arms dropped to her sides, her hands clenching. "You know about that man who killed me. That monster Joseph Branzino. How?"

"Because he's also responsible for our mother's death and since he's been in town, he's attacked me twice." Ava Mae didn't need to know the details about everything else Branzino had done.

Ava Mae's black-eyed, razor-toothed face reappeared. "Where is he?"

Harlow tried not to cringe, but that side of Ava Mae was frightening. No wonder Harlow had dreamed of a black abyss coming after her. "I don't know. That's the problem. He's holding a sixteen-year-old girl for ransom and no one knows where he is in the city."

"Pay his ransom. Make him come to you."

"No. He wants another life. The life of someone I care about."

Ava Mae cocked her head and her eyes twinkled. "Augustine?"

"Yes." Harlow expected that to be the end of Ava Mae's scary face, but it wasn't. If anything, the threat to Augustine only seemed to intensify it.

"Oh no, he will not hurt Augustine. We'll have to find Joseph Branzino then. We will rescue this girl. And then we will deal with him."

She seemed so matter-of-fact. "How exactly do you think we're going to do this?"

"Together." Ava Mae grinned, adding a whole new level of frightening to her image. "We are twice as strong and I've had lots of years to listen and learn and practice. This tree has been more than my home, it's been my teacher. He won't expect us to come after him. But we will need something of his."

"I don't have...wait. I have a business card of his."

"That will do. We need more fae. All of the same kind."

"All of the same kind? The same kind as us?"

"No, just the same as each other. They have to share a bloodline."

Harlow pursed her mouth as she thought. "Let's go talk to Augustine. He'll know who can help us."

Ava Mae's human face returned and she smiled. "The one you love."

"I don't know if *love* is exactly the right word." Even though she was a little mad at him for keeping secrets from her, her face was still heating, because *love* might actually be the *perfect* word. "I do like him very much." That much she could comfortably admit. She pointed toward the secret door. "We have to go back this way. Follow me." She slid past Ava Mae to climb through the door. "This is our mother's closet. She's not really dead, by the way. She's on the fae plane..." Harlow turned but Ava Mae wasn't there.

She stuck her head back through the door. Ava Mae was on the platform, tears streaming down her face. "What's wrong? You couldn't get through?"

"No. I tried to follow, but when I went through the door I was yanked back. I still can't leave the tree."

"That's not going to work at all." Harlow slipped through to stand beside her sister. "There's got to be a way you can come with me."

Ava Mae's tears stopped. "There is. If you will allow it."

"Allow it? What is it?"

Ava Mae pointed at Harlow. "You could let me share your body."

"That sounds..." *Weird*. "What do you mean, exactly?"

Ava Mae shifted uncomfortably. "I could fill the hollow place. Only until we find Joseph Branzino. Then I can finally be at peace."

The thought of not feeling that emptiness, even for a short while, was tempting. "And after he's been dealt with for his crimes?"

Ava Mae smiled, not the dark, scary smile, but the wistful smile of a young girl. "Then I can be at peace. Maybe I can even go be with Mama."

The idea of being able to reunite her mother and her sister almost brought tears to Harlow's eyes. "Okay."

With a happy gasp, Ava Mae charged forward like a slip-stream of air, barreling toward Harlow. Harlow braced but the impact never came.

She turned, expecting to see Ava Mae behind her. "Ava Mae?"

I'm here. The voice echoed inside Harlow's head.

Harlow tensed. "This is going to take some getting used to." At least it was temporary.

Please, Harlow. Just until we make Joseph Branzino pay.

Harlow nodded. "I know. It's okay. I'll be fine."

Thank you. I love you, Sister.

A sense of relief flooded Harlow and suddenly the hollow place inside her was no longer hollow. Her sister's presence had changed all of that. "Okay," Harlow whispered. "I can do this."

We, Ava Mae corrected.

Harlow spent the next hour or so packing some of her mother's things. Olivia had said Harlow should have her room, so why not? The relief of knowing her mother wasn't dead erased much of her guilt. They still had issues to work through and old hurts to heal, but at least now they had that time.

She could even understand why Olivia had wanted to keep Branzino out of her life in such a complete way. Harlow wished that he were still out of it. The man had brought nothing but pain and chaos into her life since he'd become a part of it.

But she and Ava Mae would soon rectify that. The soft laughter in her head confirmed Ava Mae's agreement. Her presence in Harlow's mind and body remained a bit of a shock, but it was just temporary. And a small price to pay for getting to know her sister. What a huge improvement over so many years of aching over a loss she didn't understand.

A door shut downstairs. Maybe it was Ava Mae's presence, but Harlow's senses had become more acute. Voices, Augustine's and Lally's.

Footsteps bounded up the stairs, stopping with Augustine poking his head into the room. "Finally moving in, huh?"

Ava Mae stirred. *He's pretty.*

Yes, he is. Trying not to smile at Ava Mae's assessment, Harlow finished wrapping the last framed photo and tucked it into the box. "Might as well, since my mother didn't seem to mind. I'm glad you're home. I have an idea about how—"

The doorbell rang.

"That's either Nekai," Augustine said. "Or Fenton's messenger. Either way, I have to get that. I warned Lally Nekai was coming over, so you know she's not answering the door. I just wanted to make sure you were okay after... everything."

Tell him.

I'm trying. "I'm fine. Listen, I want to tell you about my idea—"

The doorbell rang again. "We can talk as soon as I deal with him, but I don't have a lot of time. I have to get to Giselle's."

"The witch? Why are you going there?"

"She's performing the last rites ceremony for her father. After that she'll officially be the coven's head priestess. I'm going to keep an eye on things."

"Do you want me to go with you? I could explain my idea on the way."

"No, way too dangerous. I'm actually going in disguise." He put his hand on his heart. "I promise we'll talk the second I get home."

"What does Nekai have to do with it? Is he going with you?"

Augustine nodded. "No, he's the one setting me up with the disguise. The messenger is bringing a secret agent gadget from Fenton. Like your contact lens, except for me this time." He smiled. Ava Mae sighed. *Beautiful.* "We're working a little sting operation on the witches. We think Giselle Vincent is in league with Branzino—or at least might be able to lead us to him."

At Branzino's name, Ava Mae snarled and Harlow pictured her in full-on scary-face mode. *It's okay. Calm down.* "I'm glad you have a plan, but if that doesn't work—"

The doorbell rang a third time. "Hold that thought." He shot down the stairs. She followed, but stayed on the first-floor landing when he let Nekai in.

Ava Mae sniffed. *Nekai is a weaver fae?*

Yes.

Don't let him touch you. He'll sense me. He won't understand.

The weaver ignored Augustine to wave at her. "Hey, Harlow. How are you?"

"Good." Harlow waved back. Ava Mae snorted. *He reeks with the perfume of too many women.* Amazing what Ava Mae picked up on. *He did save me from Branzino's last attack*, Harlow thought.

Ava Mae's indifference became a palpable thing. *So I should like him because he did the right thing?*

Point taken. You and Augustine would get along great.

Ava Mae sighed. *I like the sound of that. I wonder if he bites? Maybe if I asked nicely...*

Ava Mae! Harlow hoped she wasn't blushing. She sat on the stairs, using the banisters as cover.

Nekai handed a small bag to Augustine. "Put this on when you're ready to go under cover. It's a mask, but it will alter your entire appearance. I added a little something extra to it to make you less noticeable. When someone looks at you, their gaze will slide off you, making you harder to see."

"Kind of like the ward on the house."

Nekai nodded. "Exactly."

"How long will it last?"

"Until you take the mask off. Be careful, though—witch magic and fae magic don't mix."

"Meaning?"

"There will be a sacred circle drawn for the ceremony. Only coven members will be invited in, so as a guest, that shouldn't pose a problem for you, but if you cross into it, your true identity will be revealed. If it's any consolation, it works the opposite way as well."

Harlow pushed to her feet, her nerves tripping with anger. "So if someone was using witch magic to change their appearance and they encountered fae magic?"

Nekai looked at her. "The fae magic would cancel out the witch's."

Augustine looked at her. "What are you thinking?"

"Branzino," Harlow said. Ava Mae hissed. "At the ball, he was wearing a fae costume very similar to mine. In fact, I even remarked that it looked like it could have been made by the same craftswoman." She grabbed hold of the railing. "What kind of magic would he use to disguise his true appearance? Fae or witch?"

Augustine snorted in disgust. "How much you want to bet

it's witch?" Augustine and Nekai looked at each other. Augustine shook his head. "Could Giselle create that sort of spell?"

Nekai tipped his head like he was thinking. "Giselle's got enough experience. But then so could a lot of the higher-ups in the coven."

Augustine's expression darkened. "But she's got the most to gain. Maybe Branzino killed her father in exchange for her help."

Nekai exhaled slowly. "Either way, with the two of them in league, you need to be very careful. There's no telling what either of them will do to protect themselves and their goals."

"All I care about right now is getting Rue home safe. Thank you for the disguise."

"You're welcome." Nekai glanced at Harlow. "Would you like me to stay?" A half smile curved his mouth. "Maybe give you another lesson in being fae?"

No way. Keep him away from us.

Harlow returned his half smile, but shook her head. "Not right now, but thank you."

Nekai looked disappointed. "You know how to reach me if you need me." With another little wave, he left.

A messenger passed him on the porch steps. Just a teenager, the kid held out a package to Augustine. "For you, sir. Guardian, sir."

Harlow walked down to Augustine's side as he accepted the package. The boy was tall and thin with a smattering of freckles.

Augustine looked at the package. He gave it a little shake. Something rattled. "Nothing damaged in here, I hope."

"No, sir." The boy tugged at his jacket. "I was very careful."

Augustine's hand was on the door. "Very good. Thank you."

"You're welcome, sir." He turned to go, then stopped, something else clearly on his mind. "Rue's in my grade and she's a nice girl and anyway, I hope you get her back, sir."

Augustine's smile was strained. "We will. I promise." He shut the door. The reminder of the situation settled visibly around his shoulders, slumping them with its weight. "If this doesn't work…"

She grabbed his arm. "That's what I've been trying to tell you. I've got a plan."

He lifted his head, a new light in his eyes. "I'm sorry I didn't have a chance to listen earlier. Giselle can wait a few minutes. Let's go into the library and you can tell me everything."

"You're sure?"

"Absolutely." He brushed a strand of hair out of her eyes, his fingers just shy of touching her forehead. "I haven't had as much time for you lately as I've wished and I'm sorry about that."

"Thanks. I appreciate you saying that."

"Does that mean you forgive me for keeping your mother's secret?"

Forgive him, Ava Mae begged.

Harlow nodded. "Yes." She had her own secrets now. "My mother is the most stubborn woman I know. You didn't have much choice."

"Truer words were never spoken." He winked at her and started toward the library. "Let's go, Harley, I'm all ears."

Smiling while Ava Mae giggled, Harlow went after him. She didn't even care that he'd called her Harley. Well, she didn't care *much*. He took a seat on the couch, patting the spot next to him. She sat, happy he was so responsive, but hoping that mood continued after he heard her idea. Ava Mae's idea, actually, and Harlow had no clue if it was even possible.

He leaned back and draped his arms over the couch. "What's the plan?"

She took a breath and began. "To use my gifts to search for Rue. I thought about trying to find Branzino the same way using the business card he gave me, but I tried to read it and too much time has passed. It's just a blank piece of paper now. But there's lots of Rue's stuff to be had."

He nodded slowly. "Okay, but your powers don't really work that way."

"Look, my mother could see futures, so why isn't it possible that with a boost, so could I?" Although she had a feeling working in concert with Ava Mae might eliminate the need for help of any kind. Even if that was the case, she'd still need some kind of explanation for why her powers were suddenly so strong.

"A boost?"

"I understand that a group of fae who share the same bloodlines can amplify another fae's powers. Like an antenna."

His eyes widened. "That's true. They have to be both related and of a like kind. How do you know about that?"

She thought fast. She couldn't very well say her dead twin had told her about it. "I think Dulcinea mentioned something about it." Now for the tricky part. "And I know you have a brother and sister…"

The hope in his eyes extinguished. "Half brother and sister. Neither of whom are exactly my best friends."

She scooted closer. *Touch him*, Ava Mae urged. Harlow put her hands on his leg. "They'd do it for Rue."

He looked away for a moment. "I wouldn't count on it. You don't know what you're asking."

"So tell me."

"Think about all the extra stuff that came through even when Dulcinea acted as a buffer the first couple of times you read something for me. Linking with them to strengthen your power means everything gets laid bare. Because of your skills, they'll see every aspect of my life. And I'll see theirs. They're not going to want that any more than I do."

"Why? What happened that caused all of you to become so estranged?"

"I don't want to go into it."

She shot him a look. "Really? After all we've been through, you can't share this with me?"

He stared at his hands, but the pain in his eyes was clear. "Blu and Mortalis and I share a father. He was a serial adulterer. Their mother, Kyrianna, was a member of the Elektos here. They're an old New Orleans family. At the time this all occurred, she was poised to be Prime. You know how the Elektos are—very proper, very by-the-rules. My father's running around was the one thing that threatened her being voted in by the rest of the council. They argued that if she couldn't maintain the sanctity of her home, how could she rule the city? So she gave him an ultimatum—cheat on her again and she'd leave him. He promised he was done. Told her he hadn't touched another woman in ages."

He scrubbed a hand across his face. "A few months later, the election meeting was held at Kyrianna's house. The Elektos were gathered to discuss her election." He sighed. "Before the vote was taken, my birth mother, who had finally managed to track my father down, showed up on Kyrianna's doorstep with me in her arms, demanding my father make things right."

"Yikes," Harlow whispered.

"Yikes is right. Until then, my mother had no idea my father was married and had another family. Not only had he used magic to make her believe he was human—"

"That sounds familiar." Harlow shook her head. Ava Mae snorted.

"But he'd lied to her about being married. When my mother realized the full extent of what he'd been hiding, she was mortified. But the damage was done. Kyrianna not only wasn't elected Prime, she was asked to step down from the Elektos until she could straighten her family situation out."

"What did she do?"

"She threw my father out, but she never really recovered from the embarrassment. From what I've been able to gather, she petitioned to have my father deemed *rek'vamus*—"

"That's a fae word, right? What does it mean?" She could feel Ava Mae huddled down, listening.

"It's like…an outcast, but more than that." Augustine hesitated. "The absolute and total removal of a person from all records. *Rek'vamus* is the equivalent of having never been born. Getting my father declared *rek'vamus* would have meant she could have asked for an annulment. That she could have reclaimed a sense of dignity in her life."

Harlow raised her brows. "But that would have made Blu and Mortalis illegitimate."

"No, fae are more concerned with maternity. But the council ruled the only way to pronounce my father *rek'vamus* was if I was declared *rek'vamus* also. I was the proof of his sins." His gaze went to a very faraway place. "Kyrianna refused. She knew that doing that would mean I'd have absolutely no chance for a life within fae society, and while she was furious with him, she refused to punish me."

"That was the act of a mother."

A sad smile bent his mouth. "It was, but Blu and Mortalis never really forgave her for that. Or me. And so, with the council refusing her request, she retreated to the fae plane and promised never to return to this world. As far as I know, she's kept that promise."

"The fae plane doesn't seem like the kind of place anyone would want to live."

"Not in the part you saw. But there are other areas that are beautiful beyond your dreams. Cities that defy imagination. I'm sure she's not suffering, but…"

"Her children are."

"And have been since she left." He sighed and nodded. "Blu

and Mortalis blame my mother and me for the loss of both their parents."

"But that wasn't your fault or your mother's. You were just the outcome of his infidelity, not the reason all that happened."

He shrugged. "They've also never been happy with the way I've lived my life, claiming that all I've done since I was born is bring shame to their family. Mortalis was civil to me at Olivia's funeral, but being civil and helping are two different things. He and Blu have more to get over than me. I get that."

She sat back. "I had no idea."

He patted her knee. "Don't feel sorry for me, I did fine without a brother or sister."

"I just can't imagine knowing they existed but that they didn't want anything to do with you."

He pulled out his LMD and checked the time. "That's nothing compared to losing your twin. Never knowing that connection...now that's something I can't imagine." He tucked the device away and leaned his forearms on his knees. "How are you doing with that? You seem surprisingly okay with it."

"I'm dealing."

Ava Mae nodded. *You're a good sister.*

"You know twins born to haerbinger fae sometimes carry a special power. More than just the ability to read futures, they can see a person's death. When, where, how...all the details. In that case, the twin with the ability is called the Gemini, but in order to maintain that power, they can only feed off the other twin's blood."

Harlow screwed up her face. "Gross."

He laughed. "That's only in the case of purebloods, which you're not, obviously, so don't freak out unnecessarily."

She shuddered. "Good. The last thing I need is a bout of vampirism."

"Just thought you'd want to know a little more about the

kind of fae you and your sister are." He stood. "I have to get to Giselle's."

"What about my idea?"

"It's a good one, but I don't think they'll do it, Harlow."

She rose to her feet, standing in his way. "You have to at least ask."

"I will, but don't get your hopes up."

You can't just let him go like this, Ava Mae murmured. *Give him some... encouragement.*

"Do your best to persuade them." Emboldened by her sister's words, Harlow grabbed the lapels of his coat, went up on her tiptoes and kissed him hard. Ava Mae cooed with delight.

He kissed back, wrapping his arms around her and making appreciative noises. When she pulled back, he smiled and ran his tongue over his teeth. "Not that you need a reason, but what was that for?"

"Encouragement." All the warm feelings that had poured into her didn't hurt either. She was on the verge of becoming addicted to that, especially now that he wasn't hiding her mother's secret anymore. The emotions came through much purer.

He laughed. "Well, I have to say I do feel very encouraged." He brushed his thumb over her cheek, sending another wave of deliciously affectionate and happy emotions through her. The hidden parts of him seemed to have disappeared. "I'll fill Fenton in on your idea and have him reach out to Blu and Mortalis. Blu might say yes, since she's Loudreux's personal bodyguard and will probably feel obligated to the family, but Mortalis, I don't know."

Harlow tapped her finger on his chest. His very hard chest. "What if you contact that woman that was with your brother at the funeral? The one with all the gold markings. Explain it to her and see if she can help you convince Mortalis."

Augustine's mouth opened slightly and he shook his head.

"You're amazing, you know that? That's brilliant. She owes me one, actually." He kissed her nose before heading out of the library. "I don't even care that you have a criminal record. Harley Goodwin, you're a keeper." He laughed as he left, leaving her giddy and warm from her toes up.

Oooo, Ava Mae moaned. *I like him a lot. Let's seduce him.*

Ava Mae, settle down. I'm still getting to know him. Harlow shook her head, slightly miffed by her twin's suggestion. But it was hard to be truly upset. Ava Mae did have an awful lot of good ideas.

Chapter Twenty-five

The enormous crowd at Evander's made blending in easier than Augustine had expected. He hung near the back, slowly scanning the crowd to catch as many people on camera as possible. Fenton was monitoring the feed back at the Pelcrum and using the com cell from Augustine's LMD to communicate with him, although Augustine had to be a little more circumspect in replying.

"Quite the crowd," Fenton said.

"Mm-hmm." Augustine turned toward the open part of the yard, where Giselle had set up the sacred circle.

"By the way," Fenton said, "Yanna's here with me. If you have any issues with that, look at the ground."

Augustine kept monitoring the crowd.

"Good. I see they took care of the weather like I predicted. Takes a hefty spell to do that. I wonder how many of them are maintaining it?"

Augustine leaned back to give Fenton a better view. Although the sky above Evander's estate was still cloudy, there was no rain. That changed at the property line, where a steady drizzle had been coming down for the last half hour. Because he couldn't have driven the Thrun here and taken the risk of being recognized, he'd walked. His umbrella now leaned against a chair on the patio with a host of others.

The crowd shifted. People moved aside, making a path. Cormier opened the door from the house, then stepped aside.

Giselle and Zara came out. Giselle wore a white robe while Zara wore one in dark green trimmed in white, both with the hoods pulled up. Giselle carried a large, ancient book and had a short bone-handled dagger tucked under her belt. Zara clasped a white rose. They walked through the crowd without speaking to anyone, eyes straight ahead, stopping only when they'd arrived at the center of the circle.

"That's chalk or lime," Fenton said. "I'm sure they did that so the boundaries of the circle wouldn't be accidentally broken by a guest."

Augustine realized he was looking at the pentagram and surrounding circle that had been mapped out on the grass in a powdery substance. Four white candles sat at even intervals around the circle while white flowers marked the points of the pentagram.

Zara stood behind and to the left of Giselle. Some in the crowd moved to stand at the circle's edge.

"Those are all coven members from what I can see," Fenton said.

Giselle lifted a hand in greeting. Her voice rose above the rain's thrum. "The circle has been cast, the four corners called. So turns the wheel of life."

The coven members repeated the phrase. "So turns the wheel of life."

"There are many here who are not of our coven. Some may have come out of curiosity rather than respect for my father. For those of you for whom that is true, I acknowledge your bravery." Her eyes took on a sinister gleam. "And your foolishness. No disrespect will be tolerated."

A little nervous laughter swept through the crowd. A few people backed up. Augustine held his ground.

"I first welcome the thirteen into the circle."

That number of men and women entered, most in black but all with a touch of white somewhere. Augustine squinted at it.

Fenton's voice filled his head. "White is the color of death for the witches."

Augustine nodded in understanding. One of the men who'd entered the circle took a position very close to Giselle, and the looks they exchanged seemed more intimate than was proper for such an occasion. "Who is that?" Augustine whispered.

"Checking," Fenton responded. "Found him. Ian Dufrene. He owns the House of Pain tattoo parlor on Magazine Street." Fenton whistled. "He and Giselle look well acquainted."

That they did. Augustine nodded slightly.

When the thirteen were in position, Giselle spoke again. "The rest of the coven in attendance may join us now."

A lot more people entered the circle, making it harder to see her, but the crowd slowly moved to the sides and back so that those outside the circle had a view.

She nodded to those around her. "Let us begin. For those of you outside the circle, I ask that you remain quiet and respectful until the ritual is over."

She opened the book. "From the book of shadows that has always led us, may the words of our ancestors guide us still." She began to read. "We grieve not for him who has gone from our world, but instead celebrate his passing into the Summerlands. In this way his death has brought him new life. Think not of sorrowful things, but rather focus on the memories of Evander Vincent that will bring you the most joy and strength. Find peace in this time and allow him to go in peace as well."

She closed the book. "Those of the coven who wish to speak or offer blessings may do so now." She stepped back and Zara moved forward.

Zara laid the white rose she'd been carrying at the center of the circle. "Go in peace, Daddy."

One by one the others came forward, each with some small offering or a slip of paper that Augustine imagined carried a spell or a blessing or whatever they called it. A few spoke of their memories of Evander. He surveyed the rest of the audience. A few looked as bored as he felt, but there was no sign of Ogun. He was about to call the plan a bust when he caught movement out of the corner of his eye.

Ogun approached the back of the crowd. Augustine looked at him long enough for Fenton to pick up on it, then shifted to Giselle. She was almost scowling, her gaze arrowed in on the voodoo doctor.

"Excellent," Fenton said. "Unfortunately, this means you're going to have to hang around long enough to see what happens between them."

"Mm-hmm." Augustine guessed that would take at least an hour, and that's about how much time had passed when the coven members had finished saying their goodbyes. Some of them were very long-winded, although most of the thirteen had been succinct. Ian had said very little. Augustine wondered if there was a correlation between those who'd supported Evander and those who'd had the most to say.

When the last of the coven had spoken, Ian stepped into the center of the circle. Giselle was behind him to one side. He bowed to her, then turned to the crowd. "May I present our new high priestess, Giselle Vivianna Vincent."

The coven behind him spoke in unison. "So mote it be."

He swept his hand out toward her, bowing again. "My lady."

Giselle returned to the center of the circle. Her eyes were on Ogun. "Thank you. I would now like to invite the rest of you into the circle to pay your last respects and wish my father a safe journey."

Fenton's curse rang through Augustine's head. "She's trying to tip Ogun's hand. If he enters that circle, any protection spells of his will be negated. So will yours. I'm sure Nekai explained it."

Augustine nodded.

Fenton clicked his tongue. "Of course, if you don't enter the circle, you could draw suspicion. It might be best to leave now while you can."

Augustine lifted his hand to cover his mouth. "Not yet." He worked his way through the crowd, most of whom were headed for the circle, until he got to the house. Cormier stood at the door. Augustine plastered on a friendly smile and pointed to the door. "Do you think I could pop inside to use the facilities? Too much coffee. You know how it is."

Judging by Cormier's expression, he clearly didn't. He opened the door anyway. "First left off the kitchen, sir."

"Thanks." Augustine went inside. He slipped into the bathroom, but as soon as Cormier shut the door, he made his way to the front of the house.

"Augustine, you're taking too big a risk." Fear edged Fenton's voice. "If you're discovered..."

"No one knows who I am. And if I'm discovered, I'll just say I was admiring the antiques and got carried away."

Taking the stairs as silently as only a shadeux fae could, he found a room that looked out over the backyard. The shelves on one side held rows of ancient books and the floor was well-worn wood that seemed to bear the markings of numerous sacred circles.

"Looks like Evander's personal altar room." Fenton made a small noise in the back of his throat. "How many spells have been cast in here?"

"Too many." As much as Augustine wanted to rummage around, the task at hand took precedence. He moved to the window. The crowd milled about, but Giselle still held court at the center of the circle. Ogun stood just at the chalk boundary.

"He's not going into that circle," Fenton said.

Augustine cracked the window, hoping to hear a little of whatever conversation might take place. "He'll have to. Giselle isn't about to move."

"You can't just sit there, waiting."

"Why not?"

"Because eventually someone will come in. Or Cormier will realize you haven't come out."

"I'll cross that bridge when I get to it." The crowd was beginning to disperse. Giselle and Ogun held their positions, although Zara was walking toward him now.

She stopped while she was still inside the circle. With a lot of the crowd gone, hearing them was easier. She spoke first. "You shouldn't have come."

Ogun puffed out his chest. "I came to pay my respects."

Zara smiled and held her hand out toward the circle's center. "Then please, step into this sacred space."

Ogun didn't smile back. "You know that's not going to happen."

Zara's smile turned into one of self-satisfaction. "Then leave."

"I need to speak to your sister."

Zara shrugged. "Well, you know where to find her." She tipped her head toward the circle's center, then walked away smiling.

"Sir?" Cormier's voice rang out below. "Sir, are you here? I can't have you wandering through the family's personal space."

"This was what I was talking about," Fenton grumped. "You've got to get out of—wait a moment. Yanna has an idea." A few mumbled words escaped Augustine. "Hold on, we're going to try something."

Footsteps announced Cormier's presence on the second floor. The phone rang. A few rooms away, Cormier answered it. "The Vincent house. Yes, this is he. Ah, I see, sir, I hadn't realized you'd left. Your umbrella? I'll check if it's still outside. Yes, I'll hold it until you return. Thank you again. Goodbye." Footsteps retreated as Cormier went back downstairs.

"He bought it." Fenton's voice was bright with an unseen grin. "Yanna suggested we use a sound synthesizer to mimic your voice, and now Cormier thinks you left through the front door, but forgot your umbrella."

"Nicely done." Ogun still stood at the circle's edge. His arms were crossed and he was staring at Giselle, who had yet to leave the center. Augustine pinched the bridge of his nose. "This is going to take forever."

A door opened and closed and a new voice sounded from downstairs. "Cormier, could you fix me a cup of tea?"

"Of course, Miss Zara."

"Thank you. Is there anyone else in the house?"

"No. There was a guest who came in to use the bathroom, but he's gone now."

"Good. On second thought, forget the tea. You should probably check on Giselle, see if she needs anything."

Augustine went back to watching the standoff. Cormier appeared, but Giselle brushed him off. Then Augustine heard more footsteps. An earthy, flowery scent followed. Zara. Damn it. She must be close.

He went into shadeux mode, a kind of wispy half-form he'd figured out as a kid that had made hiding from his mother's anger much easier, and tucked himself into the corner behind one of the tall cabinets. It wasn't perfect invisibility, but in the shadowy recesses of the room, on this kind of gray day, it was pretty close.

He could still see out the windows but the distance made it harder to hear. At least now that the crowds were gone, Giselle had stepped outside the circle. She argued with Ogun. A few words and phrases drifted up, things like "Don't threaten me" and "...die first."

Zara walked into the room. Her ceremonial robe was gone, leaving her long skirt to tangle around her ankles. He pressed against the wall. If need be, he could, according to Fenton, pass right through it in his smokesinger form, but he'd never actually done that. Fortunately, the books on the opposite shelf were holding her interest.

"Abort," Fenton growled in his head.

He shook his head slowly, trying to tell Fenton no. That wasn't really possible at the moment.

The door slammed shut downstairs.

"Zara?" Giselle's voice.

"Up here," Zara answered.

He'd either picked the very best or the very worst room to hide in.

"Get out of there." Augustine could hear panic in Fenton's voice. "Go into smokesinger form and slip through the wall and onto the roof. You can drop to the ground and walk away like nothing happened."

Easier said than done.

Giselle walked in, the book of shadows in her hands. "I released the weather spell right after Ian left. As soon as the rain started coming down, the rest of the stragglers took off. Great way to clear out unwanted guests."

"Giselle spelled the rain away on her own? Impressive," Fenton muttered.

Zara spun. "Why was Father Ogun here? He certainly didn't come to pay his respects."

Giselle popped her jaw to one side, eyes glittering with anger. "Can you believe that slimy piece of voodoo trash? Trying to intimidate me at my own father's passing ceremony. The nerve. I should—"

Zara slid the book in her hand back into place with a loud

thunk. "Tell me why he was here. If we're going to work together, there's no reason to hide anything from me."

Fenton exhaled loudly. "On second thought, hug the wall and stay right where you are."

Giselle set the book of shadows onto a small wooden stand, then put her hands on her hips and faced her sister. "There's something you need to know and you're not going to like it."

"Here we go." Fenton practically hummed with excitement.

"Just tell me." Zara sat on a small bench against the wall. Augustine could still see most of her if he looked through the glass panels of the cabinet.

"Before Daddy died, he was involved in some very questionable things."

Zara didn't look nearly as shocked as Augustine had expected. "Like what?"

Giselle pulled a velvet-tufted ottoman from a corner and sat. "You remember those vampires that got into the city, the ones that killed the last fae Guardian and that old fae movie actress?"

Anger pinged through Augustine at her casual mention of Olivia.

Zara nodded. "Yes, what about them?"

"Apparently Daddy was involved in that."

Fenton's soft curse was echoed by Yanna's louder one.

Zara thought a moment. "I still don't understand what that has to do with Ogun being here."

Giselle sighed with great dramatic flourish. "Unfortunately, our father felt he'd gotten too far in and decided to get out while he still had a chance. He bought *bokura* powder from Ogun and used it to stage the suicide of that fae lieutenant—"

"The one that was in the papers? The one who hung himself?"

Fenton snorted. "I highly doubt Evander was responsible for

that. He was never one to get his hands dirty. Giselle, on the other hand..."

"Yes. Daddy gave him the *bokura*, then commanded him to hang himself, leaving a note that took the responsibility for the vampire infestation upon himself. Ogun is now threatening to tell the police everything because they're bearing down on him and he's worried he'll end up taking the fall."

Zara shook her head. "What are we going to do? If the fae find out a witch was involved in this, we'll be regulated out of business."

"I know. That's why I'm bringing you into this. I know I'm high priestess now, but this is *our* family legacy. We're in this together."

"I agree." Zara stood and walked to the shelves. Giselle twisted to keep her eyes on her sister. Zara trailed her fingers over the books before speaking again. "There's only one real solution I can think of."

"What's that?"

Zara opened her mouth to speak, then closed it again and smiled. "Something that perhaps you should let me try before I explain any further. Do you trust me and my abilities?"

Giselle stood. "Yes, of course, but I can't let you do something that might allow all this to blow back on you."

Zara laughed lightly. "My magic is too pristine to allow blowback. Besides, I would never do anything to bring greater harm to our family. Only a clearer path for us."

Giselle looked unconvinced. "I don't know. Ogun isn't some typical human. He knows what we're capable of and he's got power of his own."

Zara grasped her sister's shoulders. "What's gotten into you? You're defeated before the battle's even begun."

Giselle shook her head and glanced around the room. "It's this house. It's like I can feel an unkind presence here."

Zara nodded. "I feel it, too. I promise you, once I've taken care of our voodoo friend, I'll smudge every speck of negative energy out of here. When I'm done, you'll have a clean slate and you'll be able to move in and make it your own."

"It's the *only* way I'll be able to move in." Giselle picked the book of shadows back up. "No point in leaving this here, I suppose." She hugged it to her chest, turning slowly as she looked around the room. "If there's anything here you want…" Her gaze slid over the spot where Augustine stood.

"I don't need anything from here."

Giselle's gaze stayed on the corner. "That presence we were feeling might be closer than we thought."

Sturka. They might not be able to really see him, but they must be able to sense him. He had only one option. Go smokesinger and pray he could maintain the ethereal form necessary to glide through the wall and out of the house.

"Get out of there," Fenton yelled in his head. "Think smoke."

Big help. But Augustine did his best. He felt lighter. Was that a sign it was working? He imagined himself able to pass through the wall. His extremities went numb. If they found him here, war would break out.

Rain dampened his shoulder. Part of him was through the wall. The realization almost broke his focus.

"Whatever it is, it's getting away. If Ogun thinks he can send one of his spirits to spy on us…" Zara stepped in front of her sister and drew a pinch of dirt from a small pouch at her waist. She tossed the soil into the air toward him. "Unwelcome spirit, I bid you leave or by this earth your powers cleave."

Augustine made one last push, the effort draining him. He leaned against the wall, his boots biting into the shingles to keep him from sliding. Rain trickled down his face. He looked up and saw sky. Exhaling in relief, he worked his way to the edge of the roof, dropped to the ground and took off for home.

Chapter Twenty-six

Harlow cut the last biscuit out of the dough and set it in line with the others.

"Those look real good, baby girl." Lally smiled. "Real good. You're a fast learner." She bumped her hip against Harlow's. "Don't you think you're going to take over my job now."

"Never." She lifted the tray of snowy white biscuits. "Can these go in the oven?"

"Mm-hmm. Bottom oven, middle rack." Lally pointed with her elbow, her hands too busy shifting the pot of greens. "Now all we need is Augie."

The door opened and Augustine came in, dripping water.

"Speak of the devil," Harlow said.

The very handsome devil, Ava Mae added. *Let's kiss him again.*

Lally threw a dish towel over her shoulder. "Land sakes, child, you're soaked."

"Rain has a way of doing that." He grinned until his gaze landed on Harlow, then his eyes narrowed. "I feel like there's something weird going on here."

Harlow froze. Did he know? Could his fae senses pick up Ava Mae's presence? "What? There's nothing weird—"

"You're wearing an apron and there's something that looks strangely like flour on your cheek. Are you...baking?" He said the word like it was *skydiving* or *belly dancing*.

Harlow rolled her eyes to hide her relief. "Lally's teaching me to make biscuits. Which you're going to eat, so I'd behave unless you want me to drop yours on the floor."

He leaned a hip against the counter, making a face at Lally. "Did you watch her closely? I'm a little afraid."

Lally threw a towel at him. "The two of you are like beans and rice."

Harlow looked at her. "What's that mean?"

Augustine bent down to whisper in her ear. "She means we go great together."

Lally chuckled behind Harlow, nudging her with an elbow. "He's right. You do."

Was Lally trying to push them together? It wouldn't be the worst thing that could happen. *Especially if it happens soon*, Ava Mae added. Harlow changed the subject. "How did it go at Giselle's? Did you get enough to bring her in and question her?"

"Not exactly. We got some new information, but honestly, it sounds more like lies. The whole thing was both more and less than I expected it to be." He sighed. "I'm willing to give your method a try. Fenton's talking to Blu as we speak and I'm going to call Mortalis tonight." He went back to leaning against the counter. "You're right that nothing in the past should matter. Mortalis and Blu and I just need to get over our issues. We've got to get Rue home."

She smiled. It was nice to be agreed with. And to finally have a plan. "Good. That makes me happy. I appreciate you doing this."

"Nothing to appreciate. I shouldn't have argued with you in the first place." He shucked his wet coat and hung it by the door. "I'm going to take a hot shower, then come downstairs and eat like a horse. Please tell me you made a lot of whatever I'm smelling."

"Crawfish pie and greens," Lally answered.

"Plus the biscuits that I made," Harlow added. "And sweet potato pie that I helped with."

"Damn skippy. This is going to be a fast shower."

Lally waved him away. "You got fifteen minutes before it hits the table."

Harlow grabbed his arm to keep him from leaving just yet. "If Mortalis agrees, how soon before he can get here?"

"Instantly. He can travel by mirror like the rest of us."

A nervous tremor went through her as she released him.

He squinted at her. "You ready for this?

She nodded, "I'm ready." *We're ready*, Ava Mae echoed. "You know that I'm doing this because I want to find Rue, but you have to understand it's also because I want to find Branzino."

"I know." The light in his eyes shifted, darkening into something feral and frightening. The look shot pleasure through her bones that this man was on her side. "And you need to understand that I have no intention of letting Branzino live. I realize we have the evidence necessary to put him in the Claustrum for the rest of his life, but that would be too merciful a reward for the things he's done."

Ava Mae tried to pet him with Harlow's hands. She stuck them in her pockets to keep from embarrassing herself.

Harlow nodded. "I'm with you a hundred percent."

"Good." He tipped his head toward the stairs. "I'm going to grab that shower now."

"Okay." She watched him leave as she ignored Ava Mae's pleas that they join him. It was good that Augustine had no plans for Branzino to survive the hunt. His being okay with Branzino's death was important. It meant that when the time came, he'd be less shocked when she was the one who caused that death.

We, Sister. When we cause his death. You're not in this alone anymore.

That's right. Harlow nodded. *And won't Branzino be surprised when his firstborn turns out to be the death of him after all?*

While Augustine was in the shower he worked out what he would say to Mortalis. Getting his brother to agree wouldn't be easy, although Augustine knew Mortalis wouldn't argue with the end result. Bringing Rue home was as good a reason as any to attempt to boost Harlow's powers.

And for both of them to finally get beyond their anger at what had happened all those years ago.

Asking full-blooded shadeux fae like Blu and Mortalis to share the emotions and memories of their childhood was like asking sharks to learn to cuddle. They were raised to be warriors and both worked in personal security, the perfect job for fae who'd been trained in the lethal arts of their kind since childhood.

Augustine dried off and got dressed, the tantalizing scents of supper wafting up from the kitchen. If Mortalis said yes, the evening's activities would take a very interesting turn. Even if projecting Harlow's powers didn't work, Augustine and his half siblings would still be subjected to the sharing of memories.

For a moment he pushed that reality aside. If Harlow couldn't find Rue via this method, he didn't know what they'd do. They could bring Giselle in, but he had a feeling she'd just shut down if they didn't have something concrete to leverage. And any action against her now that she was the coven's high priestess would have greater consequences.

His other hope, the security camera monitoring system Harlow had put in place, had turned up nothing. Wherever Branzino was hiding Rue, it was locked down tight.

Augustine picked up his LMD and scrolled through his

contacts. Not surprisingly, Mortalis was there. Fenton had anticipated possibilities Augustine had yet to imagine. He tapped the screen, dialing the number.

"Hello?"

"Mortalis?"

Silence for a second. "Augustine?"

"Yes. I have a favor to ask you."

"I'm sure you do. I can't imagine any other reason you'd be calling."

Augustine bit down the retort burning on his tongue. "The daughter of our prime, Rue Loudreux, has been kidnapped by a very dangerous raptor fae. Harlow's father, actually. We need your help. Harlow would like to try projecting her powers and—"

"And you need two other like-blooded fae to help."

"Yes."

"No."

Augustine almost pulled his LMD back to look at it. Mortalis's refusal had come a lot more quickly than expected. "You haven't even heard me out. And this is for Rue."

"What's to hear? It's a good cause, but you don't need Blu and me. Get three other fae to help you. Fenton and Loudreux and his wife. Use them. Rue's their daughter."

Augustine stared at the ceiling and tried to maintain his calm. "They're cypher fae. And Fenton's not related to them. Besides, shadeux blood is a lot stronger. You know that."

The doorbell rang. Augustine started down the steps to see who it was.

"Be that as it may, I'm not interested in the repercussions."

"I know what happened was a bad scene for you. I get that. But you're not the only one who grew up without a mother and father. At least you had some time with them. And you had other family." He hit the first floor landing. Lally was reaching for the door handle. "You're not the one who ended up on the streets."

As Lally opened the door, Hugo Loudreux burst through it. Anger and pain lit his eyes. "You." He pointed at Augustine. "If you don't find my daughter in the next few hours, I will kill you myself and turn you over to these kidnappers."

Augustine finished his descent. "Has something new happened?"

"Something new?" Spittle flew from Loudreux's lips. "This." He thrust a box toward Augustine.

"What's going on?" Mortalis asked.

Augustine reached to take the top off. "Is this from the kidnappers?"

"Yes," Loudreux ground out. Tears wet his cheeks.

Augustine lifted the box's lid. Nestled inside the tissues was a bloody piece of flesh. His stomach roiled.

"I'm guessing that's Loudreux." Mortalis's tone seemed a bit more subdued. Less combative.

Augustine stared at the slice of freckled skin. A tiny seven sat squarely in the midst of the pale triangle. He pointed to his head and told Loudreux, "I have Mortalis on the line." Then he spoke to his brother, but his gaze stayed locked on Hugo, who was in that moment not so much the Prime as a desperate, grieving father. "Hugo Loudreux has just come in with the latest delivery from the kidnappers. They first sent us a ransom note, then Rue's pinky finger. Now it seems they've sent us the tip of her ear."

"Oh." Silence followed Mortalis's soft inhale.

Loudreux lifted the box a little higher. "This came with a note. If proof of your death isn't made public by sunrise, the next thing they'll send is her body."

Mortalis cleared his throat. "I can be there in two hours."

"What? Why two hours?"

But Mortalis had already hung up.

⚜

"It really is beautiful here." Giselle stood in the midst of Zara's garden, the koi pond to her right. "If you can give me half of this at Daddy's house—"

Zara clucked her tongue. "Enough of that. It's your house now. You have to stop thinking of it as his. While I honor Mother's presence here, this is certainly not her house anymore."

"You're right. It'll be different once I get the remodel done. On my house." She smiled. Her long white ceremonial robes discarded, her ivory cashmere sweater coat now shielded her against the cool evening.

Zara tossed a handful of pellets to the koi. "I went through the same thing when I moved in here, although obviously I kept all of Mother's things. It just took me a while to think of it as mine."

"Good to know." She turned to watch the fish gobble down the food. "Thank you again for being with me during the ceremony."

"Of course." Zara smiled mysteriously, quickly shifting her gaze to the pond. "And thank you for letting me deal with Ogun."

Giselle laughed softly. "Are you going to give me a hint as to what you're planning?"

Zara shook her head. "I think some things are best left to the witch who conjures them."

Giselle walked to the bench and sat. "I still can't believe he had the nerve to show up today."

"It was disrespectful."

"I'm sure he's even less happy with me after I told him that under no circumstances would I be turning myself in. I couldn't care less that the police have been hounding him—" Giselle's air disappeared like a hand had clamped around her throat. The crystal tattooed between her shoulder blades burned. She clawed at her neck, then slapped the bench with the other hand to get Zara's attention.

Zara came running over. "What's wrong? Are you choking on something?"

Giselle shook her head as she gasped for air. Stars danced at the edges of her vision.

Zara took Giselle's face in her hands. "Wind that bends the tree and vane, make my sister breathe again. Whatever harm within her dwells, cast it out and show the spells."

Giselle's lungs filled suddenly. She coughed, hacking and hacking until she spat something out.

Zara scooped it up before Giselle could stop her. She stared at the thing in her palm while Giselle rubbed her burning throat. "I feel like I swallowed acid." Her voice was raspy and thin. "What is that?"

Zara's eyes burned with green fire. She held out her hand so Giselle could see what she'd coughed up.

She looked at the thing, then up at Zara. "Is that...hair?"

Zara dug it open with her fingernails. "Hair, feathers and a piece of black string." She ran her fingers over it. "Just as I thought. Coated in ashes."

Giselle recoiled, her hand still on her neck. "How on earth did that get in my throat? Where did it come from?"

"Everything we need to know is here. This is voodoo magic."

"How do you know?"

"Feathers to tickle the throat, string to tie it closed, black because it's meant for death, with the ashes to burn away the evidence once it's done." She picked out a strand of the hair and squinted at it. "This must be your hair. How would Ogun have that?"

Giselle coughed again, anger steeling her against the pain in her throat. "He ripped a few strands from my head as I was throwing him out of my house a couple days ago."

Zara's hand closed around the evil charm, tightening into a fist. "If he thinks his little games are any match for what we can do, he's sorely mistaken. No one takes this kind of action against my sister. You're the high priestess now. Did he think he could get away with this? Ogun is going to pay."

Giselle nodded, an idea churning in her head. Ogun clearly thought she and Zara were no threat, but he didn't know that she'd just found a way to increase her power. Hadn't he noticed how easily she held the sacred circle and maintained the spell keeping the rain at bay? Or maybe he hadn't realized she was doing all of that herself. Either way, it was time to give Zara the same opportunity Ian had given her. "He underestimates us," she rasped.

Zara nodded. "Yes, but I'm about to put an end to that. One or two more spells and I'll be ready to take him on."

"A few more spells? To strengthen yourself?"

"In a way, yes."

"What if I told you of another way to increase your power?"

Zara looked skeptical. "Let's go inside and talk. I'll make you a cup of tea that will heal your throat."

Giselle nodded and followed her sister into the kitchen. A few minutes later, with a steaming cup of tea in front of her, Zara sat down with her at the kitchen table. Giselle took a sip, the hot liquid coating her throat and instantly soothing it.

Zara pushed the crock of honey toward her. "So what's this way to increase my power?"

"Ian."

Zara grinned. "Maybe we're not talking about the same kind of power."

Giselle stood, shrugged off her sweater coat, then turned and unbuttoned her blouse, letting it slip down to reveal her back.

Zara gasped. "You let him tattoo you? I'm surprised. And impressed. I never figured you for the kind of girl who'd get inked. I've got a few myself, but—"

"But none like this." Giselle faced her sister as she buttoned her blouse up. "Ian can strengthen your powers by tattooing you with the thing your powers are derived from. Which I imagine, in your case, would be some kind of plant? You don't have to tell me the specifics. But you would have to tell him."

"And you have proof this works?"

"I maintained the sacred circle while also holding the spell that kept the rain away."

"I thought a few of the coven members had cast the weather ward."

"No." Giselle took another sip of tea. "All me."

"Okay, I'm impressed. Those are two big spells that require concentration, in addition to keeping your poise while speaking to the guests and reading the rites of passage." She nodded. "I'm interested. Especially since our enemies seem to be increasing daily."

Giselle smiled. "I'll set it up."

Zara bit her bottom lip. "As long as Ian is coming over, there is one more element I need to complete this garden and the magic I hope to work here. I know that he's yours and I wouldn't ask this if it wouldn't eventually benefit you as well, but…"

"The Great Rite." Sex magic. The kind that would imbue a place with a depth of power and stability few other rites could provide. She could see by Zara's nervous expression how difficult a thing it had been to ask.

Zara gave a little half shrug. "You know what, forget it. I can find someone else. I don't want to do anything to come between you two."

Giselle reached out and took her sister's hand. "I would be happy to let you have him. On one condition."

Excitement sparkled in Zara's eyes. "Name it. Anything."

The Great Rite strengthened with each participant. "You let me join you." She smiled. "Then I don't have to wait to benefit."

Chapter Twenty-seven

Dinner had been good, but quick. They'd gotten back to the business of finding Rue as soon as it was over. Harlow smiled. The biscuits had been a success, though.

A soft knock turned her away from watching the cam feeds.

Augustine stood in the door of her office. "Mortalis is on his way, although he's not traveling by mirror for reasons I don't know. He's also not answering my calls anymore. Fenton and Blu just got here. They're in the library with Hugo."

"I cannot believe Branzino cut off the tip of Rue's ear." Her anger at her father, at what he was capable of, only strengthened her desire to find him. And kill him. *We will.* "He deserves no mercy."

None, Ava Mae snarled in agreement.

"He won't get any from me." Augustine glanced at the monitors. "Anything?"

"No."

"Why don't you come downstairs then, and meet Blu."

She got up from her chair. "She's not going to like me."

"You don't know that."

"She knows I'm on your side. I would think that's enough."

A hint of a smile showed on his face. "Come on, it won't be that bad." He started for the steps and she followed. "Now, Mortalis…"

She kept following him until they were in the library. Hugo was in a chair in the farthest corner, a clear sign he wasn't interested in being disturbed.

He brought her to Blu. "This is my half sister, Blu."

"Nice to meet you." Harlow held out her gloved hand.

Blu glanced at it, but didn't shake it. "How soon can we do this?"

"As soon as Mortalis gets here and you show Harlow a little respect. You have no reason to be angry at her." Augustine shook his head, clearly unhappy with his sister's lack of social grace.

"I don't want to delay this any more than you do," Harlow reassured her.

Blu frowned, but gave Harlow's hand a quick shake before crossing her arms. She looked very much like a female version of Augustine, except more petite and with darker skin. And possibly the inability to smile. Blu also seemed more likely to cut you than give you a chance to explain yourself. Her head-to-toe leathers displayed a variety of weapons strapped here and there. Daggers, throwing stars, and something that looked like an ice pick, but undoubtedly had never been used in conjunction with cocktails.

Fenton stood near the Gutenberg Bible display case, the light from it casting a halo around him. He left it to greet Harlow, coming to her side as though sensing she needed him. "Harlow, thank you for being such a help in our search for Rue."

"Of course." She nudged Augustine.

He nodded. "Thank you for agreeing to do this, Blu."

Blu lifted her head slightly to look at him. "It's only for Rue."

"I know."

Harlow jumped in. "I'm going to do everything I can to keep the flow between you three to a minimum."

Blu's gaze shifted to Hugo. "Don't waste energy on that. Just concentrate on finding Rue."

She's right, Ava Mae said. *We need to concentrate on locating Branzino.*

Rue, Harlow corrected. *Branzino is the bonus.*

Lally came in. "I've got coffee going and I can make tea if anyone wants it."

Fenton nodded. "The coffee is a good idea. It could be a long night."

The doorbell rang again. Harlow headed for the door. "I'll get it, Lally. We need the coffee more."

Lally nodded and headed for the kitchen. Harlow pulled the door open. Cy, Dulcinea and Sydra stood on her front porch. "Come in. Augustine's in the library with Blu, Fenton and Loudreux."

Dulcinea and Sydra went straight into the other room, but Cy paused in the foyer. "You're really brave to try this."

She smiled. "That's kind of you to say, but we're all doing what we have to in order to get Rue back."

He shrugged, his massive shoulders rising like cresting waves. "It's still brave."

"Thanks." She tipped her head toward the other room. "We should go in."

He nodded and gestured for her to go ahead of him. When they walked in, Augustine looked up from talking to Dulcinea. "There you are. Okay, we're all assembled. Fenton just heard from Mortalis. He's flying in."

That was odd. "Why?"

"He's bringing Chrysabelle." Augustine's jaw popped to the side in obvious frustration.

"It's not like we can't use the help. I guess. Who's getting him from the airport?" Harlow asked.

Blu answered. "Amery. He's our cousin."

Harlow looked at Augustine. "You have a cousin? Why not let him take your place in the circle then?"

Blu answered. "Greater chance of it not working. He's twice removed." She slanted her eyes at Augustine. "Unfortunately, projection works best when the bloodlines are as close as possible."

"I see." She almost laughed when she saw Augustine's expression. Apparently his relationship with Blu had always required an amount of long-suffering.

Blu shrugged. "Of course, if Augustine backs out because he feels incapable of—"

"I'm not backing out," he growled. "If everyone could have a seat, I'd like to go over best- and worst-case scenarios."

Which they did, for the next hour and a half, until Augustine raised a hand. "Hold on, incoming call. Answer. Hey, Amery." He nodded, listening. Then he frowned. "Are you kidding me? *Bala'stro*. I knew he'd pull something. Give me a sec." Grimacing, he looked at Fenton. "Can you grant a special dispensation to allow a vampire access to the city?"

Harlow tensed, causing Ava Mae to jitter with nerves. *A vampire? Why would they let a vampire in? They're the enemy. I don't like this.*

I don't know, Harlow answered. *I don't like it either.*

Fenton looked as confused as Augustine looked agitated. "I can, but can I also ask why? I thought Amery was at the airport picking Mortalis up."

"He is. Mortalis brought Mal *and* Chrysabelle with him."

Harlow was on the verge of freaking out, but she couldn't help it. She backed up, sweat beading along her spine. "Of course. Chrysabelle's married to a vampire, isn't she? Is that Mal? Is he the vampire?" What if the vampire touched her? What if his touch made her raptor side take over completely? She clenched her hands to stop them from shaking. "Why would Mortalis bring them both?"

I can control that side of you now, Ava Mae said. *I won't let it hurt you.*

"Yes, Chrysabelle is married to a vampire and yes, that

vampire is Mal. As to why Mortalis would bring them, I'm assuming to help, which isn't bad in theory, but not when it upsets you like this." He moved to her side. "You don't have anything to fear from Mal. He's nothing like the vampires that invaded the city."

She blew out a breath and nodded, but he couldn't understand. Not really. "I'm going to wait in the kitchen with Lally. Just keep him away from me."

"I will. I promise."

Don't worry, Ava Mae purred. *If he touches us, I'll kill him myself.*

Their need for Ian wasn't something Giselle had wanted to discuss on the phone, but he'd happily agreed to come to Zara's at her request, even with few details. She opened the door for him when he arrived.

He smiled. "I got here as soon as I finished up with my client. You made it seem like it was urgent."

"It is. There was an incident after the ritual this afternoon." She couldn't keep the anger off her face as she closed the door.

"What happened?"

Hot, angry tears blurred her vision. She looked away, not wanting him to see her so weak and vulnerable. "Father Ogun—"

"I saw him at the ceremony. He wanted something from you, didn't he?"

She nodded, her fingers twining in the cord tying her ceremonial robe together. She and Zara had redressed in preparation for the Great Rite. "And I wouldn't give in to him, so he cast some kind of voodoo spell on me. If Zara hadn't been there, I would have died."

He cupped her face in his hands, forcing her to look at him. The metal of his rings was a smooth contrast to the rough embrace of his palms. "There is nothing I wouldn't do for you. Say the word and he is gone."

"No," she whispered, the intoxication of his touch stealing her breath. "Zara and I will deal with him. But that's why you're here. You brought your things as I asked?"

"Of course." He kissed her, more reassuring than provocative, before letting her go. "You want more ink? More power?"

"We both want one."

He nodded, smiling a little. "Excellent." He looked down the hall. "Where is Zara?"

"In the garden meditating."

"It's chilly out there."

She trailed her fingers down his cheek, his stubble rough under her fingertips. "Not for her. Set up whatever you need to and then meet us in the garden."

"You want me to tattoo you outside? I'm not sure that's such a great idea. It's kind of dark and—"

"No, set your things up in here, then meet us outside. Don't take too long."

He nodded. "I'll be right there."

Giselle went to join her sister, who knelt in the midst of a newly cast sacred circle. It was much smaller than the enormous one they'd used for their father's last rites ceremony and quite balmy inside thanks to Zara's earth magic. "He's here."

Zara stood and brushed the bits of grass off her robe. "Did you tell him?"

"About the Great Rite?" Giselle laughed softly. "Not yet. I thought we could do that together. Surprise him."

Zara smiled and nodded. "I like that. And you're sure we can trust him? There's no way he's not going to realize the real purpose of the rite."

Which was to imbue Zara's garden with another layer of power and stability so that whatever magic she planned to perform here would have a much greater chance of succeeding. If Giselle had to guess, it was chaos magic, the same kind their mother had died performing, but Zara had made it plain she didn't want to reveal what she was up to just yet. Giselle rested her hand on Zara's arm. "Ian's no fool. He's not going to betray us, not when he wants the fae oppression overthrown as much as we do."

"Well then, he'd better perform like the goddess is watching."

As they laughed, a voice interrupted them.

"This place is amazing." Ian set his bag down on the stone patio before walking onto the lawn. He stopped a couple feet from them, a sly smile curving his lush mouth. "What are you two planning?

Giselle stood shoulder to shoulder with her sister. "Come into the circle and we'll show you."

He entered. "Now I see why the cool air doesn't affect you."

"Thank you," Zara said.

Giselle waited until he made eye contact with her. "Your high priestess has need of you."

"Anything. Name it."

She looked at Zara and gave her a slight nod. At the same time, they both untied their robes and let them fall. "We'd like you to join us in the Great Rite to strengthen all magic that will be performed here."

Despite the fact that they both stood before him naked, Ian kept his eye contact with her, never faltering once. His respect for her position was astonishing. "I would be honored."

Giselle slid her hand into his hair and kissed him hard as Zara came around from behind and began to undress him. "I do love a man who obeys."

Chapter Twenty-eight

Augustine met Mortalis at the door. Mal and Chrysabelle stood behind him. Amery had wisely stayed in the car. Augustine stared his brother down. "What the hell do you think you're doing?"

"You asked me here." Mortalis shifted slightly. He was as heavily armed as Blu, and by the looks of Mal and Chrysabelle, so were they. It was a point in their favor that they'd come armed for battle, but a slim one.

"I asked you. Not them. You could have had the decency to clear it with me."

Mortalis frowned. "You would have said no."

"Exactly." Augustine glanced at Mortalis's company. "No offense, Mal, Chrysabelle, but considering Harlow's mother was killed by vampires and she was later held at knifepoint by one, you can't expect her to greet you with open arms."

Chrysabelle shook her head. "That poor woman."

Mal grunted. "I knew this was a bad idea."

Mortalis shot the vampire a look before returning to Augustine. "Inside." He held his finger up to Mal and Chrysabelle. "A moment."

Augustine didn't move. "No. Right here is fine. It's not like Mal won't be able to hear the conversation through the door anyway."

Mal snorted. "He has a point."

With a beleaguered sigh, Mortalis began. "You need the help.

These two are combat-capable. Probably more so than your sorry band of lieutenants."

"They're not sorry—"

"*And* if I'm doing you a favor by being here, you can do one for me by letting Mal participate in this."

"You already owe me a favor for helping Chrysabelle get into the Claustrum."

Mortalis shook his head. "*She* owes you that favor. As does Mal, because the actions that followed saved his life. Consider them being here as that favor being paid back."

"You're splitting hairs." Augustine stared at Mortalis long and hard. He briefly entertained the idea of calling Amery in to take his place. He shifted his gaze to the vampire. Mal was one of the most dangerous vampires he'd ever known. And not the sort to do something out of the goodness of his heart. "I find it hard to believe you'd come out of some sense of duty. There must be more to this."

Chrysabelle cleared her throat and put a hand on Mal's arm. "Augustine, you helped me and I know that caused you no small amount of trouble, so let me help you in this and make that up to you. As for Mal, he is here because I am here, but also because good deeds help him to...erase past sins. Every one he does makes his life easier and, by extension, mine. So please, let us help."

It was hard to be angry at her. This was Mortalis's doing, but Augustine's first priority was Harlow. She was about to put herself through an ordeal. She didn't need any added stress. "You can stay and help, but Mal has to keep his distance from Harlow." He shook his head. "On one hand, I appreciate the extra help. We have no idea exactly what Branzino's got up his sleeve, but he cannot continue to terrorize Harlow and this city. On the other hand, I'd like to send you both the hell home."

She nodded. "If it helps, I've killed a raptor fae before."

Augustine frowned. "I know. I'm the one who let you into the Claustrum, remember?" He stepped out of the way to let them into the house, pointing at the library. "Wait in there."

Then he went to the kitchen where Harlow was still holed up with Lally. "They're here. And they're truly here to help."

She nodded and rolled her shoulders. "I'm sure they are."

Lally wiped her hands on a kitchen towel. "I'll be in my room if y'all need me."

"Thanks, Lally." He sat down beside Harlow. "Look, I have zero intention of trying to talk you into liking either one of them. I don't like vampires any more than you do, but Mal's not exactly like the fringe that invaded the city." He was actually much, much worse. "He's a noble vampire, which means he's descended from old blood. Nobles take care of their blood needs with a comarré, which is what Chrysabelle is, a special breed of human whose blood is so much better than ordinary humans', nobles never need to bother with those humans."

Harlow slanted her eyes at him. "Really?"

Augustine nodded. "It's a pretty symbiotic relationship. But, on the slightest chance that he hurts you in some way, I'll kill him myself. You know I'm capable of that. Vampires stand no chance against shadeux fae."

She nodded, smiling a tiny bit. "You'd do that for me? I mean, he's your friend's husband and all..."

"But you're my..." He hesitated. They were more than friends, but *girlfriend* seemed like kid stuff. "You're very important to me. And I don't care if he's the president of the Southern Union, you matter more."

Harlow stared at her gloved hands, trying not to smile and failing. "Thanks. I like being very important to you. You're very important to me, too."

"So you're okay with them being here?"

All traces of a smile vanished. She sighed, then nodded slowly. "I don't want any contact with him."

"I know. Once we—once *you* figure out where Branzino is, I'll station them at the perimeters. I and my lieutenants will be the ones who actually go in."

"And me."

He tipped his head. "Harley, I know you want to be a bigger part of this, but you're already doing more than you should. It's not safe—"

She slipped a glove off and laid her hand over his, her skin as warm and soft as sun-kissed silk. "I deserve to go."

The warmth of her touch sank deeper into him. New thoughts formed in his head. Would letting her go be so bad? He could protect her. She was helping so much. For that reason alone, she deserved to go. She *should* go. He nodded. "You . . . do deserve to go."

"And no matter what your lieutenants say, you're going to stand by that, right?"

Her hand stayed on his arm. He would, because . . . they were a team. Of course they were. "Yes."

"Because we're a team."

"That's right."

She leaned in and kissed him lightly on the mouth. "Thank you." She slipped her hand off his and put her glove back on. Her smile seemed a little sad to him. "I'm ready to give this a shot if you are."

His arm felt cold where her hand had been. He blinked, the oddest sensation running through him. "You can do this. We're all rooting for you."

She nodded, smiling a little more confidently this time. "Thank you. I'm nervous, but nothing ventured, nothing gained, right? Let's go find Rue."

❧

I told you we could do it, Ava Mae said. *And Augustine just proved it.*

Harlow stared at the foyer floor. *But I didn't like doing that to him.*

We had no choice, Ava Mae reminded her. *He wouldn't have let us go otherwise.*

Augustine went ahead of her and opened the library doors. As much as Harlow disliked using her new skill of persuasion on Augustine, being the center of attention was worse, and that's exactly what she'd become by walking into the library. She stopped outside the open doors.

Breathe, Ava Mae said. *We're going to do just fine. Look how well you did convincing Augustine to let us go on the raid.*

I know, but that doesn't mean I don't feel bad for tricking him.

I'm sorry you feel bad about it, but we had to do it. We needed the practice. We needed to be sure.

Ava Mae had a point. *I guess that's true.*

What would you have done if he'd refused to let us go? I have to find my peace. I only wish it wasn't so hard on you.

Harlow shook her head. *No, it's okay. We're in this together. To the end.* Her sister deserved to find peace. For that, Harlow could deal with a little mental discomfort.

Ava Mae preened a tiny bit. *Thank you, Sister. Now we must make good on our promise to find Branzino.*

Harlow nodded in response, then realized how odd she must look to everyone watching. She lifted her head and walked into the library. The furniture had been moved back, creating an open area in the center of the room.

In one of the far corners stood the comarré, Chrysabelle, whom Harlow had first seen at her mother's funeral. At the

woman's side was the vampire. He looked like the personifica-
tion of darkness. She shivered and found another place to focus
her gaze.

"You must be Mortalis." She stretched out her gloved hand.
"We didn't get to meet at the funeral, but it was very nice of you
to come then and it's even nicer of you to come now."

"It was the right thing to do." He shook her hand.

If not for his darker skin and the more serious set of his eyes,
he could be Augustine's twin. Their shared bloodline was very
obvious. Had that contributed to the trouble between them?
How could Mortalis and Blu deny Augustine was their sibling
when the resemblance was so plain? "If you and your sister and
Augustine could..." She looked around for Dulcinea. "Have
you ever done this? I don't know how to set it up."

Dulcinea smiled like she was happy to have something to do
besides stand and watch. "I've seen it done. You need to be in
the center, with them around you."

Dulcinea held out her hand to Loudreux, who still sat at the
edge of the room. "Prime Loudreux, if you could bring the article of Rue's to us?"

He stood, heaved out a sigh and walked over. From his coat
he pulled a small, tissue-paper-wrapped object and handed it to
Dulcinea. "No one's touched it since Rue. She's had it since she
was a baby."

Dulcinea carefully peeled back the tissue to reveal a small
stuffed cat. Its pink fur was worn off in a few spots and one eye
had been replaced with a button. Loudreux sobbed once at the
sight of it, then slunk back to his chair and collapsed into it.

"I'll hold on to this until everyone's in place." She nodded to
Augustine. "Stand in front of her." Then she directed Mortalis
and Blu. "You two at equal distances from your brother and
around her."

They took their places. Harlow looked at them, but they

offered no reassurance. She turned her face toward Augustine. He smiled at her as if she'd already accomplished her task. As if failing wouldn't change a single thing between them, and in that instant, she believed that was exactly the truth.

But the light in his eyes wasn't just confidence in her. It looked like...love.

I told you, Ava Mae said. *He loves us.*

Me. He doesn't know about you.

Ava Mae just laughed. But Harlow couldn't find that kind of lightness inside herself. She couldn't even smile back.

"Hey," Augustine's voice was a soft whisper, meant only for her. "Don't be afraid. It's going to be okay." His eyes were as kind and caring as she'd ever seen them. "Don't worry about us at all. Just do whatever it is you do when you read something."

But he had no idea what she'd done to him. And no idea about the real reason Branzino wanted this house. There were secrets between them and she hated that.

Please, Ava Mae begged, as if sensing the war in Harlow's head. *You can't say anything to him, not yet. You and I have to be together on this or it won't work. We're a team now. That's the only way we're going to take Branzino down.*

Harlow nodded. "We're a team," she whispered.

Augustine's smile grew bigger. "Good."

Yes, very good. Ava Mae's happiness almost overwhelmed Harlow. *I'm ready when you are, Sister.*

Chapter Twenty-nine

Ian sat bent over Zara's prone form. He'd set up his tattoo table in the living room after they'd all come back inside. Giselle glanced at the new ink adorning the inside of her wrist. The tiny shard of crystal throbbed, but so did the new sense of power within her. Perhaps the Great Rite had done more than sanctify Zara's garden.

"Ready?" Ian asked.

"Mm-hmm," Zara replied. Her postcoital glow had yet to wear off.

The sting of his needle would take care of that, Giselle thought. Although Zara already had a few tattoos, so she might be used to the pain. A ring of ivy around one ankle, a rose on the other, and now she'd be adding a tree of life between her shoulder blades, the same place Ian had put Giselle's first. Apparently plants of any kind were the source of her power.

Ian went to work, the hum of his machine filling the space. Giselle pulled her robe around her and wandered through the house. Memories of her childhood came flooding back, each room bringing something new.

She found herself upstairs and finally stopped as she approached the door that had once led into her mother's bedroom. Surely this was Zara's room now. She put her hand on the knob, then hesitated. Just a peek. She opened it and looked in.

The room looked exactly as she remembered it. She pushed the door a little wider and flicked the light on.

Zara hadn't changed a thing.

Giselle glanced downward, the buzz of Ian's needle faint but audible even up here. There was something oddly sweet and a little sad about Zara's leaving this room exactly as it had been. Giselle had always thought Zara sentimental, but not to this extent.

She looked around the room, careful not to disturb anything, although there wasn't a trace of dust anywhere, so Zara either had bespelled the room or cleaned it regularly. What secrets had her mother hidden here? All witches had them, and her mother had loved her journals. They'd found volumes of them after her death. She'd kept track of things as random as the weather, the first simple spells she'd taught them, and the names of the neighbors who'd bothered her most.

Her spells were all written down in a different set of books: what worked, what didn't and why. By keeping all of that separate, she'd essentially created a new book of shadows, which had undoubtedly proved immensely useful to Zara, since she and their mother were the same kind of witch.

But there'd been nothing in them for Giselle, although she'd pored over them in the first few weeks after her mother's death, hoping for that one special thing, that secret something she would know her mother had meant especially for her.

Giselle sat on the bed. Now that she thought about it, there'd been no mention of chaos magic in any of them. Nothing to even indicate her mother had worked on such a spell. Not in her book of shadows and not that Giselle could recall seeing in any of the journals.

Had Zara found it? Or was she still looking, too? Was that why the room remained unchanged? Giselle glanced around with new purpose. Zara was occupied. She might sense magic being performed in her house, but Giselle could explain that away if need be.

She raised her hands. "That which is hidden, come into view. Something left for Giselle without a clue."

A candle flickered to life. It sat on her mother's old rolltop desk. The flame burned tall and bright green, then died down to the simple yellow that it should be. Giselle went closer. The sides of the wide ivory candle were cut with designs adorned here and there with crystals.

She smiled. Crystals. The source of her power, something her mother had known very well. She picked up the candle and blew it out, then held it closer to the desk lamp. The designs on the sides seemed to have some kind of pattern to them.

She took the candle back to the bed and sat to study it further.

Could these designs be sigils? Chaos magic required a sigil to focus it, otherwise the power of the spell would simply disperse and the intended object would remain largely unaffected. If they *were* sigils, were they the ones their mother had used? The chaos spell she'd tried to cast had ended up killing her.

Trying to cast the exact same spell would lead to the exact same results.

Either way, this candle was coming home with her. She glanced at the clock. She'd been gone long enough. Candle in hand, she went back downstairs.

Ian spoke without looking up. "Almost done."

"How's she doing?"

"Very good."

"Zara?"

Zara turned her head to face Giselle. She looked almost sleepy. "Hmm?"

Asking her while she was distracted by the pain might work in Giselle's favor. "I didn't mean to nose about, but I went into Mom's old room and—"

"And I'm way too sentimental, I know that already."

"No, I think it's sweet, actually." She glanced down at her hands. "Would you mind if I took this candle? I don't really have anything of hers and it would be nice to have something."

Zara smiled. "Now who's sentimental?" She closed her eyes. "Take it. I'm happy you want something of hers."

"Thanks." That hadn't been the ordeal she'd expected. Maybe Zara was keeping the room the way it was simply as a shrine to their mother and not for any other reason. For a moment Giselle contemplated keeping whatever information she gleaned from the candle to herself, but in that instant she knew she couldn't. She and Zara were in this together. Her sister deserved to know. Especially if Zara was contemplating re-creating their mother's spell.

But that would have to wait for a time when they were alone. She wasn't about to reveal any of this in front of Ian.

"That's the last of it." Ian arched his back as he cleaned Zara off. He held out a hand mirror. "Go take a look."

She pulled the sheet around herself and went to stand before the big wall mirror, turning so she could see her reflection. "Oh, it's lovely. Small, but beautifully done."

He sat back and grinned. "This is one case where size doesn't really matter. How do you feel? Anything different?"

She nodded. "Yes, maybe a little different."

"Try something," Giselle urged. "That's what Ian had me do. Anything you've always wished you could be better at?"

Zara thought for a moment. "I hate revealing a weakness—"

"We all do," Ian said. "But I hope you know I consider this a sacred trinity."

Giselle wondered if Ian also hoped they'd include him in another Great Rite. Zara was a beautiful woman. What man wouldn't want to join them in such an act again?

"Thank you." Zara took another look at her reflection in the hand mirror before continuing. "There is something..."

She reached out toward a potted ivy that sat on an end table.

As Giselle watched, the ivy withered and died. "You killed that plant." That was the exact opposite of what she'd expected her sister to do.

Zara nodded, smiling. "I know! I've never been able to do that." She shrugged. "Not that I've had a reason to, but you never know. Someday I might." She wiggled her fingers. "And now I can."

"In that case, excellent." Giselle smiled, but she couldn't help but wonder what her sister was planning on doing that might require her to kill a living thing.

The need to keep her sister close and happy had never been clearer.

Augustine let the world around him melt away to focus solely on Harlow. She'd gone from nervous to afraid in a few short seconds. Could she do this? Maybe he should call it off. Then she closed her eyes, took a deep breath and seemed to find some calm. He took a breath himself, trying to force out some of his worry and concern for her, knowing she'd pick up on those emotions the moment they touched. Those kinds of feelings would only upset her and could ruin what she was about to attempt.

Dulcinea pointed at him. "Here's what's going to happen. The three of you will connect first. Each of you will put your left hand on the shoulder of the person to your left. Then, when she's ready, you'll use your right hand to touch Harlow. Has to be skin on skin, so the four of you need to shed some clothing."

Augustine pulled off his shirt, while Mortalis and Blu took off the top layers of their leathers, revealing body-hugging vests beneath. He really needed to get some of those leathers.

Harlow unzipped her sweatshirt and tossed it aside, which left her in a black tank top. The last time he'd seen that much of her skin they'd been at the ball. With no idea what was about to happen. She'd been so happy that night. He wanted to make that possible for her again. To fix all this and get them to a place where they could have a chance at figuring out what was developing between them. Their relationship deserved that chance.

And after tonight, hopefully they'd get it.

"Now," Dulcinea continued. "After she touches the stuffed animal, then you need to put your hands on her. Not before or you'll fill her head with your emotions and make it difficult for her to read the toy.

"Do your best to clear your minds and give yourself over to Harlow. Let yourselves be her instrument. Some of what happens might not be pleasant, but you're all adults. Deal with it."

"We're prepared for that," Augustine said.

Blu nodded, but Mortalis just grunted. Augustine ignored it. His brother's problems were his brother's problems. He'd agreed to help; now he'd have to deal with whatever came from that.

"Good. And whatever you do, don't break contact until Harlow tells you to." Dulcinea looked at Harlow. "You ready?"

Harlow nodded, only the tiniest sign of stress creasing the corners of her eyes, and shucked her gloves. "Yes."

Dulcinea held out Rue's little stuffed cat, touching it only where the tissue still covered it. He, Blu and Mortalis lifted their hands to grasp each other's shoulders. It was the first time he'd ever touched Blu. He'd touched Mortalis before, but only in a way that involved a closed fist.

Harlow took the toy. She looked at it for a moment, then slipped her hand into the wrapping and pulled the cat out. The tissue floated to the floor. She closed her eyes and stiffened slightly.

"Now," Dulcinea whispered.

The siblings lifted their right hands and laid them on Harlow. She tensed beneath Augustine's fingers, her sharp gasp cutting through him.

He opened his mouth to question her, but Dulce shook her head. Her voice stayed soft. "She's fine. Don't interrupt." She pinned him with her gaze. "*Clear* your head."

He frowned but nodded and tried to ignore his own thoughts and do as Dulce told him, but the feeling that he should be doing more was hard to—a jolt rocked him.

He closed his eyes as images began to filter in. Blu and Mortalis's mother sitting in a chair staring blindly at nothing with a very young Blu crying at her feet. A man packing. Another jolt hit Augustine as he realized he was seeing his father for the first time. Then another when he understood the images in his head were Mortalis's. He was seeing through his brother's eyes, watching the most awful parts of his young life unfold.

The emotions started after that. The deep and unending ache of loss. The kind of helplessness that killed off parts of you. Anger in great waves that felt like it could only be resolved by the sort of desperate acts that ended in blood.

More images. Through a window, Augustine saw his own mother. With a baby in her arms. The gleam of a blade. A horrifying chill ran through Augustine. Mortalis had stalked them. Planned to kill. Sweat trickled down Augustine's spine.

He opened his eyes. Harlow's were still closed and her mouth was moving. He focused on her for a moment. She was whispering Rue's name over and over. He glanced at Blu. A single tear track shone on her cheek. Then his gaze shifted to Mortalis.

His brother's eyes were closed, his mouth bent in what could only be pain. What was he seeing? Feeling?

But new feelings and images swept through Augustine, pulling him back into his own head. This time he saw Mortalis and anger filled him. These were Blu's memories and emotions. A deep sense of loss and disappointment. The feeling that she was going to lose not only her father and her mother but her brother, too. Had she been the one to stop Mortalis from coming after Augustine and his mother?

Harlow's gasp opened his eyes. Hers were open now, too. She stared at him but there was no way she was seeing him. Her eyes were clouded over with white. Her hands squeezed the little stuffed cat until her knuckles paled. Her lips still moved, the words impossible to hear, but slowly the sound increased.

"...Rue, Rue, Rue, Rue..."

No object Harlow had ever read had felt like this. She knew, without question, that the power within her was born of the joining with Ava Mae. Certainly the assistance of Augustine and his siblings had something to do with it, but they were supposed to be helping her project her gifts, not helping with the actual reading of the object. As soon as her hands had come into contact with the stuffed cat, the sights, sounds and emotions from Rue had poured in.

It was like she had become Rue. Harlow's head had filled with the knowledge that Mimi, although strict, loved Rue very much. And that Hugo, for all his bluster, was wrapped around his daughter's little finger, which was perhaps why Branzino had chosen to cut off that particular digit.

She sensed Rue's crush on Augustine. Saw the picture of him Rue had accessed on her father's computer and the girlish doodling on Rue's tablet of "Rue Robelais" over and over. Harlow smelled the perfume Rue had spritzed on before the ball. Felt the nerves that had overtaken her as she'd waited backstage to be presented, then experienced Augustine's presence as he'd calmed her.

Ava Mae sighed at the warm happiness that moment of Rue's life brought into Harlow's head. *He's perfect, isn't he?*

Not entirely, everyone has flaws. Harlow wanted Ava Mae fixated on Rue, not Augustine. *C'mon, help me find Rue. We can flirt with Augustine later.*

I am helping, Ava Mae pouted. *Don't yell at me.*

I'm not yelling. I just know we won't find Branzino without finding Rue.

Ava Mae sighed. *I know. Concentrating now.*

The happiness of Rue's life was replaced by fear as Rue realized her kidnapping was real. Panic vibrated through Harlow's body. She'd done it. She'd projected her ability to read into the future. Sweat trickled down her spine and her pulse raced. One by one the old memories of Rue faded away, replaced by a swirling white fog. Ava Mae's voice rang out in her head. *Call out to Rue. There is power in a name. Use it like a beacon to shine a path to her.*

Harlow began chanting the girl's name. Over and over until the repetitions became a beam of audible light shining into the unknown. The fog in her head expanded and she understood that she'd tapped into the minds of the three surrounding her. They had become vessels and her power had overflowed and filled them. Wisp by wisp, the fog in her head cleared.

A picture began to form. Sounds and smells followed. A concrete floor with walls of wood reinforced here and there with metal strapping, but no sheetrock covering any of it. Windows of glass block too high to see through. The spicy tang of something earthy mixed with other food smells as steam wafted over her skin. Her ears filled with the ramblings of a radio DJ. Behind his voice came the jangle of bells, the squeak and moan of wheels and the clip-clop of hooves. The unmistakable odor of dung followed.

Eyes still filled with the vision before her, Harlow stopped speaking Rue's name. "I don't know this place."

She heard Dulcinea's voice in the distance whisper, "Go ahead." Then Augustine spoke. "It feels like a warehouse at the far edge of the Quarter. Somewhere past the French Market. The spice of crawfish boiling is thick and I hear the tourist carriages going by. The smell of the mules is unmistakable."

Dulcinea's voice came in a little louder. "Harlow, can you hold on to the image?"

"I don't know."

Yes, Ava Mae promised. *We can hold on to it because there's more to come. But you must tell them it will only get stronger as we get closer. Tell them! You already know Augustine won't fight us going along. We're so close! Well done, Sister.*

Harlow cleared her throat. "I can hold on to it until we find her. In fact, the closer I get to her, the stronger the image will become."

"Then we can break the connection?" Augustine asked.

Yes, Ava Mae said.

Harlow nodded. "Yes. Take your hands off me now."

The three surrounding broke contact with her. The image flickered and Harlow blinked as the next image filled her head. She gasped as Branzino's evil face came into view. She jerked back, blinking as she realized her eyes had been open the whole time. Now, without the others touching her, she could see more than just the outcome of her search for Rue. Ava Mae clung to the last images that had come through as Harlow looked down at the little stuffed cat. She understood exactly the deception Ava Mae wanted her to perpetrate.

I don't know if I can lie to them.

You have to. It's the only way we can end this. The only way I can find peace. Do it for us.

Dulcinea held out her hand. "You've probably drained everything there was out of that toy."

Harlow looked up, about to hand it over, when the room

began to spin. She opened her mouth to say something, to warn them that she felt faint.

"Grab her," Dulcinea yelled. "Her eyes are rolling back in her head."

She started to collapse, but arms caught her and Augustine's smoky scent surrounded her. His face filled her field of vision. She reached for him, but another wave of dizziness hit her. Darkness closed in around the edges. A new image swam in her head. She was looking into a mirror, but her reflection was warped. She backed away but her reflection grabbed her by the wrists and started to pull her through the mirror. She tried to get away, tried to resist, but she lost her grip and, unable to hold on any longer, fell into the abyss that had finally come to claim her.

Chapter Thirty

Giselle drove the Mercedes home, but parking the vehicle took longer than she'd anticipated. Having a car might be a convenience, but not at this address. Not to mention that a car this nice wasn't meant for street parking. Moving into her father's house would solve that, of course, but the thought of leaving this house behind filled her with a sense of melancholy.

Keys in hand, she stared at the place she'd called home since she'd moved out on her own. She remembered the day she'd paid it off—earlier than expected, thanks to a particularly needy client with deep pockets.

Then the weight of the candle in her purse brought her back to reality. It was just a house. There were much bigger things to worry about at the moment. She unlocked the front door and went inside.

Before she flipped on the light, she felt another's presence. She threw her hands out before her. *"Duratus!"* She held the spell with one hand as she turned on the light with the other. Branzino sat frozen in her living room.

She pushed the front door shut with her foot, then walked over to him. The beauty of the simple immobility spell was that it only paralyzed the body. Cognition remained unaffected. "I told you I had rules about this sort of thing. I don't care what you need from me or why you're here, I will not abide these intrusions. I thought I'd made that clear the last time, but you are apparently either very stupid or willfully noncompliant.

Either way, the moment I release you, you're leaving. Am I clear?"

His murky gray eyes stared back at her, unable to do anything else.

She dropped the spell and thrust her hand in the other direction to point at the door. "Get the hell out of my—"

His beefy hand collided with her cheek, knocking her to the carpet. "You work for me, witch. Not the other way around. Remember that. Touch me with your magic again and I will kill you. Am I clear?"

She clutched her cheek, the taste of blood filling her mouth. She blinked, unable to focus. He started sprinkling something around her. It was white and sooty at the same time. Realization shot through her. Salt and ashes. A binding circle. She scrabbled backward, but he closed the circle before she'd gone an inch.

Fear made her breath short and her heart pound. "What do you want from me?"

He crouched so they were eye to eye and smiled. "See how much easier it is when you start with questions instead of assumptions?" He stood, the smile disappearing. "What I want from you is a spell that will protect me from a shadeux fae."

"Augustine," she muttered. "I thought you had it all worked out? Wasn't he supposed to sacrifice himself and save you the trouble of soiling your hands with his death?"

The hard glint in his eyes said she'd hit a nerve. Good. "Things are not going as quickly as I had hoped, but I've taken measures to speed things along. Now, I need this spell from you and I need it fast."

"I can make something that will help you, but it will take time."

"How long?"

"Four or five hours, maybe a little less. I have to research, find out what kinds of—"

"You have sixty minutes. And that includes delivery. I don't have the time to come back here." He tossed a card at her. "Bring it to this address in an hour. Make sure you're not followed and tell no one where you're going."

The card landed on the edge of the circle. "And if I don't?"

He leaned in and for a moment, she saw a flicker of the monster who'd first appeared in her house. "You've underestimated me, just as I underestimated you the last time I visited you, but you taught me a lesson that day."

He raised his fingers like he was about to expound on a point she needed to pay attention to. "I may be fae, but in the human world, I am a very different kind of monster. One who gets things done by whatever means necessary."

A tremor of fear swept up her spine, but she was too angry to give in. "And this means what to me?"

"That my skills are not limited to the othernatural world." He straightened. "If you don't show up in an hour with the spell I've requested, you won't receive the code."

"The code for what?"

"For the explosive device I've planted in this house. But I wouldn't waste time looking for it if I were you." He glanced at his watch, then kicked a hole in the binding circle, setting her free. "Get working, witch. Fifty-nine minutes and counting."

Augustine cursed under his breath as he carried Harlow over to the sofa and eased her onto it. "Come on, Harley," he whispered. "Don't fade on me now." She'd been so adamant about them no longer touching her when she'd locked onto the image of where Rue was that he knew the strain of the reading had finally become too much for her.

Dulcinea rested a hand on his arm. "She'll be okay. Give

her a few minutes. That was a pretty hard-core read she just pulled off. I'm surprised she held on to consciousness as long as she did."

"She's amazing." He sat on the edge of the sofa, his hand resting on Harlow's leg. Her pulse thumped in his ears, punching him in the gut with each stressed beat. "Calm down, Harley, let go of all those emotions."

"She will. I know you're worried, but she just needs some time now," Dulcinea said. "I have to agree with you on the amazing part. I confess, I wasn't her biggest fan at first, but she's got guts. She's come a long way for someone who didn't even want to admit to being fae."

Loudreux approached. "Save your sentiments. We need to go. Right now. My *daughter* is in danger."

Augustine looked up. Fenton was by the door. Mal and Chrysabelle had stayed near the far wall. Blu and Mortalis were side by side but not talking. Sydra and Cy hung close as if waiting for his command. Cy's eyes held deep worry and his gaze was stuck on Harlow. Augustine stood and faced Loudreux. "I agree, we need to go. And we will, just as soon as Harlow comes to."

"What?" he sputtered. "Why are we waiting? She'll be fine. We don't need her anymore. You three have the image of where Rue is. We're leaving now and that's an order."

Fenton stepped forward. "I can stay here with her if you like, Augustine."

He shook his head but kept his gaze fixed on Loudreux. "She's coming with us." There was no way he was leaving Harlow behind. She *had* to be with them. "We need her. What if we get down there and can't find the warehouse? She said herself the image will only get stronger as we get closer. Harlow is as important as any other member of this team."

Loudreux's left eye twitched. "The only one who matters to

me right now is Rue." He pointed toward the door. "Get out there and find her or I'll—"

"You'll what?" Augustine countered. "The Prime has no more control over the Guardian than I do over you." He reminded himself that in that moment, Hugo was merely a father afraid for the life of his child. Augustine took a breath and tried to speak more calmly. "I know you're upset and fearful and you want Rue safe. I want the same thing. But right now, you'd be most useful at home. I can't have you running on emotions and risking the mission."

Loudreux opened his mouth to argue, but Augustine ignored him and kept talking. He pointed at Mortalis and Blu. "Since you two saw the same thing that Harlow did, you can each take a team and head down there. Mortalis, you take Mal and Chrysabelle. Blu, take Dulcinea, Cy and Sydra. Try your best to locate the warehouse. If you find it, do whatever recon you need to do to make sure Rue's there. If she's in danger, do whatever's necessary to get her out. Otherwise, set up a perimeter and wait for me. Mortalis, your team will be responsible for making sure none of Branzino's crew escapes the warehouse. Anyone leaves, you capture them. Alive if possible."

He shoved a hand through his hair. "Branzino's known Harlow's bloodlines longer than she has, so he must know she's capable of doing a reading like this. There's a good chance he's booby-trapped the place and is anticipating our arrival. He wants me dead and has shown he doesn't care if Rue is collateral damage. That's why I want you to wait for me to get there before you go in. If I can draw him out of the building, and keep his attention focused on me, the rest of you can get Rue to safety without incident."

Harlow jerked like she was in pain, pulling his attention for a moment, but then she lay still again. "I'm sure it's no accident he chose a spot that's not far from a tourist area. Once you've located the warehouse, some of you need to quietly start diverting any tourists away from the location. Any questions?"

A few noes were muttered. Harlow's face contorted and her hands curled into fists like she was fighting something. A remnant of the read? He waved his hand. "Then go. We'll be there as soon as we can."

They filed out. Fenton paused. "I'll be in the kitchen with Lally if you need me."

"Okay." Augustine stayed at Harlow's side, watching as she moaned and convulsed. She was definitely struggling with something. Another nightmare, maybe. He wanted to wake her, but was afraid of disrupting her recovery.

After some of the longest minutes of his life, Harlow took a deep breath and opened her eyes. "Hey."

"Hey there." He knew his concern for her showed on his face, but he didn't care. They were alone and she needed to know he cared. "How are you feeling?"

She licked her lips and blinked a few times. "Not great, but I'll live. My head's killing me, but I guess that's to be expected."

"Probably."

She ran her hands over her body like she was checking to make sure she had all her parts. She struggled to sit up. He tucked a pillow behind her as she looked around the room. "Where is everybody?"

"Fenton's in the kitchen with Lally, Loudreux's gone home, and everyone else is off to the French Quarter to find the warehouse you saw."

She nodded. "I did it, huh?"

"You sure did. I've never been so proud of anyone—"

"I was just doing my part to help." She dipped her chin.

He inched closer. "What you did was everything. We had no real lead on how to find Rue. Without your help, we'd still be at square one."

Her reply came soft and short. "Thanks." She looked up at him again. "Why didn't you leave me and go with the others?"

"Because...we're a team. I said you could come with me and I'm keeping that promise. Besides, we may still need you to help locate that warehouse."

She perked up. "We should go then."

"You feel well enough?" He'd expected her to need more time.

"I feel great."

Not the response he'd anticipated, but so be it. He held her gloves out to her. "Put these on and we'll head out."

She took them but dropped them into her lap and reached for him instead, threading her bare hands through his hair and pulling him in for a long, hard kiss. He stiffened in shock, then quickly softened under her touch. She kissed him with a ferocity he'd never felt from her, scraping her teeth over his lip and holding on to him like he might try to get away. When her hands slid through his hair to grasp his horns, he broke the kiss, barely hanging on to his self-control. "Hello."

"Hiya." She smiled and reached up to drag a bare finger over one of his horns, sending another ripple of pleasure through him. "I've wanted to do that for ages."

"You have?" The look in her eyes seemed darker than any-thing he'd seen from her before. She looked slightly drunk. Doing such a huge reading must have really taken it out of her.

"Yep." She stretched her arms toward the sky before hunch-ing toward him again. "Augustine..." She said his name like it was a brand-new word. "Are you trying to make me fall in love with you?"

He shook his head, dumbfounded by her question and the

heady implication that maybe she *was* falling in love with him. Because he certainly was with her.

For a second he was breathless with what that meant. With the weight of being that committed to one person. With the sheer lightness that filled him at the possibility that this woman could care that much for him. "I'm not trying to...make you do anything." He smiled, unable to help himself. "But if you are, I'm okay with that."

She tugged her gloves on, a very satisfied smile curving her full mouth. "Let's go get Rue, shall we?"

While she got her coat, he jogged upstairs to strap on a few more weapons. When he turned, she was leaning in the doorway, watching him with a look that could only be described as possessive. "I want a blade, too. For protection."

He hesitated. "I suppose that's not the worst idea."

"You want me to be safe, don't you?" She held her hand out, palm up, and curved her fingers in. "Something I can hide in my boot."

He thought a moment, then reached down and unsheathed the one he kept in his own boot. "Take this one." He patted the hilt of his sword. "I don't need it as much with this at my side."

She sauntered over, took the dagger and tucked it away. She certainly wasn't looking or acting like she felt any residual impact from the reading she'd done, and she'd rested for less than half an hour. Maybe the excitement of finally finding Rue was giving her an adrenaline high.

They headed downstairs, said goodbye to Lally and Fenton, who'd decided to stay at the house, and went out to the car.

Harlow coasted her fingers over the hood. "I can't wait to go for a ride. This thing is amazing."

The cell com chirped in Augustine's head just as his LMD vibrated. "Hang on, got a call. Answer."

"Boss, it's Cy. We think we found the warehouse. I just sent you the address. No way to see inside, but Blu says she's picked up Rue's scent all over the place and considering they live in the same house, she should know. Also, we can hear a radio playing and Blu says it's the same one that was playing in Harlow's read. We've got the whole joint staked out. How long before you get here?"

Augustine pulled out his LMD and looked at the address. "Less than ten minutes. If he tries to leave with Rue before I get there, do whatever necessary to save her and subdue him."

"Only subdue?"

"I'd like to be the last face he sees."

"Understood."

Chapter Thirty-one

Harlow's anger tasted bitter. *Ava Mae, stop ignoring me. You can't do this. This is my body,* she raged from the depths of the hollow Ava Mae had vacated. *You can't just take control of it.*

Ava Mae finally responded to Harlow's ranting. *I know you're upset. I thought you'd calm down by now. Please don't be angry, Sister. It's just until Branzino is dealt with. Remember, I'm the firstborn. I'm the one who's been prophesied to kill him. And this way, you won't have to bear his blood on your hands.* Ava Mae smiled at the delicious man sitting in the driver's seat. Her sister had great taste in men. Making the switch while Harlow was knocked out from the reading had been work, but easier than doing it while she was conscious would have been. Harlow had proven stronger than Ava Mae had thought. Conscious, Ava Mae wasn't sure Harlow would have let her take over.

You should have asked me. And to ignore me like that was—

I'm sorry. It's not like I've ever done this before. I guess I let the joy of having a solid form get to me. I've been nothing but a disembodied spirit for longer than I can remember. But then you wouldn't know what that's like because you weren't murdered.

I guess. Harlow seemed mollified. *But I will take control back.*

Of course you will. Just as soon as Branzino is dead.

You promise? Harlow asked.

Cross my heart and hope to . . . yes, I promise.

All right. But keep your hands off Augustine.

"I'll try," Ava Mae muttered.

"What was that?" Augustine asked.

"I said...I like to fly. Going fast is fun."

Augustine glanced over. "That must be why you look so happy."

"What's not to be happy about?" Especially now that Harlow understood letting Ava Mae have control of their body was the best possible decision. Harlow was too timid. Too afraid. And Ava Mae had been kept from this life for too long. Besides, she was the one destined to kill their father.

Eyes on the road, he arched his brows. "We still have a long night ahead of us. I wouldn't get too confident yet." He gave a little half smile. "But yeah, we're a lot closer to where we need to be than the last few days, right?"

"Right." He had no idea. If not for the fact that she was about to get the chance to kill her murderous father, she'd already be seducing Augustine. Everything about him intoxicated her. His smoky scent. The buttery roundness of his words. The way he took charge of situations. The power he wielded as Guardian. Even the speed at which he drove.

But that came to an end as he pulled the car into a space. "We'll park here and walk the next block. I don't want to chance tipping him off."

"Good idea." She got out and followed him. The stars fascinated her. She'd never seen them through real eyes before. "They're beautiful, aren't they?"

"What?"

"The stars."

He nodded. "When we get back to the house, I'll show you how to climb up on the roof. The view is amazing."

"I can't wait."

He checked his LMD, then pointed forward. "Cy, Blu, Dulcinea and Sydra should be that way." Half a block and they turned a corner to find the other fae who'd been in the library.

Augustine nodded at the big one. "Cy, anything new since we talked?"

Cy shook his head. "No movement. Mortalis and his crew are in place around the block, covering all the exits."

"Good. Gimme a sec, Harlow." Augustine went into a huddle with a few of the others, while Cy came over to talk to her.

He smiled a little shyly. "You okay? What you did back at the house was pretty impressive."

"Thanks." The big fae had a sweet, mopey grin on his face. *This one has a crush on us, huh*?

I don't know about that. We just have some things in common.

He gave her a little wink. "And now on to the main event, eh?" He glanced down the street. "Ever starward."

She nodded. "Sure." *What's that supposed to mean?*

Beats me. Harlow gave a mental shrug.

He made a funny face. "I bet you'd love to have a working light blade right about now, huh?"

She twisted her foot out and pointed at her boot. "I've got a blade. Augustine gave it to me."

Augustine came over at that moment. "We're going to move on the warehouse. Cy, if you could give Harlow and me a second?"

"Sure, boss." He nodded at Harlow. "See you later."

When Cy left, Augustine pointed at her. "You're staying here. I said you could come along, but I'm not letting you get into the thick of it. It's too dangerous and I don't need Branzino taking another hostage."

She smiled sweetly. There was no point in arguing with him. She had no intention of going farther anyway. She held her hands up. "This is as far as I wanted to go anyway."

His brows lifted. "Okay then."

She laughed softly. "Expecting a fight?"

"Yes, actually."

"I'm stubborn, not stupid."

I'd put up more of a fight than that. He's going to know you're up to—never mind. Harlow cut herself off and a wash of regret flooded off her.

Ava Mae considered her sister's words. *Thank you, Sister dear.* She tipped her head and put on a stern face. "If you don't get Branzino tonight, I may be forced to go after him myself."

Augustine smiled. "There's the Harlow I know. We'll get him, I promise."

She put her hands on his chest, went up on her tiptoes and kissed his cheek. "Be careful. I don't want you getting hurt."

Stop kissing him.

He nodded, eyeing her with curiosity. Maybe she had pushed it too far. "I'll be fine. I have a good team around me. Speaking of which, I have to go." He jerked a thumb toward the group of waiting fae behind him. "Sit tight. I'll be back with Rue before you know it."

"Actually, if it's okay with you, I'll wait in the car." She looked up through her eyelashes at him. "The night is starting to hit me in a big way. I'm feeling a little dead on my feet."

Concern filled his eyes. "Of course. I'll have Cy walk with you."

"Oh no, please, don't take him away from the action. He's really looking forward to this."

"Okay." He hesitated. "Except you're not going to be able to get into the car without my LMD and the app to unlock it—"

She laughed. "Augie, that car is basically a computer on wheels." She wiggled her fingers. "It's cute you think I can't get into it without help."

He snorted. "I forgot who I was talking to. See you in a bit." With a little salute, he headed back to the waiting group of fae.

She waved back, then headed around the corner and broke into a jog toward Branzino's real location.

Perhaps it was Ian's ink empowering her, but Giselle finished the potion for Branzino faster than she'd imagined, considering her hands were trembling with a mix of anger and panic. Still, time was running dangerously short. The very idea that her home might be lost to that despicable fae—and that she had willingly partnered with him—made her sick.

She should have killed him when she'd had the chance, but her desire to see the witches regain their freedom had been too rich a prize. She was greedy. She knew that. It was ironic, really, that her desire to rid her city of the fae had led her to join with one. *Stupid, stupid woman.*

She could almost understand how her father had done the same thing.

She stuffed the vial in her purse. At least she had the benefit of her father's car. It would buy her a few precious minutes. She ran out of the house, locking her door with a flick of her fingers.

The Mercedes purred to life and she screeched out of the parking spot, caroming down the road toward the address Branzino had given her. It wasn't far, but it might as well have been the other side of the world. With Mardi Gras only one night away, tourists clogged the streets, already celebrating.

She leaned on the horn, casting dispersion spells like shotgun blasts to clear the way when necessary. But luck was not on her side. As she approached the location, there wasn't a parking spot in sight. "I don't have time for this," she growled.

If she lost her house over this, she would kill every blasted fae she could lay her hands on. When a compact hybrid swerved into the space she'd been aiming for, she screamed in frustration, threw the car into park and jumped out.

A mounted police officer brought his horse to a stop alongside the Mercedes. "Ma'am, you can't leave your car in the middle of the road."

"Here." She tossed the keys at him. "You deal with it."

"Ma'am!"

She ignored him, hustling down an alley toward the address she'd been given. The neighborhood grew less desirable with each step. She stopped in the shadows to read the numbers on the buildings. That couldn't be right, could it? The place looked abandoned. But that was probably the point. She was about to head for the door when a woman ran past.

Something about her looked familiar. Even in the streetlights, her cranberry-colored hair shone. That hair. Giselle had read a fortune for a woman with hair like that a couple weeks ago. A woman with fae blood who hadn't seemed to realize she was fae. She'd been wearing gloves just like this one. But there was something different about this woman. A dark aura that clung to her like a bad mood. What was she doing here? Was she in league with Branzino? One of his minions?

The woman stopped in front of the building Giselle was supposed to be going into. Giselle checked the time. She had thirteen minutes. She could spare a few to find out what was going on. The woman looked around, causing Giselle to shrink back into the shadows and whisper the words to make herself vanish.

Satisfied she was alone, the woman pulled one glove off and pressed her fingers to the keypad next to the lock, but she wasn't pressing the buttons, just holding her fingers against it. She must be using some kind of fae skill to disarm it. A few seconds later, she pulled the glove back on, turned the handle and slipped inside.

Giselle held the invisibility spell while casting another to slow the door's close. She reached it just before it snicked shut, slipping in after the mysterious woman. If the woman was working with Branzino, why didn't she just punch in the code to unlock the door?

The interior was darker than was comfortable, but that wouldn't matter to the fae. They had better night vision than humans. Giselle stayed where she was, letting her eyes adjust. The space looked like an old fruit-packing plant. Rubber-coated metal stairs led off to the right. They went up to what might have been office space and a balcony that overlooked the working floor.

With no idea what direction the woman had gone in, Giselle stayed where she was and listened. Faint sobbing. Definitely female and not too far away. She took a chance and brought her LMD to life so she could read the time. Ten minutes.

Taking an even greater risk, she quietly peeled away from her hiding spot and climbed the stairs. She took each step cautiously, whispering, *"Silencio"* over and over to muffle any sound. When she reached the top, she edged along the railing until she could see down into the floor below. Moonlight filtered through the skylights, casting pale rectangles on the rough concrete.

The fae woman wasn't visible, but someone else was. A hulking figure moved out from the shadows into the dim light. "Who's there?"

Giselle tensed. Branzino. She reminded herself she had every right to be here. He'd demanded she bring him the potion, after all. She should say something. She couldn't lose her house because of this other woman. It wasn't like Giselle had really thought Branzino was working alone anyway. She prepared herself to explain why she'd been eavesdropping, took a deep breath and—

"Hello, Daddy."

Giselle froze. Daddy? Eight minutes until the device Branzino had hidden in her house detonated, but the bomb that had just been dropped here suddenly seemed a lot more interesting.

Chapter Thirty-two

Augustine threw the radio pod against the wall, smashing it into pieces and silencing the DJ's endless chatter. The building was empty. "That *bala'stro*. He moved her." They'd scoured the building from top to bottom, but there was no sign of Rue or Branzino.

Blu nodded. "They were definitely here recently. Place reeks of raptor fae." She held out her hand. In it was a piece of frosty white fabric. "Plus I found a scrap of Rue's ball gown."

"Good. We'll give that to Harlow when she gets here." He'd sent Dulcinea back to the car to fetch Harlow. There was no way around it. They needed her. Needed a new lead.

Mortalis came inside. "Nothing I can find out here, but Mal might have something."

Augustine shook his head in frustration. "Then why the hell isn't he in here telling me this himself?"

Mortalis looked nonplussed. "You said you didn't want him—"

"Get him in here now."

"I'm here." The vampire walked in, Chrysabelle behind him. His eyes glinted with silver, a sign of his noble bloodlines.

Augustine stared at him. "What have you got?"

"Blood. Fae blood, to be specific. Mortalis said the girl was wounded, so it's probably hers."

"Can you track her?"

He nodded. "But the lot of you following me through the streets might draw some attention."

"Not a problem. I have to wait here for Harlow anyway."

Mal shrugged. "So let me find her and bring her back."

"No. She's been through enough. She's not going be rescued by a damn vampire who isn't supposed to be in the city to begin with." Augustine glared at Mortalis before looking at Mal again. "How long will it take you to find her?"

"Not long. The blood smells fresh."

"Then find her as quickly as you can, vampire, and get back here."

Mal's eyes silvered a little more, the glint seeming like a challenge to Augustine's authority. "And if she's in danger?"

Augustine glared back. "Then you're already wasting time."

Mal's nod was barely perceptible. A second later he dissolved into a cloud of black smoke and vanished into the night.

Chrysabelle looked after him, then sighed and shifted her gaze to Augustine. "Mal will find her."

"If he can't, Harlow will." Augustine ground his teeth together in frustration.

Dulcinea approached from the side. She'd been gone longer than he'd expected. "Boss?"

"Where's Harlow?"

Dulcinea sighed. "About that—"

"Out with it." His patience had reached a new low.

Dulcinea glanced toward the door. "She wasn't at the car or anywhere near it, I looked. In fact, there was no sign she'd even made it back."

"Branzino?"

"No sign he'd been there either." She shook her head. "If Branzino's moving Rue, he thinks we're onto him. Not exactly the time he'd be out looking for Harlow."

"So where is she?"

Dulcinea shook her head. "I have no idea."

Augustine pointed toward the street. "Get back out there and look." He waved Cy over. "Go with Dulcinea to look for Harlow. She's missing."

He opened his mouth like he was going to say something, then shut it.

"What?" Augustine asked.

He rubbed the back of his neck. "It's probably nothing, but she didn't seem like herself when I was talking to her earlier."

"Like how?"

"She acted like she didn't know anything about *Star Alliance*, for one."

Dulcinea made a face. "That geeky holovision show?"

"It's not geeky," Cy snapped. He looked back at Augustine. "She loves that show. But she didn't even recognize the *Star Alliance* greeting."

Augustine thought for a moment. About the aggressive way Harlow had kissed him when she'd woken up. About the new swagger in her walk. The way she'd asked for a blade.

Dulcinea crossed her arms and said what he was thinking. "Maybe the reading had a bigger effect on her than we thought."

Augustine shook his head. He'd chalked up Harlow's wanting them to stop touching her to the stress of the reading, but now he wasn't sure. The place she'd led them to was empty, and now she was gone. "Or maybe she's decided to go after Branzino herself." He muttered a curse. "I pray that's not what she's done."

A whirl of black smoke filled the space and Mal materialized out of it. "I found the girl. Branzino must have backup, because there are four heartbeats in the building."

Augustine glanced at Dulcinea and Cy before answering. "I have a pretty good idea who one of them belongs to."

Branzino blinked like he'd seen a ghost. "Harlow? What are you doing here?"

Ava Mae pushed her rage down. Losing control too soon would get in the way of her goal. "Yes, I'm here. Why so shocked? Isn't that what you wanted?"

"I didn't think—"

"No, you didn't." She straightened a bit, scowling at him like he had been a great disappointment to her. An expression that required no acting. "If you had explained your plans to me, given me a chance to be a part—"

"I gave you a chance." Anger glinted in his eyes.

"Don't you dare be angry with me."

A whimper came from one of the rooms behind him. *Rue. We have to save her.*

Ava Mae ignored Harlow. "You gave me an ultimatum. Big difference."

He planted his hands on his hips. "What now then? You want to be a part of the family after all the grief you've given me? I wish your brothers were here to see this, but I've already sent them home."

"Too bad. I would have loved to meet them," Ava Mae said sweetly. "Why don't you start by telling me what you want the house for?"

He snorted. "What does it matter? I can't do a thing with that house until you own all of it. You want to be part of this? Kill Augustine. It's the only way you're ever going to own the whole thing outright."

Her hand clenched, itchy for the blade. Instead she held her smile and shook her head. "Why can't you be honest with me, Daddy? Why can't you tell me the truth about why you want the house? I'm here, trying to help you, and you're still not letting me in."

He stared at her like he couldn't quite figure her out, which was good. Having him off balance would only help. "I'm sure you know why. My record isn't exactly clean. I can't own property in this city. Hell, I can't even find a decent place to rent, and I need that to set up shop. But with that house..." He grinned. "There's a lot of money to be made in this city. I want my share."

She sighed. "I don't doubt that's all a part of your plan, but you're still not telling me the truth and we both know it."

He seemed taken aback. "I don't know what you're talking about."

"Yes, you do. Stop playing dumb or I will sell my half to Augustine."

He scowled. "There's more to that house than you know."

"Like what?"

He shook his head, clearly frustrated by what he was about to reveal. "There's a...tree."

"The lightning tree."

His eyes rounded and he sucked in a ragged breath. "How do you know about that?"

"I know more than you give me credit for."

Harlow laughed bitterly. *He had no idea.*

Branzino nodded slowly. "I guess I underestimated you. Apparently I do that a lot. So...you're ready to give me the house?"

She frowned. "No. I'm here to be partners with you. To be a family." The time had come to draw him in. She sniffled. "I thought you wanted that." She bit down on her tongue until her eyes teared up. "I thought you wanted to be my *father*."

He rubbed a hand across his forehead before coming closer. "I do. I just didn't know you wanted that, too."

Harlow trembled with rage. *I hate him.*

Ava Mae worked to control the tremors her sister's anger sent through her. She hadn't expected Harlow to have so much influence over her. Ava Mae's time in this body would be short if she didn't do something about it soon. *I know, Sister. Be strong. We're almost there.* Ava Mae sank to the floor, drawing her knees to her chin and wrapping her arms around them before putting her face down and sniffling some more. "All my life I wanted a father..." She let her voice trail off into a sob. From under her arm, she could see his feet moving closer. Using the cover of her hair, she slipped the knife from her boot.

He knelt beside her. "Harlow, baby, I had no idea—"

She lunged with all her power, shoving the blade lengthwise against his neck and knocking him onto his back on the floor. She straddled him, the blade already crimson where it pressed into the thick flesh of his throat. The tang of blood mixed with the scent of bleach. That smell was one of Ava Mae's last human memories. Old pain surged through her and Harlow cringed. Ava Mae leaned in. "You have no idea about a lot of things."

In the depths of his wide pupils, Ava Mae's black eyes and pointed teeth shone back. The face that had first made Harlow afraid. This time it didn't. He swallowed. "Look, if you want to be in charge of the New Orleans branch of the family business, fine, you can be in charge. Your brothers can stay in Chicago and—"

"You think this is about who's in charge?" She put her free hand to her mouth, bit her glove and pulled it off. Then she .thrust her bare hand into the open neck of his shirt and planted her hand against the cool, sticky skin of his chest. She dug her nails in as she opened herself up and spilled into him the pain of what he'd done to her. How it felt to be suffocated, the sensation of gasping for air but finding none. Then she let him feel the hollow longing that had plagued Harlow every day of her life, let him taste the bitter ache that had robbed the sweetness from her days.

He moaned softly. "Harlow, we can talk about this. Find some way to—"

"Your past has caught up with you and tonight, in this filthy warehouse, in this city that you so badly want a piece of, you're finally going to pay." She forced more emotion through her touch, emptying her years of suffering into him.

A new, tormented light filled his gaze. His eyes rolled back into his head for a moment. She reined the emotion in to keep him conscious. He whimpered. "You're not Harlow."

"Harlow is with me, but do you even know my name? Because you should. It was right there on my crib. You should know the name of the child you murdered. The name of the infant you left dead in her bed. It's Ava Mae." She dug her nails deeper into his flesh. "Say it." Pain flowed out of her like water from a bursting dam.

He paled beneath her. Started to shake. Sweat trickled down his temples. "Ava Mae," he whispered.

"My mother told you your firstborn would cause your death, and you know what?" Ava Mae leaned in until they were almost nose to nose. "She was right."

"Please," he begged, shaking harder now. "I can fix this. I can explain—"

"You killed me. You killed my mother. What's to explain? It's time for your fortune to come true."

He opened his mouth again, but she was tired of the sound of his voice. With a lifetime of rage and sorrow driving her, she cried out in anger as she emptied the last of her pain into him. He convulsed once, almost throwing her off.

She drew the blade across his throat. Blood bubbled from the wound as he sputtered silent words. The stench of bleach grew

CITY OF ETERNAL NIGHT   331

stronger. He lifted a hand toward her. It fell back to his side as his life's blood puddled around him.

Harlow flinched, trying not to see through Ava Mae's eyes and failing.

Ava Mae felt her sister's reaction, but her own sense of satisfaction was greater. She stood over his body. Justice had been done. Her father had paid for his sins. He lay prone at her feet, his human image flickering as it gave way to his true fae form beneath, finally blinking out as the last burble of air escaped his slashed throat.

Ava Mae shuddered as she peered closer. "Is that what we come from? I can't believe *that* runs in our bloodlines."

You killed him, Harlow whispered.

You knew that's what I planned to do. What we *planned to do.* Ava Mae's tone softened. *And at least this way, you didn't have to do it yourself.*

I know. I just... I don't know. It's so real.

There's nothing to be afraid of anymore now. Ava Mae glanced at the still-bloody weapon in her hand. *Let's get Rue and get out of here.*

What are you going to tell Augustine?

Ava Mae laughed softly. *You worry too much. No one's going to care about anything except that Rue is free and Branzino is dead.*

I don't know. Augustine's not like that.

Ava Mae bent to wipe the blade off on Branzino's suit, but then paused and straightened. She lifted the blade and slashed open the sleeve of her hoodie, then her leggings across one thigh, drawing a little blood both times. Harlow barely felt the sting of it. Ava Mae messed up her hair and yanked her hoodie down off one shoulder hard enough to tear it. *We'll tell him it was self-defense. That should be enough for him to let it go.* She started for the other room.

The door burst open and Augustine came rushing in. "What

happened?" He ran to her, grabbing her arms. "Harlow, you're hurt. Are you all right?"

Ava Mae nodded as if she were unable to speak.

More fae came rushing in behind him. "Why did you come here on your own?"

Suddenly Ava Mae collapsed against him, sobbing. "He sent me a message. Said he'd kill you if I didn't come to him. But then he tried to kill me anyway."

"Shh, it's okay, I'm here now." He pulled her close and wrapped his arms around her.

She closed her eyes and inhaled, trembling a little with the excitement of what had just happened. "He almost killed me..." she moaned.

Augustine kissed the top of Ava Mae's head. "Don't be afraid. From the looks of things, Branzino's not going to bother you anymore."

Harlow wanted to tell Augustine what really happened. That Ava Mae wasn't her. There shouldn't be these lies between them. *Give me back my body. Branzino is dead. You can be at peace now.*

Ava Mae's laugh echoed through Harlow like an alarm. *I don't think so, Sister. I have a lot of living left to do.*

Chapter Thirty-three

G iselle climbed out one of the warehouse windows and used a levitation spell to lower herself to the ground without injury. Nerves tripping with what she'd seen, she escaped down an alley undetected and kept running until she was a block from Jackson Square. She slipped into the crowds of tourists and slowed her pace to match theirs, finally catching her breath. Every once in a while she glanced over her shoulder, but there was no sign of Augustine or his lieutenants. And the vampire she swore she'd seen.

Her nerves calmed slowly. She assessed what she knew so far. There were no sirens, which she was sure she'd be hearing if her home had blown up, so Branzino's threat must have been a bluff. She also knew Branzino was dead. That was good news. And bad news. Whatever plan he'd had to rid the city of the fae's rule was done with.

But she was also no longer under his thumb.

And then there was the most interesting piece of what she'd overhead. A lightning tree. She'd heard stories, but had no real idea what the power of such a thing was. There was one person who probably would know. And if Branzino wanted it, it was worth looking into.

Her father's Mercedes was probably in the police impound lot by now. She stepped off the curb and hailed a passing cab. This was no time for a streetcar. She got in. "Garden District, Toledano Street. Right off of St. Charles."

"You got it." He punched the meter and took off.

"Was there an explosion in the Quarter tonight? A house, maybe?"

"Not that I've heard, and I woulda heard." He glanced at her in the rearview mirror. "I take it you're not in town for Mardi Gras?"

So her house must be okay. She sat back. "No, and I'm not in the mood for talking either."

The driver made a face in the mirror and went back to driving. She stared out the window as the crowds slipped away. The insanity of the evening was fading, but the feeling she'd just been handed an enormous gift only increased.

Not only was there the curious business of the lightning tree and whatever that might mean, but there was this new information about Harlow and Branzino. If Harlow, or Ava Mae, who Giselle suspected might be inhabiting Harlow and be the cause of the black aura hovering around her, was really Branzino's daughter, which she appeared to be, that meant Augustine was living with the enemy. Although Harlow *had* basically confessed to not knowing what her father had been up to. And had been angry enough to cut his throat.

How much did Augustine know? Did he know about the lightning tree? The way Harlow and Branzino had talked, the tree was connected to the house. Augustine had lived there long enough. He must know about the tree.

It had also seemed Harlow had her father's gift of transferring emotions through touch. Giselle tipped her head back, shuddering at the memory of how he'd made her feel.

Finding out what kind of fae Branzino was could be very useful in dealing with Harlow in the future.

Giselle had fled after Augustine burst into the warehouse, using the ruckus as her cover. He'd seemed shocked by Harlow's presence there, but she hadn't heard much more. There was no way she was staying to be discovered by one of his lieu-tenants. Which raised another question. Why on earth did Augustine have a vampire among his crew? That was worth investigating because it was the kind of thing that could give her leverage.

The taxi pulled to a stop. "St. Charles and Toledano." The driver didn't bother looking at her.

She swiped her LMD over the scanner, then tapped the screen to pay with a minimal tip. She got out before he could respond. A short walk later and she was at her sister's door. Zara opened after a couple of knocks.

"I didn't expect to see you again tonight. Everything okay?"

"No. Can I come in?"

"Of course." Zara moved to let Giselle in. "What's going on? Did Ogun attack you again?"

"No, it's not that." Giselle shut the door. "It's not bad news, but I don't know where to start."

Zara smiled. "Start with the most interesting thing."

Giselle nodded. Straight into it then. "What's a lightning tree?"

Zara's mouth rounded slightly. "A myth. I mean, I've heard of them, but they're like unicorns and Atlantis. Why? What makes you ask?"

"What if it wasn't a myth? What if I told you I knew where there might be one?"

Zara grabbed Giselle's hand and pulled her farther into the house. "Are you teasing me?"

"No, I'd never—"

"A lightning tree is one of the most powerful—if I had a lightning tree, me, a green witch, do you have any idea the kind of things I could do?" Zara shook her head, her thoughts clearly coming faster than she could put them into words. "Where is it? How do you know? Tell me everything."

Giselle put her arm around her sister. "Let's go get comfortable. I think you're going to want to sit down for the rest of this."

After making sure she was okay, Augustine let Blu take Rue home. There would be plenty of time tomorrow for Hugo to say thank you. Although Augustine wouldn't be surprised if that thank-you never came. If anything, Hugo would probably continue to blame Rue's kidnapping on Augustine.

None of that mattered. Right now all Augustine wanted to do was get Harlow home. He shot a text to Fenton, then sent Mal, Chrysabelle and Mortalis to their plane. The sooner he got the vampire out of town the better. He left Sydra, Cy and Dulcinea to deal with Branzino and clean up the scene. They'd transport his body to the fae plane for burial and make sure everything else was neat and tidy. This wasn't something the NOPD needed to be involved with.

He helped Harlow into the car and shut her door, then got in on the other side. He started the vehicle, but put his hand over her gloved one before pulling out. "You were really brave tonight. It's my fault you weren't better prepared. I promise you, no matter what happens, I am going to keep training you until you can fight off just about anything."

She looked up, her eyes a little red from crying. "You promise?"

"Whenever you're ready for your next lesson, you just let me know."

She brightened. "I'm ready now." She smiled. "Well, not *now*. But tomorrow?"

"Sure."

She turned her hand so she could interlace her fingers with his. "All I want now is a nice hot shower."

He nodded. "That sounds good."

Her eyes sparked with something dark. Something that looked like...desire. "Doesn't it?"

He tried to ignore his body's response to the thoughts her wicked expression had suddenly put there. The shock of battle could do things to people, make them react in ways that they'd later regret. He wasn't about to take advantage of Harlow in that state. "We'll, uh, get those cuts fixed up, too."

She shrugged and glanced at her arm. "They're already healed." She smiled. "That's the beauty of being fae."

He laughed softly as he released her hand. "Yeah, it is. Okay then. Home." With that, he checked traffic and pulled into the street. The change in Harlow from the day he'd met her to now was nothing short of astonishing, but since the reading to find Rue, she almost seemed like a different person. The way she blatantly flirted back with him was only part of it. She seemed to *want* to be fae. To have not only accepted it, but embraced it.

And for her to be able to kill Branzino...the man was nearly a full-blooded raptor fae. She must have caught him off guard. Was that possible if he'd been attacking her? A lucky shot? How fortunate she'd asked him for that knife earlier.

"You look occupied."

He kept his eyes on the road. "Still processing. Big night."

"I'd say."

He wanted to ask her about the fight, to press for details, but he didn't want to upset her again. She'd been so shaken up. He glanced over. She smiled at him as she wound a strand of hair around one finger. For someone who'd been sobbing her eyes out, she was doing okay now. His gaze returned to the road. "The fight must have exhausted you. They do that. The adrenaline builds up and then, *whoosh*, fight's over and you're drained."

"Mm-hmm. That's exactly it." She yawned. "Hot shower and

then bed. Although the shower might perk me up a little." Her quiet laugh was filled with innuendo.

And there she was again. The Harlow he wasn't sure what to do with. "Bed—that is, sleep, is what both of us need right now." He cleared his throat. "My night is far from over. Lots of…Guardian stuff still to do."

He slanted his eyes at her. She looked like she was actually pouting. Who on earth was this creature beside him?

The rest of the ride, which fortunately wasn't much longer, was spent in silence. He parked. They both got out, the silence sticking as they walked into the kitchen.

Fenton and Lally were still at the table, a pot of coffee between them. Fenton stood up immediately. "You did it."

Lally held her arms out to Harlow. "You poor child. Fenton told me what happened, but at least that man is gone."

Harlow stayed where she was. "I need a shower." She slipped out of the kitchen, her footsteps fading as she jogged upstairs.

Lally's gaze lingered on the doorway for a moment, then she turned to Augustine. "Something's different about that child, but I guess killing your own father would change just about anyone." She gave Augustine a little half smile that didn't reach her eyes. "If you'll excuse me. It's late and I know y'all got business to discuss." She left without waiting for his response, the door to her room shutting shortly after.

Augustine dropped into one of the kitchen chairs. "She's not wrong. Something's been different with Harlow since she did the reading. I think we pushed her too hard."

Fenton sat back down. "She did the reading of her own free will."

Augustine snorted. "What were her options? Not help? Let Rue die?" He leaned forward. "Branzino told her if she didn't come to him, he was going to kill me."

Fenton frowned. "We never heard about that."

"Because she never said anything." He leaned back, shaking his head. "I'm glad Branzino's dead but I'm sorry she had to be the one to do it."

Fenton's fingers rapped the table slowly. "How exactly did she manage to kill him? I know you said it was self-defense, but…"

"He's a raptor fae and she barely acknowledges she *is* fae? At least that's how she used to feel. She seems pretty okay with being fae now." He sighed, staring out the kitchen window into the dark. "I can't really tell you how she killed him. I plan on questioning her, but not tonight."

"No, of course not, not tonight." Fenton turned his coffee cup so that the handle was perpendicular to the edge of the table. "Curious, though."

Augustine got up to get a cup. "You think this will shut Loudreux up for a while?"

"About your ability as Guardian?" Fenton laughed. "No. He'll claim it was all Harlow's doing. I'd be surprised if he didn't campaign for her to take over."

"We got a problem."

Both men turned to see Lally standing in the doorway, an empty white stone box and lid in her hands.

Augustine set his coffee down. "What's the matter?"

She came into the kitchen, kicking the door shut behind her, then glanced toward the ceiling. "This box used to hold the ashes of Harlow's sister."

Augustine's hand drifted to the hilt of his sword. "And now the box is empty." The fear in Lally's eyes chilled him. "What do you think happened to the ashes?"

She looked at Fenton, then back at Augustine. "I think…" She put the box on the table and gripped the back of a chair. "Augustine, there's a lot you don't know about this house. A lot no one knows. There's power here. The kind that can raise the dead. And I think… that's exactly what Harlow's done. She's brought her sister back but the way she's done it..." She shook her head. Tears spilled down her cheeks. "Ain't no good gonna come of it. No good. Nothing but sorrow and trouble."

She sat down, covered her face with her hands and wept softly.

Augustine knelt beside her, a thousand questions burning in his brain. "What are you talking about?" He looked at Fenton, but he didn't seem to have any idea what she was talking about either. "What kind of power?"

She sniffed and lifted her head. "There is one other possibility." She put her hand on his shoulder, but turned to look at Fenton. "You're gonna have to look the other way on this one."

"Why's that?" Fenton asked.

Lally took a deep breath. "Because I know you people got a thing about humans going into your world, but I need to talk to Miss Olivia and Augustine's got to take me."

Augustine stood. "Let's go. Olivia needs to know Branzino's dead anyway."

Fenton frowned at Augustine. "You can't repeat the transgression of taking another human onto the fae plane. I won't allow that."

"Fenton—"

"No, Augustine." He got up, adjusting his tweed sports coat. "I'll take Lally through."

"That's unexpected. Thank you for doing this." Augustine hesitated. "There's a good chance you'll see some of my lieutenants there. They're taking care of Branzino's body."

"Burying him in *Hakel'dama*?"

"Where else?" The land behind the Claustrum served as a potter's field for dead criminal fae. Branzino would be put into that ground and forgotten, which was all he deserved.

Fenton shrugged. "So they see me. They're your lieutenants. They're not going to do anything to get Lally or you in trouble."

"No, they're not, but I thought you should know."

"I appreciate that." He pushed his glasses back. "Just make sure you come through the mirror after us. And if word gets out, well, no one in the Elektos will say a thing about it to me. I'll make sure of that."

"I'm ready when you are." Lally pushed her chair back and got up. "You got your mirror, Mr. Welch?"

Fenton nodded and smiled. "I can see living with Augustine has rubbed off on you. You're no one's fool, are you, Miss Hughes?"

Sadness shadowed her eyes as she touched the lamb carved into the top of the white stone box. "I hope not, Mr. Welch. I hope not."

Chapter Thirty-four

Augustine only waited thirty seconds after Fenton and Lally went through the mirror before he slipped through after them. He came out at Lally's side. The fae plane that held the Claustrum was as bleak and gray and unwelcoming as ever.

Lally wrapped her arms around herself. "This place is where Miss Olivia's at? Lord Jesus, help us all."

"Lally? Lally!" Olivia's voice broke through the softly whistling winds like the peal of a church bell, bright and clear.

Lally turned toward the sound, tears already making her brown eyes seem bigger and more luminous than normal. The two women rushed toward each other, embracing with the emotion of sisters.

Ironic, considering the reason they were here. Fenton started forward, but Augustine put his hand on the man's arm. "Give them a minute."

Fenton nodded. "Of course." A clump of dried grass blew past. "We really need to do something about getting her to a different part of the plane."

"Agreed, but I don't have the slightest clue how to do that."

"I don't either, but I know people who might."

Augustine snorted. "Is there anything you don't have a solution to? You're all right, you know that?"

The cypher smiled. "Thank you. I do my best."

Olivia stopped talking to Lally long enough to look at

Augustine. "Get over here, Augie. And bring Fartus Wanker with you so he can explain why he's here."

Augustine sighed as he started toward them. "She knows your name. I promise she does."

Fenton just shook his head and followed.

Livie's eyes shone with pleasure as Augustine approached, a clear sign Lally hadn't mentioned the real reason they were there. "*Cher*, I was about to scold you for waiting so long to visit after bringing Harlow, but considering you brought Lally to me, all's forgiven." She hugged him hard and kissed his cheek, the comforting scent of her lemon verbena perfume ever-present. She leaned back. "How is my daughter?"

"She's fine." A half-truth. But she'd know the full truth soon enough.

Still holding on to Augustine, she shifted her gaze to Fenton. "So. Why are you here?"

Augustine answered. "Fenton brought Lally so that I wouldn't get in trouble for bringing another human onto the fae plane."

"Is that so?" She let go of Augustine and approached Fenton. His left eye twitched behind his glasses, but he held his ground. She didn't stop until she was well within his personal space. "I know the dangers of skin contact with a cypher, but I'm dead so I don't know how many passwords and account numbers you could siphon off me if you were inclined to do such a thing—"

"I'm not." Fenton was as stiff as a corpse.

"Good, because I'm going to hug you now." She threw her arms around him. "Thank you. That's the nicest thing any Elektos has ever done."

"For you, you mean?"

She pulled back. "No, Fartus, for anyone. You government types aren't exactly known for your random acts of kindness."

She walked toward a cluster of boulders. "Come on, have a sit and let's visit."

Lally stayed put. "Miss Olivia, I need to ask you about something."

"About this place? Awful, ain't it?" Olivia settled in, shaking her head. "It must be a horrible shock for you to see me here."

Lally shook her head and smiled, then seemed to change her mind about having a seat. She joined Olivia on the rocks. "It's not the Ritz, but I'm happy to visit you wherever I can considering I was at your funeral a few weeks ago."

"Helluva thing." Olivia looped her arm through Lally's. "I am so glad to see you."

Lally's smile faltered and she shot a look at Augustine, then Fenton. "Miss Olivia—"

Olivia threw her hands up. "In the name of our lady Elizabeth Taylor, will you please just call me Olivia."

Lally nodded, but continued. "*Olivia*, I have something very important to ask you."

"That sounds serious."

"It is."

"Go ahead then."

Lally took a breath. "Has Harlow been here on her own in the last few days?"

"Not since Augie brought her, no."

Lally put her hand over Livie's. "Have you seen *any* signs that... she might have brought Ava Mae's ashes here?"

Olivia went as pale as a dead person could. "Why are you asking me this? What's happened?"

Augustine wanted to know himself.

"I found the box you kept her ashes in and it wasn't in your bedroom. It was..." Lally shot a brief glance at Augustine again. "Somewhere you once tried to put it before but I stopped you. You remember? Except this time, the box was empty."

Olivia's mouth dropped open and she seemed to be trembling. "Does Harlow know about..."

"Yes. I had to tell her. It's her house now and she deserved to know, especially with that man after her, trying everything he could to get his hands on that place. She had to know what was at stake. What he was really after."

Olivia shook her head. "How would he know about the—about that?"

Lally shrugged. "Your guess is as good as mine."

Curiosity burned in Augustine's soul. He cleared his throat. "Branzino's dead now, by the way. Nothing more to worry about there."

That didn't seem to have quite the impact he'd expected as Olivia's hand went to her mouth and she stared blankly toward the horizon. "That's good, Augie, that's real good." She looked at Lally. "But if the box was where you said it was and it was empty, then..." Her hands curled into fists. "Is Harlow okay?" She shot Augustine an appraising glance. "Augie said she was fine."

Lally shook her head slowly. "She's not acting exactly like herself, but she's done some hard things lately. She killed that man herself."

Olivia shook her head. "That's not my Harlow." She stood, still shaking her head. "Lally, you warned me and now...why didn't you stop her? Why didn't you tell her to stay away from that—"

"I did warn her." Lally jumped up and grabbed Livie's hands. "I told her the same things I told you. She must have taken the ashes in and made her wish. You know how grief takes over. I'll find a way to fix this, I swear."

Augustine scratched one horn. "Is either of you going to tell me what the hell is going on?"

Olivia looked at him, her horrified expression scaring him.

Whatever had happened was more serious than he'd imagined. "Harlow's done something she shouldn't have."

"I get that. But that's not telling me much."

She turned back to Lally. "Tell him. Tell him everything. Now. Or I will. I will not lose Harlow over this."

Lally's reluctance showed in the tightness of her mouth and the grim set of her eyes. "This is family business, Olivia."

Augustine raised his brows. He'd never heard Lally talk that way to Olivia. Whatever this was about, it was beyond serious.

Olivia cocked her head. "And Augustine isn't family?"

Fenton held up his hands. "I'm certain I don't need to be involved in this at this immediate moment. I'll take my leave. I should stop by the Loudreux's anyway. See if they need me to take care of anything." He looked at Augustine. "Check in with me in the morning."

"Will do."

With a nod, Fenton flipped open his travel mirror and slipped through.

"Boss!"

They turned toward the shout. Cy, Dulcinea and Sydra walked toward them. Augustine waved them over. "Everything taken care of?"

Dulcinea nodded. "He's in the ground. You should know there were five other dead fae in that building."

"His henchmen?"

Sydra nodded. "I ran them through the database on my LMD. They were all from Chicago."

Augustine nodded. "I guess he tied up those loose ends for us."

"Are you checking up on us?" Dulcinea asked. Then her gaze shifted to Olivia. "Hey, you're not dead!"

Olivia laughed. "Thank you for noticing, but technically I am."

Augustine interrupted. "I'll explain later. Look, since Branzino is dead, there's the matter of the money he gave Harlow. She wants nothing to do with it and she doesn't need it, so why don't you three take it? Give half to Beatrice—after all, Branzino's the reason she's a widow and with a baby on the way—"

"Makes sense," Cy said.

"Then you three take the other half and divide it up. Consider it a bonus for all the crap we've been through lately."

Sydra smiled a little. "That's very nice of you. Where is this money?"

Augustine pointed toward the Claustrum's gates. "Buried not far from the entrance. I'm sure Olivia can show you."

She put a hand to her chest like she was offended he'd think she'd been snooping. "Augie, you hid that money."

"Are you saying you don't know where it is?"

She pursed her lips for a moment. "No."

"Good. Take them to it. Lally and I need to get home, but I promise I'll get Fenton to bring her back for another visit."

Olivia hugged Lally before shaking her finger at Augustine. "You'd better."

Dulcinea grinned. "See you later, boss. Hey, how much money are we talking about?"

Augustine grinned back. "Eight hundred fifty thousand dollars."

The faces of all three of his lieutenants went blank for a moment. Dulcinea got a hold of herself first. "That's some bonus." She stepped aside and held her hand out toward the Claustrum. "After you, Miss Olivia."

As Livie left with them, Augustine turned back to Lally. "Now, you want to tell me what you think is going on with Harlow?"

Lally nodded. "It's easier if I just show you. Let's go home and you can see for yourself. Then I'll explain everything, including what I think has happened."

Ava Mae got up from where she'd been sitting on the landing. She'd heard everything that Augustine and Lally had said in the kitchen, watched Fenton take Lally through the mirror and Augustine follow. She had no idea how long they'd be gone, but it didn't matter. She'd heard and seen enough.

"Lally knows," she said. "Or at least she has an idea that you've done something, Sister dear." She started up the steps to her room.

Harlow laughed bitterly. *Did you think you wouldn't be found out? You're not acting like me at all*, she snapped. *Just give me my body back. I'll do whatever you want, help you in whatever way I can, just leave me alone.*

Ava Mae rolled her shoulders as the wave of Harlow's anger passed through her. *Learn to accept what's happened. It'll make things easier.*

Branzino's dead. That's what you wanted. What we wanted. Our mother's life is avenged. Your life is avenged. You said that's what you needed to be at peace. Let me go back to living mine. Please. You promised. Harlow was on the brink of sobbing, sending another wave of emotion through Ava Mae.

She grabbed hold of the railing, a little dizzy from Harlow's outburst. *Enough. All your pitiful raging isn't going to change anything. I'm here to stay and I plan on enjoying life. The life I never got to have because I was murdered.*

You have my sympathy, you know that, but you can't have my body, too. Besides, Lally knows something's wrong, Harlow countered quietly. *She's tenacious. She won't let this go until she's figured it out.*

Ava Mae stomped up the steps toward her room. *You think that old witch has any power over me? Not anymore. She stopped Mother from bringing me back once, but things are too far gone for that now. I'm more than just your sister reborn. The tree saw to that.*

Lally's not a witch. And what do you mean, the tree saw to that?

Ava Mae laughed. *You're so naïve.* Traiteur, *witch, shaman, whatever you want to call her, she's got power of her own. You've seen signs of it.*

No, I haven't. She's just a woman who was granted immortality by something her mother did. That's all.

Think, Ava Mae said. *You've never seen her do anything out of the ordinary? You've never seen her shy away from another with powers that might reveal her?*

Nekai, Harlow whispered.

See, Ava Mae said. *You have no idea what she's capable of. Better to get her out of the way before she tries something—*

NO.

The power of Harlow's response rocked Ava Mae. She swallowed against a surge of nausea. *Fine. I won't do anything for now. But if she comes at me, tries to take this life from me, nothing you can say will stop me.*

That seemed to quiet Harlow. Ava Mae hoped she stayed that way. Her sister's outbursts were having a greater effect on her than she'd expected. Either Harlow was stronger than Ava Mae had first thought, or Ava Mae was weakening under the strain of maintaining her hold on this form.

No matter, Ava Mae would have to find a way to make Harlow accept that she wasn't the one in charge anymore. Taking Augustine to bed, something Ava Mae had planned on doing anyway, might accomplish that. Especially if Ava Mae could use him to show Harlow that he wasn't in love with her, just interested in a good time.

If that didn't crush her dear sister's naïve fantasies and make her retreat into the dark, hollow place Ava Mae had first inhabited, then she'd find another way to shock her into obedience. Something that would show Harlow Ava Mae was a force to be reckoned with.

Something like killing Lally.

Chapter Thirty-five

Augustine stepped through the mirror with Lally and reappeared in the foyer, right where they'd left. "You okay? Traveling that way can make you a little dizzy."

She smiled weakly. "Child, you got no idea about the things I can handle. But you're about to." She nodded toward her room. "Follow me."

He did as she asked, and when they were in her room, she shut the door and locked it before opening her closet. She pushed the clothing aside, then looked at him. "Being that you're the Guardian and seeing all the things you've seen lately, none of what I'm about to tell you should come as too big a shock and yet I'm sure it will. But understand it was kept from you because that's just the way things have been. This wasn't Olivia's secret to share either. It's mine."

He smiled. "I'm just happy you're finally sharing it. And I can't imagine anything you show me could be that shocking."

She made a face like he had no idea what he was talking about. "Well then. You just follow me on through here." She disappeared into the closet.

He went after her. Behind the clothes that were pushed back was a small, open door. He could see her on the other side. A secret room? Not that shocking. He stepped through and stared at what lay beyond. "You have got to be kidding me."

"I tried to tell you."

"That should not exist." He glanced back at the door. "Not

in this space. Not in this *house*." He looked at her. This was so much bigger than he'd guessed. "Lally, why is there a burned tree in the center of the house? And how is that skylight there? I've been on the roof. There's no skylight anywhere."

A certain gleam lit her eyes and for a few seconds, it looked as though the wisdom of the ages lived in her. "That's all your people's magic."

"This is fae magic?"

She nodded. "Done to protect this tree. Well, more like to protect people *from* this tree." She put her hand on the trunk. "This is a lightning tree and it's got all kinds of power."

And no doubt the Elektos of earlier times had thought something this powerful could one day benefit them.

She proceeded to tell him the story of the tree and her mother and the deal she'd made with the fae. As it sank in that Lally was as ancient as days, he stood dumbstruck. She smiled gently. "I know it's a lot to take in, Augie."

He took a deep breath. "It is." He stared up at the tree. Its branches jutted into the house. "Is this thing in every room?"

"After this many years, I suppose it's in a lot of them." She moved to stand in front of it, pointing one story up. "That balcony leads from a hidden door in Olivia's closet. Harlow found it. And I found the empty box of ashes up there."

"So you think Harlow…" He really had no idea what Lally thought, or what was even possible with a tree like this.

"I think she made a wish of the tree, to bring her sister back."

"And that's a problem because?"

Lally sighed. "Because not long after I told Olivia about the tree, she tried to do the very same thing, except I caught her before it went too far. Some of the ashes were spilled and I know the tree made use of them."

"What does that mean?"

"Since it was just a tiny bit, the tree couldn't bring Ava

Mae back. Not all the way. But ever since Olivia did that, I've sensed the tree wasn't alone. I believe it raised the spirit of Ava Mae. Course, she was just a baby when she died, but once the tree woke her spirit, it probably started growing her up, too. Maybe even put a bit of itself in her."

She shook her head. "This tree was a thing of remarkable power once upon a time, but it became so twisted after what my mama did . . ." She looked away, clearing her throat. "If Harlow brought the rest of the ashes—"

"Then the tree had everything it needed to make Ava Mae whole again."

Lally faced him again. "Not whole. I've seen the tree bring things back. They ain't never whole and there's always a little something wrong with them. They might seem okay at first but as time goes by they go bad like milk left in the sun."

"So where is this twisted-up version of Ava Mae then?"

Lally's chest expanded with a deep breath. "That's the worst of it. Anything the tree touches usually can't get too far from the tree or whatever power the tree's sunk into it goes away. Myself included."

He looked up at the tree. "Where is she then? Why is that the worst of it?"

Lally's chin trembled. "It's possible that Ava Mae's spirit has gotten inside Harlow's body. That she's using Harlow as a way to get distance from the tree. And as a way to live again."

A chill ripped through Augustine. "You think Harlow's possessed by her dead sister?"

Lally nodded. "And if she is, I don't think there's anything Harlow can do to get out."

"You mean Harlow's trapped in her own body?" Heat overtook the chill as anger rose up in him. His hand automatically went to the hilt of the sword at his side. "There has to be something we can do. If Harlow's suffering—"

Lally raised her hands. "I don't even know if what I'm guessing at is true. You're closest to Harlow. You need to spend some time with her, see if you can figure it out. Ava Mae won't know everything Harlow does, she won't be able to pass as her sister for too long without slipping up in a big way. And Harlow's a strong woman. She might be able to give us a sign." Lally's hands came up to touch her necklace. "Whatever you do, don't let on like you know. We don't want to tip our hand and push Ava Mae to do something that can't be undone."

His shoulders slumped at the thought of putting Harlow in more danger. "I think she's gone to bed already, but I promise, I will spend the whole day with her tomorrow. I'll be her shadow. I will find out if Ava Mae is the one calling the shots."

"Good."

"Is there anything you can think of that might help?"

"A nice stiff drink."

"I meant help for Harlow, not me."

"I meant it for Harlow. If Ava Mae is in control, getting her intoxicated may loosen that control." Lally frowned. "Or it might just knock her out. Either way, it might give Harlow a chance to let us know what's going on."

"Okay. And now that you mentioned it, maybe I'll have one anyway."

The long hot shower had done wonders. Ava Mae turned off the water, grabbed a towel and dried off. She tossed the towel on the rack and walked out of the steamy bathroom to stand naked before the full-length mirror in the bedroom. The slice on her arm and leg had healed without a trace. She studied her new body. "Not bad." She did a little half turn. "Not bad at all."

You can't do this. I know what you're planning. I can feel it in you. See him in your thoughts. You can't seduce him and take him to bed in my body. I'm not consenting to this.

Ava Mae laughed. *How many times do I have to tell you it's my body now? And don't act like you're not going to enjoy it. You want Augustine just as much as I do. You know you do. Your heart rate goes up around him. You're just too scared to admit it, just like you're too scared to enjoy life.*

Yes, I like him and I find him attractive, but I want to build a relationship with him based on more than just physical attraction. Besides, all *you want him for is sex.*

You say that like it's a bad thing. Ava Mae fluffed her hair. The color was amazing.

It is, because you don't love him. You just want to use him.

Ava Mae raised her brows and smiled at her reflection. *So you love him, do you?*

Harlow went quiet. *Maybe I'm . . . starting to.*

You can't even admit your feelings for him. Ava Mae shook her head. *You're wasting this body.*

Whatever I'm feeling, you're going to ruin it by sleeping with him.

Relax and enjoy it. It'll be fun! And it could end up making him fall madly in love with you, you know.

You mean you, not me.

Ava Mae laughed as she dug through Harlow's dresser drawers. *Now you're catching on. Ugh. Do you actually only wear black? And what are these?* She held up a pair of boy-short underwear. *You dress like an old woman at a funeral. Where's the lace and silk and barely-there thongs? Where's the color? How could any man love a woman this boring?*

I am not boring, Harlow shouted.

Harlow's anger shot through Ava Mae and her hand jerked, tossing the panties back in the drawer.

Hey. Harlow perked up. *I did that.*

Don't get excited. It won't happen again. I was bored by your clothing selections. My control slipped.

So keeping me prisoner takes effort? Good to know.

Ava Mae was about to respond when she heard footsteps on the stairs. She inhaled. Smoke. Her mouth curved into a smile. *There's my man.*

Harlow simmered but was oddly quiet. Maybe she was finally starting to accept her fate. Or maybe she was looking forward to having Augustine in bed just as much as Ava Mae was, but couldn't admit it. Probably that.

Ava Mae went back to rummaging through the drawers for something suitably sexy. The best she could do was a silky chemise in navy. Ava Mae slipped it on, then put the bathrobe hanging on the back of the door over it. She looked at herself in the mirror and rolled her eyes. "Shopping needs to be a priority. Where's Augustine's room?"

Attic.

Harlow was angry, but at least she was answering. Ava Mae started up the stairs, her bare feet making no sound on the polished wood treads. She smiled. A few more minutes and anger would be the last thing on Harlow's mind.

Chapter Thirty-six

Helpless. The word spiraled through Augustine's mind like a dying bird. He leaned against the big window that overlooked the neighborhood, taking a draw from the bottle of Livie's bourbon he'd brought upstairs. His gaze was fixed on the lights of the next house over, but he wasn't really seeing them. The evening's events kept playing over and over in his head while he analyzed every word Harlow had spoken, every move she'd made, picking the hours apart for what was her and what might be Ava Mae.

He shuddered and crossed himself, whispering a prayer that Harlow was different because the reading had changed her in some way. And not because her dead sister had taken her over.

"Hey."

He turned. Harlow stood in the doorway, wearing her bathrobe and a slip that stopped midthigh. Her damp hair hung in soft waves around her face. Hell's bells, she was beautiful.

"Hey, Harley." He made a point of using the nickname that usually irritated her.

She smiled. "Can I come in?"

"My door is always open."

She sauntered in and took a seat on his couch, propping her feet on the coffee table so that the robe fell away from her bare legs. It wasn't like Harlow to show that much skin, for fear of being touched, but he wanted to believe she was getting more comfortable around him. "I feel like I owe you a thank-you."

"For what?"

She shrugged and the robe dropped off one shoulder. "For not giving me all the grief you could have for going after Branzino alone."

He leaned against the wall beside the window, trying not to let her naked legs distract him. "Who says we're done talking about it?"

She laughed softly, a sound he'd always loved. "That makes more sense."

"You were only doing what you thought was right. I know that. Do I like it? No. But I understand it."

She twisted to face him more, then patted the cushion beside her. "You're so far away."

He straightened, then hesitated. Next to her was exactly where he wanted to be. So long as she was Harlow. But then, if he didn't get close, how would he find out? He took the seat, keeping a little room between them. She smelled sweet and flowery from whatever fancy soap she'd used. His mouth watered. He set the bourbon on the coffee table. "I thought you were going to bed?"

"The shower did wonders." She poked him in the bicep, touching his T-shirt, not his skin. "Are you trying to get rid of me?"

He looked into her eyes, hoping to see something that would tell him this was Harlow. "I'd never try to get rid of you."

"Good." Her eyes sparkled with the same darkly wicked look he'd seen before. A look he couldn't quite buy as Harlow's. His heart sank. He decided to push her a little to see how she'd respond.

"I don't want to scare you away, but…" He leaned in and curled a strand of her pretty hair around his finger. "I have feelings for you. And they're only getting more complex as the days pass. You asked me if I was trying to make you fall in love with me." He tugged the strand lightly. "Is that how you feel?"

She glanced down at the couch. "If I say no, I run the risk of hurting you. If I say yes, I run the risk of scaring you away. You just said you didn't want to scare me and now you're asking me such a tough question?" She looked up at him again, the sprinkling of freckles across her nose and cheeks making him want to kiss her. "Why can't we just keep doing what we're doing and see what happens?"

That sounded like a very Harlow response. He clung to that new shred of hope. "Cool with me. I just thought you should know how I was feeling." He started to get up, but she grabbed his arm.

"I *do* like you. A lot. More than a lot, but *love* isn't something I can say right now."

He sat back down. "You're touching me, so you must know exactly how I feel."

She smiled and the wicked glint was back. "I do. Which is why I don't think you'll mind this." She let go of him to shed her robe completely, then shifted her position, throwing one leg over him to straddle his lap.

His initial reaction was a sharp inhale and the thought that this was *not* a very Harlow response. The hope he'd felt dissipated like smoke in the air.

If Harlow noticed, he couldn't tell. Instead she threaded her hands through his hair and kissed him, dragging the pads of her thumbs over the points of his horns. "Mmm. You taste... sweet and smoky."

The sensations shooting down his spine made focused thought nearly impossible. His hands went to her hips like that was their natural resting spot.

"It's the uh, bourbon." He lifted a hand to point lamely at

the bottle, surprised that he could get himself to do that much with Harlow—in the name of all that was holy, please let it be Harlow—planted on his lap. She was warm and lush and smelled like sugared violets.

"I've never had bourbon." She curved her fingers over the buttoned fly of his jeans and, using it for a handhold, leaned back to snag the bottle with her free hand.

His body tightened at her intimate contact while his brain tried to disconnect from all rational thought. Taking her to bed seemed the one directive that made the most sense. "Don't you want a glass? I could get up and—"

She shook her head, clearly amused by the effect she was having on him. "Why? My mouth's already been on yours. And it's going to be there again." She lifted the bottle to her lips and took a sip without breaking eye contact.

He waited for her reaction. There was no way Harlow would enjoy straight bourbon.

She made a face.

"Not to your liking?"

For a moment she was quiet. "It tastes like a tree smells. Like a burnt tree smells."

Keeping his expression from changing was a struggle. "How would you know what a burnt tree smells like?" Unless she'd spent the last two decades trapped in one.

Her confidence seemed to falter. "I don't know." She took another sip. "I like the way it tastes on you better."

"Give it time. Bourbon is an acquired taste. Your mother loved it."

"Did she?" Harlow lifted the bottle a third time. She grimaced again. "Straight?"

"No. It's the main ingredient in a mint julep." The same drink she'd gotten tipsy on with Lally a few weeks ago. But then, maybe Ava Mae wouldn't know that. He sighed.

She rolled her arm around the bottle, tucking it against her chest. "What's wrong?"

"Nothing." He forced himself to smile. If this was Ava Mae, then the next step was figuring out if Harlow was still in there. He tugged on a strand of her hair. "Why don't you put the bottle down and let me see if I like the way bourbon tastes on you?"

She grinned and set the bottle on the floor, then leaned into him, her mouth hungry and insistent. Her tongue darted across his, leaving a wake of fire behind. That fire burned into his bones and flooded him with heat, making it hard to focus on the task of determining whether this was Ava Mae or Harlow. He was starting to think this was Ava Mae, which created a new problem because while Ava Mae might be on his lap, she looked like Harlow, sounded like Harlow and felt like Harlow.

And Harlow was the only woman he'd been able to think about since she'd shown up in New Orleans.

The man he'd been before Livie's death, before accepting the Guardianship, wouldn't have cared if this was Harlow or not, just that the woman on his lap was warm and willing. As most of them were.

But that man no longer existed. And the man he was now desperately wanted a sign that his Harlow was still in there.

She ran her hands under his T-shirt, coasting them over his skin as she kissed her way down his neck. "You feel like you're a thousand degrees."

"It's my smokesinger blood." He tipped his head back, the silk of her hands on his body intoxicating him more than the bourbon. Any further and he'd lose control, forget who he was and—he bolted upright.

She hesitated. "What's wrong?"

"Nothing, baby." Especially now that he had a plan. He scooped her into his arms and carried her to the bed, putting her down on the quilt before joining her. He knelt over her and feathered kisses across her throat. She cooed and arched toward him for more. Not at all the reserved response he'd often dreamed of getting from Harlow. No, this was the kind of reaction he'd imagined would only come after he'd showered her with attention, the kind of inhibition that he'd coax from her by turning her into his goddess and worshipping her. The kind of abandon that she'd reward him with when the pleasure coursing through her body made anything else impossible.

Ava Mae apparently had none of her sister's shyness.

Pretending the woman beneath him was Harlow wasn't difficult, but the thought that every kiss, every touch, every whispered endearment was being lavished upon Harlow's twin twisted his insides. The desire to protect Harlow at any cost warred with his sense of loyalty to her. In some strange way, he had to allow himself to believe this *was* being loyal to her.

After all, he only needed to push her to the point of distraction. Enough that she'd answer to the name of Ava Mae. That would be proof enough, wouldn't it?

As she moaned in pleasure he leaned back on his knees to pull his shirt off. She stared up at him. Her amber eyes had gone oddly black. There was no question in his mind now which sister controlled the tempting body that lay beneath him. This was Ava Mae.

He grabbed her hips and pulled her closer. She inhaled a ragged breath and for a second he could have sworn her teeth had been replaced by sharp, pointed edges, but the image was fleeting. He blinked again, suddenly very aware of how much danger Harlow might really be in. He ditched his idea of getting Ava Mae to respond to her name as proof she was in control.

He had to somehow subdue Ava Mae enough to give Harlow a chance, and they were past the opportunity for the bourbon to do the trick. He reached for his nightstand and grabbed a lighter and the *nequam* cigarette he'd rolled earlier. He stuck it in his mouth and lit it up.

Ava Mae squinted. "What are you doing? What is that?"

"*Nequam*. It's like fae tobacco." Which Harlow already knew. He blew out a thin stream of smoke. "I know you've never tried it, but trust me when I tell you it will greatly enhance what we're about to do." He held it out to her.

Without hesitation she took a long drag. He smiled and nodded, taking another short one himself, then blowing smoke rings through the air before holding it out to her again. "You try."

Three more puffs and the best she could do was an oval blob, but she'd smoked enough that her lids were heavy with the *nequam*'s effects. Harlow had never tried it, so he'd expected it to hit her system hard. He wasn't disappointed.

Her eyes went back to amber. All tension left her body and she melted back into the covers with a faraway smile on her face. "Am I floating?"

"Um-hmm." He lay down beside her and blew more smoke over her. "You're dreaming, Ava Mae."

"I am?" She stared at the ceiling.

"Yes. And in this part of the dream, you're going to let me talk to Harlow." He slipped his hand into hers.

"She doesn't like me..." Her words tapered off into a whisper.

"Harlow, if you're in there and you can hear me, squeeze my hand." He prayed she had that much control, but maybe she didn't.

Her fingers twitched, pressing against his. Her mouth moved but no sound came out. He leaned closer.

"Get her out."

Hope sprang alive in his chest. He propped himself up on his elbow. "Harlow, I will, I swear it. Lally figured out what's going on, that your sister has somehow taken over your body."

A tear trickled down her temple into her hair. He kissed the tear away. "I'm going to get her out of there, sweetheart. Be brave and stay strong."

Her fingers wrapped a little tighter around his.

"You have my word, Harlow. I promise this is all going to be okay."

The only problem was he didn't know how to keep that promise. Yet. But he would find a way. Whether through proper channels or dark alleys, with the help of friends or the coercion of enemies, he would rescue Harlow.

Or die trying.

Acknowledgments

Every book is a different writing experience. Some pour out of me like a lucid dream, others are a fight for every word. But what remains the same is the need for a strong support group.

Here are a few of those people: My amazing, supportive agent, Elaine. My editor, Susan, and the entire publishing team at Orbit. The fabulous Writer's Camp home team—Leigh, Laura, Rocki. And the away team—Louisa, Amanda C., Amanda B., Julie and Kristen C. My House of Pain Street Team, one of the best groups of readers and encouragers a writer could ask for. (Melanie, you rock!) And of course my readers, to whom this book is dedicated.

Lastly, huge thanks to my family for their continuous support and to my husband who is an amazing man and a constant source of entertainment. You are all 100 percent awesome.

extras

orbit

meet the author

Kevin Roberts, Intimate Images

KRISTEN PAINTER likes to balance her obsessions with shoes and cats by making the lives of her characters miserable and surprising her readers with interesting twists. She currently writes award-winning urban fantasy for Orbit Books. The former college English teacher can often be found on Twitter @Kristen _Painter, and on Facebook (where she loves to interact with her readers) at www.facebook.com/KristenPainterAuthor. Sign up for her mailing list at http://eepurl.com/xT-9L for book news, cover reveals and giveaways.

introducing

If you enjoyed
CITY OF ETERNAL NIGHT
look out for

CHARMING

Pax Arcana: Book One

by Elliott James

John Charming isn't your average prince…
He comes from a line of Charmings—an illustrious
family of dragon slayers, witch-finders and killers dating
back to before the fall of Rome. Trained by a modern-day
version of the Knights Templar, monster hunters who have
updated their tools from chain mail and crossbows to
Kevlar and shotguns, John Charming was one of the
best—until a curse made him one of the abominations
the Knights were sworn to hunt.
That was a lifetime ago. Now John tends bar under
an assumed name in rural Virginia and leads a peaceful,
quiet life. That is, until a vampire and a blonde
walk into his bar…

extras

Prelude

Hocus Focus

There's a reason that we refer to being in love as being enchanted. Think back to the worst relationship you've ever been in: the one where your family and friends tried to warn you that the person you were with was cheating on you, or partying a little too much, or a control freak, or secretly gay, or whatever. Remember how you were convinced that no one but you could see the real person beneath that endearingly flawed surface? And then later, after the relationship reached that scorched-earth-policy stage where letters were being burned and photos were being cropped, did you find yourself looking back and being amazed at how obvious the truth had been all along? Did it feel as if you were waking up from some kind of a spell?

Well, there's something going on right in front of your face that you can't see right now, and you're not going to believe me when I point it out to you. Relax, I'm not going to provide a number where you can leave your credit card information, and you don't have to join anything. The only reason I'm telling you at all is that at some point in the future, you might have a falling-out with the worldview you're currently enamored of, and if that happens, what I'm about to tell you will help you make sense of things later.

The supernatural is real. Vampires? Real. Werewolves? Real. Zombies, Ankou, djinn, Boo Hags, banshees, ghouls, spriggans, windigos, vodyanoi, tulpas, and so on and so on, all real. Well, except for Orcs and Hobbits. Tolkien just made those up.

I know it sounds ridiculous. How could magic really exist in a world with an Internet and forensic science and smartphones and satellites and such and still go undiscovered?

372

extras

The answer is simple: it's magic.

The truth is that the world is under a spell called the Pax Arcana, a compulsion that makes people unable to see, believe, or even seriously consider any evidence of the supernatural that is not an immediate threat to their survival.

I know this because I come from a long line of dragon slayers, witch finders, and self-righteous asshats. I used to be one of the modern-day knights who patrol the borders between the world of man and the supernatural abyss that is its shadow. I wore non-reflective Kevlar instead of shining armor and carried a sawed-off shotgun as well as a sword; I didn't light a candle against the dark, I wielded a flamethrower...right up until the day I discovered that I had been cursed by one of the monsters I used to hunt. My name is Charming by the way. John Charming.

And I am not living happily ever after.

Chapter One

A Blonde and a Vampire
Walk into a Bar...

Once upon a time, she smelled wrong. Well, no, that's not exactly true. She smelled clean, like fresh snow and air after a lightning storm and something hard to identify, something like sex and butter pecan ice cream. Honestly, I think she was the best thing I'd ever smelled. I was inferring "wrongness" from the fact that she wasn't entirely human.

I later found out that her name was Sig.

Sig stood there in the doorway of the bar with the wind behind her, and there was something both earthy and unearthly about her. Standing at least six feet tall in running shoes, she had shoulders as broad as a professional swimmer's, sinewy arms, and well-rounded hips that were curvy and compact. All in all, she was as buxom, blonde, blue-eyed, and clear-skinned as any woman who had ever posed for a Swedish tourism ad.

And I wanted her out of the bar, fast.

You have to understand, Rigby's is not the kind of place where goddesses were meant to walk among mortals. It is a small, modest establishment eking out a fragile existence at the tail end of Clayburg's main street. The owner, David Suggs, had wanted a quaint pub, but instead of decorating the place with dartboards or Scottish coats of arms or ceramic mugs, he had decided to celebrate southwest Virginia culture and covered the walls with rusty old railroad equipment and farming tools.

extras

When I asked why a bar—excuse me, I mean *pub*—with a Celtic name didn't have a Celtic atmosphere, Dave said that he had named Rigby's after a Beatles song about lonely people needing a place to belong.

"Names have power," Dave had gone on to inform me, and I had listened gravely as if this were a revelation.

Speaking of names, "John Charming" is not what it reads on my current driver's license. In fact, about the only thing accurate on my current license is the part where it says that I'm black-haired and blue-eyed. I'm six foot one instead of six foot two and about seventy-five pounds lighter than the 250 pounds indicated on my identification. But I do kind of look the way the man pictured on my license might look if Trevor A. Barnes had lost that much weight and cut his hair short and shaved off his beard. Oh, and if he were still alive.

And no, I didn't kill the man whose identity I had assumed, in case you're wondering. Well, not the first time anyway.

Anyhow, I had recently been forced to leave Alaska and start a new life of my own, and in David Suggs I had found an employer who wasn't going to be too thorough with his background checks. My current goal was to work for Dave for at least one fiscal year and not draw any attention to myself.

Which was why I was not happy to see the blonde.

For her part, the blonde didn't seem too happy to see me either. Sig focused on me immediately. People always gave me a quick flickering glance when they walked into the bar—excuse me, the pub—but the first thing they really checked out was the clientele. Their eyes were sometimes predatory, sometimes cautious, sometimes hopeful, often tired, but they only returned to me after being disappointed. Sig's gaze, however, centered on me like the oncoming lights of a train—assuming train lights have slight bags underneath them and make you want to flex surreptitiously. Those same startlingly blue eyes widened, and her body went still for a moment.

Whatever had triggered her alarms, Sig hesitated, visibly debating whether to approach and talk to me. She didn't hesitate for long, though—I got the impression that she rarely hesitated for long—and chose to go find herself a table.

Now, it was a Thursday night in April, and Rigby's was not empty. Clayburg is host to a small private college named Stillwaters University, one of those places where parents pay more money than they should to get an education for children with mediocre high school records, and underachievers with upper-middle-class parents tend to do a lot of heavy drinking. This is why Rigby's manages to stay in business. Small bars with farming implements on the walls don't really draw huge college crowds, but the more popular bars tend to stay packed, and Rigby's does attract an odd combination of local rednecks and students with a sense of irony. So when a striking six-foot blonde who wasn't an obvious transvestite sat down in the middle of the bar, there were people around to notice.

Even Sandra, a nineteen-year-old waitress who considers customers an unwelcome distraction from covert texting, noticed the newcomer. She walked up to Sig promptly instead of making Renee, an older waitress and Rigby's de facto manager, chide her into action.

For the next hour I pretended to ignore the new arrival while focusing on her intently. I listened in—my hearing is as well developed as my sense of smell—while several patrons tried to introduce themselves. Sig seemed to have a knack for knowing how to discourage each would-be player as fast as possible.

She told suitors that she wanted to be up-front about her sex change operation because she was tired of having it cause problems when her lovers found out later, or she told them that she liked only black men, or young men, or older men who made more than seventy thousand dollars a year. She told them that what really turned her on was men who were willing to have sex with other men while she watched. She mentioned one man's wife by name, and when the weedy-looking grad student doing a John Lennon impersonation tried the sensitive-poet approach, she challenged him to an arm-wrestling contest. He stared at her, sitting there exuding athleticism, confidence, and health—three things he was noticeably lacking—and chose to be offended rather than take her up on it.

There was at least one woman who seemed interested in Sig as well, a cute sandy-haired college student who was tall and willowy, but when it comes to picking up strangers, women are generally less likely to go on a kamikaze mission than men. The young woman kept looking over at Sig's table, hoping to establish some kind of meaningful eye contact, but Sig wasn't making any.

Sig wasn't looking at me either, but she held herself at an angle that kept me in her peripheral vision at all times.

For my part, I spent the time between drink orders trying to figure out exactly what Sig was. She definitely wasn't undead. She wasn't a half-blood Fae either, though her scent wasn't entirely dissimilar. Elf smell isn't something you forget, sweet and decadent, with a hint of honey blossom and distant ocean. There aren't any full-blooded Fae left, of course—they packed their bags and went back to Fairyland a long time ago—but don't mention that to any of the mixed human descendants that the elves left behind. Elvish half-breeds tend to be some-what sensitive on that particular subject. They can be real bas-tards about being bastards.

I would have been tempted to think that Sig was an angel, except that I've never heard of anyone I'd trust ever actually seeing a real angel. God is as much an article of faith in my world as he, she, we, they, or it is in yours.

Stumped, I tried to approach the problem by figuring out what Sig was doing there. She didn't seem to enjoy the ginger ale she had ordered—didn't seem to notice it at all, just sipped from it perfunctorily. There was something wary and expectant about her body language, and she had positioned herself so that she was in full view of the front door. She could have just been meeting someone, but I had a feeling that she was looking for someone or something specific by using herself as bait... but as to what and why and to what end, I had no idea. Sex, food, or revenge seemed the most likely choices.

I was still mulling that over when the vampire walked in.

introducing

If you enjoyed
CITY OF ETERNAL NIGHT
look out for

FULL BLOODED

Jessica McClain: Book One

by Amanda Carlson

It's not easy being a girl. It's even harder when you're the only girl in a family of werewolves. But it's next to impossible when your very existence spells out the doom of your race... Meet Jessica McClain—she just became part of the pack.

Chapter One

I drew in a ragged breath and tried hard to surface from one hell of a nightmare. "*Jesus*," I moaned. Sweat slid down my face. My head was fuzzy. Was I dreaming? If I was, this dream hurt like a bitch.

Wait, dreams aren't supposed to hurt.

Without warning my body seized again. Pain scorched

through my veins like a bad sunburn, igniting every cell in its path. I clenched my teeth, trying hard to block the rush.

Then, as quickly as it struck, the pain disappeared.

The sudden loss of sensation jolted my brain awake and my eyes snapped open in the dark. This wasn't a damn dream. I took a quick internal inventory of all my body parts. Everything tingled, but thankfully my limbs could move freely again. The weak green halo of my digital clock read 2:07 a.m. I'd only been asleep for a few hours. I rolled onto my side and swiped my sticky hair off my face. When my fingers came in contact with my skin, I gasped and snapped them away like a child who'd just touched a hot stove.

Holy shit, I'm on fire.

That couldn't be right.

Don't panic, Jess. Think logically.

I pressed the back of my hand against my forehead to get a better read on how badly I was burning up. Hot coals would've felt cooler than my skin.

I must be really sick.

Sickness was a rare event in my life, but it did happen. I wasn't prone to illness, but I wasn't immune to it either. My twin brother never got sick, but if the virus was strong enough I was susceptible.

I sat up, allowing my mind to linger for a brief moment on a very different explanation of my symptoms. *That scenario would be impossible. Get a grip. You're a twenty-six-year-old female. It's never going to happen. It's probably just the flu. There's no need to—*

Without so much as a breath of warning, another spasm of pain hit clear and bright. My body jerked backward as the force of it plowed through me, sending my head slamming into the bedframe, snapping the wooden slats like matchsticks. My back bowed and my arms lashed out, knocking my bedside table and everything on it to the ground. The explosion of my lamp as it struck the floor was lost beneath my bona fide girl scream. "*Shiiiit!*"

Another tremor hit, erupting its vile ash into my psyche like a volcano. But this time instead of being lost in the pale haze of sleep, I was wide awake. I *had* to fight this.

I wasn't sick.

I was *changing*.

Jesus Christ! You've spent your whole life thinking about this very moment and you try to convince yourself you have the flu? What's the matter with you? If you want to live, you have to get to the dose before it's too late!

The pain buried me, my arms and legs locked beside me. I was unable to move as the continuous force of spasms hit me one after another. The memory of my father's voice rang clearly in my mind. I'd been foolish and too stubborn for my own good and now I was paying the price. "*Jessica, don't argue with me. This is a necessary precaution. You must keep this by you at all times.*" The new leather case, containing a primed syringe of an exclusively engineered cocktail of drugs, would be entrusted to me for safekeeping. The contents of which were supposed to render me unconscious if need be. "*You may never need it, but as you well know, this is one of the stipulations of your living alone.*"

I'm so sorry, Dad.

This wasn't supposed to happen. My genetic markers weren't coded for this. This was an impossibility. In a world of impossibilities.

I'd been so stupid.

My body continued to twist in on itself, my muscles moving and shifting in tandem. I was locked in a dance I had no chance of freeing myself from. The pain rushed up, finally reaching a crushing crescendo. As it hit its last note, my mind shattered apart under its impact.

Everything went blissfully black.

Too soon, pinpoints of light danced behind my eyelids. I eased them open. The pain was gone. Only a low throbbing current remained. It took me a moment to realize I was on all fours on the floor beside my bed, my knees and palms bloodied from the shards of my broken lamp. My small bedside table was scattered in pieces around me. It looked like a small hurricane had ripped apart my bedroom. I had no time to waste.

The dose is your only chance now. Go!

The bathroom door was five feet from me. I propelled myself forward, tugging myself on shaky arms, dragging my body behind me. *Come on, we can do this. It's right there.* I'd only made it a few thin paces when the pain struck again, hard and fast. I collapsed on my side, the muscles under my skin roiling in earnest. *Jesuschrist!* The pain was straight out of a fairy tale, wicked and unrelenting.

I moaned, convulsing as the agony washed over me, crying out in my head, searching for the only possible thing that could help me now. My brother was my only chance. *Tyler, it's happening! Ty, Ty…please! Tyler, can you hear me? Tyyy…*

Another cloud of darkness tugged at the edges of my consciousness and I welcomed it. Anything to make all this horror disappear. Right before it claimed me, at that thin line between real and unreal, something very faint brushed against my senses. A tingle of recognition prickled me. But that wasn't right. That wasn't my brother's voice.

Dad?

Nothing but empty air filled my mind. I chastised myself. *You're just hoping for a miracle now.* Females weren't meant to change. I'd heard that line my entire life. How could they change when they weren't supposed to *exist*? I was a mistake, I'd always been a mistake, and there was nothing my father could do to help me now.

Pain rushed up, exploding my mind. Its fury breaking me apart once again.

Jessica, Jessica, can you hear me? We're on our way. Stay with us. Just a few more minutes! Jessica . . . Hang in there, honey. Jess!

I can't, Dad. I just can't.

Blood.

Fear shot through me like a cold spear. I lifted my nose and scented the air. Coolness ran along my back, forcing my hair to rise, prickling my skin. I shivered. My labored breaths echoed too loudly in my sensitive ears. I peered into the darkness, inhaling deeply again.

Blood.

A rumble of sounds bubbled up from beneath me and I inched back into the corner and whined. The thrumming from my chest surrounded me, enveloping me in my own fear.

Out.

I leapt forward. My claws slid out in front of me, sending me tumbling as I scrabbled for purchase on the smooth surface. I picked myself up, plunging down a dark tunnel into a bigger space. All around me things shattered and exploded, scaring me. I vaulted onto something big, my claws slicing through it easily. I sailed off, landing inches from the sliver of light.

Out.

My ears pricked. I lowered my nose to the ground, inhaling as the sounds hit me. Images shifted in my brain. *Humans, fear, noise . . . harm.* A low mewing sound came from the back of my throat. A loud noise rattled above my head. I jumped back, swiveling away, searching.

Then I saw it.

Out.

I leapt toward the moonlight, striking the barrier hard. It gave way instantly, shattering. I extended myself, power coursed through my body. The ground rushed up quickly, my front paws crashing onto something solid, my jaws snapping together fiercely with the force of the impact. The thing beneath me collapsed with a loud, grating noise. Without hesitation I hit the ground.

Run.

I surged across hard surfaces, finding a narrow stretch of woods. I followed it until the few trees yielded to more land. I ran and ran. I ran until the smells no longer confused me, until the noises stopped their assault on my sensitive ears.

Hide.

I veered toward a deep thicket of trees. Once inside their safe enclave, I dove into the undergrowth. The scent pleased me as I wiggled beneath the low branches, concealing myself completely. Once I was settled, I stilled, perking my ears. I opened my mouth, drawing the damp air over my tongue, sampling it, my nostrils flared. The scents of the area came quickly, my brain categorizing them efficiently. The strong acidic stench of fresh leavings hung in the air.

Prey.

I cocked my head and listened. The faint sounds of rustling and grunting were almost undetectable. My ears twitched with interest. My stomach gave a long, low growl.

Eat.

I sampled the air again, testing it for the confusing smells, the smells I didn't like. I laid my head down and whimpered, the hunger gnawing at my insides, cramping me.

Eat, eat, eat.

I couldn't ignore it, the hunger consumed me, making me hurt. I crept slowly from my shelter beneath the trees to the clearing where the tall grass began. I lifted my head above the gently waving stalks and inhaled. They were near. I trotted through the darkness, soundless and strong. I slid into their enclosure, under the rough wooden obstacle with ease. I edged farther into the darkness of the big den, my paws brushing against the old, stale grass, disturbing nothing more.

Prey.

The wind shifted across my back. They scented me for the first time. Bleating their outrage, they stamped their hooves, angry at the intrusion. I slipped under another weak barrier, my body lithe and agile as I edged along the splintered wood. I spotted my prey.

Eat.

I lunged, my jaws shifting, my canines finding its neck, sinking in deeply. Sweet blood flowed into my mouth. My hunger blazed like an insatiable fire, and my eyes rolled back in my head in ecstasy. The animal tipped over, dying instantly as it landed in the dirty hay. I set upon it, tearing fiercely at its flesh, grabbing long hunks of meat and swallowing them whole.

"Goddamn wolves!"

My head jerked up at the noise, my eyes flickering with recognition.

Human.

"I'll teach you to come in here and mess around in my barn, you mangy piece of shit!"

Sound exploded and pain registered as I flew backward,

crashing into the side of the enclosure. I tried to get up, but my claws slipped and skidded in the slippery mess. *Blood.* I readjusted, gaining traction, and launched myself in the air. The pungent smell of fear hit me, making my insides quiver with need.

Kill.

A deep growl erupted from inside my throat, my fangs lashing. My paws hit their target, bringing us both down with a crash.

Mine.

I tore into flesh, blood pooled on my tongue.

"Please...don't..."

No!

I stopped.

No!

I backed away.

"Bob, you all right out there?"

Danger.

Out.

I loped forward, limping along in the shadows. I spotted a small opening, jumped, and landed with a painful hiss. My back leg buckled beneath me, but I had to keep moving.

Run.

I ran, scooting under the barrier. A scream of alarm rent the air behind me. I ran and ran until I saw only darkness.

Rest.

I crawled beneath a thick canopy of leaves, my body curling in on itself. I licked my wound. There was too much damage. I closed my eyes. Instantly images flashed through my mind one by one.

Man, boy...woman.

extras

I focused on her.
I *needed* her.
Jessica.
I called her back to me.
She came willingly.